# WHERE SUCH UNMAKING REIGNS

# WHERE SUCH UNMAKING REIGNS

For Rich
+ Brenda Hostetter Meyer
I am a better person
for having known you

*[handwritten inscription]*

## Kathleen Kern

**To order additional copies of this book, contact:**
Xlibris Corporation
1-888-795-4274
www.Xlibris.com
Orders@Xlibris.com
19573

This book is dedicated to the memory of
Elias Jeraisse, Yochanan Lorwin, and Inbal Perelson—
three people who cared more about justice than nationality

# ACKNOWLEDGEMENTS

Voltaire, Emile Habiby and Joseph Heller taught me that humor can cut through the crap of a thousand empires. I am especially indebted to the late Emile Habiby for the character of Sa'eed and encourage people to look for his *Secret Life of Sa'eed: the Ill-Fated Pessoptimist* (London: Zed Books, 1985), now out of print. I got the idea of using Adrienne Rich's poem, "Natural Resources" from Deena Hurwitz's book *Walking the Red Line: Israelis in Search of Justice for Palestine.* (Philadelphia: New Society Publishers, 1992.)

Thom Metzger, Jamey Bouwmeester, Carolyn Schlicher, Jane Adas and John Mahoney were the first to read the manuscript and offer comments. Maxine Kaufman-Lacusta read the manuscript from the perspective of a Canadian-Israeli who has worked many years in the human rights field, and with the meticulous eye of a copy editor. My mother, Marilyn Rayle Kern, helped with additional proofreading and Rick Polhamus provided the cover art.

I have worked with Christian Peacemaker Teams for ten years. Most of my time with CPT has been spent in Hebron or in North America writing and speaking about Hebron. I want to thank all of the CPTers I worked with in Hebron for their camaraderie, courage and senses of humor. If they, and our Israeli and Palestinian co-workers, recognize snatches of conversations or aspects of their personalities in the characters of this book, I want them to know that only the things they like about the characters are based on my experience in the field. All the things they don't like about the characters were invented to advance the story line. Likewise for readers from CPT's church constituency—behaviors of which they might disapprove were invented to conform to the the realities of the publishing world.

Bruce Cockburn provided most of the soundtrack for the writing process and the Barenaked Ladies provided most of the soundtrack for the editing process.

Finally, I want to express my gratitude to the Palestinians and Israelis who have worked sacrificially for decades on behalf of human rights and a just peace between their peoples. They were the true inspiration for this book, and they deserve the Nobel Peace Prize far more than any of the actors in the Israeli-Palestinian conflict who have received one to date.

*This is what I am:* watching the spider
rebuild—"patiently," they say

But I recognize in her
impatience—my own—

the passion to make and make again
where such unmaking reigns . . .

My heart is moved by all I cannot save:
so much has been destroyed

I have to cast my lot with those
who age after age, perversely,

with no extraordinary power,
reconstitute the world
Adrienne Rich, "Natural Resources,"
*Dream of a Common Language: Poems: 1974-77*

*People like us*
*We're going to make it because*
*We don't want freedom*
*We don't want justice*
*We just want someone to love*
Talking Heads, "People Like Us," from *True Stories,*
Sire Records, 1986

# PREFACE

The non-fiction portions of this book are 98% true. The fictional portions are only half true.

# CHAPTER 1

Tess had seen Yiphat's expression on other faces before. It meant, "What does my brother/son/husband/fiance see in you?"

Tess smiled at her. Yiphat dropped her eyes and began sorting the papers on her desk into piles as she waited for the person she had called to come to the phone.

"Eugie, hi." Yiphat rolled her eyes. "Yes, I know, but I really need your help. My mother's flying in from New York. She told me that she was going to make reservations on the next flight to Tel Aviv after she got off the phone. You know what my apartment's like."

While Yiphat listened to the person on the other end, Tess examined her nails. Maybe now that Yossi was in the hospital she could buy some nail polish. He didn't like her to wear makeup or nail polish, but it bothered her that the half-moons of her nail beds were not symmetrical.

"Yeah. Yossi's going to make it. That's what the doctor said, but it's probably better if you didn't come up right away. The doctor told me no longer than fifteen minutes. God knows how he's going to keep my mother away. No, I haven't heard anything on the news about who they suspect. Yossi's girl friend—" Yiphat looked up from the phone. "What's your name again?"

"Tess MacAdoo."

"Tess said she saw the guy who did it, but she didn't know whether he was speaking Arabic or Hebrew."


The man had been saying something like, "Hamsy, hamsy."

Yossi had been putting on a condom when the door blew in, knocking him to the floor. "What the fuck was that?" he said, as he tried to sit up.

"Tessie?" He seemed to have difficulty focussing on her. "Can you take a look outside? Maybe it's another bus bomb." He shook his head and winced. Falling back onto one elbow, he slid his fingers into his black curls and then stared at the smear of blood on his hand, "But then why did the door—"

Tess ran to the window. The panes were gone, and she looked down into horrified faces looking up at hers. A tall man pointed a camera at her. She realized she was naked, her hair uncombed. Stooping below the window sill, she turned back to survey the damage in their hotel room.

Yossi now lay on his back, moaning, his tanned face ashy.

"Yossi?" She knelt down beside him and laid her hand on his forehead, recoiling when she touched the cold sweat.

She wiped her hand on the bedspread, put on her night gown, brushed her hair and went to get help. She would suggest that Yossi demand a refund from the management of the hotel, once he had received medical attention.

Stepping gingerly over piles of rubble in her bare feet, she came to a large man lying naked on the floor of what had been the room three doors down from theirs. His skin looked like it had been boiled. He thrashed about like a seal; one leg had had the foot blown off and the other had lost everything below the knee. One hand was gone and on the other the fingers hung as though on open hinges. Water sprayed up, fountain-like, from an exposed pipe.

At the insistence of her first husband, who had driven an ambulance, Tess had gone through Red Cross first aid training. She thought she ought to apply direct pressure to the stumps of his legs. However, they weren't bleeding and she knew that she wasn't supposed to touch a burn victim. According to the Red Cross manual, most victims of serious injuries were supposed to be covered, and she supposed she could do that, although she hoped she wouldn't have to get too close to all that sticky flesh. She ran back into her room and grabbed a sheet off her bed. When she came back, the hotel manager was standing by the thrashing man asking him questions—at least she assumed they were questions.

Whenever the manager said something, the man kept answering, "Hamsy, hamsy."

The manager had looked askance at her when she and Yossi had gotten their room the previous night. Yossi told her later that one of the men in the lobby asked the manager if they were married.

"Of course not," Yossi heard him respond in Arabic. "They're Americans."

Tess threw the sheet at the hotel manager and told him to cover the man's arms and legs. Instead, he covered all of the twisting body as though the man were already dead.

Israeli police came up behind her.

"My fiance," she said, relieved she could focus on Yossi now. "He's been hurt too."

"Is he Arab or American?"

"He's American."

All four police officers made a U-turn and followed her into her room. They stood there looking down at Yossi until the hotel manager came to the doorless entrance, yelled at them, and pointed down the hall toward the man without hands or feet.

They yelled back at him and then ignored him.

"You are married?" one of the policemen asked Tess. She shook her head. Another policeman dug an elbow into his fellow officer's ribs.

"What happened here?"

"We were . . . well, and then there was an explosion and the door blew in."

Yossi opened his eyes and looked up at the four policemen and Tess. He muttered something and one of the policemen kicked him.

"I thought you said he was American!" One of the policemen turned toward her. "Why is he speaking Arabic?"

"Tessie, don't cooperate with them," Yossi said, barely moving his lips.

"But Yossi, I don't know Jerusalem. Who else is going to take you to the hospital?"

One of the policemen picked up their passports from the bureau.

"Yossi Berger," he read out loud. "You are Jewish."

"I am a Communist," he said.

"Yes," said the policeman, "but you are a Jewish Communist."

The paramedics carefully lifted Yossi on to a stretcher. Tess followed the ambulance attendants outside, cutting her foot on one of the glass shards that littered the sidewalk.

The police would not let her enter the ambulance, and motioned for her to move halfway down the block and stand with the other people who had been in the hotel.

"Tessie," Yossi called. "Go find my sister, Yiphat, at Tzedek. It's near Jaffa Gate. Tell her what happened and tell her I asked her to take care of you."

"You must go over there." The policeman took her arm and pointed.

"But Yossi . . ." Tess looked over at the frightened crowd milling around in pajamas.

"Tessie, I love you. Everything's going to be okay."


Tess smiled as she settled more comfortably into the black vinyl chair in Yiphat's office. That was the good thing about men. They usually had such good ideas when it came to her comfort and security. And when they stopped having such good ideas, there were others who came along with new ideas.

As Yiphat drummed her fingers on the desk while listening to the speaker at the other end of the phone line, Tess looked around the office. The dingy white walls were hung with several pictures of children behind bars wearing black and white scarves. One little girl, wrists manacled to the bars, raised her fingers in a "V" sign. Over Yiphat's desk hung a poster of a Seurat painting. Looking out the window, Tess watched men and women passing—some with tattoos and shaved heads, wearing miniskirts and jeans, and some wearing hats and long skirts and black suits. On the white cement buildings, the sun shone blindingly, and Tess thought the men in black suits and hats must sweat a lot. As she thought of the smell, she wrinkled her nose. The lower left pane of the window had a sticker showing a dove with an olive branch in its beak flying through the bars of a cell. The caption read, "There is no peace until all the prisoners are free."

She turned around and looked at the Seurat poster again. The women with parasols lounging by the river did not match the rest of the decor. She thought Yiphat should find another picture with a prison theme to hang there.

"Eugie," Yiphat's speech became slow and deliberate. "I appreciate the position you are in. I know things are crazy right now in Hebron. But this is an emergency. I have two hundred Bedouin facing eviction, four families in Bethlehem who have just received land confiscation notices, and one 15 year old kid from Ramallah who disappeared when soldiers took him three nights ago. My brother is lying comatose in Hadassah Hospital. My mother, God! MY MOTHER! is coming. She's going to blame me for this, you know. I have to appear in court Sunday morning. I've got a stinking headache. And frankly, Eugie, I think you owe me. How many times have I helped YOU out when you guys got arrested?"

Yiphat scrabbled around through the papers on her desk until she found a pack of cigarettes. Tess looked away so that Yiphat would not see her disapproval. Smoking caused wrinkles, and it was obvious that Yiphat spent too much time in the sun as it was. Her face was long and narrow, lines already forming between the corners of her mouth and her nostrils. Because Yiphat was Yossi's sister, Tess, out of loyalty, took note of her striking gray eyes and dark, curly hair. Tess wished she had naturally curly hair. Her lovers had told her, however, that hers was so dark and glossy that they could almost see themselves in it. Her second husband, who had an artistic eye (and was the reason she recognized the Seurat painting in Yiphat's office), had told her that her hair made her pale complexion glow in a way that blonde hair never could.

Yiphat lit her cigarette, inhaled and closed her eyes while she listened to the voice on the other end of the line.

"No, that's okay, Eugie. I'm sure that I would feel the same way if someone suddenly saddled me with—" At the break in the conversation, Tess, turned away from the picture of the little girl handcuffed to the bars. She looked over at Yiphat expectantly.

"Listen, we'll talk about this later, okay? As far as I'm concerned, we're even if you can do this for me. She seems—" Yiphat raised her left eyebrow as she looked at Tess "—like she'll stay out of your way."

Tess smiled. This was a quality that lots of people liked about her.

"Okay, Eugie. I'll see you in a couple hours. I want to see Munir as long as I'm coming down there. Are our friends at Kiryat Arba still stoning his house?" Yiphat tapped her cigarette on a green metal wastebasket. "Uh-huh. Uh-huh. Yeah, well we can't give him any money either, but I'm bringing some papers to sign so he can give me power of attorney."

Yiphat inhaled again. Tess wished she could open a window.

"I have no idea what my legal services are worth. We don't charge for human rights cases." Yiphat crushed her cigarette butt against the side of the trash can. "Okay, I'll make something up. See you."

Yiphat hung up the phone and leaned back in her swivel chair, putting her tasselled loafers up on the desk.

"So, it's all settled," she said. "You're going down to Hebron for a few days to stay with the RAPTors. Yossi worked with them for a month."

"Okay," said Tess.

"Yossi told you about them?"

"No."

Yiphat gave her another look that Tess had seen before on other faces. It meant, "Don't you think you ought to be asking me a question?"

"Well, they're good people. I mean they're religious and everything—R.A.P.T. stands for Reformed anti-Baptists or something like that—but they do good work. They stick their necks out."

Tess smiled and nodded.

"So you're Christian, too, I guess."

"I was raised Catholic."

When she and Yossi had gotten engaged, and she had heard about his mother's reaction, she asked him if he wanted her to convert. He had told her that he had thought she had grown beyond superstition and magical thinking, so she had decided she had grown beyond them.

Yiphat sat up and began straightening out the piles of papers she had messed up when she was looking for her cigarettes.

"So, what did the police say when you talked to them?"


After Yossi left in the ambulance, Tess had waited for two hours with a group of Egyptian Copts who told her they were in town for Coptic Easter—whatever that was—before the police came over to talk to her. The men had all been wearing striped night gowns with open necks and the women had worn bathrobes with sequins. Many of them had put henna on their graying hair. Tess had longed to recommend a more appropriate hair color—maybe soft, light brown highlights—but she spoke no Arabic.

"You had the closest room to the terrorist," the police began. "Did you know him from before?"

"No. I've never been here before."

"Why were you staying in an Arab hotel?"

"I don't know. Yossi picked it. I didn't know it was an Arab hotel." The policeman snorted. "Your boyfriend. He loves the Arabs?"

"Which Arabs?"

The policeman pounded his desk. "Do not pretend that you do not know! You may think you are clever, but I know people like you. You kiss the Arabs' behinds!"

No one had accused Tess of being clever before. She was flattered.

"If I knew more, I would tell you, officer, but now I must go find Yossi's sister and tell her what happened.

"Go. But I want to know where I can find you."


"And you gave them our address?" Yiphat asked. "Great. That's just great. They already think that we work with terrorists. Hey, Shabak," Yiphat addressed a corner of the ceiling. She began speaking in Hebrew, ending by giving it the finger.

"You speak Hebrew?" Tess asked, impressed.

"I'm an Israeli. I'm a lawyer," Yiphat snapped. "How do you think I could work in the Israeli courts if I didn't speak Hebrew?"

"I suppose that would be difficult," Tess said with equanimity.

Yiphat rubbed her left temple with her index and middle fingers and then began hunting for another cigarette. "Yossi didn't tell me much about you," she said. "Just that he really wanted me to meet you. How did you guys get together?"


Yossi had been a friend of Stan, Tess's third husband, who had been writing a minimalist opera based on Noam Chomsky's writings. He had just finished "World Orders, Old and New," when he had moved out with all his equipment. He told her that her existential non-being had suctioned the Muse from his creative womb.

The evening that Stan had moved out, Yossi had come and found her sitting in the middle of the apartment, looking at herself in a hand mirror.

"I still look the same as I did when I met him," she said, one tear trickling down her cheek.

"He's crazy," Yossi said. "He just doesn't realize what he's got." He put his arms around her and they made love on the cold, hard floor.


"We met through a mutual friend," Tess said to Yiphat.

"And why did he bring you here?"

"He said that I needed to see this place because he wanted to teach me about colonialism and because I was still brainwashed by the Zionists."

Yiphat put her head and crossed arms on the desk like a delinquent school child. After a few moments, Tess wondered if she had fallen asleep. She took the opportunity to look at her nails again.

Yiphat lifted her face from her arms. It was red, but her voice was steady. "Listen. Something you should know about Yossi. He doesn't stick with things. I mean he doesn't know what it's like for those of us who live here, no matter how much I've tried to tell him. He doesn't have the patience to put up with all the shit I put up with every fu—every day."

Tess smiled in a way that most men thought was enigmatic.

Yiphat frowned. "You don't get it, do you?"

"Not quite," said Tess.

"How long have you known my brother?"

Tess thought a moment. "Six weeks and three days."

"And you dropped everything to come over here? Why?"


Tess had kept the books for a small community college in the Bronx, a job at which she excelled because of her photographic memory. (Stan had once told her that if she would stop remembering everything verbatim she might be able to have an original thought.) She enjoyed her job—entering raw, uninteresting numbers into the computer and watching the computer organize them into elegant columns. The office had recently gotten a color printer, too. Still, her mother always told her that the key to living a comfortable life was indulging men in the small things. So she had quit her job and told Yossi she would come with him.

"You're not smart, Teresa Marie, but you have what counts to make it in life," her mother had said. "As long as what they ask you to do don't go against the teachings of the Church, there's no harm in letting them have their way."

By removing the parameter of Catholic teaching, Tess had succeeded with men in a manner far beyond anything her mother had imagined.


"Because I love Yossi," she told Yiphat. "Because I want to be where he is."

"It must have been horrible for you, this morning," Yiphat said. She gouged at one of her eyes with the heel of her palm. "Last year, the son of my landlady was killed in the bombing in Ashkelon. You never think it's going to happen . . . My mother—Oh god, my mother—this will be the final proof she needs that you can't trust Arabs. And no one sees where all that anger comes from. I mean some of us do and some days I feel like—" Her face crumpled and she started to sob. "Damn you, Yossi."

Tess folded her hands in her lap and let a tear trickle down her cheek. The thought had just occurred to her that she was going to be alone if Yossi died, and she had nowhere to go. She thought about him in the hospital, and wished she could be by his bedside instead of traveling to an unknown destination to stay with unknown people. It sounded less comfortable.

"Let's go," Yiphat said, after searching for her car keys.

*     *     *


Eugie closed the cellphone and stared at the crack in the flap. A couple months ago, Frank had thrown a cucumber at one of his Palestinian jock friends who was using the phone. The resulting damage thus far had not interfered with the phone's function.

"So is he going to be okay?" Felicia asked.

Eugie touched the side table to make sure it was solid before she laid the phone down. The red surface, cluttered with cameras, papers and other paraphernalia, seemed to be dissolving into a mass of swarming black spots.

She and Yossi had managed to keep the full extent of their

involvement with each other from Felicia and Frank, so she had some incentive not to faint. Sidling over to a chair in the doorway of Frank's bedroom, she sat down, closing her eyes and holding her head in her hands. Not as good as putting her head between her knees, but it seemed to help.

"He's dead," Felicia said flatly.

Eugie lifted her head. Felicia was working her jaw and twisting a lock of black hair around her finger. Frank's mild blue eyes had tears in them. He turned his back and wiped them on his bare arm.

"No," Eugie said. "He's still unconscious, but the doctors think he'll survive. We just need to pray for him."

Felicia grimaced. "That'll help," she said. "Knowing people are praying for him just might piss him off enough he'll come out of the coma."

"When you said 'We can't because we're too busy' to Yiphat, what was that about?" Frank asked.

"Yossi's fiancee was with him," Eugie replied. "Yiphat can't put her up in her apartment because her mother's coming. She wants us to take her in for a few days."

"Guess you got a roommate." Felicia stood up and stretched. When she put her head back, her black mane hung past her buttocks. Eugie wondered how she could stand to have all that hair on her neck in the summer. Felicia had grown up in the lowlands of Colombia; maybe she had inherited heat tolerance genes from her mother along with the clear brown skin and black eyes.

"I need a smoke," Felicia said and went outside, pulling the heavy metal door behind her with enough force to make it resound like a gong.

"You okay?" Frank asked.

Eugie raised her head and searched his round, tanned face for hidden meanings in the question. No, she decided. He just thought she, like he, was upset that a former teammate of theirs had been injured.

"Yeah," she said. "It was just a shock, that's all. I didn't even know Yossi was in the country." She took a deep breath and exhaled. "Or that he was engaged."

"Me neither," Frank said.

"Guess I'd better finish that land expropriation report," she said and walked into the office.

She wanted to put her fist through the flying toasters screen saver. Instead, she savagely jiggled the mouse until the report on which she had been working came up. She saved it and then stared at it for a few moments. Hadn't they already included the confiscation of the Beit Ummar vineyards north of Hebron in last month's report? She went down to the little multicolored window icon, selected, "Find" and then entered "Confiscation." Nothing came up. She tried "Expropriation." Still nothing.

Damn Microsoft. Damn it all to hell, she thought. The tears came and she leaned her head and arms on the computer monitor and tried to sob without making any noise.

When she recovered, she blew her nose—again as soundlessly as possible, hoping Frank could not hear. Staring at the screen, she moved the mouse to keep the flying toasters at bay with one hand and traced her lips with two fingers of the other. When she realized she was touching her lips the way Yossi used to—he would stroke her lips for what seemed like hours as though preparing the foundation for the best kissing she had ever known—she bit the middle knuckle of her index finger hard.

For a moment, the pain from the bite stopped the molten lead from dripping into her chest cavity. She stared at the red imprints of her incisors on her finger. Then she bit a hangnail off of her ring finger.

"You're a lot stronger than you think you are," a co-worker at the human services agency had told her once. During times when she wanted to be weak, Eugie reminded herself of this. The hearty Swiss peasant stock she came from had cursed her with a big-boned, robust exterior that hid the frail, fluttery woman she was inside—the kind of woman who, in Victorian novels, fainted at every emotional upset and eventually died of a broken heart.

Eugie sighed. People with broken hearts should be so lucky.

*    *    *

At the Bethlehem checkpoint, a long line of cars was waiting to enter the town. Soldiers in khaki uniforms and dark green wool berets paced up and down the line of cars, looking carefully at the drivers.

"This is strange," Yiphat said as she shifted into first. "Normally they only stop people coming into Jerusalem."

Tess watched as a man with gray hair got out of the seven-passenger Mercedes taxi in front of them and hoisted himself over a ten foot stone wall on the right side of the road. He disappeared into a grove of trees.

"That's Tantur." Yiphat gestured toward the wall. "It's owned by the Vatican and sits on the border between Jerusalem and the West Bank. He doesn't have a permit to be working in Israel, so he's sneaking in. Can you imagine having to sneak through a checkpoint to get to your own home?"

Tess shook her head and looked sober, since that seemed to be the response Yiphat was looking for.

"That's Jebal Abu Ghneim or Har Homa, depending on your politics," Yiphat said, pointing out the driver's side window toward a round wooded hill that stood out among other brown hills. "They want to build another settlement on it. Of course they're calling it a neighborhood of Jerusalem. Even if you don't give a shit about human rights and confiscating land, it's such a crime to bulldoze all those trees."

When they finally got up to the orange plastic barricade, a soldier poked his head through the window. He reminded Tess a little bit of Yossi.

"Good afternoon!" he said, looking at Tess.

She smiled back him and noted his Adam's apple bobbing up and down. Yiphat asked him something in Hebrew, and nodded without facial expression when he responded.

"May I see your passports?" he asked in English.

"I don't have mine," Tess said. "The police took it."

"You didn't tell me that!" Yiphat said.

"You didn't ask me."

"Shit. Listen," she said to the soldier and launched into a long explanation, in what Tess assumed to be Hebrew.

The soldier looked doubtful, said something in Hebrew, and walked a few feet away. He pulled out a walkie-talkie and began speaking into it, looking back at their car several times.

"He's calling his commanding officer. I think they're checking for Kachniks," said Yiphat. "Let me do all the talking. Do you have any kind of identification at all?"

Tess fished out her Visa card from her purse. Yiphat raised her eyebrows as she took it and shook her head.

"A driver's license would be better," she said. Don't you have some kind of photo ID?"

Tess took a photo of her and Yossi out of her wallet. She was seated on a boulder and Yossi stood behind her with his arms around her. An old college friend of Yossi's had taken the picture when they had driven out to visit him in Ithaca, New York.

"That's not a photo ID," Yiphat said. "That's just . . . Wait. This probably won't work, but I do have a photo of Yossi in my wallet.

Maybe—."

The commanding officer, a heavy-set man with a dark, weathered face, approached their car. He barked something in Hebrew. Yiphat responded and handed over her own ID in a blue plastic jacket. The officer looked at Tess and his expression softened.

"*B'seder*," he said to Yiphat. "Welcome to Israel," he said to Tess.

Yiphat handed the photo, which the officer had not bothered looking at, back to Tess. For the next couple miles, Yiphat fumed.

"'Welcome to Israel.' God, if you hadn't been without a passport I would have told them . . . Do they still have Yossi's, by the way?"

"I think so."

"Shit. They're just so damn arrogant. And what really pisses me off is that arrogance always wins. I mean, every time I go back to the United States, I hear people talking about Bethlehem and East Jerusalem like they're a part of Israel, and they don't even think what it means for people to stop calling them the Occupied Territories."

Tess, who had assumed that Bethlehem was a part of Israel, thought it best to keep silent.

"You know, a couple of years ago, someone vandalized the door of the office of the Alternative Information Center in Jerusalem and wrote, 'Go back to Palestine.' The next day, someone from the office hung out a sign that said, 'We ARE in Palestine.' And they're in West Jerusalem."

Tess smiled—again, because it seemed like the most appropriate response.

"We are now passing the settlement of Efrat," Yiphat said gesturing on her left toward a group of pleasant looking white houses with red tiled roofs, laid out in staggered rows on low, brown hills.

Several minutes later, they passed another cluster of houses. "This is still Efrat," Yiphat said as they drove by. Several minutes later another cluster appeared. "And this is STILL Efrat," Yiphat said. "God! I was at the demonstration outside of Al Khader last year—that's an Arab village near Bethlehem. Efrat said it needed the land to expand, but when you stood on the hill they were trying confiscate, you couldn't even see Efrat from there."

She drove in silence for a few moments and then said, "Al Khader was the last demonstration I went to that wasn't totally lame."

Tess nodded. "Yossi told me about Al Khader when he started talking about coming over here."

"It can get pretty lonely, here," Yiphat said. "You make friends, you fall in love, but then people burn out and go home. I thought if Yossi were here—well, it's a lot easier feeling alienated with someone who feels alienated, too. But Mom, even with all her Hadassah work, didn't really want him to make *aliyah*. Of course, maybe she doesn't want her own son over here betraying '*Am Yisrael* like her daughter. She's going to blame me for all this. I just know it."

She turned and looked at Tess. "Yossi hasn't introduced you to my mother, has he?"

"No."

"I didn't think so. I would have heard about it. Oy! Would I have heard about it!"

"He said we should aim for *fait accompli* like the Zionists do."

One corner of Yiphat's mouth went up.

On the horizon, the minaret of a mosque appeared and then a cluster of white, square buildings.

"Halhul," Yiphat announced. "It's sort of a suburb of Hebron. You know, you're not like the kind of girls my brother usually gets interested in. I mean they're usually more politically—you know."

Tess traced her involvement in leftist politics to her second husband, who had mistaken her for a deep soul because she had memorized all the lyrics on the Pete Seeger, Peter, Paul and Mary, Bob Dylan and Phil Ochs albums that one of her boyfriends had owned. In fact, the same ability for memorization had won her prizes for catechism in parochial school and recognition from the Daughters of the American Revolution and the Veterans of Foreign Wars, but she had never told her subsequent lovers on the left about these awards. Operating on her mother's advice and her own observations, she found that she almost never needed to talk about herself or her past when she was involved with a man.

"I had friends at school who were involved with Central American stuff," she said. "I went to Nicaragua in 1986 and it changed my life." Mostly, she did not add, because she had gone with Barney and that had been the last straw for her first husband.

"Would you look at that," Yiphat said, nodding her head toward a large, red Star of David that had been painted on the front door of a square white house. "We're entering Hebron, by the way. The gas station is where Halhul ends and Hebron begins. That's the glass factory on the right."

Tess caught a fleeting glimpse of a low building with blue glass globes hanging from the awning and brightly painted plates hanging on the walls.

A green and white bus roared past them, enveloping their car in charcoal-colored fumes.

"Gross," Yiphat said. "It's so dusty here. Worse than Jerusalem.

I'm going to park by the mosque so we don't have to drive downtown," she continued. "Traffic there has been a bitch ever since they closed down Dubboya street. Actually it was always a bitch, but now it's worse.

The streets were filled with chunky, pale blue Peugots that made Yiphat's white Volkswagen seem even smaller. Tess noticed that most of the woman on the sidewalks were wearing white scarves that fastened under the chin, long flowing coat dresses, and high heeled shoes. Not a bad look, she thought. It could be slimming on a heavy person. Of course the white scarves called attention to the face, so a woman would have to be careful about her makeup.

Yiphat gave a group of small boys some money to watch her VW when they finally parked. She said it was about a quarter of a mile from the parking lot of the Il Ibrahimi Mosque to the alley in the marketplace where the RAPTors had their apartment.

Hundreds of men and women bustled through the streets. Most of them seemed to have children in tow. The sun gleamed on white buildings and the white headscarves of the women. Unshaven men in soiled clothes kept coming up to them and saying, "Taxi?" Yiphat ignored them.

In front of what appeared to be a vegetable market, one small pushcart stood, with a wok-like pan containing boiling oil. A man dropped miniature ice cream scoopfuls of a pale green mixture into the oil. The end result of the deep fat frying looked like chunks of dog food. The vendor stuffed them into a round pita and topped the sandwich with tomatoes and french fries. Another vendor's cart stood next to his, with three choices of beverages—all in poisonous-looking colors.

Yiphat and Tess walked on, passing a checkpoint at the intersection of three roads. Four soldiers were taking everything out of the trunk of a blue Peugot while its driver leaned against the hood of his car and smoked, looking away from the soldiers. A block up from the checkpoint they turned into an alley. Live chickens, in plastic crates of various colors, stood out in front of shops on either side of the street. A stream of what looked like a mixture of blood and urine pooled beneath an ancient Volvo delivery truck. As she tried to avoid a mound of chicken droppings and feathers, Tess stepped on a bloody rabbit tail.

"It really stinks here this time of year," Yiphat told her as they passed through a narrow iron door painted yellow with large black diamonds. Someone had spray-painted a Star of David on it.

After they walked up a steep flight of concrete stairs, Yiphat pushed through sheets and towels hanging on lines stretched across the small landing and walked into an apartment without knocking. Two women and a youngish-looking man sat around a table splotched with different colors of paint, eating stuffed pitas.

"Tess MacAdoo, these are the RAPTors," Yiphat announced with a wave of her arm. She sat on a low bench that had been draped with a ragged quilt. "Where's Margaret?"

"Up on the roof," said the older of the two women. She had large dark eyes and nondescript brown hair plaited into a messy braid that hung to her waist. "I wish you wouldn't call us the RAPTors, Yiphat. It's not an image we would like to project."

"I don't know," said the young man. "I think it's kind of cool. I can imagine lots of kids wanting to join a group called the RAPTors. Especially in Toronto. They've got a new basketball team there and they're called the Raptors."

"Yeah, you told me that," said the woman with the braid. Tess noted that she was wearing high-topped basketball shoes with her long, navy blue skirt. She was too old to get away with that sort of look, Tess thought.

"I still think it's kind of a dumb name for a basketball team," the woman said, pressing her elbows to her rib cage and holding her hands up limply. "I mean, how could a dinosaur sink a basket with those silly little arms?"

Yiphat laughed. "Well, I refuse to call you the RAP team, Eugie. I mean, that can't be in keeping with your image, either."

"Reformed Anabaptist Peacemaking Teams got its name before anyone on the board had heard about rap music," Eugie said as she walked into a dark kitchen one step up from the room in which they were eating.

She returned with a damp wash cloth and began wiping the table. "Felicia, do you want to do the introductions?"

Felicia, a younger woman with olive skin and billows of black hair, pulled a pack of cigarettes out of the pocket of the man's shirt she was wearing over a brown t-shirt with bleach spots.

"I am Felicia-Inez Erb," she said, offering Yiphat and then Tess cigarettes.

"No thank you, I don't smoke," Tess said.

"Yay!" Eugie said under her breath.

"This is Frank," she said, gesturing to the young man who had offered his chair to Tess and now stood leaning against the side of a doorway that led into a bedroom. "And that is Eugie," she said. "You'll meet Margaret—"

"Sister Margaret," Yiphat added.

"She prefers to be called Margaret," Felicia said, "—later."

"So," Eugie said, continuing to wipe the table without looking up.

"What is the news on Yossi?"

"No news since I talked to you," Yiphat said. "I'm going to stop in at Hadassah Hospital on the way back. Which reminds me, I really need to see Munir before I leave. Do you think I'll get any hassle driving through the checkpoint?"

"Not with a yellow license plate," Eugie said. "Frank, why don't you go with Yiphat? We haven't been by to see Munir in over a week, and I'm feeling a little guilty."

Frank, who had not taken his eyes off Tess since she had come into the room, said "Sure," automatically. Then he shook his head as if to clear it. "Um, go to Munir's? I promised Samir and Abed that I was going to play basketball with them." He looked at Tess again, "Unless—maybe it would be a good idea for Tess to meet Munir."

She smiled at him, and he turned red.

Yiphat pursed her lips and nodded thoughtfully. "You know, I have a feeling Tess wouldn't mind meeting Samir and Abed afterwards either."

"Yeah!" Frank said. "I could tell them I was late because I had to introduce you to Munir! Would you like to come?" he asked her.

"I'd love to," she said. Most of her lovers had liked basketball.

"I had a feeling you would," Yiphat said. "Eugie, will you come up to the roof with me a minute before I leave?"

# *Interim*
# Diary of an Israeli Human Rights Lawyer
# by Allegra Pacheco

It's been over a year since my caseload doubled. Following the second stage of the Oslo accords (the signing of the interim agreement in September 1995), the Israeli government accelerated land confiscations, house demolitions, arrests, tortures and administrative detentions, all in the name of implementing the peace process. The land and houses stood in the way of bypass road construction; the Palestinian opposition had to be arrested and tortured for fear they would undermine the Oslo accords; and the political prisoners in administrative detention could not be released because they might sway the masses to reject Oslo . . .

Just a glance at my caseload during the week-and-a half leading up to the clashes sheds some light on what the peace process has meant for Palestinians.

## September 15, 1996

Bethlehem. I meet with George Abu Zulof, 29 years old, from Beit Sahour. A human rights worker and former colleague of mine, George is two weeks late in traveling to Holland. He had received a scholarship to attend a three-month management training program. George is late because he cannot obtain a permit from the Israeli security authorities to exit the West Bank and use Ben Gurion airport. The airport is George's only way out of the country; the Jordanian government will not let him exit through the Allenby bridge. We appeal to the ministry of Justice and galvanize the international human rights community to write on his behalf, but to no avail. The Israeli authorities state with their typical Kafkaesque logic—that since George poses a security threat to the area he is prohibited from leaving it. George has not been able to leave the West Bank for over 10 years. His chances for professional advancement are crushed for now.

# September 17, 1996

I travel to the village of Sur Ba'her, which is divided in half by the newly expanded municipal borders of Jerusalem. One side of the village is in Jerusalem and the other is in the West Bank. I am there to visit nine houses that the Israeli government intends to demolish. I go from family to family, looking at the little children and the desperate parents who tell me the same story over and over again: this is their only home, they own the land, they have nowhere else to go, there is no more money to build another house.

These houses are located high up on a furiously windy hill— dust is flying everywhere. I feel the anger of the village in the wind.

# September 18. 1996

Megiddo prison, northern Israel. I meet with the Palestinian administrative detainees. Administrative detention is a legal euphemism for long term imprisonment without trial. Currently, there are over 300 Palestinian administrative detainees inside Israeli prisons. None of the detainees have been tried or convicted of any offense; they are being held for having opinions critical of the Oslo Agreements, views held today by many Palestinians and even members of the Israeli government. Although administrative detention is meant to be used as a temporary, extreme measure, many of the detainees have been sitting in prison for over a year; dozens for over two years.

Instead of releasing the detainees (as is called for in the Oslo Agreements), the Israelis are summarily extending their detentions. Last month these imprisoned men began a boycott of the military courts which serve, they argue, as rubber stamps for the Israeli security services ("Shabak"). Several detainees are now on a hunger strike. More are considering this. Frustration from being held indefinitely without charges and the long term separation from families is fueling the fire for a showdown in the prison.

That evening at my home, I receive a call from Ihsan al-Aza, who wants to know if her brother Dirar will be released from administrative detention. The al-Azas live in a refugee camp in Bethlehem. Dirar has been in administrative detention for a year and four months. His case is a typical example of how administrative detention rips apart a person's life. Two weeks before Dirar was arrested, his mother died. Last month his father died, leaving Dirar and his three sisters orphaned. With no other brothers around, the sisters are struggling financially. While Dirar went through the mourning period in jail, he and sisters were consoled by the fact that his detention was set to end on September 24.

After he has sat in detention for a year and a half, what danger can Dirar pose to the Israelis, Ihsan asks me, especially now that their refugee camp is no longer under Israeli control? I have no answer.

## September 19, 1996

Two families from the Jerusalem neighborhood of Issawiya arrive at my office in the late afternoon with 24-hour house demolition notices signed by Mayor Ehud Olmert. The houses may be destroyed the next day because they were built without permits. It is the weekend before Yom Kippur—the municipality and all the courts are closed. The families have invested all their money in these homes. They built without permits because the housing shortage is acute and the Jerusalem municipality hardly ever grants building permits in poor Palestinian neighborhoods. One couple sleeps on a couch in the living room of the three room house where they live together with the husband's family of 10.

I stay late to draft a request to the court to halt the demolitions.

## September 20, 1996

The next day, Friday, the courts are closed. I find the one judge on call. He looks at my papers and tells me that I haven't made any legal arguments. Of course I've made no legal arguments—because I have none. Israeli building law is drafted to facilitate demolitions in Palestinian neighborhoods; it is legal to destroy these homes.

The judge says, "I want to help you, but you don't provide me with any way out." I ask him to consider the moral issue of demolishing a house. He balks and shakes his head. There is no room in judicial discretion for the inhumaneness of forced homelessness, dispossession and impoverishment of Palestinian families. I feel that I'm about to lose this case. I ask for just a few days' delay until after the holiday. He gives me five days to try to stop these demolitions.

## September 22, 1996

The Shabak announces that it will extend the detention of my friend and former client Imad a-Sabi, leaving his wife and year-old daughter husbandless and fatherless for another half year. Imad has been in administrative detention since December, 1995. I send a letter to the Israeli security services asking them not to renew Dirar Al-Aza's detention based on humanitarian grounds. I write that Dirar has been punished enough.

## September 25, 1996

Back in court for the house demolitions, I am granted a two-week delay. As I leave the court, Ibrahim Sheqarna's uncle calls to tell me that Ibrahim's detention has been extended for six months. The eldest of twelve children and newly-married. Ibrahim supports the family. His father is not at home when I call; he left at the crack of dawn to wait for his son at the Jenin checkpoint. But the father waits in vain all day; Ibrahim never arrives.

I hear that clashes have begun in Ramallah.

I go to Bethlehem for a meeting. From there I call the legal advisor's office in the Civil administration (the Israeli body that administers the military occupation in the West Bank) to find out about Dirar. I hear giggling in the background as my name is announced on the other end of the phone. My cousin is doing his army service as a clerk in this office; it is apparently the staff joke that he is related to me, a lawyer from the "other side."

Although it is not his job to report on administrative detentions, they transfer the call to my cousin. I am very nervous; I know how Dirar and his sisters will suffer if his detention is extended. Perhaps my appeal to the Shabak helped. After a few minutes, my cousin returns to the phone and tells me that Dirar's detention has been extended for six more months. I am torn in two. I want to scream— once again I see that nothing has really changed for Palestinians; they are still under Israeli military occupation. The peace process is a farce.

That night, Palestinians in Bethlehem are throwing rocks and burning the newly-constructed security wall in front of Rachel's tomb. This wall, built to protect Jewish visitors to the site, stands in the middle of Bethlehem's main artery. In the shadow of the fire, I see silhouettes of Palestinian boys with their arms stretched back, bodies twisting to hurl another rock. Fixed to my spot, I watch—silhouette after silhouette, stone after stone. The rage streaming from their bodies as they stand meters from the Israeli guns is not limited to this site—it is an accumulation of anger, feelings of betrayal, loss of hope for the future. It's for the brother in prison, the unemployed father trapped by the closure, and for the family's demolished house.

The peace process scatters into the smoke-filled wind, along with the tear gas, as the prospects for these young rock-throwers, the next generation of the "new era of peace" grow dimmer by the moment.

Reprinted from *Challenge* Magazine, November 1996

# CHAPTER 2

When they reached the top of the stairs, Eugie heard what sounded like a gunshot; she and Yiphat raced across the cement roof to look over the wall.

"I think someone dropped something," said Margaret, who was sitting in the sun on the opposite side of the roof, reading a three-month-old issue of *The Nation.* Without looking up from her magazine, she put her plastic water bottle between her knees, unscrewed the cap with one hand, and took a sip.

Seven soldiers in the camp that the building overlooked continued to play basketball. Others ambled between trailers and prefabricated buildings that served as eating and sleeping facilities. Eugie assumed Margaret was right about the gunshot.

"It must have been the ramp on the delivery truck," Eugie said as she watched a Palestinian boy back a dolly heaped with multicolored crates of squawking chickens out of a truck parked directly below.

"I live in DC. I can tell the difference." Margaret flipped a page.

"So he's really going to make it?" Eugie asked Yiphat.

"The doctors say yes," Yiphat said. "Tess told me that the police took both of their passports. I have to get back to Jerusalem and see if I can get them to give them up."

Eugie began picking off split ends from her braid and fought to keep back tears. She marveled at Yiphat's self-possession. Yossi and his sister were close, she knew, and yet Yiphat was behaving only a few degrees more brusquely than usual.

"So did Geoff get off okay?" She asked, hoping that changing the subject would help.

Yiphat lit another cigarette and blew smoke in the direction of the army camp.

"Yeah."

A soldier sunk a basket, elbowing another out of the way. The ensuing argument held Yiphat's attention long enough for Eugie to wipe her eyes on the sleeve of her blouse.

"I was going to drive him to the airport, but we had a huge fight two days before he left and he told me he'd rather take a Nesher taxi. He's such a bastard." She inhaled and blew a malformed smoke ring. "So, Munir says his house hasn't been stoned in over a week?"

"Yeah. So maybe the *Ha'Aretz* reporter did some good after all. I told you that the day after his profile appeared in the newspaper, some guy from Kiryat Arba told him they'd kill him if he ever talked to reporters again?"

"Uh-huh." Yiphat considered her cigarette, started to crush it against the wall, then reconsidered and took another puff. "I called Gideon at *Ha'Aretz* and told him. He was really concerned. You know you guys came across as being a little crazy in his article."

"Oh well, you know, fools for Christ."

Yiphat raised her left eyebrow.

"Oh, sorry . . ." Eugie began to search for words to extend the apology and Yiphat cut her off.

"It's okay. We all have our vices. I smoke, you have religion, *nu*, so how else would we survive here?"

Eugie smiled briefly. She could not have given up her religion even if she had tried, and she had considered trying when she lost Yossi.

"What about Tasneem?" Yiphat asked.

"She's still having the nightmares. Did I tell you she was in the hospital last week?"

"No." Yiphat threw her butt to the concrete floor of the roof, staring at it while Eugie continued.

"She had had a fever for four days and the doctors said she was dehydrated. Munir is convinced it's because she can't sleep at night because of the stoning and the threats."

"Christ! No four-year-old should have to put up with that! Do you think he could get her to Bethlehem for a psychiatric eval?"

Yiphat asked. "It would help when I bring his case to the high court."

"I'll ask him, but I doubt he has the money for it." Eugie sighed. The team had offered to sleep on Munir's roof and try to videotape the settler punks throwing stones and shouting death threats, but the conversations always ended with Munir pleading for money and the team explaining that RAPT policy forbade handouts.

"I'll see if I can get some funds from the office for it," Yiphat said. "If I say we need it for evidence, Lipschitz may think it's okay. Listen, I really have got to go. Are you sure you're okay with having Tess here? I forgot that you and Yossi had had a little bit of a thing going there for awhile. I assumed you weren't really serious."

"No," said Eugie. "It's okay. I mean we both knew pretty early on that it wasn't going to work out."

"Yeah. You know, I sort of had that figured out about Geoff after I found out that he liked the Three Stooges. Anyway, I'm not sure why Yossi's so crazy for her. She wasn't what I expected from everything he said about her. I REALLY have to go."

As Yiphat disappeared down the stairs, Eugie called after her, "I'll try to get up to Jerusalem next week." The noises from the chicken market covered up any response from Yiphat, if she had indeed made a response.

Yiphat wasn't the sort of person one hugged good-bye. Eugie picked up the cigarette butt and walked over to the instant coffee jar that Felicia used to dispose of her butts.

"She doesn't know everything about you and Yossi, does she?" Margaret asked without looking up from the magazine.

"No. I guess Yossi never told her."

But he had told his sister about Tess.


Eugie's given name was Unmerited Grace, bestowed by her mother over her father's objections. After three boys, her mother had been grateful to God for a girl, a gratitude that waned after three more sisters succeeded Eugie.

Her mother called her Grace, and members of her Reformed Anabaptist congregation in Pennsylvania still called her that, but due to her brothers' persistence, she became known to most of her family and friends as U.G. In college, she had begun spelling her name "Eugie," to avoid becoming known as "Ugh," as her peers had called her from junior high on.

Yossi had been the latest in a series of disastrous relationships beginning with her Social Work professor at Redemption College, a small Reformed Anabaptist school in Indiana.

She had developed a huge crush on Professor Schwenkfeld after he called her into his office and asked her to tell him the story of her life. No one had ever asked her that before and she became flustered when she realized that her life was not all that interesting.

He had encouraged her to transcend the boundaries of her limited religious upbringing and share her gifts with a hungry world. When he put his hand over hers and talked to her in his office, his gray eyes never leaving her face, she felt a warm feeling spreading through all her internal organs, and desperately wanted to kiss him.

At some point she started to have fantasies about his wife dying, and she knew that she was in trouble. She could have gotten beyond that, she thought, if he hadn't started having an affair with her roommate. Or maybe if he hadn't started talking about the affair in her group therapy class.

Confidentiality being the overriding concern in Professor Schwenkfeld's class, and the most important thing they would learn that semester, he said, he felt free to share about the relationship he had begun with Donna and about the pressures he was feeling from his wife and daughters.

It was Eugie's job to make excuses for Donna on those nights that she didn't come back to their dorm room. She lied to Donna's parents when they asked her whether the rumors they had heard about Donna and Professor Schwenkfeld were true.

On the day after he had brought his family to hear the Choral Society's annual rendition of *The Messiah,* and she had seen his wife looking tight-lipped and miserable, Eugie challenged him in the group about the consequences of his behavior.

After a moment's silence, during which Eugie tried not to throw up, he said, "I have to say it doesn't surprise me to hear you saying this, Eugie. I have sensed a real spirit of judging coming from you over the last few weeks. I haven't felt 'safe'"—he made quotation marks with his fingers—"around you for a long time, and as you know, this class is supposed to be about helping people in a group therapy situation to feel safe, so what are you going to do about that?"

It had been too late to withdraw from the class at that point. Eugie never forgave herself for violating her conscience in order to keep up her 3.9 grade-point average. She had refused to attend the wedding, though.

After the fallout from the broken engagement in her senior year of college, she had had approximately one significant relationship with a man every two years. She nearly became engaged to a Methodist who worked at the same social services agency she did a couple years ago. When he turned out to be gay, she vowed never again to become involved with someone who was not a Reformed Anabaptist.

Yossi was the first to test her resolve after making that vow. She failed the test miserably.

They had met in Chicago. She had given a presentation at a church group about her experience with RAPT in Haiti, and he had come up afterward to compliment her on her talk. When she alluded to her stammering problem, he had said that it made her presentation seem even more authentic. Later he told her that he thought her stammering was adorable.

"You're daydreaming," Margaret said, again without looking up from her magazine.

Eugie put her hands in the pockets of her skirt. She had been moving them inadvertently as she remembered what it was like to run them through Yossi's dark, springy hair as his head lay on her breasts.

"Do you think it would be okay if I took Tess out on night patrol, tonight? It's Friday."

"I don't see why not." Margaret took off her black plastic spectacles and began to wipe them with the hem of her T-shirt. "She has to learn sometime. Now tell me again how Yiphat talked you into taking her in?"

"I guess the last thing Yossi said to Tess was that she should look up Yiphat. Yiphat can't take her. Her apartment's about the size of one of our bedrooms. And really, we owe her and Hillel and the others."

"Well, you're the *mudeera*," Margaret said.

Eugie winced. "I am not the *mudeera*. I'm the facilitator. There's a difference between a director and a facilitator, you know." When Yossi had worked with the team for a month, he had had a habit of saying "You're the *mudeera*," when she had disagreed with him in strategy sessions. Knowing how he felt about authority, she would react as though he had slapped her—at least she did on the inside. She hadn't wanted the others on the team to know how it affected her.

"I know," Margaret said. She rose from the floor of the roof, stretched, and brushed off pants that may have been blue at one point.

Rolling up her copy of *The Nation*, she tucked it under her arm and picked up the denim jacket on which she had been sitting.

"My turn to cook tonight. Better get the lentils started," she said, making her way down the stairs.

"Okay, I think I'm going to lie down and read for a little bit," Eugie said, leaning against the wall and watching the army camp. Directly below her, the chicken vendors had begun lowering their awnings and slamming shut the heavy metal doors of their shops.

Over the loudspeaker of the mosque around the corner from their apartment, the recording of the muezzin began to sing, "Allaaaaah-ah-ah-ah-ah-ah-aaaaaahu Akhbar." Soon other voices, some recorded, some live, from Hebron's sixty-plus mosques joined it, all at different time intervals. When Eugie had first come to Hebron, the calls to prayer had struck her as a cacophony, but now she found them soothing. You could count on the calls to prayer sounding, even when the political situation was uncertain, rumors of massacres abounded, and relationships within the team were stormy.

By all rights, Margaret should have been in charge of the group, Eugie thought. Her age, and her experience in anti-war movements spanning five decades would have made her the natural choice. However, Margaret had joined RAPT on the condition that she would never be expected to serve as a coordinator. Felicia, likewise, had no interest in leading a team, despite her enormous self-certainty, and Frank was new. Also, as Felicia pointed out, it would have looked bad for the only male on the team to be in charge, to Felicia, anyway, and Eugie was inclined to agree with her. Their director in Minneapolis had told her they needed more women in leadership positions. Some people on the RAPT steering committee thought it would push the Reformed Anabaptists into ordaining women.

Trudging downstairs to the women's apartment, she thought that it was hard enough symbolizing America and Christianity for the people in Hebron. It didn't seem fair that she had to symbolize womanhood, too, for the people back home.

An hour and a half later she appeared in the front/living/dining room area of the lower apartment. Margaret was chopping cucumbers for a salad, and Felicia was reading a historical romance. With her hands clasped on her lap, Tess was sitting on the couch looking as though she were enjoying Frank's conversation a good deal. Eugie wondered how Tess got her dark, glossy hair to curl under symmetrically. Years ago, when she had tried her hair in a pageboy, the ends on either side of her head always curled in the same direction instead of toward each other. Tess's large brown eyes looked into Frank's placid blue ones as though they had known each other for a long time. There was not a zit on her.

When she heard Eugie come in, Felicia raised her head, looked over at Frank and Tess, looked meaningfully at Eugie, and then went back to her book.

"How was Munir?" Eugie asked.

"Huh?" Frank said. Then he turned and looked at her. "Oh, he wasn't in. Yiphat was really p.o.-ed, but she went over to his brother's house to leave a message. We got to the school too late, I think. Samir and Abed must have gone home already. I'll check with them tomorrow and apologize."

"Good," Eugie said. "Hey, ask them if they'd be willing to translate for us next time we go visit Munir. So who's on for night patrol tonight?" she continued. "I thought I could take Tess around to the mosque. Would two of you mind looping up toward Beit Hadassah?"

"I'll go," said Margaret, who always went on night patrol.

"I went last night," Frank said to Felicia.

"Yeah, yeah," said Felicia. "I'll go."

As Eugie watched Tess eat about a half hour later, she began to understand what Yossi saw in her. A spiritual centeredness radiated from those calm, dark eyes fixed on Frank as he talked about his parents' farm in Minnesota. Eugie wondered how Tess could maintain her composure after having so recently seen a man get blown up. Slender and dainty, more of a listener than a talker, Tess was, Eugie thought, everything Eugie herself wished to be: tranquil, beautiful and thin. And loved by Yossi.

Under the surface, Tess was in torment, Eugie knew. She had seen it before dinner, when she had shown Tess the room in which they poured cold water over themselves in lieu of a shower, and the squat-toilet in the small bathroom that never lost its smell even though Eugie and Margaret threw dish and laundry water onto the floor twice a day and squeegeed it down the toilet.

As Eugie had explained the dynamics of squat-toilet usage (i.e., throw toilet paper in the wastebasket, not down the pipe; pour a jug of water down when you're finished), she had looked up and seen two large tears rolling down Tess's cheeks. Enfolding Tess in her arms, Eugie let her cry on her shoulder. Tess had soon recovered and asked to be shown her room.

Eugie had not been with Yossi for half a year, and she was still a mess. And furious with herself for being a mess. In the last three months she had come to the gloomy conclusion that perhaps her disastrous relationships were God's way of letting her know she should be single.

"You don't have your passport?" Eugie asked. "Maybe you shouldn't go out."

"I think it would probably be better if she stayed back," Frank said. "Nonsense," Margaret said. "She's going to have to leave the apartment sometime while she's here. We'll just tell the soldiers the truth."

"Oh yeah," said Felicia. "That will look really good. 'Our new team person doesn't have her passport because she was involved in a suspicious bombing incident at an Arab hotel.'"

"I have Yiphat's card," Eugie said. "If anyone asks, I'll tell them to call our lawyer. And," she said, smiling as she buckled her black waistpack around her middle, "we will be VERY charming. Who's got the pelephone?"

*     *     *

Frank continued to protest that Tess should stay back, until he realized that he would have to go with Felicia if Tess remained in the apartment. He told her that RAPT policy dictated that team members always patrol in pairs. Tess had told him that she would rather go out anyway. Since coming into the country, she had not had any sort of aerobic exercise, and she could sense she had put on some weight. Frank offered to take Felicia's place.

After she and Eugie parted from Frank and Margaret, Eugie asked her, "It's been a rough day for you, hasn't it?"

"What doesn't kill us makes us stronger," Tess responded.

"I hope that you feel welcome here," Eugie said, as she waved to a soldier, who smiled and touched the brim of his red wool beret. "After what you've been through. I mean, when I was talking to Yiphat, it wasn't that I didn't want you in particular to come. It's just that things can get really crazy here. But it looks like you're pretty good at dealing with crises."

"Yes," said Tess. "Things usually have a way of turning out for the best."

"Wow," said Eugie. "It's been a long time since I met someone that optimistic. I wish I could feel that way. I mean, all day we're dealing with people—"

A young man with long sidecurls and a black velvet skullcap came charging toward them on a bicycle. Tess started to step out of the way, but Eugie grabbed her arm and forced her to remain in the path of the bicycle. The young man swerved at the last minute and ran into a squad of four soldiers on patrol, who began yelling at him—presumably in Hebrew." Eugie appeared not to notice.

"*Det var som svarte.* You have good nerves, yes?" A male voice boomed behind them. Tess turned and smiled upward. The tall square-jawed man with sandy hair smiled back at her, but then ignored her and focused on Eugie.

He must have something on his mind, Tess thought, not being able to explain the shift of focus in any other way.

"Oh, you mean Goldstein-pin guy?" Eugie asked. "Well, the first five times he did it, we would get out of his way, but now we figure it's his own fault if he runs into us."

"His name is Goldsteinpin?"

"Oh. I don't know his name, but the first time we saw him he was wearing a pin with Baruch Goldstein's picture on it. I suppose sometime we ought to introduce ourselves to him. Do you know who Baruch Goldstein is?" she asked Tess, but before Tess could respond, the tall man interrupted.

"Have you seen Wisam lately?" the tall man asked.

"No. She doesn't come around much anymore. She's awfully busy with her job and with school."

"I have been to the municipality three times this week," the man said. "She was never in." He tugged absentmindedly at an identification card pinned to his blue nylon vest. "I think she may not want to see me."

Eugie started to put her arm around him and then caught herself. "Oops," she said. "I keep forgetting I'm not supposed to touch men in public here. Listen Erland, Wisam is very religious. You know that. And I just don't think her family would let her get involved with you. And I know she would not move back to Norway with you."

She turned back to Tess. "Erland is with TIPH."

"Temporary International Presence in Hebron," Erland said to Tess. She smiled at him as a way of thanking him for the explanation, although it had done nothing to make her more interested in the subject. And he still seemed more interested in Eugie.

"Wisam would not let her family get in the way of her happiness. She said that arranged marriages were part of Arab culture, not of Islam."

"Well, yes, but there you go. She probably doesn't think it's the best idea to get involved with a non-Muslim."

"I hate religion!" Erland said. They stopped to watch some teenage boys play soccer in the alleyway. "You know, there were some settler girls throwing rocks at the boys who were playing here last night." He whipped out a notepad and wrote a few comments in it.

"Yeah, I know. I guess the guys made some really rude remarks—at least that's what the police told us. But anyway, if you hate religion, it's just not going to work out with you and Wisam."

"But I don't have any objection to her religion," Erland said. "I think we could be happy, and I would not stand in the way of her God. Tell me, if you really loved someone, would you let religion stand in the way of your happy life?"

Eugie bit her lip. "I was in love with someone once," she said after a pause. "He was Jewish. It didn't work out, and religion was a big reason for why it didn't work out."

"Does not that prove that religion is not a good thing for human happiness?" Erland asked.

"I could not be happy without my religion, either," Eugie said. "And neither could Wisam. We're going on up to the mosque. Want to come with?"

"No, I will stay here and watch the game. Call me if you see problems."

"Okay," said Eugie. "Chin up, Erland."

It was such a big chin, Tess thought. It had not been tactful of Eugie to call attention to it.

As they approached a swinging gate in the middle of the road, Tess wrinkled her nose. Eugie noticed and said, "There's a guy down there that skins sheep," gesturing toward a wooden door at their left, four steps down from street level. "*Erev Tov!*" She called out.

"*Erev Tov.* Good evening," a soldier in a dark green wool beret said to them. When he looked at Tess, his eyebrows went up and he said, "And good evening to you, too."

"Hi," said Tess.

"You are together?" he asked.

"Yes," said Eugie. "Tess will be with us for a little while."

"Tess," said the soldier, drawing out the "s." "Welcome to Israel, Tess."

"We're in Hebron, not Israel," Eugie said, still smiling.

"We shall see," the soldier said, also still smiling.

"Well bye. Come on, Tess."

They walked past an enormous rectangular building, set back from the road on their left by dozens of broad, shallow steps. Weird shadows cast by the trees that lined the staircase seemed to creep toward the building. A trailer with metal steps leading up from the street sat in front of the building's grounds. Tess realized that the grass around the building was the first green, growing thing she had seen since coming to Hebron.

"That's the police station," Eugie told her. "And THAT monstrosity is the il Ibrahimi mosque—or the Cave of Machpelah, depending on your political or religious affiliation."

Tess looked at the brown stone structure awash in floodlights and thought it looked like half of a castle. On the long side facing them, there were regularly spaced stone humps lining the edge of the roof. On the short side, square zig-zaggy ridges, which she normally associated with castles, lined the roof. Two slender towers with loudspeakers jutted from opposite corners of the building, but no respectable turrets. And no drawbridge.

"Some day I'll take you up close so you can see the Herodian stonework. You've heard of Baruch Goldstein, right?"

"Yes." Yossi had told her about him when he had described his adventures in Hebron.

"Well that's where he killed the people while they were praying at the end of Ramadan in 1994."

Tess again said nothing, and Eugie continued. "Whenever people come to visit us in Hebron, they always want us to bring them here. Since we're Christian, we can go into either the Jewish or the Muslim side. There's a part of me that can really relate to Erland or to Yossi when they talk about religion being this evil thing. I mean, I don't care if I never see another holy place as long as I live."

Tess followed Eugie as she walked into the small park that lay across the street and sat on a stone bench facing the mosque.

"Those are settlers," Eugie said, pointing to elegantly dressed women in hats and men in white shirts and black pants walking up the broad, shallow steps under the yellow light. A group of five soldiers sat in chairs at the base of stairs, legs spread, with guns in their laps, talking and laughing.

"Sometimes, I like to just sit here," Eugie said, "and watch the people come and go."

A black rat scurried under the broken stone bench to their left, chased by a cat that appeared, in the dim light coming from the police station, to be the same color.

Suddenly, two soldiers yelled at the top of their lungs and began charging, guns pointed at something behind where Eugie and Tess sat. They ran for about thirty yards, then gave up, laughed, and trotted back to their comrades.

"Drill," said Eugie.

"So you were in love with a Jewish boy?" Tess asked. She was bored.

"Yeah. I guess I'm not quite over him."

"There's more room in a broken heart," Tess said. Her second husband had loved Carly Simon.

"Well, that's one way of looking at it," Eugie said. "The work does help. It's only when there's down time that I start wallowing in self-pity."

Tess had been feeling pretty sorry for herself ever since she saw the primitive shower and toilet, but it could be worse, she reflected. She had someone who adored her, and Eugie didn't. And Eugie looked like she needed to lose ten pounds, too. But then, she thought charitably, she knew men who could overlook that sort of thing.

Eugie's pocket rang. She pulled out the cellphone. "R.A.P.T.," she sang out. "Eugie speaking. Hi, Erland, something up?" She made a face at Tess. "Sure, Erland, I'll tell her next time I see her. You know, you should get up to Jerusalem for some fun soon."

She flipped the phone shut and stuck it back in the pocket of her skirt.

"He is so hung up on Wisam," she said. Standing up, she brushed herself off and said, "Life sucks."

When they returned to the apartment, two people whom Tess had not yet met sat at the table. One, Eugie introduced as Nayif, a journalist, and the other introduced herself as Lisa. Lisa wore a loosely draped, black headscarf and blue jeans. Margaret looked at Eugie and Tess with a frozen smile, and Felicia appeared to be enjoying herself a good deal. In the next room, Frank was working on the computer.

"I LOVE Louis Farrakhan," Lisa announced, tucking a strand of silky blond hair behind her ear. "I have all his tapes. Most of my friends are black, you know, and everything that the white media says about Farrakhan is just a lie."

Nayif looked at Eugie with a beseeching expression. The longest eyelashes Tess had ever seen on a man fringed his grey eyes. "We were talking about Islam in the United States. Margaret was speaking of Malcolm X," he said.

"Yeah, he—" began Eugie.

Lisa interrupted her. "You know the sort of propaganda the U.S. puts out about people like Farrakhan. It's like the propaganda about those American nuns who were supposedly killed in El Salvador. I mean really. I've hitchhiked through El Salvador and some of those soldiers are the nicest people. I met some of them in a bar and we went dancing and they told me I was the only person who had treated them like real human beings."

Margaret's smile grew broader and more fixed. Eugie stared hard at Nayif, who shrugged his shoulders. Pausing only to breathe, Lisa continued talking for twenty more minutes. Felicia went through three cigarettes.

Finally, Nayif cleared his throat and told Lisa that it was late and they must get back to his parents' house. Eugie asked them if they wanted coffee. Lisa opened her mouth but Nayif interrupted.

"No, we want to go," he said, opening the door to the apartment and making an "after you" gesture toward Lisa.

She sailed out and Nayif muttered "I am very sorry" as he followed her and closed the door.

"What is Nayif doing with her?" asked Eugie. "I thought she was staying with Wisam."

"Lisa said Wisam's parents kicked her out for using bad words," Margaret said. "I think Nayif is thinking about marrying her to get to the United States."

"I'LL marry him if it comes to that," Felicia announced, stubbing out her cigarette on a small blue saucer. Noticing Eugie watching her, she said, "Hey, the rule is that if guests smoke in our house, I'm allowed to smoke inside while they're here."

"No, no," Eugie said, rubbing her brow. "I wasn't looking at you, I was thinking of something."

From the street below their apartment, they heard Lisa's voice rising. "Leave us alone you dumb prick, it's none of your business why we're out walking. I can be with all the Arabs I want."

Eugie and Frank ran out of the apartment and down the stairs. Tess and Margaret walked over to the window in the computer room to watch them in the alley below.

Touching the hand that held his automatic weapon, Eugie was talking to the soldier and smiling. After a few moments, his scowl changed to a reluctant grin. Then Frank began speaking to the soldier, as Lisa and Nayif walked away. The soldier made a gesture with his foot as though he were playing soccer, and Frank kicked the phantom soccer ball back to him.

Tess smiled. Frank was very nice.

# *Interim*

Myron was a young Border Policeman obviously ill-suited to
military life. On the strap of his M-16 he had written with a ball-
point pen, "R.E.M.—Losing My Religion."

He first made our acquaintance because he wanted to talk about
music. He knew every American concert act that would be coming
to Israel for the next year and told us about his favorite Israeli
artists as well.

"Have you heard of Aviv Geffen?" he asked. When we shook
our heads, he said. "It's not true, you know, that he told kids to
commit suicide. They would have killed themselves anyway." The
next day, he brought in a picture of Geffen, done up in KISS-style
makeup to show us.

One afternoon we passed him in the street and saw that he
had a large gauze bandage taped over his right eyebrow.

"Myron!" we said. "What happened to you?"

He held his finger over his lips and motioned us to the side,
away from his fellow Border Police. With his back to them, he
lifted up a corner of the bandage just enough so that we could see
his new eyebrow ring.

"I told them that I got into a fight when I was home," he said.
"We are not allowed to have these in the army."

"What are you going to do?" I asked, "keep a bandage over
your eye for the next two and a half years?"

"Why not?" he asked.

# CHAPTER 3

The next morning, they left at 8:30 to walk down to the park in front of the mosque for worship. When they passed a harness-and bridle-maker's shop, two little boys dressed in matching knit sweaters and pants ran up to them to shake their hands.

"Ah, it is the beautiful Christian ladies!" a voice rasped behind them.

Tess turned and saw an old man with light, sparse hair. He looked as though he had always been short, and had become even shorter from years of walking hunched over and peering at the ground.

"Hey! What about me?" Frank asked, laughing.

The old man cackled and put his hand on Frank's arm. "You are the handsomest Christian man, too," he said.

"*Kief halak*, Sa'eed. How are you?" said Eugie.

"*al Hamdulillah*," replied Sa'eed, raising his hands to the sky. He shook everyone's hand but Felicia's. She regarded him coolly as she exhaled a cloud of cigarette smoke. An anxious look crossed his face and he turned back to Eugie.

"And this—Who is this beautiful lady?"

"Tess MacAdoo, this is Sa'eed," Eugie said.

"Ah she is almost as beautiful as my Yuaad. I have spoken to you about my beautiful Yuaad?" Sa'eed said.

Margaret spoke without looking at him. "Many times, Sa'eed. We really must get to the park to pray."

"Yes, some people think you are crazy. Some think you are spies, but I, Sa'eed, know that you are doing the work of God."

As they passed the checkpoint across from the vegetable market, Felicia muttered, "And look who he's talking to."

Tess turned and saw Sa'eed bobbing and gesticulating in front of a group of five soldiers at the checkpoint.

"Oh Felicia, he talks to everyone," Eugie said. "If we refused to talk to anyone that someone else accused of being a collaborator, we wouldn't have any friends."

"Still, it doesn't hurt to be careful," Margaret said. "And I tend to trust the people who have told us to be careful of him."

"Yeah, well what about *satyagraha*?" Eugie demanded. "Truth force. If we're open with everyone, how can we be subverted?"

"We are not leading a nonviolent mass movement like Gandhi was," Margaret said. "And we have friends whom we could get into serious trouble by repeating what they tell us."

Eugie looked distressed. "Well—of course we're not going to talk about people in front of him."

"He gives me the creeps. Always has," Felicia said. "I know his kind from Colombia. In a lot of ways they're all alike. My father couldn't tell the difference. None of the other American missionaries could either. But I always knew."

Eugie walked faster and Tess could tell she was angry. It was an awkward situation, Tess thought, because she could not tell whom she should support. Eugie seemed to be in charge, but she noticed that Eugie deferred to Margaret. Felicia spoke with more authority, but seemed to hold herself aloof from team functions. Tess smiled. Of course, why hadn't she seen the obvious? She would do whatever Frank did.

At the moment he seemed to be looking at her. She smiled up at him.

"So, you get to see what we're like when we argue," he said. "So far there hasn't been any bloodshed."

She laughed in a way calculated to make him think he had said something clever.

"Oh brother," Eugie said, looking at the barrier across the road leading to the mosque.

"Shit," Felicia said. "Just what we needed."

Tess saw they were looking at a dumpy woman with shoulder length hair the color of margarine, laughing with the soldiers standing at the checkpoint. Four men with short haircuts stood around her clutching Bibles.

"Maybe we can cut down the alley and come up through the park from the parking lot," suggested Frank.

It was too late. The blonde woman had seen them. She pointed at them as they approached, and appeared to be explaining something to the soldiers.

"Well here they come," she said. "The so-called 'Christians.'"

"I hate it when they talk in quotation marks," Eugie said under her breath.

"I was just telling these fine young men here what a bunch of Arab-lovers you are," the woman said. "I told them you don't believe that Jews have a right to come home."

"Oh, you are so full of it—" Felicia began.

Margaret nudged her, and Felicia focussed her furious eyes on the rusting trash dumpster at the boundary of the park, across the street from the mosque.

"Why, lookee thar," one of the men said, pointing at Felicia. "They got an Ay-rab with them right now. No wonder they hate Jews."

"*Yo soy Colombiana,*" Felicia said, "or you can just call me a spic, if you want."

Eugie addressed a small soldier with big ears. "We've talked before. Have we ever given you the impression that we hate Jews?"

"No," the soldier mumbled.

"He is Druse," a larger soldier with red hair said. "Why would these people lie about you in this way? They seem like very good people to me." He folded his arms across his chest and looked amused.

Eugie smiled up at him. "Yeah, well, ask them what they think Zechariah 13:7-9 means."

"But I am not religious," the soldier said, "It is not important for me."

"But it is for them," Eugie said. "And it will show you what their agenda is."

"I do not know this word, 'agenda,'" the soldier said. He was beginning to look bored.

"The Bible clearly states that it is God's plan to bring his people home. There are over seven hundred places in the Bible that testify to this," the blonde woman said.

"Okay, but I think you should tell them how you people interpret Zechariah 13:7-9."

The blonde woman looked sideways at one of the men with her and murmured something.

"Okay, I'll tell him, since we have got to go," Eugie said. "These people are Christian Zionists and they think that in order for Jesus to return, all the Jews in the world will have to move to Israel. They think that when that time comes, two-thirds of the Jews are going to die and the rest are going to convert to Christianity. Now tell me, is that the sort of thing a real *mensch* would think?"

The soldiers said something to each other in Hebrew and laughed. "I am sorry, we must go," the red-haired one said.

"Well, you boys just go right ahead," the blonde woman said. "Don't pay attention to these Arab-lovers."

Frank looked at Tess with an expression of disgust. She nodded at him.

"You are new," the short Druse soldier said to Tess.

"Yes," she said, smiling at him.

"Well, good luck," he said. "Do not mind about them," he jerked his head in the direction of the blonde woman and her friends, who were walking back to their bus. "Come and see us again."

"Yes," said the red-haired soldier. "Please visit. Come sometime to my house in Tel Aviv. I can take you to some clubs."

Tess smiled and waved back at them as she and the other RAPTors walked toward the stone benches in the park.

"Those people just make me so mad," Eugie said as she stomped toward the bench.

"All I can say," said Margaret, smiling, "is that for all the faults of the Catholic Church, we've never come up with that."

"But the crusades and inquisitions were your fault," Eugie said. She laughed and said, "I used to date a Catholic guy who told me, 'Oh you're just jealous because you don't have your own crusades and inquisitions.'"

"Are you ready, Felicia?" Eugie asked, as they sat down. "Here, sit in the middle where we can all hear you."

"I wanted to open with 'My Life Flows On,'" Felicia said, after they had arranged themselves on the stone bench. She handed around paperback hymnals.

Tess had not heard this song before, and did not read music, so she listened. Felicia had a strong soprano voice, a little husky from the smoking, and sang with gusto. Eugie sang in a quavering alto. Frank sang melody with Felicia, and Margaret mumbled tunelessly.

> My life flows on in endless song
> Above earth's lamentation
> I hear the sweet though far-off hymn
> That hails the new creation
>
> No storm can shake my inmost calm
> While to that Rock I'm clinging
> Since love is Lord of heav'n and earth
> How can I keep from singing?

Partway through the refrain, Tess heard singing coming from the direction of the mosque. The blonde woman and four men had started in with

> Come we that love the Lord and let our joys be known
> Join in a song with sweet accord, join in a song with sweet accord
> And thus surround the throne and thus surround the throne.
>
> We're marching to Zion, beautiful, beautiful Zion
> We're marching upward to Zion the beautiful city of God

The rest of the team began to sing louder. Even Margaret's monotone took on a strident volume.

"What though joys and comforts die?" sang the team

"The hill of Zion yields a thousand sacred sweets," sang the Christian Zionists.

"The Lord my savior liveth.

What though the darkness gathers round," sang the team.

"Before we reach the heav'nly fields," sang the Christian Zionists.

"Songs in the night he giveth."

"And walk the golden streets and walk the golden streets."

Tess noticed that a crowd of soldiers, policeman, Palestinians, and people she now knew to be Israeli settlers had gathered in front of the mosque to watch the sing-off. Some of the Israeli women began swaying front to back with prayer books, waving their hands in the direction of the team.

"We're marching to Zion, beautiful, beautiful Zion."

"No storm can shake my inmost calm," sang the team through clenched teeth. "While to that Rock I'm clinging."

"We're marching upward to Zion, the beautiful city of God."

"Since love is Lord of heav'n and earth, how can I keep from singing?"

Margaret spoke up. "This is ridiculous," she said. "Let's move over to the steps."

The team got up and moved toward the large parking lot in back of and below the park—where Yiphat had left the car the day before when she had brought Tess down to Hebron. Cheers and catcalls followed them. Felicia sat on a stone wall demarcating the end of the park, and the rest of the team sat on the broad, shallow steps leading down into the parking lot. The Christian Zionists continued singing behind them, but the team members were able to hear Felicia when she began to read.

"I'm continuing on with Chapter Ten in Walter Wink's *Engaging the Powers*," she said. "The chapter opens with a poem by Bertolt Brecht that I liked."

For we knew only too well:
Even hatred of squalor
Makes the brow grow stern.
Even anger against injustice
Makes the voice grow harsh. Alas we

Who wished to lay the foundations of kindness
Could not ourselves be kind.[1]


"Can we have some silence, Felicia?" Margaret asked. "I would like to think about that a little bit."

"No problem," answered Felicia.

"Hello, hello!" a voice boomed behind them.

"Hi, Abu Hani," Eugie said smiling up at him from the step on which they were sitting. "We're trying to pray right now. Can we come over and talk to you later?"

"Yes, yes of course. You must pray. Come to my house and drink tea?"

"*Mara tani*, another time," Eugie said. "But now we must pray."

"Yes yes, it is good to pray," Abu Hani said. "You have a new friend now."

"Yes, this is Tess," Eugie said. "But we must—"

"Would you like to see inside the mosque?" Abu Hani directed his question toward Tess. "Forty years I have been a tour guide. I have taken British, German, Portuguese peoples through the mosque. I will show you, too. For no money."

"Another time," Margaret said.

"Yes Haji. Today, tomorrow, anytime."

"Lord Jesus," Felicia prayed out loud with her eyes closed. "We just praise your name for this beautiful day and for all the people. We ask you to draw them closer into your precious light."

Tess bowed her head and closed her eyes when she saw that everyone else had, too.

"Lord, we ask you to hear our prayers, to just anoint us with your spirit."

"You can stop now," Frank said. "He's gone."

"Okay." Felicia's head snapped up. "Where was I? Uh . . . Chapter 10. On Not Becoming What We Hate."

---

[1]    (Minneapolis: Fortress Press, 1992) p. 195

> In the previous chapter I suggested that "Resist not evil" is
> better rendered "Do not return evil for evil," Do not mirror
> evil," "Do not respond to evil in kind." This refusal of reactive
> opposition is one of the most profound and difficult truths
> in Scripture.

Tess watched as five boys in ragged shirts and pants began
looking through the dumpster in the parking lot and pulling out
glass bottles. One of them pointed at the team sitting on the stairs,
and the boys approached them, standing a couple steps below
where they sat.

"Ignore them; just keep reading," Margaret said.

> Since our hate is usually a direct response to evil done
> to us, our hate almost invariably causes us to respond in
> terms already laid down by the enemy. Unaware of what is
> happening, we turn into the very thing we oppose, Felicia
> continued.

"Hello. How are you?" one of the boys said, measuring his words.

Eugie smiled at them and raised her finger to her lips. The
boys mimicked her and laughed.

"The arms race was the supreme example of this process. We
felt threatened by the Soviets, so we increased our weapons."

"Give me one dollar," another one of the boys said.

Eugie again put her finger to her lips and ssshed them.

"Sssssh. Sssssh. Ssssh," the boys all said in unison.

"*Ana bidi asaali*," Eugie said.

"I think you mean, '*Ekhna bidna asaali*,'" Frank said. "We
want to pray. Not 'I want to pray.'"

"Except then it wouldn't be '*asaali*.' Nasaali? Asaalna?" Eugie
rubbed her brow.

"No matter how much more powerful our resistance to evil
became," Felicia continued in a louder voice. "Soviet resistance
grew at the same pace. A.J. Muste deduced an axiom from this
behavior: 'If you arm yourself, you arm your enemy.'"

The boys began jeering at them in Arabic. One of them pushed another down the stairs. He was on his feet in seconds and lunged at the one who had pushed him.

A voice began yelling from behind them. Tess turned and saw an older man wearing a white scarf fastened around his head with black cords. He wore a long robe made out of a navy blue, pin-striped business suit material. He hastened toward them, limping and waving his cane at the boys.

They yelled something back at him, but ran away across the parking lot.

"Thanks," Frank said to the man.

"For nothing. For nothing," the man said, with a tired expression on his face. He walked away, waving his hand back as though dismissing them.

"He's one of the men who got shot in the mosque," Eugie whispered to Tess.

"I met A.J. Muste in New York shortly after I took my final vows," Margaret said.

"Who haven't you met?" Felicia said. "Look. Should I go on or should we just blow off worship for today?"

"No. No," Eugie said. "I'm sorry. Go on."

In this mimetic rivalry, we took on some of the very qualities in the Soviets that we claimed to be resisting.

A shadow fell across Tess's feet. She looked behind her and saw a little boy and girl with hair so golden that the light hitting their heads almost hurt her eyes.

"That's Mo'amar and Islam," Eugie whispered. She offered her hand to Mo'amar who shook it gravely.

> To keep communism from spreading in Africa, Asia or Latin America, we felt we had to move in with our troops or manipulate elections, or unseat legitimately elected regimes, or assassinate leftist leaders, Felicia continued.

Mo'ammar and Islam walked over to what once had been playground equipment. There were no swings in the swingset and the jungle gym had several of its metal crossbars missing. Islam attempted to climb the jungle gym and Mo'ammar pulled her down. Tess heard the hollow metal tubing of the jungle gym resound like a gong when Islam's head hit it. Islam picked up a rock from the ground and flung it at her brother, missing him by several feet. Mo'ammar picked it up and ran at her, his hand and rock poised to come bashing down on her head.

"*La'! La'!*" Eugie and Margaret shouted together and raced across the sparse grass. Margaret snatched the rock from his hand.

"Don't worry," Frank said to Tess. "He's always doing that. I've never seen him actually hit her yet."

Islam ran away crying, and Margaret and Eugie rejoined the group.

"Go on," Eugie said to Felicia.

"'You always become the thing you fight the most,' wrote Jung somewhere, and we have done everything in our power to prove him right."

"Hullo, Peacemakers," said a voice behind them. Tess turned and saw Erland walking toward them with a blonde man whose long neck and receding chin made him resemble a turtle.

"That's it. I give up." Felicia said, slamming the book shut.

"Aw geez, it's the annoying Swedish guy," Eugie groaned, when she turned and saw them approaching.

The so-named annoying Swedish guy approached the team and looked down on them, bristling with disapprobation.

"You told me that you do not invite visitors to stay with you," he said, pointing at Eugie.

Eugie glared at Erland, who looked apologetic.

"I am very sorry," he said. "I thought you—"

The Swedish guy spoke up again. "He told me that you had three Norwegian journalists staying with you last month and yet you would not make room for me, a fellow Christian peace activist."

"Look Olaf," Eugie said. "We are sort of in the middle of a lot of things right now, and we just didn't have the time to play host to you."

"But I do not understand; I do not think this is very hospitable of you," Olaf said.

The five Palestinian boys who had been cavorting around them earlier walked up to the group, arms on each others' shoulders, listening as if they understood the discussion.

Erland spoke to them in Arabic and moved away from the team and Olaf, drawing the boys into conversation. Eugie frowned in his direction.

"You have not given me a good reason not to let me stay with you," Olaf continued. "If you let Norwegians stay with you, you should let me, yes? Or is it that you do not like Swedes?"

"It's not a question of liking you or not," Margaret said. "We just cannot have you staying with us at this time.

Another bus pulled up in front of the mosque, discharging another large group of Americans. Tess noticed that many of them were wearing the crocheted snoods that some of the Israeli settler women wore, but they had not tucked their hair inside as the Israeli women did, so the sacks perched on their heads like scrota. The blonde woman and the four men with her engaged the group and then pointed at the team. Twenty of them began walking across the park toward them.

Olaf was not to be bought off by polite answers. After the third time he began a sentence with, "I don't think that's very—" Felicia snapped, "Look, we don't really care what you think. We have better things to do than babysit you. The last time you were here, you asked us to carry your baggage back to our apartment for you while the soldiers were closing in on the Hebron university students' demonstration. You're just going to be in the way."

"Look, Olaf," Eugie pointed to the approaching group of Christian Zionists. "Those people are Christians. Why don't you ask them if they'll put you up? We really have to go."

Frank had already pulled Tess down the broad steps and into the parking lot by the time the Christian Zionists reach the group. Eugie, Margaret, and Felicia ran to catch up with them. When Tess looked back, she saw Olaf making pathetic gestures as the Christian Zionists stood around him, shaking their heads in sympathy. Erland stood with the five Palestinian boys, watching the approaching Americans. The boys smiled sweetly at the assembled throng and continued to do so after the men and women responded to these smiles with baleful glares.

# *Interim*

Some selections from literature picked up at the Third Christian Zionist Congress:

From Gary Cooperburg's *Project Shofar* brochure:

> The shofar blast is a symbolic warning that we must all stand up to the challenge and fight the attempt to thwart the Divine Process of Redemption. Christian Zionists can work together with observant Jews in this effort. It is a holy effort which brings Divine grace upon those who involve themselves with it.

> Project Shofar salutes the participants of the Third Christian Zionist Congress taking place under the auspices of the international Christian Embassy in Jerusalem. We welcome your recognition that the only peace plan is the one which G-d promised to the Jewish People through our father Abraham.

From Cooperburg's brochure, *What's a nice Jewish boy doing in a place like this?*

> The Christian Embassy, which established itself as an embassy in Jerusalem for the express purpose of showing the nations of the world that Jerusalem is the exclusive, eternal capital of the Jewish State has put the Israeli government to shame. It has consistently spoken out against our rejection of the countless miracles performed for us which they recognize and our leaders fail to see. They call for a "not one inch" peace plan. They spoke out against the infamous "Oslo" underground sellout of the Jewish State. They have reached into their pockets to help bring Jews home from the former Soviet Union. "They cry out to the Jewish government to act like Jews and maintain their Jewish

integrity. They have initiated an annual feast of tabernacles convention which, among other things, seeks to comfort the Jewish people and remind us that we are still G-d's Chosen. And now, just as the leadership of the Jewish people is seeking peace at the expense of Zionism, we see the Christian Embassy sponsoring the third Christian Zionist Congress in Jerusalem.

From Cooperburg's brochure, *God's word is our guarantee*:

The cunning Arab squatters, whose ancient historical connection with the Land of Israel spans nearly 100 years, include among their slander of the Jewish people, their complaint that Jews have come from other countries and taken away what is rightfully theirs. If one would but trace the history of these fraudulent Arab migrants and thieves, he would discover an abundant lack of authentic history, or legal acquisition of the land upon which they live. But rather than waste time on trivial mundane pursuits, one has but to open his Bible to clearly see what is taking place in the Promised Land today . . .

From Richard A. Hellman's *The Vision of CIPAC* (Christians' Israel Public Action Campaign):

. . . Judea and Samaria, the biblical names for the so-called occupied territories of the West Bank are the heart of biblical Israel. Israel obtained them by legal right and has no need to give these lands over to anyone . . .

. . . Biblically speaking, I don't believe that Israel should concede land for peace. I believe that Israel and the Jewish people have been given this land, have been restored in their land, and that this should be in perpetuity. However, the nations of the world in the United Nations and even America have brought pressure upon Israel to concede land for peace . . . . But the way I read the Bible, Israel has title

deed from Dan to Beersheva, from the River of Egypt to the
Euphrates River, from the Mediterranean Sea virtually to
Saudi Arabia, including present-day Jordan.

From Ramon and Zipporah Bennett's *Arm of Salvation* newsletter
Vol. 5, No.4

Continue to pray for complete success with the ARROW
antimissile system and for the production of large numbers
of missiles and launchers.

Continue to pray for a revelation of the TRUTH about
JESUS and for Israeli hearts to be open and receptive.
Pray for protection and a HEDGE OF FIRE to be all around
Ramon for having written *Philistine*.

From "The Five Lies of Islam," *Middle East Intelligence Digest,* vol. 7
#3:

#1 Allah is God

Islam's big lie, which underpins all the falsehoods upon
which it stands, holds that the source of revelation imparted
to Muhammad is the God of the Bible worshipped by
Christians and Jews.

In fact, Allah was the name of the pagan moon-god to whom
temples were built across the Middle East . . .

To deceive non-Muslims, Muslims back up the claim that
they worship God by pointing out that the word, "Allah,"
appears in the Arabic language Bible. But while the noun
"allah" does mean "god," as a proper noun it has no connection
to the Name of the God of Israel, the One who calls Himself
YHWH. [Author's note: You mean like the English word,
"god?"]

# CHAPTER 4

Tess cut her cucumber into delicate circles before eating it with a fork. Others on the team were munching them like bananas. Frank was on his third. They all dipped their cucumbers and pieces of bread into a common bowl of *hummous*—a paste-like substance made from chick-peas and *tahini*. Eugie had poured olive oil on top of it, and Tess figured that it must be loaded with fat. She was glad she didn't like it and therefore didn't have to tell people that she wasn't eating it because she didn't want their germs. She also thought that Eugie might take it personally if she mentioned the fat content.

Eugie had expressed concern when Tess had tasted and rejected the *hummous*, and had gone into the kitchen to fetch her some salty white cheese. After Frank told her it was made from either sheep or goats' milk, she convinced Eugie that she wasn't hungry. The cheese tasted the way goats smelled.

Surreptitiously, she pinched a small fold of flesh from her waistline. She could tell by doing so that she had put on exactly three pounds. She willed herself to feel content with cucumbers, salt and bread.

"So who's first for Dubboya Street this afternoon?" Eugie said, licking *hummous* off her fingers.

No one responded. After a moment, Felicia said, "How long are we going to keep doing this? Nothing's happened there for weeks."

"Yeah," said Eugie. "But remember the one week we weren't there Ahmad's son got beaten up."

Felicia slumped in her chair and looked annoyed. "I'm sick of sitting there for hours and watching Palestinian kids whale on each other—practicing their English. Saying the same things over and over—'Hello. How are you. What is more beautiful, Hebron or America?'

I'm sick of Yehudit Levine coming up to us and shaking her finger and saying, 'Don't say I didn't warn you.' You know that retarded kid who's always asking us for our pins that have the picture of a broken gun on them? He was pointing at mine a couple days ago and Yehudit comes up later and says, 'I saw that Arab grabbing for your breast.'"

"Is it much of a walk?" Tess asked. "I would like to get some exercise."

"It's only a few blocks away," Frank said. "But if you patrol up to Tel Rumeida, it's a really steep hill."

"Okay," said Tess. "I'll go if someone will go with me."

"I'll go," said Frank.

"I'll go, too," Eugie said. "Margaret and Felicia, you'll switch with us around two?"

"Sure, "Margaret said. "I'll go up and take my nap now, in that case."

Felicia said nothing, but followed Margaret out the door.

Eugie rubbed her forehead. "Frank, what do you think about Dubboya Street? Am I being too pushy on this? I just get these bad feelings that something's about to happen."

"Yeah, but you feel that way all the time," Frank said. "Remember a couple Saturdays ago when we got invited to Jericho by some of the university students? Felicia really wanted to go and nothing happened that day. We all could have gone to Jericho."

"I told Felicia she could go," Eugie said.

"Yeah, but you said it like 'Well, if you REALLY feel like you need to go, Felicia, that's fine. The rest of us can probably make do. Go on. I don't mind. Have a good time while we're getting spit on by settlers.'"

"I did NOT say it like that," Eugie said.

"Well, that's how it came across," Frank said, peeling a banana. "Besides, she couldn't have gone with just her and me. She would have been the only girl with five guys."

"Well, Margaret and I didn't want to go," Eugie said.

"Yeah, but you're the ones that need the vacation the most. You really ought to unwind a little, Eugie. I mean, people sort of go along with what you want just because they don't want to see you tense up."

Eugie's lips disappeared as her mouth set in a straight line. She threw the piece of bread she had been about to dip in the *hummous* onto her plate, got up, went into the computer room, and closed the door.

Frank made a "Gee-I'm-sorry-she's-mad-but-it-had-to-be-said" face at Tess. She smiled at him and reached for his hand. It closed around hers, thumb moving against her palm. She knew that he relished its softness. She made a point of taking very good care of her hands. She had read in *Glamour* magazine that one should always put sunblock on one's hands when going out, even in the winter. It had taken her a long time to find the hand lotion that had the right SPF *and* moisturized well.


Eugie, Frank and Tess set out around one. As they came out of their apartment, they saw a young Palestinian man spread-eagled against the wall on the opposite side of the alley. One of the chicken vendors from a cave-like shop on the same side of the street pointed at the young man and shouted something in Arabic.

"What is he saying?" Tess asked.

"I have no idea," Eugie said as she strode up to the young man.

It took Tess longer to cross the street because she was trying not to step on chicken entrails and droppings. A young Palestinian man with a push broom ran from one of the shops when he saw her picking her way across the street and pushed a pile of offal to the gutter as she sidestepped it. A chorus of male jeering broke out along the street and he shouted angrily back. Smiling at her, he said, "Welcome. Welcome," and then bowing his head in embarrassment, ran back into his shop.

Eugie had begun a lively conversation with a dark-skinned soldier, while Frank slumped against the wall and chatted with the young man, who still had his hands up. The soldier obviously did not understand English very well. Another soldier from the checkpoint across from the entrance to the alley strolled over and began interpreting.

"No talking!" he said, pointing at Frank.

"Good afternoon," Frank said with a bland smile.

"What is the problem here?" the other soldier asked Eugie. He was very tall, with high cheek bones and bad acne.

"Well, the problem is that this is the fifth young man we have seen against this wall in the last three days," Eugie said. "Why do you keep stopping *shebab* here?"

"You do not understand the situation here," the taller soldier said. "You do not understand the Arab mind."

"Well that is true," Eugie said, "But we're trying. Tell me. Do you have any Arab friends?"

"No."

"Have you ever shared a meal with an Arab?"

"No."

"Have you ever visited Arabs in their homes?"

"No."

"Have you ever babysat their children?"

"No."

Frank chimed in. "Have you ever played basketball or soccer, I mean football, with Arabs?"

"No."

"Then maybe," Eugie said. "we know a little more about Arabs than you do."

The dark-skinned soldier asked the taller one something in Hebrew and he grunted a monosyllabic reply. Gripping the barrel of his gun, he looked at the ground.

"I know that your work here is very frustrating," Eugie said, laying a hand on his elbow. He jerked away. "But your life—his life," she said, nodding her head toward the young man against the wall, "They are both really important to me."

"Why?" the soldier asked.

"Because you are both children of God," Eugie said.

"I do not believe in God," the soldier said.

The young man with his hands against the wall said in a clipped, British accent, "He's quite right, you know. There is no God. How could there be? It's not rational."

Taking his hands from the wall, he gestured at the men and boys in the chicken market, who were watching the proceedings with great interest. "Look at them. These good fellows pray five times a day to Allah and where has it gotten them? Their religion makes them passive; it distracts them from the reality of the Occupation!"

"It also makes them suicide bombers," the tall soldier with acne said.

"Oh come on," Eugie said. "Would you want me to say that all religious Jews are murderers because of what Baruch Goldstein did? Do you like Ariel Sharon?" she asked the soldier.

"No. I do not agree with him."

"Well then, how would you like it if I told people that all Israelis were like Ariel Sharon?"

The Palestinian man interrupted her. "What about the settlers here?" he asked the soldier. "What do you think of them?"

"They are fanatics."

"Correct. And why are they fanatics?"

"Because of their religion."

"Agreed. So why are you here defending them?"

The soldier looked at the ground for a moment and then said something in Hebrew to the other soldier, who pulled a piece of orange plastic out of his pocket and handed it to the Palestinian man.

Frank wandered from the alley out onto the main road and looked toward Beit Hadassah. "We'd better get up there," he said. "I don't like the look of this."

Following him out onto the street, Tess saw what seemed like hundreds of young settler men—a sea of white shirts and black pants—milling around ahead at the entrance of Beit Hadassah. She, Eugie and Frank, walked past a group of about 12 soldiers at the entrance of the soldiers camp who were also watching the assembled settlers.

"Don't rush," Eugie said, quickening her pace. "Act calm."

The settlers parted to let them go through. Women standing along both sides of the road smiled at Tess and she smiled back at them. When she did so, the women began laughing and pointing.

As they approached the black iron gate and army checkpoint at the entrance of Beit Hadassah, Tess heard the sound of breaking glass.

The road leading to Beit Hadassah branched into a Y shape, with one of the arms heading downhill past Beit Hadassah into the marketplace, and the other arm, called Dubboya Street, leading uphill. The soldiers from Beit Hadassah had gone down to the gate that separated the settlement from the market and seemed to be struggling with a large group of settler youth.

"They're throwing bottles at people in the market," Frank said as a distinctively shaped Coca Cola bottle flew over an iron gate topped with chain-link fencing and concertina wire.

"Get pictures," Eugie ordered. "I'm going around the other side to make sure people are okay there."

"Wait," Frank said. "I think we should stick together."

But Eugie was already out of hearing. Tess watched her dash around the corner of a V-shaped building, and nearly trip over the removable iron spikes at the roadblock that marked the entrance to Dubboya Street. Frank had explained to Tess the previous evening that soldiers would drag them off the road to allow settler, police and army vehicles to pass.

Frank flattened himself against the wall and took a small camera out of his pants pocket. "Wish I had a zoom," he muttered, as he aimed at the seething mass of soldiers and teenagers and clicked. On the other side of the fence, four journalists with video cameras, Nayif among them, raced in and began taking footage of the melee. The teenagers began aiming bottles at the journalists, who seemed to be able to duck and continue filming at the same time. For every bottle that soldiers succeeded in wresting from the grip of one of the smaller settler boys, two more would go over the fence. Shaking his fist at the settlers, one of the taller journalists began shouting.

"He's Israeli," Frank told Tess. "He and Nayif work together."

An egg flew over the fence and struck the grey vest of the irate Israeli journalist. The yellow yolk balanced for a moment on a pocket bulging with a camera lens and then slid off. Grabbing him by the arm, Nayif pulled him behind the other Palestinian journalists.

Tess thought she heard a whistle shrilling on the other side of the building against which she and Frank were leaning. She looked up and saw settler women standing on the roof of Beit Hadassah with their arms folded across their chests, laughing and pointing at the boys throwing bottles below.

One soldier came up beside Tess and Frank, put his hand over one ear to block the noise, and began shouting into his walkie-talkie.

"He's calling the police," Frank said, shouting so Tess could hear him over the crowd. "Soldiers aren't allowed to arrest settlers."

"Come, please. Please, come," Tess heard a voice to her right. A Palestinian boy in a Minnesota Twins t-shirt was peering around the point of the v-shaped building, motioning at them to follow him.

Tess heard the whistle shrilling more loudly. She nudged Frank and pointed at the boy, whose brown eyes were wide with fear.

"Come, please," he said again. "Your friend. Come. Please."

Frank said, "Tell her to come here." He pointed toward the ground at his feet.

"No. No," the boy repeated. "You come. Now."

"Do you mind going and seeing what Eugie wants?" Frank asked. "Tell her we need her here."

As Tess walked up the hill toward the point of the V intersection, the young boy grabbed her hand, pulling her so hard that she, too, almost stumbled over the spikes. As she rounded the corner, she realized the noise she thought was a police whistle was actually the sound of a woman screaming.

\*       \*       \*

Eugie held her breath as she walked through the crowd of men in white shirts and black pants. They sneered at her, pointing and making comments in Hebrew. Once again, she was the fat girl with glasses in third grade. The girl who had cooties. The girl who got spit wads thrown at her because she cried so easily.

Ahead on the street she saw Wisam's Aunt Amira, beckoning at her, distraught. "Eugie, please hurry. They are coming." She looked behind her and saw twenty or so of the men she had just passed walking purposefully up the street. She willed herself to remain calm and not to run. They mustn't see her panic. She concentrated on her breathing.

Behind her a roar went up and she heard the sound of running feet. Someone yanked hard at the red-checked keffiyeh she kept tied to her knapsack so that the Palestinians would not mistake her for a settler. ("No. I'm not PFLP," she would say to the Palestinians who teased her about it. "I'm Christian." Sometimes, depending on who was present, she would tell them it meant she was Communist.)

Another hard yank caused her to lose her balance, and she fell over backward landing on her knapsack. Large men stood over her and spat on her, shouting in Hebrew. She was aware of the sounds of breaking glass up and down the street as more men rushed past. When there was no one left standing over her, she struggled to her feet and began snapping pictures—aiming in the general direction of the men who were fleeing. One wearing a blue vinyl baseball cap, who looked to be about 300 pounds, turned and saw her. He shouted, "No, no pictures," and once again she was surrounded by men grabbing at her camera. She held on more firmly. One of them, a bald man with dark glasses, grabbed her by her hair and made a fist, grinning. In the time it took for the fist to connect with her left ear, she wondered why he wasn't wearing a *kipah* like most of the other men.

The punch didn't hurt, but it knocked her over and disoriented her. She strengthened her grip on the camera and was dragged along the ground by the strap. Noticing that there were no soldiers at the Beit Hadassah checkpoint, she thought maybe she should start shrieking to attract their attention. By the time she had second thoughts—because she was, after all, a pacifist and rejected the principle of being rescued by those who relied on the force of arms—her vocal cords had gone on automatic and continued shrieking anyway. People kept kicking her, but it still didn't hurt until they connected with the back of her head. Pulling herself into the fetal position, she held the camera close to her abdomen.

From what seemed like a distance, she heard Felicia yelling, "Hey! What are you doing! Stop that!" and then she began cursing in Spanish. *Ahimsa*, Eugie thought. Harmlessness. Cursing violated it. Gandhi would disapprove. But then she felt Felicia's strong hands joining hers. Now they were both on the ground. Together they would save the camera.

A booted foot came down hard on Felicia's hand, ripping out a clump of Eugie's hair in the process. Felicia screamed, and Eugie no longer felt her body next to hers. She didn't have the strength to hang on any more, and the camera was gone. As she sat up in the middle of the road, she saw the bald man running away, camera held high over his head, as though he had just completed a touchdown. All the young settlers around him followed him into the Beit Hadassah complex, laughing and cheering.

Someone helped her up. It was Wisam's Aunt Amira with tears in her eyes.

"It's okay," she said. "I'm okay." She felt tears on her own face.

Felicia was sitting on the cement stoop of one of the houses. Face contorted with pain, she held her hand against the small of her back and accepted, with bloody fingers, a cigarette from Nayif. She seemed to be trying to joke with the young Palestinian man with the English accent. Had the soldiers let him go? Oh yes, she remembered that they had handed him his identity card with the orange plastic casing. Exactly how long ago had that been?

On the other side of the street, Frank stood with Tess, who had blood streaming down her left temple. She was leaning against him with her eyes closed, and Eugie felt a pang of guilt. It was too bad that Tess had had to deal with this on her first Saturday on Dubboya Street. She wondered whether the Palestinians on the street would be shocked seeing Tess and Frank touching each other, but then decided not to care.

"I call Wisam," Amira said. "She will come."

"Thank you. Thank you very much." Eugie wasn't sure why Wisam should come, but it seemed like a good idea.

Now there were settler children standing around her. Some wide-eyed, some contemptuous. The Israeli soldiers walked up—most with grim faces, some grinning with embarrassment. In the distance a blue light flashed.

"The *bolis*. They come," Wisam's aunt said. "They would not come until we say that *azhnabia* was hurt. They do not come for us. They say we must come there. But for Americans they come."

"Sorry," Eugie said.

"No, no, it is good," Amira said, patting her on the shoulder.

Sa'id appeared with a little bottle and began dabbing mercurochrome on her elbow with a piece of cotton.

"It is bad," he said. "It is very, very bad. Now turn your ear please."

He dabbed her ear lightly, and a shaft of pain shot through it. She gasped.

"Very sorry. Please forgive," he said. "You come to my house and drink tea? Yes?"

Two little boys pulled at her arm, "Come, please," they said. "Come to my mother." Eugie looked up and saw their mother beckoning urgently from a wrought-iron balcony.

The police arrived. They first went up to Frank and Tess and spoke with Frank. He nodded and allowed them to lead Tess to the police van. Eugie realized there were tears and mucus dripping down her chin and she wiped them away with her sleeve.

The settler children began laughing and pointing at her as though she were a performing animal in the circus. Felicia got off the stoop with Nayif's help and walked toward her, limping.

"My tail bone hurts like hell," she said. "That's where they kicked me hardest."

Eugie took a deep breath, "Anywhere else? What happened to Tess?"

"I think she just got knocked against a wall."

Tears kept pouring down Eugie's face. She laughed. "I must really look pathetic."

Felicia grinned. "No problem. It's not my style, but I'm with you, comrade."

Hand trembling, she took a deep drag on her cigarette. "I am SO annoyed that I let go of the camera. What a bunch of bastards."

"Your hand is bleeding."

Felicia help it up in front of her and looked surprised, "Yeah. That guy stomped on it."

"He wasn't wearing a *kipah*."

"He was bald. Maybe it fell off."

The police were now surrounded by men and women who lived on Dubboya Street. They began pointing at settler men. One of the policemen came over to Eugie and Felicia.

"Do you know which of these men attacked you?"

Eugie looked around for the bald guy without a kipah. He wasn't there. There were a lot of large men with beards and sidecurls, but Eugie couldn't be sure that they were the ones who spat on her. Then she saw the one with the blue baseball cap.

"He spat on me, I think," she said pointing to him.

The one she pointed to began edging away, but was detained by one of the police officers, an older man with a round, Slavic face. A number of Palestinian men and women pointed to another very large man with a black velvet *kipah* and side curls.

"Did he hurt you, too?" the police officer asked Eugie.

"No. Maybe. I don't remember."

"He definitely kicked me," Felicia said, rubbing her tail bone. An explosion of Hebrew erupted as the police ordered the man to get into the van. The police at Eugie and Felicia's side went over while the man in the black kipah shouted and gesticulated.

Nayif came up to them with his video camera. "Excuse me please, Eugie, Felicia, I want to ask you some questions."

The red light on his video camera began blinking.

"What is your name?"

Felicia snapped, "Nayif, you know what our names are."

"Yes, but CNN does not." Nayif repeated the question, "What are your names?"

"Felicia-Inez Erb."

"Grace Yoder."

"Where are you from?"

"Capuchay, Colombia."

"Intercourse, Pennsylvania."

The young Palestinian man with the British accent snorted, and then put his hand over his mouth when Nayif scowled at him.

"Can you tell me what happened here today?"

Eugie and Felicia began talking at the same time and then stopped, simultaneously took breaths, and began talking at the same time again.

"Felicia, tell me what happened," Nayif said, coming to their rescue.

"Frank called me and told me there were some settler kids throwing bottles at people in the marketplace. We live about two blocks away. When I got to the place where the road divides, I saw Frank surrounded by a bunch of soldiers. Then I heard screaming and went around the corner and saw this guy trying to grab Eugie's camera, so I went to help her, but we couldn't hold on."

"Did the settlers attack you?"

"Yes, they kicked me in the back and in the head, and one guy stomped really hard on my hand." She held up her fingers, beginning to crust over with scabs.

"Eugie, did the settlers attack you as well?"

"Yes, one of them socked me in the ear and I think I got kicked, too, but I don't remember."

A police officer approached them and pushed Nayif out of the way.

"Please go in there," he ordered the two women, pointing to the interior of the police van.

Eugie and Felicia peered in. Tess sat on a grey metal bench on the right side of the van; the very large settler in the blue baseball cap was sitting on the other side.

They climbed in beside Tess and sat for several minutes in

silence. Eugie felt small whimpering sounds rising again in her throat and she clenched her teeth as she tried to prevent their becoming audible. A fresh flow of tears made her gasp with the effort to stop crying.

The police officer turned, observed her for a second, and said, "You want some water? I will get you some." He disappeared, and Eugie continued trying to suppress her sobs.

"I say, are you all right?"

Turning in the direction of the British accent, she tried to smile. "Oh yeah. I'm fine. Just a little shaken up, that's all."

Felicia spoke. "Hussam, this is Eugie Yoder and this is Tess MacAdoo."

"Very pleased to meet you, I'm sure. I didn't get a chance to thank you for what you did when they had me up against the wall. It was really quite decent of you. Wish you had been around earlier, when they did the same thing to me at the mosque. Tess!" he said after getting a good look at her, "A lovely name, that. From the Thomas Hardy novel?"

Tess smiled at him and said, "No, I don't think so. It's short for Theresa Marie."

"Looks like you got quite a scrape there!"

Tess put her hand to her head. "Do I really look awful?" she asked.

"No, it's not that bad," Eugie assured her.

A young Palestinian boy walked up to Hussam and began speaking to him in Arabic. His eyebrows flew up and he gestured toward the large settler sitting on the bench opposite the three women. A young police officer with dark curly hair pushed Hussam and the boy out of the way and handed Eugie a flimsy plastic cup full of cold water as he climbed into the van and sat by the settler. Eugie took a sip of water and then passed it to Tess, who shook her head. She then handed Felicia the cup.

"I say! They're taking you to the police station in the same wagon with the fellow who attacked you?" Hussam exclaimed, as the van began pulling away. It occurred to Eugie that perhaps Hussam was right. Perhaps it was inappropriate. She raised her red, swollen eyes to the settler, who looked away. The young police officer looked at her directly.

"Shabbat shalom," she said, for lack of a better thing to say.

He grimaced. "Shabbat fucking shalom. These fucking people . . ." he said, shaking his head. He looked at Tess.

"Is your friend okay?" he asked. "She doesn't look so good. Her boyfriend told me to take good care of her, when I talked to him."

Felicia sighed and patted her pockets. She found her pack of cigarettes. "Only one left," she said gloomily. "I should have asked Nayif for a couple more. I have a feeling it's going to be a long afternoon."

The van stopped at the Beit Hadassah checkpoint while soldiers pulled the iron spikes back so it could proceed.

Settler men, women, and children surrounded the van as it passed through the checkpoint. A dainty woman with a scarf wrapped around her head stepped up to the back of the wagon and began shrieking at the police officer. Eugie caught the words "photo" and "Shabbat" and guessed that she was telling the police officer that their attack was a natural reaction to people who had been violating the sabbath by taking pictures.

Goldstein-pin guy, the young man who had tried to run into them with his bicycle the previous day, now came up to the back of the van and Eugie burst into fresh tears.

"What happened?" he asked, his voice full of concern.

Eugie looked away and tried to stifle her sobs.

"What happened?" he repeated. "Why is she crying?"

"You were there," Eugie said. "You saw what happened."

"No I wasn't," he said. "I didn't see anything."

"You were there. I saw you."

Felicia finally said, "We were attacked on the street by settlers."

Goldstein-pin guy laughed and said, "Ah, very good," and walked away.

A woman in a purple turban who looked as though she were in her sixties, walked up to the back of the van and spat at their feet.

"If you say anything to the police, we will kill you," she said.

"Yeah, we know, Mrs. Levine. You've told us before," Felicia said.

"Don't say I didn't warn you," she said.

"No, Mrs. Levine. We won't say you didn't warn us," Eugie and Felicia said together, drearily.

Eugie turned to Tess. "Are you okay?" she asked. "What happened?"

"I heard you screaming," Tess replied. "But I couldn't see you. There was a crowd of men standing around you, and one of them stepped back suddenly and pushed me into a wall."

"We should put some ice on that lump," Eugie said. "I wonder if the police have some."

"By the way, I got hurt too," Felicia said in acid tones.

Eugie untied the *keffiyeh* from her backpack and wadded it up in a bundle. "Here. Put this behind your lower back," she said. "Let me see your fingers."

Felicia rolled her eyes and muttered, "Never mind."

"Come on," Eugie ordered. "Show them to me."

After examining them, Eugie rooted around in her knapsack for the packet of baby wipes she always carried with her and began clearing away coagulated blood from Felicia's hands. The second and third fingers on her right hand were swollen, and the silver rings on these fingers appeared to be cutting into the flesh.

"Those rings may have to be cut off," Eugie said.

Felicia jerked her hand away. "Uh-uh," she said. "They stay on."

"Well, we should at least splint your fingers," Eugie said.

The young police officer returned to the van, shouted something in Hebrew to the large settler, who had been sitting silently in the van and jerked his thumb over his shoulder. A cheer went up from the crowd as the fat man climbed out.

"Fucking settlers," the police officer sighed as he climbed into the van with them. "They beat up women on Shabbat, but they won't ride in a truck."

He stared at Felicia, Eugie, and Tess and shook his head. Eugie thought he seemed angry with them as well.

"You are Christian?" he asked.

The three women nodded as the van began to pull away from the crowd of settlers in front of Beit Hadassah. Several meters down the road, they passed the man with the black velvet *kipah*. Eugie was even less sure now that he had been one of the attackers.

"You sure you saw him?" she asked Felicia.

"Yeah, I'm sure. And so were about five other people on the street."

Eugie caught herself before she said, "They all look alike to me," and giggled instead. The police officer looked at her askance and she stopped.

When they passed the IDF camp near their apartment, the van stopped and about six curious soldiers gathered around the back of the van and peered in. They looked a little frightened, Eugie thought. The policeman in the van said something to them and they all shook their heads.

Continuing past the old vegetable market—closed since the Baruch Goldstein massacre—the van drove up the street to the mosque. Eugie heard the gate at the checkpoint in front of the mosque area open, and after the van drove through she saw a couple of Ethiopian soldiers closing it. The soldiers stared at them as they traveled the fifty meters or so from the checkpoint to the police station in front of the mosque.

Felicia, Eugie and Tess climbed the rickety iron stairs leading up to the police trailer and sat at the picnic table in front of the two rooms that served as offices. Several teenaged settler boys walked over from the mosque. Standing at the base of the iron staircase, they stared up at the women. Eugie began crying again. Another glass of water appeared and she received it with shaking hands.

"*Shukran. Shukran,*" she said, and when she realized she was speaking in Arabic, she said, "I'm sorry. I mean '*Todah.*'"

The young police officer who had ridden with them in the van squatted in front of her and said, "That's okay. You can say *shukran* to me."

Eugie burst into fresh tears at this kindness and he looked frightened. "More water?" he asked.

She shook her head. Felicia took over.

"I'm Felicia," she said, extending her right hand and then wincing when he shook it.

"My name is Tony. Oh sorry," the policeman said when he saw her swollen and discolored fingers.

"Not your fault," Felicia said as she inhaled sharply, her olive skin turning ashy.

"You need a doctor?" the officer stood up and prepared to move away.

"No. No," Felicia said. "I'll be fine. So you speak Arabic?"

The police officer looked down at the group of five settler boys as though gauging whether they were within hearing distance. He then bent over and whispered, "I am Druse."

"Oh," said Eugie who had managed to get herself under control once again. "I assumed you were Jewish because of this." She pointed to her own throat, and Tony's hand went to the Star of David hanging around his neck.

"My girlfriend gave it to me," he said. "She is Jewish. She said I would be more safe here if I wore it."

A voice called from inside one of the rooms. Tony called back and then appeared to evaluate the three of them. "You and you," he said, pointing at Felicia and Tess. "Come with me in this room. You," he said, pointing at Eugie, "go into that room."

Eugie walked to the room where he pointed and sat in one of the metal folding chairs. The florescent light that went the length of the ceiling was not on, and Eugie wondered why the balding Slavic police officer chose to write a report in the dim light. Nine feet across from her, in a metal folding chair sat one of the fat settlers who may or may not have kicked her and spat on her.

"Do you speak English?" she asked him.

"No," he said.

She burst into tears again. The balding police officer rushed out of the cubicle-sized office and returned with yet another plastic cup of water and handed it to her. If she didn't stop crying soon, she thought, she was going to be in desperate need of a bathroom.

She asked the police officer, "Do you speak English?"

He held up his thumb and index finger. "Very little," he said.

"Could you tell him," Eugie said, pointing at the fat man, "that I don't usually take pictures of people on the Sabbath? I only do it when I see someone attacking someone else? I didn't mean to offend his religious beliefs."

This remark provoked a tirade in Hebrew that lasted nearly a full minute. As the officer yelled at the fat man, he waved his hand, palm upwards, at him, gestured toward Eugie, and then shook his hand at the settler yet again.

Eugie was sorry she had said anything. She sat for the next ten minutes in the dim room without anyone speaking to her. It reminded her of the times that she had gone to the ophthalmologist when she was younger and had had to sit in a dark room for what seemed like hours after the doctor had put drops in her eyes. Sometimes her mother would sit with her and sometimes she wouldn't. She was glad her mother was not with her now. She made a point of describing her work with RAPT to her parents in breezy tones (travel! adventure! language study!)

"Where are the Americans?" a woman's voice broke the silence.

"I'm Colombian," she heard Felicia's voice call from the next room.

"Felicia, Eugie. Where are you?"

Hearing Wisam's voice made Eugie choke up again. She left the office, ignoring whatever it was the policeman was saying to her in Hebrew, and stood on the porch area in front of the police trailer. Blinking against the sunlight, she finally focussed on Wisam, who was peering around the corner of the next office. Someone from inside the office shouted something harshly in Hebrew, and Wisam answered in Arabic in precisely the same tone of voice. Felicia and Tess stepped out and Wisam exclaimed in dismay, "Your head! Ay! Your hands. *Ya haram!*"

She turned and looked at Eugie. "And Eugie! You are bleeding. This is bad. It is very, very bad!"

Tears began streaming down Eugie's face yet again, and Wisam's voice changed. "Eugie, stop crying. You must be strong. Do not let them know they have hurt you." She gestured toward the settler youth assembled at the base of the black iron stairs.

"Once a soldier pulled me down the street by my hair and tore some of it out, and I said it was illegal for him to treat me that way. But I never cried, even though it hurt me very greatly."

Eugie wiped her eyes on the sleeve of her cream-colored blouse—which was beginning to look grubby.

"There, that is better." Wisam smiled at her. Eugie noticed that her eyes matched the flowing, mossy green coat dress she was wearing. Even with the white scarf pinned under her chin, Wisam seemed cool in the heat of the afternoon.

"You will want some water," she continued briskly. "I will ask the police."

"No, no," Eugie said. "I'm fine. Have you talked to Frank?"

"Yes, I stopped in at your apartment and he was making many phone calls. My aunt said you were badly hurt when she called."

"No, it's not too bad."

"I have spoken to the mayor. He was very upset that this terrible thing has happened to you, and he has made a complaint to the Civil Administration."

Eugie rather doubted that the mayor had become so emotionally exercised. She suspected Wisam had written a nasty note to the Israeli authorities and handed it to the mayor for his signature.

Tony came out of the office on the right-hand side of the trailer and entered the room in which Eugie had been sitting. He appeared again in a few seconds with a sheaf of papers and nodded his head back toward the room.

"Fucking dick-head is praying in there. I hate these people."

Wisam drew herself up and glared at him.

"Excuse me," she said. "There are women present."

Shrugging, Tony turned to Eugie and Felicia. "You will need to come up to the administration building. We want to take photos of where they hit you and have you look through some pictures of settlers to see if you can pick out the man who beat you."

He gestured toward the jeep. Felicia, Eugie, and Tess went back down the iron stairs, climbed back in the van, and sat on the hard, grey benches. Standing outside the van, Wisam continued talking to them.

"This should be very big news," she said, smiling with satisfaction. "It has already been on the radio. Now maybe people will regard the threats of the settlers in a more serious way."

"Have you talked to Erland lately?" Eugie asked.

Wisam looked at the ground and shook her head. "It is too difficult," she said.

Nayif approached and climbed in the van with them. "They broke my camera," he said. "After you left, they broke my camera. Hussam thinks that he can still get the tape to CNN. I hope so." He slumped on the bench.

"You're going to make a complaint, too?" Felicia asked

"Damn right. My boss had better pay for a new camera, too."

The bald police officer climbed behind the steering wheel. Tony joined them in the van. He said something to Nayif in Arabic. Nayif held up his camera and replied. Tony then responded with more Arabic, and Nayif jumped out of the van.

"What did you say to him?" Felicia asked as the van pulled away from the police trailer in front of the mosque.

"I told him that this car was for foreigners only. He has to pay for a taxi if he wants to make a complaint."

Looking out from the back of the van, Eugie watched Nayif take out a cigarette with shaking hands and stare at the ground, his face burning with humiliation. She then saw Erland walk up to Wisam and begin speaking to her. Wisam gestured at the departing van and then turned her back on Erland. Approaching Nayif, Wisam said something to him that made him nod at her, and the two of them walked away in the other direction. Erland's shoulders slumped as he watched them disappear down a side alley into the market.

Eugie began to cry again.

# *Interim*

## One Saturday Afternoon on Dubboya Street
## by Kathleen Kern

Early in the afternoon, I was sitting outside an Arab home on Dubboya Street. At any given time, there are twelve or more children in the three-story house, many of whom peer through the bars of a small bay window and drop things—sometimes by accident and sometimes to see if the people below will pick them up.

As three adult male settlers were passing by on the opposite side of the street, one of the children dropped an empty plastic soda bottle from the window. It landed directly under the window, about twenty feet from the settlers. Nevertheless, one of them hailed a passing military jeep, pointed at the bottle on the ground and insisted the soldiers do something about it. Reinforcements arrived about four minutes later, and eight heavily armed soldiers got out of their jeeps and sent a young man who lived there inside to fetch his father. The father came to the window to speak to the soldiers, which seemed to satisfy them. They left after barking what sounded like a stern warning.

## II

Two male settlers in their late teens or early twenties walked past singing in Hebrew, with mocking expressions on their faces. One then began singing in nearly perfect English, "All we are singing is 'Give war a chance.'" When he passed by again about two hours later, he sang, "If I had an Uzi, I'd shoot 'em in the morning. I'd shoot 'em in the evening, all over my land." Then, speaking, he said, "It's MY land. It's not their land. "It's MY land." He later identified himself as Azrael ben Israel.

## III

Between 2:00 and 2:30 pm, a confrontation occurred between Palestinian youth and Israeli soldiers near the checkpoint at one end of Dubboya St. This was one of several clashes that erupted after the settler attack on Qurtuba girls school. As I watched, some soldiers shot in the air and threw sound bombs [concussion grenades.] One soldier smiled and waved at two settlers who approached the checkpoint. A few minutes later, Azrael ben Israel walked past me briskly, muttering, "There should have been fifty or sixty dead Arabs by now."

## IV

Another young Israeli also became interested in events at the checkpoint and asked me about the explosions. "They were sound bombs," I said. He asked for a definition of sound bombs and then inquired whether the army or the Arabs had thrown them. I told him that only the army uses sound bombs. "It doesn't matter," he said. "Pretty soon the *Mashiach* [Messiah] will come and [the Arabs] will all move to Jordan. I'm not like the others," he continued. "I don't want to kill them. I only want them to leave."

Then he asked, "Are you Jewish?"

"Christian," I replied. His face stiffened. "The Messiah will come and kill all the *goyim*—Arabs and Christians—and drink their blood," he said as he walked away.

## V

The young messianic hopeful was joined by Ben Israel. He noticed a group of Palestinians watching him and his friend. "Why don't we invite ourselves for coffee?" Ben Israel asked. "I hear they are very hospitable people." Abruptly changing his tone, he pointed at them and said, "First, we'll deal with you and then we'll deal with the Germans."

"They are the same people," his friend said.

"Let's go," Ben Israel said. "It's making me sick to look at them."

As he walked away, he called over his shoulder, "Go back to Greece."

## VI

Around 3:45 pm, about eight girls walked onto the street from the settlement of Beit Hadassah and began yelling insults at Palestinians watching from balconies across the street. Several began throwing stones at their homes. A soldier tried to cajole the girls into leaving. They ignored him and continued shouting and throwing stones.

They were joined by several small boys and a teenager in a prayer shawl who began reading from a prayer book. Another soldier approached the group, and the two of them ordered the children to leave. They ignored both soldiers. The girls began chanting the name of Baruch Goldstein and saying, "Goldstein is our father" in Hebrew. Then they began throwing rocks and spitting in our direction.

A visiting Quaker professor engaged one of the settler men who was watching the children, and told us later, "I asked him how he, as a parent, felt about the children throwing rocks at Arabs and yelling, 'Goldstein, Goldstein.' He spent the next twenty minutes not answering my question."

## VII

After the girls dispersed, Carmen Pauls, Wendy Lehman, Hedy Sawadsky, and I sat near the Beit Hadassah checkpoint. Ben Israel and the young man who had talked about the Messiah again passed the group. Ben Israel proclaimed loudly, "We should gas them all. Does anyone know where we can get Zyklon B? I heard you can get it in Germany. I think we should take some Zyklon B, put all these—I don't know what you call them—they're not human. Take all of them and put them into little camps and gas them."

Joe, the visiting Quaker professor, asked, "So you think what the Germans did to the Jews justifies the Jews using the same tactics against the Arabs?"

"Absolutely. We've learned our lesson. I'm a member of the Jewish Nazi party." His friend tried to hush him. "I'M not," the friend said. "Well, I am," Ben Israel said. "I'm a Jewish Nazi."

He then told the CPTers that he had no particular desire to kill Arabs. "We'd be much happier shooting Rabin and Peres."

After a pause, Ben Israel told us that the people living on Dubboya Street had roots that went back only about 100 years. "They're not from Ishmael. They're mixed. Mostly they're from Greece. The Ottoman Turks brought them over."

"Where are you from?" Wendy asked.

"I'm from here," he said.

"I mean, where were you born?"

"I was born in Romania," said Ben Israel, "but I don't see what that has to do with anything."

Carmen and I went further up the street at this point and the two young men continued their conversation with Wendy and Hedy. "We're at war. We are at war with these people," ben Israel told them, pointing at the Palestinians up the street.

Hedy tried to tell him that all people—Jews, Arabs, Christians—have the breath of God in them. "So does a dog or a goat," said ben Israel's friend. "These people are immoral," added ben Israel. "Terribly immoral. Homosexuality came from these people."

He continued, "We know what we're doing is between us and God. If I kill an Arab, I will know I am doing it for the right reasons. Not because I hate him, but because he'll kill me."

Ben Israel ended the conversation by saying he had one uplifting thing to share. "We're going to rebuild our temple. We're going to keep our land. They can't take our land. The world can't take our land. We are going to retake Jordan, retake Lebanon, retake Syria.

"Soon," his friend added.

"Yes," agreed ben Israel. "Very soon."

# VIII

A young man dressed like the settlers had watched quietly while the girls from Beit Hadassah had shouted insults and thrown rocks. He came over to a group of Palestinians on the street and began talking to them in fluent Arabic. At first skeptical, the Palestinian young people began asking him rapid-fire questions. A journalist friend, interpreting, told us that he was telling the group that his family had come from Iraq, but that he had been born in Jerusalem. A young woman brought a newspaper out of her house and asked the young man to read aloud to test his Arabic.

The journalist shouted, "What do you think of the situation in Hebron?"

"It is very beautiful here," he said. "But Nablus is more beautiful."

Soldiers approached and tried to drag the young man away. I called out "Shabbat shalom."

"God helps you," he called back.

He resisted the soldiers' attempts to remove him. "But they're my friends!" he protested. As the two soldiers each took one of his arms and physically forced him to walk away, he called back to the assembled Palestinian young people, "Come visit me in Jerusalem."

It was the only time that long afternoon that the soldiers intervened to prevent an Israeli from making contact with Palestinians.

Our journalist friend, as he watched the young man being dragged away, said, "He was very crazy."

# CHAPTER 5

Eugie looked at her left ear for the eighth time that day. The part that had gotten folded over her sunglasses' ear piece had turned blue. Tess had shown her how she could fluff her hair out to cover it. Although they had not gotten back from the Civil Administration until after 2:00 A.M. three days ago, Tess had combed out her own hair and, using Margaret's sewing scissors, had given herself bangs to cover up the scrape on her temple.

Eugie felt as though she had dreamed the conversations she'd had with the police at the Civil Administration building that night. The lurid yellow color of the walls in the interrogation room had matched the yellows in the Salvador Dali-esque dreams that sometimes struck when she had migraines.

The police had looked skeptical when she told them that her attacker had not worn a *kipah*. After they developed the picture that Felicia had snapped before joining Eugie in her struggle to retain the camera, they saw that the assailant had had his *kipah* in his mouth. Given that she so clearly remembered the grin on his face as he drew his fist back to punch her, Eugie wondered why she had not noticed the kipah. She thought one of the pictures in the police book looked something like the man who had punched her, but she couldn't be sure, because the man in the mug shot was not wearing dark glasses.

While leafing through the pages that contained pictures of Hebron settler women who had been charged with various acts of mayhem in the past, she ran across a picture of Maxine, an Israeli friend from the Hebron Solidarity Movement, who had returned to Canada. She laughed and wished she could phone Yiphat and tell her that Maxine had been filed with dangerous settler women.

When the policeman in the cubicle opposite her asked what was so funny, she said, "Nothing," and flipped the page.

Eventually, the police sent her to a medical officer, who examined her injuries for purposes of documentation. He berated her for walking in dangerous neighborhoods. What did she expect, he said, walking down Dubboya Street dressed as she had been?

It hadn't made sense to her, because her long navy blue skirt and cotton blouse with sleeves rolled to the elbows was just as modest as the outfits most of the settler women wore. The next day, when she spoke to Hillel Cotton, a rabbi who worked for Human Rights: Past, Present and Forever, she mentioned the puzzling conversation. He groaned and said, "He assumed that Arabs had attacked you."

Hillel told her that the story of their attack had appeared on the second page of the *Jerusalem Post*. The impending verdict in the OJ Simpson trial took up the front page. The mention of OJ brought back memories of the summer of '94 in Haiti, when she and the team had listened to Voice of America on the radio every night out on the balcony of an unfinished rectory—the home of a priest who was in hiding because of right-wing paramilitary death threats. All that summer, the American invasion had been on and then off several times. They had gone as long as nine nights without hearing anything on the Voice of America about Haiti. But every night that summer there had been an update on the OJ trial. LeCaire, their Haitian translator, had never heard of OJ Simpson, and it was difficult to explain to him why OJ figured so prominently in newscasts.

Eugie sighed and fluffed her hair over her ear again. To see if her jaw still hurt, she opened her mouth as wide as she could. It did.

She also had a pimple over her left eyebrow—the kind that never came to a head but just ached for days, until it became an invisible but palpable lump under the skin. She knew that no one could see the pimple, but it still made her feel ugly. No one noticed the bristly little hairs that grew on her chin either, but they drove her crazy until she got to her tweezers and plucked them.

"You picking your face again?" Felicia asked as she entered the room and threw her backpack onto the hideous blue vinyl couch that had come with the apartment.

Eugie put her hands behind her back and looked away from the mirror over the sink.

"I ran into Yehudit Levine on the street," Felicia said, flopping down beside her backpack on the couch. "She said the soldiers are saying we sleep with Arabs for money, and asked me if it was true. I said, 'Of course not,' and she said, "Oh it isn't for the money, then?'"

"How are your fingers?" Eugie asked.

Felicia held up her right hand. "The swelling is gone, but they hurt to bend. Good thing I'm left-handed. Anyway, Yehudit started in again about how the Arabs were going to rape us and slit our throats and I said, 'That's funny. The only people who have attacked us so far are a bunch of settlers,' and then she said, 'Oh, so it's always the Jews. It's always their fault all over the world . . . '"

Sitting on a scratchy brown-and-white ottoman across from the couch, Eugie watched Felicia, who had stretched one leg out on the coffee table, fiddle with her cigarette lighter. They had talked more in the last three days than they probably had for the last two months. Eugie wondered if it was wrong for her to like Felicia better now that she seemed more insecure. She noted that Felicia had thick ankles and then felt guilty for noticing.

"How do you think Tess seems to be handing everything?" Eugie asked.

Felicia smirked and raised one eyebrow. "Well, she's either handling it really well or she's moved on to thinking about something else. I don't think she's able to think about more than one thing at a time."

"She's just quiet," Eugie said. "I think she feels things pretty deeply and just doesn't let on."

"You're analyzing again," Felicia said. "You know what I think? I think you're really upset that Yossi got involved with her right after you and he broke up, and you feel really guilty about being upset and so you're over-compensating by making her out to be some sort of Mother Teresa or something."

"Now who's analyzing?" Eugie bit off a hangnail. "Besides, did you hear about Mother Theresa accepting that award from Papa Doc Duvalier?"

"Yeah. Remember, I was there when Yossi told us?"

"Oh."

Frank's voice echoed up the stone staircase outside their apartment.

"Eugie, Felicia. You up there? We just got a call from Yiphat. Something's up near Kiryat Arba."

Across the hall from the women's apartment, Umm Rishad, the mother of eight children (the youngest of whom tortured cats), poked her head out of the door.

"What is? Who is?" she asked, groping in the air as though hoping to find the English words there.

"*Mish mushkelleh*, Umm Rishad, It's nothing," Eugie said as she and Felicia hurried down the stairs and entered the apartment on the main floor.

Frank was scribbling a note, and Margaret was clearing up the sections of a *Jerusalem Post* scattered on the chairs, table and couch. Tess was examining her nails.

"Yiphat heard rumors that there are houses going down around Kiryat Arba and Harsina," Frank said. "She asked us to check it out."

\*    \*    \*

Tess did not want to go out in the noonday sun. The official RAPT baseball caps did not provide adequate coverage for the back of the neck. She abhorred tan lines and she did not like the greasy feel of the cheap communal sunblock the team used. She wished she had thought to buy an extra tube of the Clinique City Block before she had left the country with Yossi. It never clogged her pores.

They spent over an hour and a half looking for the house threatened with demolition. The taxi dropped them off at the entrance to the settlement of Giv'at Harsina, where a bulldozer and several jeeps full of soldiers were parked. While a man with an automatic weapon and a crocheted *kipah* eyed them from the guard house at the entrance of the settlement, they had knocked on the doors of five small stone houses in the area to find out where the demolitions were taking place. A woman at the fifth house had just told them she didn't speak English, when they got a call on their cellphone from Yiphat, who told them that one of the houses belonged to the Abu Jaber family. The frightened-looking woman at the door, with three children clutching at her dress, looked relieved when they said "Abu Jaber." She pointed toward the western horizon and disappeared inside her house.

They had had to ask directions two more times from people on the street, and had walked down a dirt path meandering through lush vineyards, when they came upon the house.

All the family's possessions—clothes, cooking utensils, sleeping mats—lay strewn on the rocky ground outside. A young woman with a baby on her hip wiped her eyes on the corner of her white head covering. As the team approached, a group of five wide-eyed, pre-school aged children stared at them, and a man with greying hair came out of the house carrying a canister of propane cooking gas.

"*Salaam aleykum*," Eugie said, placing her right hand over her heart.

"*Aleykum salaam*." The older man put the gas canister down, and two boys in their late teens or early twenties drifted to his side. As they murmured to each other, Eugie, catching one of the words, said quickly, "*La'. Mish moustautineen.* We are not settlers."

A flurry of hand gestures and single-word sentences followed. Tess noted that Felicia moved her hands in fluid motions, while Eugie's gestures seemed to jerk and stammer, just as her speech did.

Margaret had crouched down beside the five cowering children, who regarded her as they might a vicious dog on a short chain.

Frank walked over to the doomed house and seemed to be gauging its proportions. In two easy movements, he pulled himself up by the grating across one of the windows, balanced on the concrete windowsill and hoisted himself up on the roof.

Eugie pointed to Frank and asked the man a question. He nodded and his face folded into deep creases. Tess did not know whether this expression signalled sorrow or happiness. Eugie held up her right hand, thumb and fingers pressed together in the Middle Eastern guesture Tess had come to recognize as, "Wait a minute." Motioning for Margaret and Tess to follow, Eugie and Felicia walked over to the house, so that they could talk to Frank.

"Mr. Abu Jaber says we are welcome to stand on the roof of his house, but I don't know whether he understands that we want to do that when the bulldozer comes. I think we really need to be sure he's given us permission to do that," Eugie said.

"I think he knows what we mean," Felicia said. "I said we wanted to stop the soldiers. You know, we really need to learn the Arabic word for 'bulldozer.'"

"Well," said Frank, looking off into the distance. "The journalists are coming, so maybe they can translate. And there's TIPH, too."

One of the young men from the household appeared around the corner with a ladder. He bowed slightly and swept his arms toward it to invite them to climb up, and then disappeared.

"Okay, who's going to go up and who's going to stay down?" Eugie said.

"I'd better stay down," Felicia said. "If they arrest me one more time, I might be deported."

"Okay," Eugie said. "You and Tess stay down and take pictures. Margaret and I will go up with Frank. Margaret, you come up behind me, since I'm wearing a skirt."

"All the men are looking away on purpose, I think, so you can climb up," Margaret said. "But go ahead. I'll follow."

"Come on," Felicia said to Tess. "Let's go talk to the journalists."

Tess reflected on the fact that Frank had climbed onto the roof without consulting her first. It was a bad sign. On the other hand, he probably would have wanted her to come up, and she had no desire to stand there with the sun's heat and light reflecting at her from the white concrete roof. She also thought that she probably would not like to get arrested, although she could not pinpoint the exact reason—aside from the possibility that the toilet facilities in prison might be even more hideous than those at the RAPT apartment.

She smiled at Frank and waved, then joined Felicia, who was already deep in conversation with the journalists. Nayif put his camera on his shoulder and began filming Felicia, who laughed and put her hand over his lens. A female journalist, clad in royal blue knit stretchpants and matching top embroidered with sequined teddy bears, extended her hand toward Tess.

"Hello. I have not met you."

"My name is Tess." She stared with fascinated horror at the teddy bears.

"My name is Kefaah. Felicia," she turned, and as she did so, some of her black waist-length hair whipped Tess in the face. "See, Tess wears lipstick. You told me it was against official RAPT policy for women to wear lipstick."

Felicia scowled at Tess. "Tess sort of joined us by accident. Anyway, why should women wear lipstick? It's like saying our own lips aren't good enough."

"But it is very beautiful to wear lipstick!" Kefaah protested. She smiled at Tess, who was staring at the flecks of lipstick on Kefaah's large, yellow front teeth.

"Yes, it is very beautiful," Nayif agreed, looking at Tess. The two cameramen with him nodded their heads vigorously. Two days earlier, Tess had met them on the street during night patrol. One filmed for CNN and the other for a French television company. The short heavy one with curling light brown hair who worked for French TV was Wisam's brother.

"Kefaah, come here," Eugie called from the roof. Tess watched as Kefaah picked her way on stiletto heels through the rocks and rubble around the house, shielded her eyes with the yellow legal pad she was carrying, and looked up at Eugie.

Another car pulled up behind Tess and Felicia on the dirt road. Tess turned and saw Hussam, the Palestinian with the British accent, get out of the car with several more journalists.

"Hullo, hullo," he called as he strode over to join the others. Wisam's brother said something to him in Arabic, and he shrugged in response. Nayif then asked him a question, which received a longer response in Arabic.

"So you're with BBC?" Felicia asked a tall man with straw-like hair and bulging vest pockets. Tess was impressed that Felicia understood that much.

"I'm actually with WTN," he said, not taking his eyes off Tess as he continued responding to Felicia. "Jack here is with BBC, and Horst . . ." He looked behind him and then toward the house. A young man with wire-rimmed glasses was being pulled up onto the roof by Frank and Eugie. "Horst over there is with German TV. Now where did those Norwegians go? They were a half a kilometer ahead of us."

Kefaah was now standing on the roof, calling directions to one of the young men from the family. He nodded, removed the ladder from the house, and disappeared into the vineyard with it.

"Good job!" Felicia said. "That will slow them down a little."

One of the journalists pointed up the road to a group of three figures dressed in white, standing beside a house that had already been demolished some time ago. Wisam, in her moss green coatdress and white headscarf, was with them. The roof of the house looked intact, as though some giant had pulled it off the house, kicked the walls down and then carefully replaced the roof on top of the rubble.

"Pancake," the journalist named Jack said. "That's what's going to happen to this one. You think you and your friends will be able to stop it?"

"No," said Felicia. "But maybe we can slow them down."

"Heads up!" Eugie called from the roof. "Here comes the bulldozer. Felicia, come here and take the phone."

Tess walked with the journalists out onto the dirt road to watch the bulldozer, accompanied by about a dozen jeeps, approaching from about a half kilometer away. Wisam and the TIPH people hurried to their car and sped down the last meters of dirt road to arrive before the soldiers did. Hussam said something in Arabic to Nayif, who nodded and began walking toward the house.

Kefaah paced the roof, talking into her cellphone. Felicia paced in the opposite direction on the ground below speaking into the team's cellphone. Eugie sat crosslegged on the roof, facing Frank and Margaret. They held hands and bowed their heads. Margaret appeared to be speaking, but Tess couldn't hear anything.

"I simply do not understand why anyone would start praying at a time like this," Hussam said.

The bulldozer, followed by several dozen soldiers in jeeps arrived at the house. Wisam walked toward the commander, her white headscarf and green dress billowing in the wind, followed by Erland and the other two TIPH people.

"Captain Ziv, you must not destroy this house." Wisam's voice rose above the commotion. "An assistant to the prime minister has told the mayor that he will call shortly and issue a desist order."

Captain Ziv looked at Wisam with contempt and then looked away. Erland and another TIPH Norwegian, whom Tess did not recognize, began speaking to the Captain, but their voices did not carry as well as Wisam's.

Tess looked back to the doomed house. The father of the family sat on a pile of clothes thrown on the ground, his head in his hands. The women of the household stood with their backs against the front door of the house, shrieking in Arabic and gesticulating. Horst, the German journalist, sat nonchalantly on the edge of the flat roof, and appeared to be carrying on an amicable conversation with an Israeli soldier below him on the ground. Eugie, Margaret, and Frank stood toward the center of the roof, arms folded across their chests, talking to Kefaah, whose black hair flapped behind her like a flag.

On the ridge above the house, next to the fence that separated the settlement of Kiryat Arba from the Palestinian homes and vineyards, stood a group of settler men. As Tess watched, their numbers steadily increased. Several laughed and pointed down at the activities below. The concrete high-rises of Kiryat Arba made the little house seem even smaller.

"Charming, aren't they?" Hussam said to Tess. "Tell you what—why don't you join us on the house over there." He motioned toward a two story house across the vineyard from the one targeted for destruction. Wisam's brother, one of the British journalists, and Nayif were already on the roof, pointing their cameras toward the doomed house. "That's where all the journalists will be filming. Felicia!" he shouted. "Come with us!"

Talking on a cellphone, Felicia walked toward them. "Uh-huh. Sure I can call back in five minutes," Tess heard her say as she approached. "That was someone from Meretz," she told Tess and Hussam. "There's already a call in to the prime minister. He said to call again in five minutes if it looks like they're still going through with it."

As the three of them walked up the red dirt road toward the two-story house several meters ahead, it occurred to Tess that Hussam was far more interested in Felicia than he was in her. He had come by the apartment twice since the incident on Dubboya Street, and each time, he and Felicia had ended up off in the corner talking about Castro and Che Guevara. Since she was usually with Frank when Hussam came by, Tess had attributed his casual reaction to her to a desire not to encroach.

Now she wondered if he might be gay.

By the time the three of them had been shown up the stairs to the roof by the anxious-looking owner of the last standing house in the vicinity, some sort of violent confrontation seemed to be going on below. A soldier pushed a woman in a fuzzy pink housedress to the ground. When the young man who had hidden the ladder in the vineyard started to run toward her, soldiers hit him on the side of the head with a gun butt, knocking him to the ground. One of the soldiers knelt with his knee in the young man's lower back and put plastic handcuffs on him.

Kefaah now stood at the edge of the roof of the house across from them and was shrieking at one of the soldiers below, who waved a piece of paper at her.

"He's telling her that it's a closed military zone," Felicia told Tess.

"If they don't leave, they'll be arrested."

By now, Eugie, Margaret, and Frank had linked arms and were sitting on the roof. Horst, the German reporter, had climbed down by himself, using the wrought-iron grating on the window as a ladder. Kefaah gestured toward the ground and then shrugged, palms up.

Nayif laughed. "She is telling the soldier that she cannot get off the roof because there is no ladder and she is just a woman. Kefaah always say she can do what men do until the Israelis tell her to do something, and then she is 'just a woman.'"

Hussam sighed. "Poor Kefaah. It must be difficult being a single woman here."

Nayif said, "It is her choice. Many men have talked to her parents about marriage. But she refuse them all."

"Well jolly good for her, then!"

"Hey Nayif," Felicia said as he hoisted his camera to his shoulder. "What is it I hear about you and that Lisa? Are you really thinking about marrying her?"

Tess watched as a deep red stain spread over Nayif's face.

"She is very crazy," Nayif said.

"I'll say!" Felicia said.

"But I am very tired of living here."

"They're making their move," the journalist with the straw-like hair said. He hoisted his camcorder to his shoulder.

Several dozen soldiers climbed up on to the roof of the house opposite them. Two took Kefaah by the elbows and handed her down to two other soldiers below. Tess saw Wisam shouting at the captain and waving a cellphone in his face. He knocked it out of her hand and it went flying over the vineyard trellises. Wisam shrieked and kicked him in the shin. Swiftly, soldiers surrounded her, and Tess saw her fall to the ground. Nayif grabbed Wisam's brother by the arm as he slung the camera off his shoulder and prepared to dash down the stairs. They began shouting at each other in Arabic.

"Tell him that Erland is keeping them off Wisam," Felicia said.

Standing in front of her, Erland stretched out his arms protectively while Wisam crouched behind him like a crab on the ground, her flowing green dress blending with the scrubby vegetation. Tess had not thought Erland attractive before, given the disproportionate size of his jaw, but she thought he looked dashing at the moment, in his white TIPH suit, ready to spring at any soldier who dared lay a hand on his beloved.

Frank and Margaret and Eugie remained huddled together on the roof of the opposite house as soldiers tried to pry them apart. Eventually two soldiers succeeded in detaching Frank from the two women, and then Margaret was handed down to the ground as well.

Eugie remained seated and seemed to be trying to reason with the one soldier left on the roof. He touched her gently on the shoulder and gestured with his other arm toward the ledge, like a maitre d' waiting to escort her to a table. After a few moments of conversation, she stood up and walked to the edge of the roof, her head hanging in defeat. Tess saw her disappear behind the far wall of the house.

When the roof was clear, Captain Ziv shouted an order to the driver of the bulldozer, who lowered the scoop on his machine and approached the house. A scream went up from one of the women of the household and she darted in front of the bulldozer, but her husband and son followed and pulled her back.

The walls of the home crumbled as though made of sand. When the first wall caved in, the roof slowly wilted until one corner almost touched the ground.

"Hard to believe it's made of concrete," Felicia said. As soon as she said the words, chunks of concrete began separating from the reinforcement bar in the roof and crashing down.

Two women from the house crumpled to the ground, sobbing. The men remained standing, shoulders sagging. A roar of laughter and cheers went up from the soldiers present. Some began ululating.

Tess looked at Nayif. A tear ran down his cheek, but his face remained unchanged as he kept filming.

"Oh well done. Destroy their home and then make fun of them." Hussam kicked the ledge on the roof and then began lighting a cigarette with shaking hands. "Oh shit. Look over there," Felicia said, pointing to their right.

Five children with bookbags came trudging down the road. Instead of racing to the house when they saw the jeeps and bulldozer, they walked even more slowly. When they finally arrived and saw the far wall of the house fall outward, they dropped their books. A boy who looked about eight fell into a sitting position on the dirt road, as though the gravity had become too much for him. His mouth hung open, but otherwise his face was blank. Three of the girls moved toward their mother, who was still sobbing as she lay on the ground. Staring at the rubble that had been her home, the older girl awkwardly rubbed her mother's shoulder. Two soldiers continued to laugh and joke with each other, as though the woman at their feet were invisible.

"What a nightmare," Felicia said. The cellphone shrilled in her hand. She looked at it for a moment before opening the receiver and speaking into it. "It's too late," she said, after listening to the person on the other end. "The house is down." Another pause. "We saw the mayor's assistant try to give the phone to Captain Ziv, but he wouldn't take it. It looks like they've arrested her." Pause. "Yes we tried to stop it, but they carried some of our people off the roof. I think they've been arrested too. I'm not sure. EUGIE!" she yelled down at the forlorn figure in a blue skirt leaning against the police van. She had to yell again before Frank nudged Eugie and motioned up toward the roof where Felicia, Tess, and the journalists were standing.

"EUGIE, HAVE YOU BEEN ARRESTED?" Felicia called. Tess watched as Eugie put her hand on a policeman's shoulder and talked to him.

"NOT ARRESTED. DETAINED," she yelled up to Felicia. "They're just detained for now," Felicia said into the phone. "Yeah. Uh-huh. Yeah. Oh. They're getting into the van now. We should probably follow. Yeah. I'll call from the police station."

Nayif offered them a ride in his Volkswagon Beetle. Tess didn't think Hussam and Wisam's brother needed to go with them, but they did and she had to sit on Felicia's lap.

"See those two chaps?" Hussam pointed at two men dressed in suits, who stood out among the crowd of Palestinian day laborers, women and children who had gathered around the grieving family. "They're Arafat's men. They're checking to see whether anyone is blaming the Chairman for this. Fascists!" No one in the car responded.

Tess had been in the back of a windowless police van the first time she had been driven to the Civil Administration, and hadn't noticed how the charcoal-colored building on the crest of the hill loomed above the white houses dotting the hillside.

"This building really gives me the creeps," Felicia said. "The British built it during the Mandate period and the Israelis took it over for their Civil Administration building later on. You know, the first time I came to Hebron, there was a storm brewing, and I looked up and there was this black building against a totally red sky, and I thought it was the most evil looking thing I had ever seen."

"Tacky" was the word that came to Tess's mind, but she did not speak. She wondered whether she ought to ask what the Mandate period was, since people on the team always seemed to expect her to ask questions, but then decided she was too physically uncomfortable to bother.

Dozens of Palestinians were waiting in a structure that looked at first glance like a picnic shelter. However, a wall closed the back end of the shelter, and a chain-link fence with a barred gate stood in front, making it look as though the people there were in a cage.

A soldier told them to stand by the concrete block marking the entrance to the Civil Administration compound while he went inside to check with his superiors regarding the arrest of Frank, Eugie and Margaret. Felicia thanked the journalists for the ride and told them she would call as soon as there was any news.

Pulling a tube of Clinique City Block out of her pocket, Tess applied some to her face, careful to spread it more thickly around the areas where crows' feet might appear.

"You know, a tan isn't going to kill you," Felicia said. She flung herself back against the concrete block and winced. Standing up straight, she rubbed her injured tailbone.

"I'm fair complected. I need more protection from the sun than you do," Tess said with equanimity.

They waited for over an hour, during which time soldiers permitted only one person to enter the compound. Felicia suggested that they go wait in the cage with the Palestinians, but Tess said she would rather wait outside. Two minutes later, Felicia said she was going to wait in the cage whether Tess accompanied her or not. Tess watched her disappear into a labyrinth of concrete and iron that led to the back entrance of the cage. When she finally emerged into the shelter where the rest of the people were waiting, there were no empty spaces on the benches. A man offered her his seat and she slumped down beside a woman in a white scarf and black coat. Tess thought that the cross expression on her face accentuated the sun damage evident from the lines on her forehead. She knew that even olive-skinned people ought to wear lotion with an SPF of at least 6.

A little white car pulled up at the gate across the road. Yiphat got out and called, "Tess! Are you all right?"

"They won't let us in to see Eugie, Frank, or Margaret," Felicia called from the cage.

Yiphat began yelling in Hebrew at the soldier manning the gate. He looked bored and answered in monosyllables. Finally, he heaved himself out of his little guard booth and opened the fence across the road. Yiphat and Tess walked through. Yiphat pointed toward Felicia in the cage, and the soldier grunted as he unlocked the door to let her out. Dozens of Palestinian men and women rushed forward when he opened the gate, but he shouted at them, and they fell back as he relocked it.

"How is Yossi?" Felicia asked.

"Still in a coma. Why don't you guys ever call me when you're planning these things? I have twenty cases on my hands right now and my mother is staying with me. She's way too close for my

comfort when she's in New York and I'm here. Can you imagine
what it's like to have her staying in my apartment?"

Tess felt annoyed with Felicia for asking about Yossi. He
was her fiance, after all, and it should have been her prerogative
to ask.

"What do the doctors say? When will he be better?" she asked.

"All they can say is that he's not in a deep coma, that he
responds to pain, and that he's stable. I'll call you when he comes
out of it."

She walked so fast that Tess and Felicia had to break into a trot
to keep up with her. As they walked around the side of the building,
four settler men, including Goldstein-pin guy, came out of the
entrance to the police station. Tess and Felicia stopped short, but
Yiphat kept walking.

"Come on. Ignore them," Yiphat muttered.

As they passed each other, a young man with blonde curls and
a crocheted *kipah* bellowed in Felicia's ear, "GO HOME!"

Wincing, Felicia clapped her hand over her ear. Yiphat turned
and began shrieking at the men in Hebrew, who laughed and jeered
as her face became a deep plum color. Goldstein-pin guy shouted
at her and began shaking his two index fingers at them almost
rhythmically.

Yiphat raised her middle finger at him and then said to Felicia
and Tess, "Come on. Let's go."

"What did he say?" Felicia asked as they entered the filthy
waiting room of the police station.

Tess sighed. She wondered whether the police, when choosing
the decor for the room, had purposely sought out the ugliest and
most uncomfortable furniture possible.

"You don't need to know what he said," Yiphat told her as she
sat down on an orange plastic bucket seat bolted to the wall.

"We do too need to know," Felicia pressed. "I mean, for the
record and everything."

Yiphat leaned over, elbows on knees, and rubbed her temples.
Then she sat up and stretched, rotating her head and neck.

"Okay." Yiphat said. "You want to know? I'll tell you. He said that I should tell my friend in there that if she testifies against the guy who attacked her, he would kill her. Satisfied?"

"Oh," said Felicia. She looked disappointed. "He didn't say he would kill me too if I testified? I mean, I was attacked too."

# *Interim*

*"We have everything here: land, water; it could be very beautiful.
What we are missing is love between people. There is enough for
everyone if everyone is willing to share. Engineers should be
studying how to grow bread in the desert, not inventing new
weapons. Palestine needs factories to make medicines to heal
diseases, not to manufacture weapons."*

Atta Jaber—whose home was destroyed twice, on August 19,
1998 and September 16, 1998. The second time, he was arrested
and charged with "assault by infant," because he thrust his baby
son Rajeh into the arms of a soldier overseeing the demolition and
said, "Here, you take him; I can no longer take care of him."

Date: Mon, 23 Mar 1998 12:10:43 +0300
To: The British Ambassador to Israel
From: Jeff Halper, the Israeli Committee Against Home
Demolitions
Subject: The al-Atrash Family's Arrest

To: His Excellency the British Ambassador, Mr. David
Manning

A Protest Against the Brutal Treatment of the Al-Atrash
Family of Hebron by the Israeli Authorities

The Israeli Committee Against House Demolitions wishes
to register its protest against the brutal treatment, going
back over ten years, of the Palestinian Al-Atrash family of
Hebron by the Israeli authorities.

On March 4, 1998, the home of the Al-Atrash family was
destroyed FOR THE SECOND TIME. They were given
only an hour to evacuate their possessions. Whatever was
left of the furniture, toys, and other things were bulldozed

together with the house. On March 22, after attempts of the Al-Atrash family to rebuild their home, the Israeli army seized their equipment and brutally man-handled them, leading to the arrest of four members of the family.

There cannot be a better example of arbitrary and completely superfluous cruelty as this case. Here is a family with 10 children, reduced to poverty by what is euphemistically called "the closure," the forbidding of most Palestinian workers to come into Israel during the day for purposes of employment — even though Israeli policy of the past 30 years was designed to transform them into a work-force completely dependent upon Israel by preventing the development of Palestinian industry, agriculture, business, or even an adequate infrastructure in the West Bank and Gaza.

Yusef Al-Atrash, an experienced construction worker, now sews boots in Hebron for a salary of $350 per month. All he wanted to do was build a house for his family ON HIS OWN PROPERTY which has been in his family since Ottoman times (and for which he has all the proper documentation). No politics involved, in a rural area far from any Israeli settlement, army base or by-pass road, yet on a hillside from which he could point out another eight or nine houses also slated for demolition, and a school building the Israelis will not allow to be completed.

Why was he denied the permit? Well, the reason given by the Civil Administration was that only one house was permitted on "his" property according to the 1942 British planning policy — and a relative of his had already built one.

But what is "his property?" The Mandate plan was intended to ensure that agricultural land was not overwhelmed with building — although the Al-Atrash property is on a steep and rocky slope that has never been cultivated. As time passed fathers passed on their holdings to their children, thus subdividing the land as happens naturally in every country. Yusef inherited his plot of six acres from his father, had it carefully surveyed and marked with border markings and officially registered with the authorities. When he travelled to the Israeli Civil Administration to obtain a building permit, however, he was told that the boundary is not recognized and that all the land going back 100 years was recognized as one undivided unit, upon which a house had already been built, thus foreclosing any other building in the future.

Taking out his maps, Yusef protested that his plot was legally marked and registered, but was waved out of the office of the Israeli clerk Yossi Hasson (who has a reputation of dealing curtly with Palestinian petitioners seeking permits), who told him: "I don't care." The trek to the Civil Administration north of Jerusalem, the wait to see Hasson and the trip back took between 7-8 hours; the meeting with Hasson took less than a minute.

The Al-Atrash family refuses to concede its rights to decent housing as guaranteed by human rights covenants signed by Israel itself — and to build on its own land. On March 20th members of The Israeli Committee Against House Demolitions, a coalition of various Israeli peace and human rights groups, visited the Al-Atrash family and helped them begin the rebuilding of their "illegal" house for the third time. On March 22, 1998, the Israeli army confiscated their building equipment and, in the process, brutally man-handled the family, leading to the arrest of Yusef and Zuhur Al-Atrash and two of their children, a son Hussam, 17 years old, and their daughter Manaal, 16. The Al-Atrash's eight other children, including a year-old baby, were left in the tent occupied by the family on the chilly hilltop.

The Israeli Committee Against House Demolitions protests this action on the part of the Israeli authorities and calls on people and governments of good will to raise their voices as well. Indeed, we should together raise the issue of mass house demolitions — a cruel and completely unnecessary application of a Kafkaesque policy of planning in which Palestinian homes are demolished because they are "illegal" yet making it virtually impossible for Palestinians to obtain building permits — onto the international agenda. Over 1000 Palestinian families on the West Bank and in Jerusalem face the loss of their houses in this increasing aggressive campaign to clear most of the West Bank of its Palestinian residents.

Simply on a human level it is one of the most shameful aspects of Israeli occupation, one that violates fundamental rights of people to decent shelter as guaranteed in human rights covenants signed by Israel itself. And it victimizes primarily the poor and defenseless, causing untold suffering as it destroys any possibility of reconciliation between Israelis and Palestinians.

The policy of home demolitions for punitive and political reasons (Israel being the only country in the world following such practices) illustrates more than other elements of our tragic situation how good people with their own history of persecution and suffering can so easily become the perpetrators of persecution and suffering when they gain power over others. We seek in our efforts not only to end the gratuitous pain and misery caused by our government's actions, but to try to reclaim that basic humanity that we ourselves invoked as a justification for having a state of our own.

We call on you and your government to aid us, Palestinian and Israeli together, in combatting this inhumane policy that only undermines any chance for peace. Protesting the brutal and arbitrary treatment of the Al-Atrash family is a place to start.

THE ISRAELI COMMITTEE AGAINST HOUSE DEMOLITIONS

# CHAPTER 6

The Gaza-Jericho Agreement, except for Article XX
(Confidence-Building Measures), the Preparatory Transfer
Agreement and the Further Transfer Protocol will be
superseded by this Agreement,

Tess read in a low voice. She found it easier to memorize material
when she read it aloud.

It was Margaret who had set her to memorizing the *Israeli-Palestinian Interim Agreement,* which everyone else referred to as "Oslo."
Tess could not bring herself even to touch the scrub brush the team
used to clean in and around the squat-toilet. She had blanched when
she had tried to wash dishes in cold water and bleach. (How could
anyone even think of putting one's hand in cold water and bleach
without rubber gloves?) She had not felt able to write up a report on
the home demolition five days ago. Nor did she feel ready to brave the
open market and purchase food supplies.

Margaret, having exhausted every other chore that might have
been helpful to the team, finally asked Tess how well she read. As
Tess stared at her blankly (she read fine—unless Margaret meant
that she was supposed to understand what she read), Margaret
snapped, "Do you think you could read this?" She shoved a white
paperback book about the size of *Elle's* fall fashion issue at Tess.

Tess read the title, *The Israeli-Palestinian Interim Agreement . . .*
and smiled into Margaret's tight-lipped face.

"Yes. I can read this," she said.

"Can you read it in such a way as to be able to report on its
contents to the team?" Margaret's face and tone remained severe.
Tess had already written her and Felicia off as people inclined to
become disenchanted with her and thus not really worth charming.

"You mean memorize it?" Tess asked.

"If that's what it takes."

It was the perfect job. She could stay out of the sun and she didn't have to worry about breaking her nails. And it made Frank less anxious because she was doing something the others perceived as useful. She had become alarmed when he offered to go find rubber gloves for her to do housework. Fortunately, rubber gloves were not so easy to come by in the market.

Tess read,

> 5. Permanent status negotiations will commence as soon as possible, but not later than May 4, 1996 between the Parties. It is understood that these negotiations shall cover remaining issues including: Jerusalem, refugees, settlements, security arrangements, borders, relations and cooperation with other neighbors and other issues of common interest.
>
> 6. Nothing in this Agreement shall prejudice or preempt the outcome of the negotiations on the permanent status to be conducted pursuant to the DOP. Neither Party shall be deemed, by virtue of having entered into this Agreement, to have renounced or waived any of its existing rights, claims or positions.
>
> 7. Neither side shall initiate or take any step that will change the status of the West Bank and the Gaza Strip pending the outcome of the permanent status negotiations.

Margaret was scrubbing away at the tiles in the bathroom. Felicia had gone out to buy food for dinner, and Eugie clacked away at the computer in the next room with the rapidity of automatic weapon fire.

Frank was hanging his clothes out on the patio—a tiled patch open to the sky, which they shared with people in the neighboring apartment. If she and Frank ever became a couple, Tess thought, she would have to see about getting him some nicer clothes. It pleased her male admirers when she selected clothes for them— even if they generally preferred to wear garments that belonged in the rag bin. She never told them that she thought it reflected badly on her if she was accompanied by men who looked like homeless people. Choosing colors and styles that both enhanced the appearance of the men and did not clash with the clothes in her wardrobe took a lot of thought.

"Hello hello!" a woman's voice sang from the patio.

"Oh. Hi Madeleine." Frank's voice was not enthusiastic.

Tess looked up from her book and smiled uncertainly at a woman who appeared to be over six feet tall. Or maybe it was the long, coarse brown robe she was wearing that made her look that way. From her freckles and invisible eyelashes, Tess guessed that she must have red hair, although there was no way of knowing for certain, given that she wore a white, nun-like veil.

"Are Eugie and Felicia here?" Madeleine asked. "I just heard the terrible news about what happened last Saturday. I brought them something." She set two small blue glass vases on the dining room table.

"I'll be right with you, Madeleine," Eugie called wearily from the next room.

"Where is Felicia?" Madeleine asked.

"Out," said Frank, walking through the front room of the apartment with the black plastic bucket he used as a laundry basket. He disappeared into his bedroom.

"Would you like some tea, Madeleine?" Margaret called from the kitchen as she washed her hands.

"No, no. I just wanted to drop some things off. Hello, how are you? I am Sister Madeleine." Madeleine extended her hand to Tess, who flexed her fingers after Madeleine loosened her grip.

"This is Tess." Arms crossed, Eugie leaned against the door frame leading into the computer room. "She'll be staying with us for a while."

"Excellent!" Madeleine responded. "I just stopped in to drop off a little consolation gift, as it were. I feel just terrible. David Fogel told me several weeks ago that some people were planning on attacking you folks, and I just didn't take it seriously."

"Yeah, well, we're okay." Eugie said. Her face remained expressionless.

Tess kept her face from reflecting her outrage. They were most certainly NOT okay. Did this woman realize that she had had to cut her own hair to cover the scrape on her temple? Although she looked good in bangs—they imbued her with a sort of *gamine* quality—they were a nuisance to keep up with. Not to mention expensive, because she preferred to have her hair cut by a stylist and her hair grew fast. And Felicia had come very close to getting her rings cut off.

As a matter of fact, Felicia's fingers still looked discolored, and she had adopted the habit of holding them up and observing them often. Tess would have tried to use some concealer on her hands if her fingers looked like that.

"David Fogel said he was going to look into who had done this to you."

"David Fogel is a settler in Kiryat Arba," Eugie explained to Tess.

"Yes! And he's a GOOD peace person," Madeleine said, throwing a sparkling smile in Tess's direction.

Margaret walked between Madeleine and Tess without looking at either of them and entered the computer room.

Eugie looked back over her shoulder. "I'm not done with the report on the house demolition," she said.

"I just want to look at e-mail quickly," Margaret said.

"There was a house demolition? When? That's awful!" Madeleine said.

"Yes. It was." Eugie looked Madeleine in the eye. "It was one of the more horrible things I've seen since I've been here. Twenty-two people left homeless so that Kiryat Arba can expand."

"Now you mustn't blame the settlers," Madeleine said. "Some of them are good peace people. David Fogel and his friends are against demolishing homes. As a matter of fact he was talking about getting the Palestinian families who lived near Kiryat Arba to participate in one of his dialogue groups. Maybe if they hadn't all refused, that house would still be standing."

"And maybe if David Fogel is really against demolishing those homes he should try stopping it. I didn't see him and his friends around yesterday."

"Well, I'm sure if they had known about the demolition, they would have tried to stop it. But I didn't come here to argue. I wanted to give you a copy of my newest press release. She handed Tess and Eugie each a sheet of paper from the sheaf she held under her arm.

The release was entitled, "Release the Sleep Bomb Now!"

> It has come to the attention of the Hebron office of Peace and Friendship, that a new technology has been developed that would render enemy soldiers immobile without injuring them.
>
> Called the Sleep Bomb, this technology, when dropped near enemy forces, would put them instantly to sleep, thus rendering them harmless. Tests have shown that human beings exposed to the Sleep Bomb will remain unconscious for up to two hours, with no negative effects to their physical or mental health.
>
> The Hebron office of Peace and Friendship is asking all parties who really value peace to demand that their governments release the technology of the Sleep Bomb, so that bloody attacks so detrimental to the cause of peace may be effectively rendered extinct.

There followed the addresses of the President of the United States and the head of the U.S. Department of Defense, along with the addresses of various cabinet members in the Israeli government.

A sample letter began,

> "Dear President/Prime Minister/Minister _____."
> Like me, I know you are a good peace person and that

it grieves you personally to watch the blood and destruction currently wrought by conventional weapons of war. Therefore I urge you to immediately release the technology called the Sleep Bomb . . ."

"I thought you could get your office in Minneapolis to distribute this over the Internet," Madeleine said.

"Umm, well I guess we can send it to them," Eugie said. "I've got to finish writing this report on the home demolition first, though."

"Of course! Whenever it's convenient for you." Madeleine sounded as though Eugie had just made the most gracious of offers. "Are you sure some of you folks don't want to participate in the next dialogue group with me and David Fogel?"

"We really can't," Eugie said. "It's just not what we do."

Madeleine looked disappointed but still cheerful. "Very well. Another time, then."

"Bye, Madeleine," Eugie said.

"It was nice to meet you," Tess said. She thought if they ever met again, she would suggest that Madeleine try using mascara. Unfortunately, she had brought only black mascara and Madeleine would really need a medium brown. Tess's brow furrowed. She tried to remember an article she had read in *Mademoiselle* last year that told how women could work with their freckles instead of trying to hide them or diminish them. Too bad she hadn't saved the article, but she hadn't thought she would need it, given that a freckle had never blotched her perfect complexion.

"It was nice meeting you, too," Madeleine said, looking a little taken aback. Tess realized she was still frowning as she thought of the long-lost *Mademoiselle* article, and her brow cleared. Madeleine mirrored back to her the pleasant expression and said, "Please come by our office sometime. The others can tell you where it is."

"Peace to all of you," she sang as she bustled out the door of the apartment.

"SISTER Madeleine," Margaret exploded from the next room. "I hate her using that title. It gives all nuns a bad name, and she isn't even a nun."

"No, she's Jewish, Christian, AND Moslem," Eugie said.

"Yeah, that's what she says," she explained to Tess. "She goes to Friday prayers at Al Aqsa, Friday night and Saturday morning prayers at some synagogue in Jerusalem, and to church at St. George's on Sunday."

Tess realized that Eugie was responding to her own quizzical expression as she tried to recall what the article had said about whether blusher should be used on freckled complexions. Her photographic memory failed her when she only skimmed articles. She would take a more disciplined approach to beauty articles in the future, even if they did not seem to apply to her.

"Oh really?" Tess said, because it seemed like the response that Eugie wanted so that she could continue ranting.

"Yeah. She says there's no difference between Judaism, Christianity, and Islam—except for the Apostle Paul. She said if we just got rid of the Apostle Paul there'd be no difference between the religions."

"I started to challenge her once on that," Margaret said from the office, "because I did my Masters work on Paul, but she interrupted me and said she knew it was true because she had written a paper on it once."

"I'm surprised she showed up," Frank said as he came out of his bedroom. "The last time she was here, Yossi lost his temper and accused her of sleeping with David Fogel."

"That was so bad," Eugie said, laughing. "The look on her face." She sobered up. "It's really not true," she said to Tess. "She's too much of a puritan for that. As a matter of fact, that's what she uses to show that Judaism, Christianity, and Islam are identical. They all hate fornicators, adulterers, and homosexuals."

"Careful," Margaret said. "We're in Hebron, remember."

"I ran into her at St. George's a couple of Sundays ago," Frank told Tess. "She pulled out this check from the Christian Embassy. Said she wanted to prove to us that the Christian Zionists were good peace people. It was for $10,000! They gave it to her center. That's actually when we decided we needed to be careful around her."

Tess turned back to her reading so she would not feel required to ask questions about the Christian Embassy.

The phone in the office rang three times. Tess had learned that they didn't pick it up, because it was almost always for their neighbors. Shortly after the third ring, however, there was a knock on the door.

"It is Felicia the phone," announced Nasseem, their next door neighbor. She was somehow related to the upstairs neighbors, Tess had learned. She was also by far the most beautiful woman she had seen here—almost as good looking as herself. If she hadn't been hugely pregnant, Tess thought, she might have been jealous of her.

"*Shukran*, Nasseem," Eugie said, as Nasseem turned to go.

"Hello?" Margaret said. "Yes, Felicia, she's gone. You can come up now . . . Oh dear! You've been making him wait, too? Yes, by all means, come at once."

Moments later, Felicia came through the door followed by a man who appeared to be in his fifties. He wore the traditional long robe with a matching suit jacket. A snowy white kefiyah covered his head, and he carried a silver-handled cane.

"This is Abu Yussuf," Felicia announced. "It was his sons' house that got bulldozed the other day."

"*Ahlan wa sahlan*, Abu Yussuf," Eugie said, coming forward. She waited for him to extend his hand and then she shook it. That was one of the first things she had taught Tess. When it's a man, wait for him to offer his own hand. Tess felt comfortable with that, since she generally didn't think to shake hands with either women or men—unless she needed to size up an unknown man's attraction to her.

"We saw Madeleine going through the door just as we came around the corner," Felicia said. "And then Abu Nizam—"

"He's our landlord," Eugie explained to Tess.

"Called over from his shop," Felicia continued, "and invited us to drink tea. So it seemed like really good timing. Abu Yussuf's daughter is married to some relative of Abu Nizam's."

Margaret emerged from the office. "I'll make tea," she said, disappearing into the kitchen.

"So how can we help you, Abu Yussuf?" Eugie asked, bringing a wooden chair with the same color of chipped paint as the table over to him.

Abu Yussuf sat down, folded his hands over the top of his cane and began a long monologue in Arabic.

Tess read,

> 2. In order to maintain the territorial integrity of the West Bank and the Gaza Strip as a single territorial unit, and to promote their economic growth and demographic and geographical links between them, both sides shall implement the provisions of this Annex, while respecting and preserving without obstacles, normal and smooth movement of people, vehicles, and goods within the West Bank and between the West Bank and the Gaza Strip.

Eugie and Felicia attempted to communicate with two word sentences and hand gestures. To every stammering attempt, Abu Yussuf responded with a stream of excited Arabic.

"I'll go up and see if Ahlam is in," Eugie said. She held her hand up, fingers pressed together into the "wait a minute" gesture and pointed up with her left index finger.

Abu Yussuf smiled and nodded and then continued speaking in Arabic to Felicia for the several minutes that Eugie was upstairs. Margaret plied him with tea and wafer cookies, which also seemed to inspire a stream of commentary.

> g. With a view to preventing friction and to enabling the two sides to deal with possible incidents, both sides shall ensure that the relevant DCO shall immediately be notified of any of the following events:
> (1) routine, scheduled or unscheduled activity or deployment by the Israeli military forces or the Palestinian Police that directly affects the security responsibility of either side. This includes activity or deployment in the proximity

of settlements or Palestinian populated localities, as the case may be.

Ahlam, the neigbors' oldest daughter, came down wearing a white *hijab* and a pantsuit made of some silky material. Tess could tell that the suit was homemade—but it looked quite attractive on Ahlam. It would have looked good on her, too, although she would have preferred a more tailored jacket. She stared at the outfit hungrily.

When Tess had appeared in a perfectly presentable outfit of jeans and a bodysuit her first morning in Hebron, Eugie, Margaret, and Felicia had all impressed on her the importance of modesty. Eugie had gone through the clothes Tess had managed to salvage after the bombing incident in the hotel and pronounced all but two of her tops unsuitable for wearing around Hebron. Tess had had a hard time making do with clothes Eugie had loaned her and clothes left behind by previous RAPT members. She did not understand why the RAPT women, as well as the men, seemed to take pride in the shabbiness of their clothes. Neither did she understand why Palestinian women felt such a need to be modest. On average, most of them had better figures than American women.

"Ahlam's on her way to work," Eugie announced, "so this will have to be short."

Ahlam kept her eyes on the floor and pushed her glasses up on her nose. She asked the old man a question without looking at him. He said something to her that made her smile, look up, and meet his gaze.

The conversation then became more serious. "He says that it was the house of his two sons that was destroyed yesterday," Ahlam said.

The team members nodded their heads in unison at Abu Yussuf. The identical expressions of sympathy on their faces made them look, Tess thought, as if they were all somehow from the same family.

After another long stream of Arabic and several muted questions from Ahlam, she turned to the team and said, "He says can you help him?"

"What else did he say?" Felicia asked.

"Oh it is not important," Ahlam smiled tightly and looked at the floor.

The RAPTors looked at each other uncertainly.

"Could you tell him that we have no money and no *wasta*?" Eugie asked.

Ahlam looked horrified. "I could not tell him that! It would be quite—how do you say—rude?"

Again there was silence.

> "6. *Joint Liaison Bureaus*," Tess read in an undertone. "Joint Liaison Bureaus established by the two sides shall operate at crossing points and at terminals as described in Articles V, VI and VIII of this Annex."

"Ask him how his grandson is—the boy that the soldier hit with his gun when he tried to help his mother," Eugie asked.

Ahlam put the question to Abu Yussuf, who shrugged his shoulders and gave his shortest response yet.

"He says that he is in jail for seven days."

"Shit, what are we going to do?" Felicia muttered. "No, no—don't translate that," she said as Ahlam opened her mouth.

Eugie went over to the table that the team threw most of their junk on and which Margaret tried to neaten, in vain, every day. Selecting a business card from a pile next to the cellphone recharger, she circled something on it with a pen. She handed it to Abu Yussuf and addressed Ahlam.

"Can you tell him that this is our phone number, and we don't know what we can do, but we will talk to some people?"

Ahlam translated and the old man sighed. He smiled at the team sadly, and with a half wave, left the apartment.

"*Maa salaam*," Eugie called out after him. He did not respond, but they heard the dull knock of his cane on the concrete stairs as he made his way down to the street.

"I must go," Ahlam said. "I must teach my computer students."

"We're really sorry if we made you late," Eugie said.

"Thank you so much, Ahlam," Margaret said.

"For nothing, for nothing," she said. "You must come up to visit soon."

The team nodded and smiled at her as she left, and said nothing for a few moments while they listened to her light footfalls on the steps.

Felicia broke the silence. "God, I hate this job."

"I've GOT to get this report sent out," Eugie said. "Minneapolis should have had it yesterday."

"You were in jail yesterday; they'll understand," Margaret said.

"b. In the West Bank, the Palestinian Police will possess the following arms and equipment," Tess said under her breath.

> (1)  up to 4,000 rifles;
>
> (2)  up to 4,000 pistols;
>
> (3)  up to 120 machine guns of 0.3" or 0.5" caliber; and
>
> (4)  up to 15 light, unarmed riot vehicles of a type to be agreed on between the two sides in the JSC.

"Frank, what did the police officers tell you when they shoved your face in the dirt?" Eugie called from the computer room.

"Eat, eat."

"Not 'eat dirt?'"

"No just 'eat. eat.' They probably didn't know the English word for 'dirt.'"

"How are your wrists?"

Tess looked up as Frank held his hands up and looked at the backs and fronts of his wrists.

"You can kind of see the marks from the plastic handcuffs, but don't write about that. It might seem like I'm whining."

"On the other hand," Margaret said, "it might call attention to the kind of damage that plastic handcuffs can do."

"Yeah, but they finally took mine off when I asked them to for about the fifth time," Frank said. "They wouldn't have done that for Palestinians."

"I'm just going to write that they put you in plastic handcuffs," said Eugie from the next room.

Tess tucked the Oslo book underneath her arm and walked over to Frank. "Let me see your wrists." She stroked them. "I have some aloe vera lotion upstairs that will help."

Frank flushed a bright red and gave a tight smile. "No. Really, Tess, they're fine."

"I'll be back in just a couple of minutes." She smiled at him and saw from his expression that he would not refuse her again.

When she returned from the upstairs apartment, Sa'eed, the man she had met on the way to worship the first morning, was sitting in a chair and eating all the cookies that Abu Yussuf had left behind.

She began applying aloe vera lotion to Frank's friction burns. Sa'eed stared at her. "Just like my beautiful Yuaad," he sighed. "So, what is your news?" he asked. "I heared you were at the place where the house was destroyed yesterday. It is very, very bad."

"How is your wife?" Margaret asked.

"Very well, thank you, but about this house. How did you hear about it?"

"How did YOU hear about it?" Felicia sat in a chair opposite Sa'eed and looked at him coolly. He looked at the ground.

"It was in the newspapers," he muttered.

"News has a way of traveling very fast, doesn't it?" Felicia asked.

There was a knock on the door.

"AAAAAUGH!" Eugie wailed from the next room.

Tess had finished applying lotion to Frank's wrists and went to open the door. Lisa, the Louis Farrakhan aficionado she had met on her first day in Hebron, walked in, followed by three young Palestinian men.

"Hi, Hitler!" Frank said. "Hi, Samer!" He extended his hand to the third young man wearing jeans and a Hard Rock Cafe T-Shirt and said, "I'm sorry, I don't believe we have met."

"My name is Abdel Raouf," he replied, with a formal tip of his head.

"Hello, Frank. Hello, Margaret. Hello, Felicia." The young man who had been addressed as Hitler shook everyone's hand. Tess noticed that his nose had been flattened against his face. The three young men looked at Sa'eed uncertainly and did not take his hand. Sa'eed continued to look at the ground.

"Lose something, Sa'eed?" Frank asked.

It took a moment for Sa'eed to understand the question.

"Ah," he said. "You ask why I look down all of the time. It is a habit of my family's. We have found much lost money this way. When I was young, I chose to look to the sky instead of the earth, so I did not become like my father and my father's father and my father's father's father."

He exaggerated his hunched-over posture to demonstrate what he had unsuccessfully tried to avoid.

"Sadly," he continued, "looking to the sky did not help me. It brought a different curse upon me, so I have returned to the ways of my fathers."

The three young Palestinian men scowled at him, and Tess went back to her reading.

### 7. Movement

> Movement of Palestinian policemen between the West Bank and the Gaza Strip will be conducted in accordance with Article X of this Annex.

Lisa began talking about Farrakhan again in a high nasal voice that retreated to the background of Tess's consciousness like a mosquito hum. She was dimly aware that the young man named Hitler kept trying to interrupt her and disagree with her. The other two young Palestinian men disagreed with him.

Samer came over and offered her a cigarette. She smiled at him, which made him flush. "No thank you, I don't smoke," she said.

"It is a bad thing," Samer said. "Do you think I should stop?"

"Oh yes," Tess said. "It is very bad for you."

Samer squashed out his half-smoked cigarette in the chipped saucer that Margaret had brought out as an ash tray.

"What is the book you are reading?" Hitler asked.

Tess held up the heavy paperback for them to see.

"The in-ter-im agree-ment," he began sounding out.

"It's the Oslo Accords," Felicia said.

"Oslo is very, very bad." Abdel Raouf shook his head.

Hitler said something to him in Arabic which started an intense discussion with lots of handwaving. Lisa wandered into the computer room and began talking to Eugie, who responded in monosyllables.

"I am sorry for this arguing," Hitler turned back to Tess, "we disagree about Oslo. It is not a fair agreement, but what else can we do? There has been too much killing. We must begin making peace."

"Peace, peace, peace. The Jewish talk peace all the time," Abdel Raouf said. "You see the soldiers and the settlers with their guns saying 'shalom' when they pass each other in the street. If that is peace, then I want war."

Hitler shook his head. "It is a very bad thing, the war." He turned his attention back to Tess. "You see my nose? It got this way because soldiers would stop me in the street and ask my name. When I told them, they kept punching me in the nose. I don't know why." (Like most of the Palestinians Tess had met, he pronounced it 'woi.') "My father tells me that Hitler was a freedom fighter; that he was trying to keep the Jewish from taking over the world. But when I went to the university, I read about Hitler. He was a very bad man. My father should not have given me that name—but what can I do? For twenty years everyone has called me Hitler."

"You know the guy who runs the falafel stand near the municipality is called Eichmann?" Frank said.

Lisa came out of the office and launched into tirade mode. "You know, all that stuff about Hitler is mostly propaganda. I mean, no one really believes that Hitler killed six million Jews. They inflated that number so people would feel sorry for them. Really, they can't prove that more than four hundred people died in the camps. Louis Farrakhan says—"

"*Ay de mia!*" Felicia said. "Out! Right now! Samer, Hitler, Abdel Raouf, you can stay if you want, but she has to go."

Frank began, "Felicia, wait a minute."

"No!" Felicia said. "We don't allow fascists in this apartment."

She stormed in to the office, followed by Frank. The door closed and Tess heard the low mumble of urgent voices. Margaret slipped out of the kitchen and into the office.

Sa'eed, who had been sitting at the table drinking his tea for the bulk of the conversation, said, "Please permit me to offer my help. I will walk this lovely young lady home."

"Sure," said Lisa. "I know when I'm not welcome. Fascism!" Her eyebrows flew up. "Now, fascism has gotten a bad name . . ." she began, shaking her index finger at no one in particular.

Samer spoke sharply to Sa'eed in Arabic. The older man stared at the floor, shoulders hunched, and murmured something in response.

Tess read, "a. Joint Patrols led by a Palestinian vehicle will operate on each of the following roads, as indicated on map no. 4," then realized that Lisa was still lecturing about fascism. Eugie, Margaret, Felicia, and Frank were still in the office arguing. Samer, Abdel Raouf, and Hitler stood in a huddle by the couch, speaking in low voices and glancing at Sa'eed. Sa'eed continued to stare at the floor. As far as Tess could tell, no one was listening to Lisa, but she kept on talking.

> (8)  the main north-south road (Route No. 60) crossing Bethlehem
>
> (9)  the main east-west road crossing Beit Jala
>
> (10) the main north-south road (Route No. 90) crossing Jericho; and
>
> (11) the road crossing Hebron, as set out in Article VII (Hebron) below

The cellphone rang and the door to the office opened. Eugie called back over her shoulder, "We'll talk about it at the meeting this evening," as she hurried to pick up the phone.

"Oh hi, Hillel," Eugie said. "No. We're all out. They're not pressing charges for getting in the way of the demolition. In fact, the police told us when they released us that they really hoped we were still going to follow through and testify against the guys who beat us up—oh I'm over-dramatizing again. I should say the guys who socked me in the ear and stomped on Felicia's hand." She listened for a few moments. "Yeah, I think the family would be okay with that. How many rabbis would be coming with you? Listen, we'll go out to the family and check with them to make sure it's okay." Again, a few moments of listening. "That would be great!" Eugie said. "You want to talk to Hitler? He's here right now."

She held out the phone to Hitler. "Hitler, it's Rabbi Cotton. He wants to come to the University and talk to some of the students in your peace group."

Hitler smiled and took the phone. "*Salaam Aleikum,*" he said, and began a conversation half in Arabic and half in English.

There was a knock on the door. "Hello, hello!" Erland called. He walked into the apartment, followed by three other TIPH people in white suits.

Felicia opened the door to the office and poked her face out. "Oh hi, Erland," she said, sighing. "Come on in."

The door opened wider and Frank came out. "Hey dude!" he said, extending his hand.

"I wanted to bring some of the new people in our group to meet you," Erland said. Emilio, here, is from Italy. Sven is from Norway like myself and Abed is from Denmark."

"Denmark?" Frank asked.

"I was born in Gaza," Abed responded in near-perfect English.

Tess watched as Lisa, Abdel Raouf, Samer, Sa'eed and Frank exchanged handshakes all around with the newcomers. Felicia and Margaret then came out of the office and did their share of hand shaking. Then Hitler finished his phone conversation and did the same. Tess decided that it was not incumbent upon her to shake hands.

"I see you are busy," Erland said. "We will go."

"No, no," said Hitler. "We want to go."

"Hey Samer!" Frank said. "Basketball this evening?"

"Ab-so-loot-ly, dude!" responded Samer, pronouncing each syllable with relish.

"All right!" Frank said, high fiving him.

Tess sniffed. Once again, Frank had not consulted her. He should have asked her whether she wanted to watch them play basketball.

"I must talk to Eugie," Erland said, beaming.

"In here," Eugie called from the office.

Erland closed the door behind him and Tess heard him say something in a low voice, followed by a shriek from Eugie. "That's wonderful! I'm so happy for you Erland!"

Frank and Margaret disappeared into the office for a few moments and Tess heard Frank say, "All right, man!"

Tess looked up from her book. All their visitors were looking at each other uncomfortably except for Sa'eed, who was examining something on the floor again. Felicia was watching the smoke from her cigarette waft up to the ceiling. The ribbed collar of her baggy, green t-shirt had begun to separate from the rest of the shirt. Tess surveyed her own neat plaid blouse and matching chinos for a moment. She hoped that Felicia's appearance would not reflect badly on her.

As soon as Frank and Margaret came out, Felicia stubbed out her cigarette and went into the office. Abed, the Danish-Gazan, began to speak quietly in Arabic with Abdel Raouf, Hitler, and Samer. Frank and Margaret had big smiles on their faces. Frank looked at Tess and jerked his head in the direction of the office.

Tess closed her book and went into the office.

"Close the door," Felicia hissed.

"You are making, how do you say, a big thing about nothing," Erland was saying to Felicia and Eugie, a huge smile on his face.

"No, it's not nothing. You know it's not," Eugie said. "Wisam has invited Erland to dinner with her parents," Eugie said to Tess.

This was definitely more interesting than either the Oslo Accords or the people sitting in the next room. Of course, Wisam's parents, once they saw what Erland looked like, might have second thoughts. Wisam was so much better looking than Erland. It would have to make them nervous, wondering whether the children would look more like Erland than Wisam.

"Congratulations," she smiled at Erland.

"Thank you very much. I am very nervous."

"Tea's ready," Margaret called from the kitchen.

"Don't worry. You'll do fine," Eugie assured him.


It was another two hours before the TIPH people, Sa'eed, Lisa, Samer, Hitler, and Abdel Raouf left. As Margaret closed the door behind their visitors, Felicia slumped in her chair and Frank stretched out on the couch, glassy-eyed.

"You hear that?" Felicia said.

"No, what," Frank said, closing his eyes.

"Exactly."

Tess read,

> a. Passengers exiting through the Rafah passage to Egypt and through the Allenby Bridge passage to Jordan shall pay a passenger fee equivalent to 26 USA dollars
>
> b. This passenger fee will be collected by Israel. The Council may sell passenger fee vouchers to passengers passing through the Palestinian wing of the terminals, after having purchased them from Israel by means of a letter of guarantee given by an Israeli bank for each quota of vouchers transferred to the Council, or any other method of payment to be agreed upon. The design and content of the vouchers or stamps used will be agreed. c. Diplomats and children under two years of age will be exempt from the passenger fee.

"If I have to smile and nod one more time, I think I'll puke," said Frank.

"Yesssss," Eugie said from the next room. "The article is finished and I am printing it out. You guys want to read it?"

No one responded.

> 3. *Miscellaneous*
> a. The Council will be responsible for the 90 Palestinian personnel employed in the Allenby Bridge crossing by the Director-General and the 20 Palestinian personnel employed at the Rafah crossing by the Director-General, in accordance with the provisions of paragraph 2. a of Section C of this Protocol, Tess read.

*     *     *

Margaret answered the cellphone when it rang. Frank was clearing away the supper dishes. Eugie was doing a final proofread of the article about the home demolition and the arrests, and sighed when Margaret said, "It's Yiphat." Her editing seemed to miss at least one clunky sentence in every one of her articles. She wished she had the luxury of letting them sit for a week before they got posted on RAPTnet.

"Okay, coming," she said.

"She says she wants to talk to Tess," Margaret said as Eugie came out of the office.

"Oh."

It must be Yossi. Yiphat must have some news of Yossi. Oh please, God, let him be all right. If he had died, would Yiphat have asked to speak to Tess first or to herself? If Yossi had died, wouldn't Yiphat have asked her to break the news to Tess? Oh God, what if he was dead? She had told him she never wanted to speak to him again the last time they had talked. What if he had died thinking she was still angry with him? She had told him she wasn't angry; she just couldn't speak to him for reasons of emotional self-preservation. But she had lied. She was furious with him. How could he have acted like they were old, platonic buddies that last time they had met in Philadelphia? How could he have acted as though they hadn't slept together? As though she hadn't set aside all her beliefs and mores in the vain hope that love would conquer all (and because, while the Bible was clear on adultery, it left some wiggle room in the definition of "fornication")? God, he'd made her furious. Oh God, what if he was dead?

Tess had replied in monosyllables to Yiphat, and then she said, "Hi Yossi."

Eugie hadn't realized that she was clutching the door frame. She tried to make her way across the room to the couch, and banged her thigh hard on the corner of the table. Limping, she made it to the couch in time to put her head down on her knees.

When she had stopped seeing black spots in front of her eyes, she sat up and saw Frank standing in the doorway leading from the kitchen. His face was white as he watched Tess smiling into the phone.

The thought occurred to Eugie that there was something perverse in the fact that Yossi's regaining consciousness caused both her and Frank to feel stricken.

"I love you, too, Yossi," Tess said and clicked the flap on the phone shut. She then sat down and picked up the Oslo accords and resumed reading.

"Well?" Felicia said, exasperated.

Tess looked at her blankly for a moment. "Oh, you want to know about Yossi?"

"Yes, of course we do," Margaret said.

"He said he is feeling a little weak and that I should come up to Jerusalem tomorrow. Yiphat said I should wait a day." She resumed her reading.

Frank went back into the kitchen. Seconds later, they heard tea glasses shattering.

"Shit," Frank said.

Tess put the book down and went into the kitchen. Eugie

slumped against the wall, aware, without looking, that Margaret and Felicia were staring at her.

"I think I'll go to bed," she said. "I have a bad headache."

The trudge up the stairs to the women's apartment left her feeling breathless, as though her lungs had shrunk, or as though there were a hard ball of something in her stomach swelling, squeezing her lungs so that she could not get enough air in. When she got to the door, she realized that she had left her key in her waistpack downstairs. She placed her forehead against the door for a few moments. Don't cry. Don't cry. Don't let them see you cry.


When she re-entered the downstairs apartment, Felicia and Margaret looked up. She thought Margaret was asking her if she was okay, and she nodded, but after she nodded, she wasn't sure whether Margaret had asked her anything at all.

Back up at the women's apartment, the key didn't seem to work. She dropped her keys twice before successfully turning the right one counterclockwise.

Her hair needed washing, but the idea of heating up water for a bath seemed too daunting. She lay on her floor mat for about ten minutes reliving the look on Tess's face when she picked up the phone, the look on Frank's face, the fact that Yiphat had not thought to talk to her—that Yossi had not asked to talk to her . . .

Abruptly she sat up, undid her braid, and began brushing with a vengeance. She pulled a snarl of greasy hair, coated with dust and lint, from her hairbrush and stuffed it into the plastic bag that served as her wastebasket under the chair that served as her nightstand. Then she cleaned her face and neck with witch hazel, noting how black the cotton ball became after cleaning the back of her neck. It went into the bag with the other blackened cotton balls and hair snarls.

Off came the clothes; on came the faded blue T-shirt with "Freeze All Nuclear Weapons Now" written in vinyl letters cracked from many years of washing and drying.

She picked up the book of Oscar Romero quotations, which she had been using for devotions, and read

> We have never preached violence
> except the violence of love,
> Which left Christ nailed to a cross,
> the violence that we must each do to ourselves
> to overcome our selfishness
> and such cruel inequalities among us.
> The violence we preach is not the violence of the sword
> the violence of hatred.
> It is the violence of love,
> of brotherhood,
> the violence that wills to beat weapons
> into sickles for work.[1]

She closed the book, put it on the chair beside her floor mat and turned off the dim lightbulb that hung from the ceiling. Her throat constricted, and tears began to drip from the outer corners of her eyes onto the pillow. She did not know whether she grieved for Yossi or for her own pathetic shallowness. Here Archbishop Romero was defending the Christians of El Salvador, who had been accused of inciting violence because they spoke out against the kidnappings, torture, and murder. How many Christians had died for their faith in El Salvador?

And here she was, thinking, yes, love is violent. It makes me want to take a big knife and slash and slash and slash away at my arms until I am covered with blood, because I love Yossi and Yossi doesn't love me. He loves Tess.

God, she was loathsome. How could God even stand to be in the same room with her?

It was funny—not ha ha, of course. Even though she had made a conscious decision to become an agnostic when she was thirteen,

---

[1]    *The Violence of Love: The Pastoral Wisdom of Archbishop Oscar Romero* San Francisco: Harper and Row, Publishers, p. 14.

because the position seemed to have more integrity to it than the say-the-magic-words-and-become-a-Christian youth camp approach, she had never really stopped believing in God. She had never really stopped believing that Jesus loved her. At sixteen, when she had finally given in and said, of course there is a God and Jesus was who he said he was, she felt she was a little closer to reality, a little closer to truth. Even during the hollow times, when the dirty cloud enveloped her, and the lump sat in her chest so she could hardly breathe, she never again felt as though there were no God or that God had deserted her.

But she did feel, at times like these, that God was standing there looking down on her, wringing his hands and thinking, "What am I going to do with her?"

When she had worked with developmentally disabled adults, she had seen so many of them make self-destructive choices again and again. DeeDee would continue hiding her seizure medication and swear up and down she had been taking it. Paul would continue pursuing Rita, even though he knew that Rita would dump him as soon as she found a boyfriend who would abuse her. Todd would continue calling in sick to work, even though he knew he would lose his placement and have no money.

God! What had made her think she could do anything to help them? She had at least forty IQ points on most of them and yet, each time she fell in love, she saw at the very beginning reasons that she shouldn't, but always, ALWAYS managed to convince herself that this time would be different. That the intensity of her feelings gave authenticity to the relationship.

Yossi had been so attentive and so charming. He really listened to her, or at least, so it seemed at the beginning. She had never had anyone say, "I adore you" to her before.

So what if he didn't believe in God and had slept with about a hundred other women? He made her feel different and special. God would want her to be happy, right? And if she gave Yossi her unconditional love, maybe he would start feeling a little bit of God's unconditional love for him through her.

Yuk. She was disgusting. How could she have even begun to think that someone as smart as Yossi would fall for her? He wanted someone like Tess, who was beautiful and thin and quiet and totally put together.

She, on the other hand, was so . . . gross. Why did God even bother putting up with her?

She had to blow her nose. She'd better get control of herself before Margaret came in. What was she doing here anyway? How could she possibly think that anything she could do or be could add anything positive to the team or to the situation? She was such a fraud.

Dutifully, she began her nightly prayers with the same phrase she had used since she was seven years old and visualized God as a little girl praying, because that was the shape of her nightlight.

"Dear God, thank you for this day and all the wonderful things you have given me—" Here she was a healthy thirty-five year old woman who had a job she loved and family and friends who loved her. Objectively, she understood that people did not assume she was loathsome when they first met her. The vast majority of people in her life would never think she was loathsome. Heck, Yossi and all the other men didn't think she was loathsome. They had just decided at some point they didn't want to be with her anymore. That wasn't the same as their thinking she was revolting to be around. Only she knew how disgusting she really was.

She made a fist and hit her head several times. She knew she had to stop the downward spiral or she would be no good to anyone. There was work that needed to be done. She could have the luxury of collapsing when she got home. She could go stay with her younger sister and her five nieces and nephews, who thought their Aunt Eugie was a sort of demi-goddess, only more fun. They didn't realize she was fat and ugly and disgusting.

God, she had to stop this. She began praying for each of her brothers and sisters, for their marriages, for their children. She prayed for her parents, for her friends, for everyone on the team, for the people in Bosnia, for Wisam and Erland, Yiphat—for Yossi and Tess.

"Grant to them the light they need." It was the most useful prayer she had ever been taught. When you didn't know what to pray for people who made you furious, who caused you to grieve, who were falling deeper and deeper into a pit of self-destruction, it was a prayer that always applied.

When she was young, her nightly prayers had always ended with, "Please, God, don't let me have any bad dreams." About once a month, she would pray for God to let her have a nightmare, because she didn't want Him to think she was greedy. On those nights, she always had one.

Now that she was older she rarely had bad dreams anymore— and when she did, they were no worse than the nagging sorrows that seemed to dog her when she was awake. Wearily, she closed with the mantra she had begun saying the last few months: "God, please help me to want Jesus as much as I want Yossi."

Four years of therapy, and she still found it soothing, as she fell asleep, to imagine that she was cutting her wrists, over and over again.

# *Interim*

## THE HARROWERS[2]
### by Nizar Kabani
### translated by Sammir Habash

1.  The last walls of shame fell
    We were elated
    And we danced.
    We were blessed by the signing of the cowards' peace
    Nothing frightens us . . .
    Nothing shames us . . .
    The veins of pride have stiffened within us

2.  For the fiftieth time
    Our innocence fell.
    We neither shook nor screamed
    Nor were frightened by the sight of blood.
    And we entered the era of dashing . . .
    We stood in lines, like sheep before the guillotine
    We ran, we heaved . . .
    And we raced to kiss the shoes of the killers

3.  They starved our children for fifty years
    And when the fast ended
    They threw an onion.

4.  Granada fell
    For the fiftieth time
    Away from the hands of the Arabs

---

2    "Harrowers" has been substituted for Habash's choice of "Dashers" as per
     the suggestion Khaled Amayreh, a journalist in Hebron who writes for
     *Middle East International*. The original Arabic title is *al Muharwilun*.

History fell from the hands of the Arabs
Pillars fell . . . and so did the soul and the thigh of the tribe
All the songs of chivalry fell
Seville fell
Antioch fell
Hittin fell without a fight
Amoriah fell
Mary fell at the hands of the militias
And not a man saves this heavenly symbol
There is no manhood . . .

5.  The last of our fortunes fell
    In the hands of the Romans
    What are we defending?
    In our palace not a single maid is left . . .
    To make coffee and sex . . .
    What are we defending?

6.  In our hands not a single Andalus is left to own
    They stole the doors
    And the walls
    The wives and the children
    The olives and the olive oil
    The stones of the streets
    They stole Jesus Son of Mary
    While he was still suckling
    They stole the memory of the lemon of the apricot and the mint
    The lamps of our mosques

7.  They left a can of sardines in our hands called Gaza
    A dry bone called Jericho
    A hotel called Palestine
    No roof, no pillars
    They left our bodies boneless
    Our hands without fingers

8. There are no more ruins to weep over
   How can a nation cry . . .
   The ducts of its tears were clogged . . .
   They gave us a homeland smaller than a grain of wheat
   A homeland we can swallow without water
   Just like an aspirin

9. After fifty years . . .
   We now sit on ruined land
   Without a home
   Like thousands of dogs

10. After fifty years
    We found no homeland to hold
    Except a mirage
    No peacemaking is this that pierced us like a dagger
    This is rape!!

11. What does harrowing benefit?
    What does harrowing matter?
    When the people's conscience is alive as the fuse of a bomb . . .
    All Oslo's signatures will not be worthy of a mustard seed

12. How we dreamed of a green peace
    And a white crescent
    And a blue sea
    And proud fortresses
    And suddenly we found ourselves in a garbage dump

13. Who will ask them
    About the peace of cowards?
    Not the peace of the strong and able
    Who will ask them
    About the peace of sale by installments
    And by deals
    The merchants and the investors?
    Who will ask them
    About the peace of the dead . . .

They silenced the streets
The(y) assassinated all questions
And married without love the woman who once ate our children
And who chewed our livers
Yet we took her on a honeymoon
We were intoxicated . . . and we danced
We recited all that we remembered of romance's poems
Then we produced unfortunate handicapped children
That look like frogs
We mutinied on the sidewalk of sorrow
No country to embrace or a child!

14. There were no Arab dances at the wedding
    Or Arabic food
    Or Arabic singing
    Or Arabic shame
    The town boys were not present at the wedding

15. Half of the dowry was in dollars
    The diamond ring was in dollars
    The wedding clerk's fees were in dollars
    The cake was a grant from America
    The bride's veil, the flowers, the candles and the Marines' music
    All were made in America

16. The wedding ended . . .
    Palestine did not attend the celebration
    She saw its picture transmitted on every channel
    She saw its tears cross the ocean towards Chicago, Jersey and Miami
    And she, like every slaughtered bird . . . screams . . .
    This wedding is not mine. Never . . . America
    Never . . . America
    Never . . . America

Reprinted from *Challenge Magazine* [Jan.-Feb., 1996, No. 35, Vol. VII No. 1, pp. 20-21]

# CHAPTER 7

It seemed as though her uneasy sleep had lasted only moments before she heard the crackling speaker of an Israeli jeep broadcasting the words, "*MAMNOUA ITTJOWAL*"

She was on her feet in seconds, pulling on her clothes. If they were calling a curfew, something bad was happening. Margaret flipped the light on and peered at her travel alarm as she groped for her glasses. "It's three in the morning, what could they possibly be up to at this hour?"

Throwing nearby items into her backpack, Eugie said, "I'm going downstairs to call Nayif."

She forgot to bring her keys along to the downstairs apartment and had to run back up to the women's apartment to grab them. "Frank, wake up, they're announcing curfew," she called as she entered the darkened apartment.

She heard Frank groan from the next room as she punched Nayif's number into the cellphone. As soon as the phone connected with Nayif's, she heard an ear-splitting boom, both from the phone receiver and outside, followed by the sound of Nayif swearing.

"Nayif, it's Eugie. What's going on?"

"Meet me in five minutes in Baab iZawiye," Nayif ordered. "They are blowing up houses by the gas station." The phone clicked shut. Eugie began shuffling through her backpack to see if she had everything. Camera, extra film—she zipped the phone into a side pocket.

" . . . . *Mamnua itt jowil* . . . . " the loudspeaker intoned.

Frank stumbled out of the bedroom, glassy-eyed. He looked like he had been drinking, but Eugie knew that he simply was not a morning person.

"Coffee?" he whimpered.

"No time. Get the video camera."

He shuffled around in the office as Felicia, Margaret, and Tess entered the apartment with backpacks on.

Felicia dropped onto the couch and curled up in the fetal position. She yawned. "So what did Nayif say?" she asked.

"Not much. He just said he would pick us up at Baab iZawiye."

"There's a shitload of soldiers down in the alley," Frank said, emerging from the office with a video camera.

All of them except Tess trooped into the office to take a look. About eight soldiers wearing helmets, rifles poised, were standing near the checkpoint. Two more appeared from the opposite end of the alley after having conducted a satisfactory surveillance around the deserted carrot juice stand.

"Shit," said Felicia. "They'll never let us out. What now?"

In the distance they heard the sound of sleighbells drawing closer. The soldiers went out of the alley and onto the main thoroughfare to watch the approach of the vegetable vendor in his horse-drawn cart.

"Santa Claus!" said Eugie. She had fond feelings for the grizzled, one-eyed man and his boney gray horse, especially since last December, when she had had to spend the holidays in Hebron. One of the chicken delivery trucks played "We wish you a Merry Christmas" as a warning that it was backing up, which had also made her feel good.

"Listen," Felicia said. "I'm starting my period and would just as soon not be sitting around God knows where today. Margaret and I will go down and talk to the soldiers, and you guys try to slip out."

The maneuver worked surprisingly well. The one-eyed vendor, as anticipated, was stopped and yelled at by the soldiers. Felicia and Margaret walked out to intercept.

"Is there a problem?" Margaret asked. She and Felicia walked over to the other side of the cart. The soldiers also moved to that side, clustered around them, and yelled at them in Hebrew.

"But I don't understand. What's going on?" Felicia said as Eugie, Frank and Tess slipped out of the apartment door and to their right. Floodlights made the greasy asphalt shine as the three of them skidded around the corner and out of sight. They surprised three feral dogs devouring a pile of chicken offal. The animals flinched, accustomed as they were to being kicked or having stones thrown at them when humans appeared.

The RAPTors half walked, half ran through the market, keeping abreast of the jeep broadcasting the curfew announcement as it drove slowly up a parallel road.

They emerged into the small open area of vegetable stalls. To the left was a *yeshiva* that was perpetually under construction, since there seemed to be some disagreement under the Hebron Accord as to whether construction on the school could continue. A crane with the sign *Beit Ahad* in Hebrew loomed against the sky, dangling a giant cement block over the incomplete fourth floor of the school.

Soldiers at the checkpoint in front of the school shouted at them as the jeep with the loudspeaker turned off the parallel road and seemed to barrel toward them. Eugie held her finger up to her ear and smiled, indicating that she couldn't hear and ran up the final stretch of road to Baab iZawiye, the city center.

Smoking nervously, Nayif leaned against his car. As they ran toward him he jumped in and started the engine. Frank ran around to the front seat of his VW bug, allowing Tess and Eugie to squeeze into the back first.

"The soldiers were by here just one minute ago," Nayif said. "I told them I was driving foreigners to Jerusalem. They said if I was still here when they got back, they would arrest me."

"What's up?" Frank asked.

"The IDF shot a wanted man, a Hamas man, outside houses at Ras iJura. They shot missiles into two of them."

Just before the gas station at the northern entrance into Hebron, Nayif turned right and then left, stopping the car at a partially constructed two-story concrete building. "We are filming from the roof," Nayif said.

Eugie looked up and saw Wisam's brother—she never could remember his name—Hussam, and a couple of cameramen she didn't recognize on the roof. Kefaah emerged from the shadows of the doorway. Eugie couldn't make out the color of her outfit in the dim light, but saw that her black stretch pants had spangles on them, as did her shoes.

"Eugie, Frank, and—I do not remember your name—it is . . . ?"

"Tess," said Eugie and Frank in unison when Tess did not respond. "Yes, the one who wears lipstick. Come." She linked her arm with Tess's and they began bushwacking through an overgrown olive grove toward yellow search lights and sounds of soldiers shouting. Eugie never ceased marvelling at Kefaah's ability to walk over rough terrain on stiletto heels.

Another explosion. They all crouched and clapped their hands over their ears.

"Holy shit," Frank said. "What was that?"

"It is a, how do you say, like a bomb that you shoot it from a gun," Kefaah said. "They caught a wanted man named Kafishe outside the houses here. They say he helped to plan the bombing of the bus in Ashkelon last year."

"Hamas?" asked Eugie.

Kefaah shrugged. "That is what they say."

Wails of women and the crying of children now punctuated the soldiers' shouting. As the four of them peered around the corner of a stone house, they heard a woman screaming in English.

Wearing an over-sized T-shirt and jeans the woman stood in front of two soldiers with a baby slung on her hip.

"You bastards," she shrieked. "My passport is in there. My husband is an American citizen. We will tell the ambassador, we will tell the president, we will tell our congress—" Her chest began heaving with sobs and she could not continue. She fell on her knees before the soldiers, one of whom asked the other for matches so he could light a cigarette. Kefaah left Eugie, Frank, and Tess and picked her way over to the woman, wrenching her arm out of a soldier's grasp as he tried to prevent her from approaching. She knelt and took the baby from the woman and pulled her to her feet. Arm around the woman's waist, Kefaah led her behind a line of soldiers, where the women in bathrobes wailed, children cried, and men stood with their arms crossed over their chests, surveying the ruins of the two buildings.

The houses that had been hit with missiles stood about fifty meters apart. Unlike the bulldozed Abu Jaber house, these two houses had parts of their roofs and walls intact. A bulldozer was ripping up the vineyard that stood between the houses and the road. A piledriver was smashing a tractor about the size of a riding lawnmower.

Eugie moved away from Frank and Tess to try to get closer to the houses. A soldier grabbed her arm. "No," he said. "It is too dangerous for you." She looked up into the face of a teenager with curling hair and serious, dark eyes.

"I know you, don't I?" she asked.

"I have talked to you on the street near your house," he said.

"Why are you destroying these people's homes?"

Without conviction, he said, "There was a terrorist here. They should not help terrorists."

When Eugie gave talks in churches, she told audiences that witnessing to soldiers was one of the most important things that RAPT did in Hebron. "They've been groomed from the cradle to be soldiers," she would tell them. "Pacifism is a dirty word to them. They've been taught to associate it with the Jews in Europe who 'allowed' themselves to be slaughtered by the Nazis. We might be the only people they'll ever meet who question the right of the military to kill people."

But right now, she didn't have it in her to seize the teachable moment.

Turning in the direction of new shouting, she saw a group of about six soldiers run across the furrows of the ruined vineyard toward the house closest to the gas station. At a bellowed command they halted, formed a semi-circle around the front of the house, and began spraying a rude wooden hut on top of the house with automatic weapon fire.

When blood began dripping out of the slats of the structure, the soldiers broke into cheers. One of them boosted a comrade onto the roof. Eugie wondered if it was safe, given that half the roof was gone, but the rebar and the concrete held. The soldier opened the door to the structure and several dead pigeons fell out. He stuck his head inside, looked down at the others, and shrugged his shoulders.

"They thought maybe there was another wanted man inside." Kefaah's voice startled her. She hadn't heard her approach. "But I talked to the two families who live here. They did not even know that Kafishe was here. He was down by the road, in the grapes"— she pointed to where the bulldozer was destroying the last of the vineyard—"when they shot him. The daughter who lives in the United States told me the soldiers came three hours ago and told everyone to get out. They thought the soldiers would only break many things, as they do when they are normal; they did not know about Kafishe until the soldiers shot the bombs into the houses. All of their gold is under there," she pointed. "The soldiers did not give them enough time to save their gold."

"It is very terrible," Kefaah concluded, almost nonchalant. Eugie looked again at the young soldier, who had been listening to Kefaah as well. He met Eugie's eyes and then looked away.

"Come, Eugie," said Kefaah. "You must talk to the families."

Eugie turned to tell Frank and Tess where she was going and saw them holding hands as they watched the destruction and ruin in front of them. Her heart lifted. So Tess did not love Yossi, after all. She loved Frank. Then her heart sank. Even if Yossi and Tess were not together, she could not have Yossi. They had been all through that. She would drive him crazy. He had driven her crazy— almost literally. Then, as she walked toward the families who had just seen their homes and livelihoods destroyed, as she saw a young mother, mouth open in soundless anguish, rock her screaming child, Eugie was filled with a self-loathing so intense that she gagged.

*     *     *

Tess sat by the hospital bed working at her nails with an emery board. She had had to borrow nail polish remover from Yiphat before going to see Yossi. Given his weakened condition, she had decided not to bother wiping off her mascara and blusher. She was pretty sure he wouldn't notice that she had them on, and she had been right.

It had been almost two weeks since the army had blown up the two houses at the outskirts of town. Yossi's mother was still staying at Yiphat's apartment, so Tess took service taxis up to Jerusalem at times, prearranged with Yiphat, when their mother was doing something else ("Like solidarity visits with the settlers in Gaza," Yiphat had said, sighing) and returned to Hebron on the same day.

Yossi still needed to sleep for a large portion of the day, but seemed well when he was conscious. He had been so happy to see her, Tess smiled with satisfaction; and when he was conscious, he said and did all the right things. He was so proud of her, he said, for pitching right in to help the RAPTors—even though they were religious—and told her he thought she was just about the bravest woman he knew.

But he still did not want to introduce her to his mother.

This was not the greatest of her problems, however. She frowned at an aberrant cuticle on the little finger of her right hand. Then, remembering that frowning causes wrinkles, strove to push her perplexity inward as she pondered her three current dilemmas.

Dilemma 1: She was almost out of Clinique City Block, and the only place she knew that carried it was the duty-free shop at Ben Gurion airport. None of the sunblocks she had investigated in Hebron or Jerusalem promised that they were noncomedogenic. She supposed that UVA and UVB exposure were worse for her skin than blackheads, but she wasn't sure. And she didn't know how she could sneak up to the airport without Yossi, Yiphat, or the team in Hebron finding out. Besides which, she had very little money left.

Dilemma 2: Frank was pushing her to decide between him and Yossi. Fortunately, he had been busy the last two weeks helping to rebuild the houses of the families whose homes had been shelled. As she sat in the shade with Felicia and Eugie—who grumbled about not being able to help the men, despite the damage such work would do to their hands—she watched Frank hauling buckets of cement with a wiry grace and thought that maybe she ought to choose him. He had blue eyes, and she thought she might like to have blue-eyed children. He was also much calmer than Yossi. His eyes did not bore into her with Yossi's passionate intensity and force her to think of something intelligent to say.

Now, however, as she sat by Yossi, admiring his black curls fanned out over the white pillow, and the olive skin with golden undertones, she thought that maybe she would miss sex with him. Yossi always made sure she came before he began to thrust inside her. She liked that. And he said the most romantic things, while Frank just swallowed hard when he stared at her.

Of course, she and Frank had not had sex yet, which ought to factor into her decision.

Dilemma 3: When Tess told Yossi that she was working with Eugie, he grinned and said, "No shit! Hey! Tell her to come up and see me. Tell her I really miss her."

At that point it had not occurred to Tess that Yossi and Eugie might have had a prior relationship, but later, when she told Eugie what Yossi had said, Eugie had turned pale and said, "Oh. Tell him we're pretty busy right now," then burst into tears and ran upstairs to the women's apartment.

Tess asked Yossi about Eugie, and he had said, "Oh yeah. We had a little thing going for awhile there. It was after I broke up with Susan and we were both feeling a little alienated. You spend so much time working and living together, sometimes you get involved when you shouldn't. Eugie has this religious thing going that got on my nerves and confidentially, between you and me, she can be a real basket case. But it was a mutual decision to break up. We're still friends."

Tess smiled understandingly when he said this, but the thought occurred to her that maybe it was better for Eugie not to come up and visit Yossi in the hospital. In his weakened state, romantic memories might make him consider a reattachment. Eugie was not ugly by any means, although she didn't know how to dress or fix her hair becomingly. And she was a little chunky.

On second thought, she decided not to worry about Eugie. Realistically, there was no contest between the two of them, and Eugie didn't want to visit Yossi anyway.

But she needed to be more alert about the whole situation.

There were so many things happening in her life right now and she wasn't sure she liked it. She was never bored, but neither was she getting enough time to take care of her hair, skin or nails. The cuticle on her little finger was definitely ragged because she hadn't caught it in time.

Sighing, she looked over at Yossi breathing steadily and then picked up the Oslo Agreement.

> 2a. The Palestinian Authority will have all powers and responsibilities in the sphere of import and customs policy and procedures with regard to the following.
>
> (1)   Goods on List A1, attached hereto as Appendix I, locally produced in Jordan and in Egypt particularly and in the other Arab countries, which the Palestinians will be able to import in quantities agreed upon by the two sides up to the Palestinian market needs as estimated according to para 3 below.
>
> (2)   Goods on List A2 attached Hereto as Appendix II from the Arab, Islamic and other countries, which the Palestinians will be able to import in quantities agreed upon by the two sides up to the Palestinian market needs as estimated according to para 3 below.

With her cellphone to her ear and an irritable expression on her face, Yiphat walked into the room. She indicated with her hand that Tess should remain seated, although Tess had not attempted to stand up.

"Yeah, Eugie, uh huh. No, I called the Civil Administration. The spokesman says they're just being detained. Not arrested. For Christ's sake, what are they going to charge them with, walking in front of a water truck? . . . Uh-huh, uh-huh. No. He didn't. Christ!"

Tess resumed her reading, turning to the appendix cited in the text.

| TARIFF | ITEM DESCRIPTION |
|---|---|
| 76.01 | Unwrought aluminium |
| 1000/7 | Aluminium, not alloyed |
| 2000/6 | Aluminium alloys |
| 76.02/6 | Aluminium waste and scrap |
| 76.03 | Aluminium powders and flakes |
| 1000/3 | Powders of non-lamellar structure |
| 2000/2 | powders of lamellar structure; flakes |
| 18.01/0 | Cocoa beans, whole or broken, raw or roasted |
| 25.23 | Cement |
| JE 1090/9 | Cement clinker, not white |
| JE 2900 | Portland cement, not white |
| | Bars and rods of iron or non-alloy steel: |
| JE 72.13.1000/1 | Containing indentations, ribs, grooves or other deformations produced during the rolling process |
| JE 72.14.2000/9 | Containing indentations, ribs, grooves or other deformations produced during the rolling process |

"You need to get back to Hebron," Yiphat told her. "Felicia and Frank have been detained for accompanying a water truck up in Tel Rumeida. Also, my mother should be here in an hour."

Tess picked up her purse and the Oslo Accords and prepared to depart.

Arms crossed over her chest, Yiphat leaned against a closet door and glanced over at Yossi's sleeping form.

"So you want I should tell you about it?" Yiphat asked.

Tess met her eyes. She wished she could remember that Yiphat was always expecting her to ask questions. Men were so much easier. Most of them didn't expect you to ask questions. They just wanted you to listen. When Yossi had told her not be afraid to talk to Yiphat, she had known that Yiphat had raised the subject with him.

"I thought Eugie could tell me when I got back," Tess said.

"Yeah, right." Yiphat sat in the chair that Tess had vacated and put her hand on Yossi's forehead. "He's been asleep the whole time?" she asked.

"No, he was up a couple hours ago. He ate lunch and we talked a little."

"Good. Now let's just hope he can stay asleep when my mother gets here," Yiphat said.

When Tess walked into the apartment in Hebron an hour later, Eugie was on the phone and Margaret was serving tea to Hitler, the university student who had visited a couple weeks before.

He leapt to his feet and extended his hand to her. "Hello, Tess," he said, drawing the last consonant out into a hiss. "It is good you have come. It is very bad what happened to Frank and Felicia."

"What happened?" Tess asked. "Is Frank all right?"

"They are not hurt badly," Hitler said. "They did put plastic handcuffs on Frank and make him sit in the sun. They permitted Felicia to sit in the shade, but she refused and demanded that she be put in the sun too. She is a very strong woman," Hitler said.

"Hitler's uncle lives by Tel Rumeida," Margaret said, "and he brought them water. Hussam stopped in when we got the phone call, and he's up at the Civil Administration now, translating the Hebrew for them."

"Hussam is the cousin of my uncle's wife," Hitler said. "He has been in prison many times and speaks Hebrew as well as he speaks English.

It is in prison that he became a Communist."

He shook his head. "Communism is a very bad thing, you know. They do not believe in God or Prophet Muhammad, peace be upon him."

Eugie came out of the office, wearing beige cotton slacks and a beige over-sized T-shirt. Tess had told Eugie that since her coloring made her a "winter," according to the *Color Me Beautiful*[1] guidelines, she ought to wear bright colors and jewel tones. Her skin blended in with the clothes she was wearing, making her seem more blobby than usual. Tess shook her head. If only Eugie would try harder, she could be very attractive. But given that Yossi was now conscious for a good part of the day, perhaps it was better that she not encourage Eugie to work on her appearance.

"They're on their way back from the Civil Administration," Eugie announced, taking a cup of tea from Margaret. "The police said there would be no charges. We really must think of something nice to do for Yiphat. I suppose she filled you in on what happened?" She turned toward Tess.

"No."

She felt Margaret, Eugie, and Hitler all staring at her. "Something happened to a water truck at Tel Rumeida?" she asked.

"You remember last week, when Abed said they were out of water and that the municipality had stopped delivering water to people who lived near settlements, because the settlers kept breaking the windshields on the water trucks?" Eugie said.

Tess was grateful that the question was rhetorical and that Eugie kept right on talking, because she had no memory of having been told these things. She must have been thinking about something more important.

"Well, right after you left this morning, we got a call from Abed, and he said the municipality would deliver water to the people in Tel Rumeida if we walked with the truck. So Margaret and I were up at the university with Hitler doing a nonviolence workshop, and Felicia and Frank were here, so they went up to Tel Rumeida and walked up with the truck, and settlers pulled their cars across the road so the truck couldn't go up, and the soldiers detained Frank and Felicia and they said they were going to arrest them because Frank called one of the officers a Nazi."

"That is very bad. The Nazis were not human people," Hitler said.

---

[1]    Carole Jackson, *Color Me Beautiful* (New York : Ballantine Books, 1981.)

Eugie rolled her eyes. "Of course he didn't call them Nazis," Eugie said. "He just said that if he had been in Germany during the Third Reich and the Nazis wouldn't let the Jews have water, he would have done the same thing for the Jews. Which I guess wasn't too swift on his part," Eugie added.

Margaret laughed. "They said that Frank cursed the officer in every known language! FRANK! Can you imagine?"

"Like Frank even tries to speak anything but English," Eugie said. She frowned. "You don't suppose Felicia . . ."

"Well, the thought crossed my mind," said Margaret. "But according to Yiphat, only Frank was going to be charged."

Hitler looked at his watch. "I want to go," he said. "When Hussam comes, tell him to telephone me."

"Will do," Eugie said. "Thank you so much, Hitler, for staying with us."

"No. Thank you for what you have done for our people," Hitler said.

The three women sipped their tea in silence for a moment after he left.

"Oh, the *Ha'Aretz* guy said he thought this story would be on the front page," Eugie said.

"That's good," Margaret said. After another moment, she added, "It seems that things always happen just when I'm ready to leave the country."

"Yeah." Eugie gulped the last of her tea. "Well, Bruce gets in tomorrow or the day after. I guess I should reserve a spot at the Faisal Hostel."

Tess was conscious that Eugie kept looking at her and beginning to say something and then deciding against it. She recognized the look of longing and knew then that it would be a good thing to discourage contact between Eugie and Yossi.

"How is Yossi doing?" Margaret asked, finally.

"Well, he was awake when I got there, and he said he was really glad to see me," Tess said, with a sideways glance at Eugie.

Eugie began picking up tea glasses and carried them into the kitchen.

Margaret looked at her for a moment and then in the direction of the kitchen.

"What do the doctors say?"

"They think that he should be out in another few days. He'll go stay with Yiphat."

"I suppose you will be moving back up to Jerusalem then?"

"I suppose so."

"Well, feel free to stay as long as you want, Tess," Eugie's voice came from the kitchen.

"Thanks, Eugie."

Margaret continued to watch her with an unreadable expression and shook her head.

"You have no idea what you've gotten yourself into, do you?" she asked.

"I love Yossi and he loves me."

Margaret said, "I'd better go pack. I think perhaps you ought to do the same."

*     *     *

Eugie's prayer mantra for the last few weeks had been one of gratitude. She was so grateful to God that all the members of the team were running around like chickens with their heads cut off. Frank was still busy helping the two families at the head of town rebuild their houses, and the university students were organizing an action that involved breaking open the gate to the campus that the Israeli military had sealed shut during the Intifada.

She had had a lot of writing to do involving the fall-out from the destruction of the houses and the water truck incident and had had to make many trips up to Jerusalem to talk to Israeli lawyers and peace groups. The lawyer prosecuting the man who had attacked her and Felicia had also asked them to come in and give a deposition.

In the past, when she had gone up to Jerusalem to stay with friends, her overriding thought had always been that she could take a hot shower there. In the last couple weeks, however, the overriding thought had been that she was NOT going up to visit Yossi.

And every time Tess went up to Jerusalem to visit Yossi, a blade of ice tore through her heart. She wished that she had not gone off antidepressants. She had tried talking to Rabbi Hillel Cotton about what she was going through, but discovered that he was not that sort of rabbi.

It helped when Bruce Lapp arrived two days after Margaret left. Bruce was also Reformed Anabaptist, and they had friends and relatives in common. He had just come from the RA biennial convention in Orlando and was able to fill her in on how the rank and file were feeling about RAPT these days. Several churches had urged RAPT to think of more substantive ways to involve the church constituency in the issue of home demolitions, and Eugie and Bruce stayed up late one time thinking of a campaign that would involve Israeli and Palestinian NGO's as well as the churches.

One evening they had been singing hymns together for recreation, and then Bruce, with Eugie's encouragement, had begun talking about his wife and three daughters, whom he missed desperately. For Eugie, it was like listening to a wonderful fairy tale. Long ago she had dreamed that someday she would have someone who talked about her the way that Bruce talked about Nadine (who was a second cousin of Eugie's sister-in-law.) She realized, as she listened to Bruce, that this was not going to happen to her. But for her right now, it was enough to know that such relationships existed.

Bruce's arrival seemed to have the effect of making everyone on the team like each other better. Frank and Felicia stopped bickering. Eugie no longer felt that she was imposing an unpopular diktat upon the rest of the team at their meetings. It wasn't that Bruce always agreed with her, but even when he disagreed, he made her feel that he appreciated her point of view.

He also at one point said, "You mean Yossi was with you, and he chose HER?" after Eugie had poured out her secret agony, and that made the pain seem a whole lot less.

Bruce, Felicia and and Frank went up to the University the morning before Tess was to move to Jerusalem. (Yossi's mother had finally gone home.) Eugie stayed behind, sick in bed.

Yossi had called the night before and asked to speak with her. He had sounded so happy to talk to her on the phone.

"So what the fuck's the matter with you?" he had asked cheerfully. "What is this cold shoulder business? I'm lying helpless in the hospital here, and you don't even have the simple human decency to come alleviate my suffering!"

Eugie said, "Well, I understood from Tess that you had enough company. And believe it or not, we actually had things to do here while you were slacking in bed. Oh SURE you were unconscious. That's what they all say."

"Oh fuck you and the horse you rode in on," Yossi responded. "You want I should get down on my knees and beg you to come up? We're friends, right? So I'm an inveterate anarchist slacker and you're a superstitious neurotic—that doesn't mean we can't be friends, right? Right?"

It had seemed so easy to agree with him over the phone. And maybe at that moment she had agreed with him, but in the morning she woke up with one of the worst migraines she had had in years.

On her sixth trip to the squat-toilet, she was no longer bringing up even bile—she was just retching. At home, she would have put a heating pad over her face, but there was nothing here that could serve as even a poor substitute. The nausea was worse than the pain. She couldn't take codeine, because she couldn't hold down anything.

Years ago, when she had first started having migraines, the doctors had ordered a CT scan to rule out a brain tumor. Although the results had come back negative, it was hard to believe there wasn't a hard lump of something pressing against her eye. As she lay on her mat, she imagined sticking a needle behind her eye and drawing out the liquid pain from the tumor that wasn't there into a large syringe. She visualized the tumor shrinking, ever so slowly...

When she woke up, it was almost noon. At first she thought the pounding on the door was coming from the neighbors, because very few people ever came upstairs to the women's apartment, but after a moment she heard Tess open the door and admit Sa'eed.

Feeling lightheaded with relief from the pain, she staggered out of her room. "Sa'eed, you shouldn't be up here. This is the women's apartment."

"Quickly, quickly, they are destroying the house. The house near Kiryat Arba. Near Harsina."

"Which is it?" Eugie asked.

"It is close to both. It is the house of my mother's sister. You must come quickly."

"Hold on. I have to get dressed. Tess, can you go downstairs and get the cellphone? Oh shoot. They probably took it to the University. Well, would you mind checking anyway?"

Eugie wished she had followed up with the friend who worked with the Palestinian police force in Bethlehem about getting some handcuffs. The team had thought that they might be just quick enough to lock themselves to the grille of a window before a house went down. It was probably too late by now anyway. It was almost always too late.

She threw her arrest kit (towel, toothbrush, *The Gulag Archipelago)* into her knapsack and snapped on her waistpack. She met Tess coming up the stairs, who informed her that Bruce, Felicia, and Frank had indeed taken the portable phone with them.

"Sa'eed, where is this house? I have to leave a note for the team."

"There is no time!" Sa'eed grabbed her arm and pulled her down the stairs, a gesture at odds with his usual deferential manner. "You must come now!"

Eugie and Tess started to go to the stand where they generally caught taxis to Kiryat Arba.

"No, no, this way. The son of my mother's sister has a car. This way is quicker." Sa'eed looked nervously around him as he guided them deeper into the intricate caves and tunnels of Hebron's old market.

"Sa'eed—this can't be right. It's got to be faster to go the other way." Eugie and Tess were now trotting to keep up.

"Yes, yes. This is the way." He dashed ahead of them and then made a sharp left into a tunnel.

It was dark, and she smelled urine. "Sa'eed, wait," Eugie called. And then someone grabbed her from behind.

# **Interim**

Page 251 of *Israeli-Palestinian Interim Agreement on the West Bank and the Gaza Strip* (The Oslo Accords)

LIST A1 (cont.)

| TARIFF ITEM* | DESCRIPTION | QUANTITIES | (TONS) |
| --- | --- | --- | --- |
| | | Annual | 3 months |
| JE 57.02.1000/5 | Carpets and other textile floor coverings, woven, not tufted or flocked, whether or not made up, of the type of "kelem" "Schumacks," "Karamanie" and similar handwoven rugs | (b) UNITS | (b) (d) |
| JE 84.22.1100/5 | Dishwashing machines of the household type | 3000 | 750 |
| JE 84.51.4091/2 | Washing machines of the household type | | |
| JE 73.21.8131/8 | Gas and fuel heating stoves | | |
| JE 73.21.8210/0 | Liquid fuel heating stoves | | |
| 85.16.2000 | Electric space heating apparatus and electric soil heating apparatus | 2000 | 750 |
| JE 2190/4 | Storage heating radiators, non industrial | | |
| JE 2990/4 | Other heating apparatus, having a capacity of less than 5000 watts | | |
| JE 85.16.6090/2 | Electric ovens, cookers, cooking plates, boiling rings, grillers of the household type | 2,000 | 500 |
| JE 73.21.1111/7 | Gas and fuels cooking appliances of the household type | | |
| JE 85.28.1000 | Colour television receivers | 3,000 | 750 |
| JE 85.28.2000 | Black and white or monochrome | | |
| JE 84.15 | Air conditioners of the household type | 1000 | 250 |
| 1090/2 | | | |
| 8190/3 | | | |

| JE 84.18 | Refrigerators and freezers of the household type | 1000 | 250 |
|----------|--------------------------------------------------|------|-----|
| 1020 | | | |
| 2000 | | | |
| 3010/2 | | | |
| 4010/1 | | | |

---

(\*) Items marked JE may be imported only from Jordan and Egypt

(a) Quantities will be approved according to Palestinian proved needs

(b) to be discussed by the Joint Sub-Committee

(c) 50% of estimated market need

(d) Agreed absolute numbers

# CHAPTER 8

Tess had the good sense to scream when these folks had grabbed them. For about the three thousand ninety second time, Eugie wondered whether any of the preparation she had received through RAPT could be relevant to any given RAPT project assignment. Their month of training in Minneapolis involved a lot role-playing: What to do if someone was screaming threats at them, or waving a gun in their face. How to use a fax. How to use a video camera. How to write a competent press release.

The participants in her training had never discussed what to do if they were kidnapped. As soon as the hand went over her mouth and the sweaty male arm encircled her around the waist, squeezing the breath out of her, she began considering what the most appropriate response to this action should be, drawing on past memories of role-plays. Tess had simply screamed, and seconds later, there were sounds of doors and windows opening and Arabic exclamations. Whoever had grabbed them had fired his gun—in the air apparently—because a shower of concrete and grit from the tunnel roof fell on her head immediately afterward. The gun shot silenced the voices, but at least it meant there would be witnesses, she hoped.

Whoever had thrown her on the ground to cuff her hands behind her back and then half dragged and half carried her inside some building had shouted at her in English to keep still or he would shoot her. It sounded like an Australian accent. Would the witnesses in the market be able to tell the police it was an Australian? At least they could tell the police the men involved spoke English.

If they bothered telling the police. Palestinians in Hebron didn't normally turn to the police as a first resort; chances were good that the witnesses might be dragged in for questioning themselves. Probably even the team would not go to the police for a couple days. One of the ongoing discussions amongst RAPT constituents and members of other historic peace churches—like the Mennonites, Church of the Brethren, and the Quakers—was whether pacifists could in good conscience apply to civilian police for help, given that, like the military, civilian police backed up their authority with guns. The Reformed Anabaptists had a more difficult time with the discussion than the others, because Calvinist theology advocated being subject to secular rulers, and Anabaptist theology asserted the primacy of conscience over obedience to secular authority. Many Anabaptists had been drowned or burned alive in the sixteenth century for refusing to take up arms and join the mercenary armies whose services the Swiss government auctioned off to other European rulers to fight their endless petty wars.

The idea of dying for her faith had always been somewhat attractive to Eugie. It seemed a positive channel for her otherwise self-destructive behaviors. And getting shot seemed like not such a hard thing to deal with, after reading accounts of the Anabaptists who had been burned alive or crushed between large stones.

The thought of the Anabaptists who had been drowned by the authorities in a cruel parody of baptism was the scariest for her, though. It brought her back from the sixteenth century to the present as she struggled to take a deep breath through the duct tape and rag that had been stuffed into her mouth. With her tongue, she had been able to work the rag away from the back of her throat, so she wasn't gagging, but she still felt oxygen deprived.

The blindfold cut into her forehead and the plastic handcuffs cut into her wrists. Her ankles had been tied with something softer after she and Tess had been dragged inside and forced down several flights of stairs. She had tried wriggling around to find Tess, but had been slapped hard and told in Israeli-accented English to sit still if she knew what was good for her. Whoever it was had then unfastened her waistpack and taken it away.

(Oh geez, she thought, it's going to be such a pain getting a new passport. Then she wondered whether she might very well be spared that trouble by her captors.)

The wriggling had hiked her long skirt up around the back of her thighs, and she tried to work it back down again. The thought had occurred to her, while her abductors were tying her feet, that she was glad she didn't have to go to the bathroom—which had cued her bladder to start making soft, insistent pleas for relief.

As she thought of Felicia saying, "I don't want to be the one who said 'I told you so—'" her jaw clenched. Drat that Sa'eed. Now that he had abused her trust like this, how was she ever going to be able to sort out the real collaborators from those who had gotten stuck with the label by other Palestinians who didn't agree with their political philosophy? Half the people they worked with— okay, I'm probably exaggerating, she admitted—many of the people they worked with had been accused of collaboration at one time or another.

Hoping to catch the end of the duct tape and pull it off, she began to rub her cheek against her shoulder. The tape had caught on her hair, which was uncomfortable, but which also meant that it wasn't stuck completely to her skin.

She heard voices echoing in another part of wherever she was. The hollowness of the sound and the damp smell of her surroundings made her think she was underground. With her tongue, she pushed the rag hard against the duct tape and felt it give a little, but since the voices seemed to be approaching, she stopped struggling and sat still.

The conversation was in Hebrew between two men. She heard "Felicia-Inez Epp," pronounced "Feh-leesha Aynez-Eh-yep," by one of them. It occurred to her then that one of the men was speaking Hebrew with a broad accent from the American South. She felt a sudden longing for Felicia. If she were here right now, she would insist that whoever it was pronounce her name right. Where was Tess?

"Now young lady, Ahm gonna take your gag off, but Ah want you to know that if you make the littlest ol' peep, Ahm gonna put it right back on again. Understand?"

She nodded her head, and felt the duct tape pulled off her mouth, taking some of her hair with it. She took a deep breath.

"Thank you," she said. "Would it be possible for me to use a bathroom?"

"Inna minit." He reached behind her head to untie the blindfold; his armpits gave off an odor of profuse sweat and English Leather cologne.

An almost geometrically round head, gleaming in the light of a single overhead lightbulb, peered at her after the blindfold came off. Even though he was perspiring heavily, the man was wearing a black tie. His neck overflowed the collar of his white short-sleeved shirt.

Eugie looked around the room. Tess, blindfolded and duct-taped, was sitting against a rough concrete wall ninety degrees to her left. She wondered where the Australian was.

"Hi," she said. "My name is Grace."

"Unmerited Grace, actually," he said. "What Ah want you to tell me is who is that young lady over there."

Eugie turned to look at Tess. She considered whether she should tell the man her name.

"Ah guess what Ah am really asking is, is that your friend Felicia?"

There was no way that Tess could convince anyone she was Felicia, and besides, Eugie thought, it wasn't very satyagrahic. What would Jesus say? What would Gandhi say?

"No," she said. "That's not Felicia."

"Shit," he said, drawing the word out to two syllables. "Who is she, then?"

"Just a visitor. Her name is Tess. She's engaged to an Israeli friend of ours."

Now that really was a lie. Yossi would have taken violent objection if someone had referred to him as an Israeli. He was still annoyed with Yiphat for having taken Israeli citizenship. However, since all Jews could technically become Israeli citizens almost as soon as they asked to . . . and since "Jewish friend" had too many uncomfortable connotations of "Some of my best friends are—"

"Yeah, like you have any Israeli friends," the man said. He heaved himself up from a squatting position, knees cracking.

"So what's your name?" Eugie asked brightly. She glanced over at Tess, who was making muffled noises and kicking at the air with her bound feet. Eugie noted that Tess infused even so futile a gesture with grace.

The man glanced over at Tess as well. "You don't need to know my real name," he said. "But you can call me John, because I have been sent by the Lord to the House of Israel on the behalf of one whose sandal thongs I am not worthy to untie."

Eugie debated pointing out that John the Baptist had been mighty critical of the House of Israel before Herod had him beheaded, but she spent so much time at home pointing out that Jesus, the disciples, and the earliest members of the Christian church were Jewish to anti-Semitic Reformed Anabaptists that she decided not to.

"Well, John, to what do we owe the pleasure of this visit?" Eugie widened her eyes to achieve a consciously ditsy look.

He looked down at her with what seemed like barely concealed rage. Okay, scratch ditsy, Eugie thought. It was not what was called for at the moment.

"I think you know," he said.

"Umm, no, actually," she said. "Sa'eed told us there was a house going down. We followed him, and the next thing I knew, we were bound and gagged and here."

"Oh," John responded. "So it never even entered your head that this has something to do with your intention to tes-tee-fy against one of God's Chosen People."

"Testify?" She looked at him blankly for a moment and then said, "Oh, you mean that guy that stole my camera on Dubboya Street. Yeah, the prosecutor—who is also one of the Chosen People, just so you know—wanted Felicia and me to come up to Jerusalem and give early testimony, since we'll probably be leaving the country before the trial."

"Bingo!" John said. "And you're telling me that this young lady here is not Felicia."

"Yeah, I think we've covered that." Eugie tried very hard not to make that remark sarcastic, but knew she had failed.

John grunted, walked over to Tess, and ripped the duct tape off her face. She whimpered a little and bent her head forward to make it easier for him to remove her blindfold. When Tess looked up at John, he stared for a moment into her dark fawn-like eyes that were filling with tears. Then he squatted down in front of her and patted her shoulder.

"Don't cry, Hon," he said. "You just didn't know what you were getting yourself into, did you?"

She shook her head and continued to look pathetic.

"Is it true? Are you really engaged to a Jewish boy?"

She nodded.

"And you don't have anything to do with these 'so-called' Christians like that woman over there."

Pretend you don't, Tess. Pretend you don't, Eugie willed Tess to say.

"Not really," said Tess. "My fiancee was hurt by a bomb and is in the hospital. His sister had to find me a place to stay and she sent me here."

Eugie sighed with relief. Over the last couple weeks it had crossed her mind that maybe Margaret was right. Maybe Tess wasn't all that bright. But she had just shown that she was pretty clever after all. Not only had she upped her chances of getting released so she could find help, she had cleverly managed to mislead John with the truth.

(The issue of truth-telling had caused one of the arguments that had started Eugie and Yossi on the downward spiral of their relationship. Yossi believed not only that it was permissible to lie to illegitimate authority, but that one was obligated to do so whenever one could. Eugie felt that when people of goodwill lied, they added to the matrix of deceit that systems of domination used to stay in power. Yossi responded by telling her that if she told the truth with the intention to mislead the authorities—e.g., writing Rabbi Cotton's address in the "Address in Israel" space on her tourist card instead of Hebron, because Hebron wasn't in Israel—it was the same as lying. She had said, then, that if the authorities wanted to get in touch with her for a legitimate reason, Hillel could contact her, so it wasn't the same as lying.)

She sighed as she remembered Yossi with his left eyebrow raised, looking at her in a way that suggested this was the dumbest argument he had ever heard.

John misunderstood the sigh and said, "Really sorry if I'm boring you Miz Grace, but we're in a bit of a pickle here. We meant to nab your friend Felicia and not this young lady here."

"Well, if you had let me know ahead of time, I could have arranged for her to be with me. Some people—" She shook her head. "They just think they can waltz in and kidnap a person without giving them a chance to arrange their schedules. Of course, I suppose kidnapping does warrant a certain amount of spontaneity."

She smiled and blinked several times.

"Listen Miz Smart Mouth, if I was in your position, I wouldn't be making so many smart-alecky remarks."

"Yeah, well, when you're as smart as I am, sometimes you just can't help it."

John ground his teeth, making the rolls of fat on his neck jiggle.

"If you're so smart, how come you're sitting there tied up and I'm not?"

Eugie debated saying that she hadn't been aware that not being tied up was a function of one's intelligence, but then realized that she did feel pretty dumb about following Sa'eed into the bowels of the marketplace, that Jesus probably wouldn't have been snotty to this man, and that it was not likely to help their cause.

"Sorry," she said. "It's been a rough week."

"Don't I just know it," John responded, slumping against the wall.

"Tess really doesn't have anything to do with us. She's telling the truth. Her fiancé's sister sent her to us."

"So this sister of his, she Jewish too?"

"Oh yeah. She's an Israeli lawyer."

John frowned, a roll of fat looping down onto the bridge of his nose. "How's that possible—that one of God's Chosen People would have dealings with you-all?"

"Well, truthfully," Eugie said, "we have a whole lot of Israeli friends. I mean, we like to think that we're supporting the work of Israelis and Palestinians . . ."

"No such thing as a Palestinian." John jerked his index finger at her in a savage motion.

"One of the premises of our organization is that we support the work of people who are living in this region, rather than coming in with our own agenda."

"And what exactly is this work you do with the Jews and the Arabs?"

"It's a little complicated. I mean, we go through phases. Sometimes we're doing mostly violence deterrence. Sometimes we're doing mostly networking."

"Do you witness?"

Eugie considered him before she answered. "We believe that the best way to witness about Jesus is to try to love the people around us as unconditionally as Jesus would love them."

"But do you WITNESS."

"If you're asking do we hand out tracts and tell people they'll go to hell if they don't believe in Jesus, no we don't do that. And you know what? Neither did Jesus."

"Some friend you are," John sniffed. "You claim to love the Arabs and you're just sending them on to Hell by making them think they don't need Jesus."

"We were talking about Jews AND Arabs here a minute ago."

"With Jews it's different. They're God's Chosen People. And I firmly believe that when Christ comes again in Glory, they will recognize him as Lord and Savior."

John looked up to the ceiling with a beatific expression. Eugie looked up too and felt a twinge of relief that Jesus wasn't descending as they spoke. It wasn't that she didn't long for the return of Jesus. She was willing to be judged and judged sternly, if only Jesus would set to rights all the suffering in the world. She just didn't want the Christian Zionists to be proven right in their silly eschatology.

"You don't believe that Zechariah 13:7-9 indicates that one-third of the Jews will convert and the other two-thirds die?"

"No, no, no. That's a very common misinterpretation that some of my brothers in the Lord hold to. The two-thirds that the prophet is speaking of were the people who died in the Holocaust. The Lord's going to save all the Jews."

"Well, that's okay by me," Eugie said.

"You know why the Holocaust happened, don't you?"

"Ummmm, because the economic deprivation that the Allies subjected the Germans to after World War I gave rise to a militant nationalism that pandered to the latent anti-semitism in German culture?"

John blinked at her. "It's because the Jews were not faithful to God's clear commandment in the Bible that they ought to be living in Eretz Israel. If the Jews in Europe had emigrated to Israel like they were supposed to, and possessed the land like God commanded them to, then they wouldn't have died."

"You're saying the Holocaust was the JEWS' fault?"

"Absolutely not." He again pointed at her. "You think you're pretty clever don't you? You'll just twist my words into something nasty like the other so-called 'Christians' do. But I put my faith in the word of the Lord." He raised a clenched fist and then thumped at the invisible Bible in it with his other hand.

Eugie considered telling him she had had two years of seminary. (Calvin-Manz had a dual Masters program in Bible and Social Work) but thought better of it.

"The sad thing is," John continued, forgetting to be angry with her, "that another Holocaust is going to happen soon. It'll be in the United States, and we've just got to get the Jews in the U.S. over here before it happens. That's why what you're doing is so misguided," he said. "I mean, there's eight million Jews in the U.S. Where are we going to put 'em if the Arabs stay here? Tell me that, missy."

"So why aren't you working in the U.S. to prevent this Holocaust from happening?"

"I can't stop what is foretold in Holy Scripture!" Affronted, the man stepped back a few paces.

"John, did it ever occur to you that when the prophets talk about the Jews returning from Babylon, they really meant Babylon and not the U.S. and not the Soviet Union? And speaking of the Soviet Union, has the thought occurred to you—"

He sneered at her. "You just can't see what's right in front of you when you read the Bible."

"Well, I guess I just interpret it too literally. Hey. Think you can take me to the bathroom now?"

He got up with difficulty and tied the blindfold on her again. He then spun her around as though they were playing Pin the Tail on the Donkey. Standing behind her, he placed both hands on her shoulders and guided her outside of the room and through several hallways. Eugie tried to note when they were making right turns and left turns, but gave up after the fifth turn or so. From the hollowness of their footsteps, it sounded as though they were in a tunnel.

One of the engineers at the Hebron Municipality claimed that the settlers were building a tunnel under Hebron to connect the settlement enclaves in the city with Kiryat Arba outside the city. The Israeli government denied that such a tunnel existed, but there was construction work going on that had damaged the foundations of several Palestinian homes. The Israeli government had also denied the existence of the tunnel near Al Aqsa Mosque in Jerusalem until its opening set off riots throughout the West Bank.

When the team debated whether to publicize the tunnel on RAPTnet—since they weren't one hundred percent sure it existed— Nathan, a college student who spent a January inter-term with them had said, "It would be so cool—just like the end one of those old Scooby-doo episodes—the settlers will say, 'And we would have gotten away with it, too, if it hadn't been for you RAPTers.'"

An American archeologist who had recently visited the team was outraged when they told him about the tunnel rumor, because of all the ancient archeological strata under the city. He told them that Hebron might be the oldest unwalled city in the world. As they walked him around Hebron on a guided tour, he would dart to stone walls or piles of rubble in olive groves and pick up pottery shards and parts of pestles and mortars that were lying out in the open. Eugie had written "Roman era" and "Byzantine era" in pencil on the shards that he had identified and handed to her. She hoped she wouldn't be doing anything illegal by carrying them out of the country.

They ascended a short flight of stairs. Eugie had the impression that they were in a room that had direct sunlight coming through a window, but they soon walked into darkness again.

"Wait a minute," John said. There was the sound of a door opening and then the smell of an air freshener covering up the odor of a bathroom that needed cleaning.

"Toilet's to your left."

"Can you untie my hands?"

"Uh-uh. You'll just have to make do."

John gave her a light push into the room and then closed the door. Eugie sat down and managed with difficulty to pull her bound hands over her rear end and then over her legs and feet. At one point, as she lay on her back, all her limbs wriggling in the air, she thought that she must look like a large cockroach, recently poisoned. The bathroom floor was very dirty.

The pressure on her plastic handcuffs as she pulled her legs through made them cut even more deeply into her wrists. She touched her tongue to the skin bulging around the cuffs to see if she could taste blood. They hadn't broken the skin—yet—but the area around the cuffs felt warm and inflamed. She had heard young Palestinian men speak of having plastic cuffs left on for days. They usually had scars to prove it.

She stood up and felt around for the toilet with her foot. It was a porcelain bowl with no seat to pull down. However, she had used pit toilets in Palestinian homes and latrines in Haiti that had smelled worse. She crouched over the toilet without touching her rear to the bowl as her mother had taught her to do in public restrooms, and urinated.

"Is there a sink in here to wash my hands?" she called.

"It's over against the right-hand wall," John responded from the other side of the door.

He didn't comment when she came out of the bathroom with her hands clasped in front of her. The advantage of the plastic cuffs, Eugie thought, is that the only way you can remove them is to cut them off. John and his cohorts must not have another pair to spare.

"Thanks, I needed that," she said, thinking of Paul's reference to coals of fire in Romans 12:20.

"Always happy to oblige a lady," John said.

He spun her around again and guided her back to the underground room. She asked to have the blindfold removed, and he told her he thought it was best for her to keep it on.

After he had helped Eugie sit on the floor, Tess asked, "Can I go to the bathroom now?"

"Of course you can," he said. "Here, let me help you up."

"Can you take off the blindfold?" she asked. "I really need to look in a mirror."

Good going, Tess, Eugie thought. He would probably find it plausible that Tess was more concerned with her appearance at a time like this than about how to find a way out of their predicament. With her phenomenal memory, she should be able to remember the way out exactly.

"Afraid you'll have to wait until we get you to the bathroom young lady," John said. "But of course I'll let you fix yourself up once you get there."

Oh well, Eugie thought. At least she'll be able to see something.

It was hard to estimate how much time had passed before Tess came back from the bathroom. Eugie thought maybe fifteen minutes.

"All set?" John asked cheerfully as he and Tess entered the room. "You wait here for a minute and let me get you a chair."

"Tess," Eugie whispered after she heard him shut the door behind him. "Were you able to see anything? Do you have your blindfold on now?"

"No."

"Check the door. Did he lock it behind him?"

Tess took six steps. Eugie heard her jiggle the door handle.
"Yes."
"What did you see when he took your blindfold off?"

*   *   *

What Tess first noticed after John took her blindfold off and
pointed her toward the mirror in the bathroom was that her part
was crooked and she had little bits of broken hair standing at
awkward angles to her scalp where the duct tape had been pulled
off. She pulled out the comb she always kept in her pocket. Wetting
it, she started at the bottom of her shoulder-length page boy and
drew the comb through to avoid making the snarls worse. She
rounded the ends of her hair so her right and left sides angled
toward her chin.

She was really going to have to get a haircut soon. Although her
glossy, dark tresses had natural wave in them, it was only with difficulty
that she was able to get them to curl symmetrically at the ends.

There was some sort of soap, but she was not sure that she
dared wash her face with it. An article she had read last year in
*Glamour* had said that one must NEVER wash one's face with
deodorant soap. She picked up the grayish green bar and sniffed
it. It had a heavy perfume smell, which did not bode well. On the
other hand, her face just felt so dirty she didn't think she could
stand it any longer. She cupped a small pool of tap water in her
hand and stirred the bar into it, just enough to make it cloudy.
She then rubbed the diluted soap mixture on her face and neck
and splashed them with water until she was sure all the residue
was gone. There was a stained towel hanging on the rack next to
the sink. She swallowed hard, held her breath, and then used the
towel to pat her face dry.

She used the toilet, holding her breath for that procedure as
well. Tears stung her eyes for the first time that day. When Yossi
brought her to Israel, he didn't tell her that she was going to have
a rag shoved in her mouth and duct tape stuck to her face and hair,

that she was going to be hauled around like a sack, that she was going to have to use FILTHY toilets.

Ever since they got here, there had been nothing but discomfort, she realized as she remembered the bombing at the hotel.

Maybe Frank is the one she should choose. Frank wouldn't put her in situations like this.

"You okay in there, Hon?" John asked.

He sounded genuinely concerned. If only he weren't so fat, she might consider using the leverage she had with most men when they first knew her. On the other hand, she might never get out of this mess if she didn't use such leverage. She thought of the heroism involved in coming on to a fat man. It would be something she could tell her daughter some day. (Tess usually thought in terms of having daughters with long, dark hair whom she could dress in pinafores and ribbons. Occasionally she thought about having sons, but she didn't think it would be nearly as rewarding. She couldn't teach them how to be pretty, or how to manage their affairs with men, could she? Unless they were gay, but that could lead to all sorts of inconveniences.)

"I'm almost finished, John."

She examined the wrists from which John had removed those horrid cuffs and noted with displeasure that there were red lines imprinted on them. Neither Yossi nor Frank would mind. They'd probably tell her she had been very brave, and kiss the markings with adoration. But she thought they were ugly. She wondered whether the concealer she used to even out the skin tones under her eyes would cover the marks on her wrists as well.

John gently retied the blindfold and, with his arm around her shoulders, guided her back to the dreary room where Eugie waited for her.

After John left, Eugie pressed her for details. Had she noticed anything on her way there? Was she able to get some idea of where they were?

Tess closed her eyes and visualized again her face in the mirror and the damage the duct tape had done to her hair. She then switched her memory to audio and replayed the tape of John's heavy-footed shuffling outside the bathroom door and voices coming from the outside—voices in English, but with an accent like Erland's, talking to soldiers about something that had happened the night before, a "molly toff" cocktail being thrown at soldiers. (As she replayed the conversation, she wondered where Palestinians in Hebron had gotten such a cocktail, given their very sensible rejection of anything alcoholic. After ultraviolet radiation, alcohol was one of the biggest factors in premature aging of the skin.)

"I heard a man with a Norwegian accent talking to a soldier somewhere outside the bathroom," she said.

"Really? You heard TIPH people?" Eugie brightened. "That must mean we're near a checkpoint somewhere. I wonder if we're under Beit Hadassah or Avraham Avinu? Or maybe Beit Romano, where the yeshiva is?"

Tess hugged her knees to her chest and surveyed their surroundings. The concrete room contained nothing besides a pile of posters and placards with Hebrew lettering on them stacked in a corner. There were no windows. It was all very disagreeable.

"Uh, Tess, could you take my blindfold off?" Eugie said. "Oh wait a minute. John's coming back with a chair for you, probably better leave it on."

"Are you sure?" Tess asked. The blindfold had scrunched Eugie's hair into awkward loops. Never in the best of order, Eugie's hair did not need any help in looking disheveled.

"Yeah. Let's wait until we have some time to ourselves to discuss how we get out of here."

"Of course the room could be bugged," she sighed after a moment.

They heard footsteps in the hall and a key in the lock. John appeared with two straight-backed chairs, set one down beside Tess, gently assisted her to her feet and helped her into it. He then put the other one down near the far corner of the room, swung his leg over the seat with difficulty, and sat facing them both, chin resting on his arms on the back of the chair. Tess noted that this posture was straining the fabric on his slacks, and tried very hard not to show her distaste.

"So here we are," he said.

Eugie inclined her blindfolded head in his direction and smiled pleasantly. Tess took the cue and smiled at John as well.

"You really just have no idea how much trouble you're in, do you?" John continued. "You see, we really don't want to kill you. We asked, since you claim to be our brothers in Christ, that the ones who want you dead let us try to talk some sense into you first."

"I take it that's 'brothers' in the inclusive sense?" Eugie asked. "Who is it that actually wants us dead?" She continued to smile as though this were some sort of tea party. Tess hoped that meant that Eugie had thought of a way of getting out of this uncomfortable situation. If Eugie really thought they were in danger of getting killed, she wouldn't be so calm. At least Tess hoped this was the case.

"You don't need to know their names," John said. "Let's just say that they are men who really have a heart for their own people and take the Torah real seriously."

He turned toward Tess. "The Torah is what Jews call the first five books of the Bible."

Tess saw Eugie's eyebrows raise over her blindfold and heard her emit what sounded like a sigh of disgust.

"So it's fair to assume that the people who want us dead are settlers?"

"Listen Missy, these are people who are being obedient to the Lord, who told them to possess the land and drive out the Hittites and the Hivites and the Amalakites. They are NOT settlers. They are the Chosen People, who are reclaiming their inheritance promised to their father Avraham."

"So it is settlers who want us dead."

Tess frowned in Eugie's direction. This did not seem a particularly clever strategy for getting them set free.

"Listen," Eugie said. "I could argue about the prophets and the primary expectations that God has for Jews and Christians, but there wouldn't be much point to it, would there? I mean, you're convinced that you're right and I'm convinced that I'm right and I think the real question is what would Jesus want us to do in this situation."

"Jesus was a Jew, missy, and don't you forget it."

"No . . . . really?" Eugie smacked her palm up against her forehead—an awkward gesture, given that her hands were still bound. "And all these years, I thought he was a Zoroastrian."

"See . . . it just goes to show you that they don't really teach Bible in your liberal Godless seminaries up north. Jesus was not a Zorro-whatever. He was Jewish. Read your Bible."

"I actually went to Calvin-Manz Biblical Seminary for two years in Indiana," Eugie said. "Trust me. It's not a hotbed of radical thought."

"It is if they let women attend."

"Oh yeah. I forgot." Eugie arranged her skirt around her knees as she crossed her legs. Tess wished she would stop arguing about all this Bible stuff and get to the part about what they would do to avoid getting killed.

"Jesus said that our primary obligations were to love God and love our neighbors as ourselves. He said that 'on these hang all the law and the prophets.' So, John, how do you figure supporting the modern nation-state of Israel, when it denies people human rights we would insist on for ourselves, fits into that—not to mention kidnapping and cold-blooded murder?"

John's face was turning very red. Tess wished that Eugie had her blindfold off, so that she could shoot her a warning look.

"Well, I ask you Miz Grace, how are YOU showing love to your neighbor by spending all your time with terrorists? Can't you see that the Ayrabs are just using you to fulfill their ultimate goal?"

"And that would be . . ."

"Pushing all the Jews into the sea. That's all they want to do, you know, kill all the Jews they can. Read the Koh-ran; it's in there."

"You've read the Quran?"

"I've talked to people who have."

Eugie sighed. "Look. All I can tell you is we've lived a couple years in our apartment building, and I'll tell you what our neighbors want. The nineteen-year-old girl upstairs wants to go to university, but her parents want her to get married. Her younger brother wants a Walkman. Our neighbors across the hall want the safe delivery of their second baby, because last year they had a miscarriage when she was four months pregnant. They also both want raises at their jobs. Other 'Ay-rab' friends of ours want to wake up in the morning not worrying about whether their houses are going to be demolished or whether their teenage sons will come home in the evening. I can't speak for all Arabs, but that's what these Arabs want."

"You think you're pretty smart, don't you?"

Eugie tilted her head upwards, pursed her lips and expelled a puff of air. She appeared to consider the question for a moment. Tess still didn't like the way this conversation was going.

"Yeah, I'd say pretty smart. No rocket scientist, of course, but relatively smart."

John shook his head. "I don't think you're taking all this seriously enough. Do you understand you could die?"

"And what would I need to do to prevent that from happening?"

The color on John's face lightened and he looked relieved.

"Finally you're asking the right questions. If you and your friends don't want to die in real unpleasant and painful ways, you need to get out of Hebron in the next week. We will send a message to your friends saying if they want to see the two of you alive again, they will have to pack up their stuff and never darken the door of this holy city ever again. Then we'll see to it that you and the young lady here get dropped off at Ben Gurion airport."

"Did it occur to you that my co-workers might very well call the police?"

"They won't if they know what's good for you—and for them. Your Jew-hating friends aren't the only ones who know how to make bombs, you know."

Eugie leaned her head back against the wall. "Well, one doesn't exactly have to be a rocket scientist to know that stuff, does one?"

There was a moment of silence as John's face reddened again.

"I just don't get you," he finally said. "You don't think I'm serious, do you?"

"Oh yeah, I have no doubt that you're serious." Eugie was silent for a moment. "Just one thing. Tess here really isn't involved with us. She might even be a Chosen Person one day, if she decides that she doesn't want her children to be *mamzers*. *Mamzer* means bastard in Hebrew," she added in the exact tone of voice that John had used to define "Torah" for Tess. "Whatever you think of us, you shouldn't punish her for it."

"Well now, if you're all that concerned for her personal well-being, maybe you should just think about what I said before."

Tess frowned at John. Eugie was at least trying to get her out of this mess. He could make a little more effort, himself.

"You could hold her until after you disposed of me and then send her to Ben Gurion. Whatever you think of me, you shouldn't take it out on her. Seriously, what would Jesus do, John?"

Tess sighed. It might be very uncomfortable having to stay cooped up alone for several days with this *really* unappealing man. Nor did she want to get put on a plane without a chance to talk to Frank or Yossi. If they were here, they would get her out of this mess. But—Eugie was probably doing her best, she thought. She just wasn't as good at getting men to do what she wanted as Tess was.

Oh. Maybe she could say something at this point to convince John to let her go. But what? She sort of hated to leave Eugie behind, but Eugie didn't seem to mind discomfort the way she did—and she could always get help, if John let her go. But what if John made it a condition that she couldn't get help for Eugie if he let her go?

It wasn't often that Tess wished she were smarter, but she thought it might come in handy at this point

John, meanwhile, just stared at Eugie with his mouth open. "You understand that I am perfectly serious? That you will die if you and your Jew-hating friends don't leave Hebron."

"Oh yeah," Eugie said. She yawned. "Like I said before. I'm pretty smart. The question is, are you going to let Tess suffer for what you perceive as our sins? I am asking you as a fellow believer to let her go. Your beef is with us, not her."

"You are NOT a believer. Not in our Lord Jesus Christ," he added with a significant tilt of his head.

He stood up and tried to swing his leg back, but became entangled with the chair. Tess heard a ripping sound and saw John turn the color of a ripe plum.

"You had your chance." He stalked toward the door, holding the chair behind him to cover the tear in his pants. Tess heard him set the chair down outside, and then his head appeared again in the door. "You are Amalek," he snarled.

# *Interim*

E-Mail received at the Chicago office of Christian Peacemaker Teams.
All misspellings are *sic;* names and addresses have been changed.

Resent-From: CPTsupporter@nowhere.com
X-Sender: elisha@nowhere.org
Date: Sun, 05 Apr 1998 07:16:40-0400

Subject: CPT in Israel
To whom it may concern,
    I was sorry to see what appears to be "Christian" discouragement
of the people of the people of Israel—discouragement designed to
hinder God's chosen people, Israel, from living in all the land the
God of israel and the God of Messiah Jesus has given to them—
forever.
    Please understand, Arabs may live in Israel, but they must do
so with a full recognition that Israel, and no illegal (from a scriptural
perspective) Palestinian regime, is sovereign. In truth, Arabs fair
much better under Israeli sovereignty than they might dare to
imagine living under despots such as Arafat, Assad etc. God spoke
clearly to Abraham—a blessing to those who bless you and a curse
to those who curse you. I do not desire that anyone should be
cursed of God; yet, His word will accomplish its purpose.

In His love,
JH

Resent-To: <CPTsupporter@nowhere.com
From: someDoctorguy@nowhere.net
Subject: wake up brother
Date: Sat, 4 Apr 1998 14:35:02-0800

why don't you send chriistians to defend arab christians against
the real threarts and murderous behavior of the animuslims . . .
when christians wke up and begin to do the rigth thing then maybe

jesus will return to help out. In the meantime your insane programs do nothing to help the cause of peace which is an oxymoron for arabs who live in dreaded fear because of the horriffic backward and animalistic docrine called islam. Read the warning signs . . . . just listen to arab rhetoric and wake up= and stop your sick behavior and dumb propaganda.

Doctors for real peace.

From: "Col. Mustard@vaguelybiblicalname.com
Subject: What are you attempting to prove??

What exactly is your organization trying to prove by supporting the enemies(Palestinians) of the Chosen People, the Jews. My advice to you is to get out of our land. You seem to support the blatant murders of the Jewish people. You claim to be Christians when in fact you are proving to be the tools of Satan and the False Messiah (Anti-Christ). There are a lot of Jewish believers in the Messiah and as believers we hold to the entirety of the word of G-d, not the doctrines of the catholic sponsored and written doctrines. We will soon completely remove you as well as your Palestinian allies from our home land. You Christians are Anti-Judaism, anti-Semite groups of vile hatred and have no inheritance with the Chosen People of G-d. You place yourselves in a place of dictatorial rule and force your demonic beliefs upon those who follow the ENTIRETY OF THE LAW OF G-D. We hold NOT to the Pagan ways of the Christians instead we do as was commanded by G-d to our fore-fathers. We were intrusted with His Holy Word because we were the only ones found to be responsible enough to ensure that it not be perverted. So how dare you enter into our homeland and try to convert us into paganism.

Remember the Messiah Yeshua will return and destroy those who try to pervert His fellow Jews and His Holy Land Yisrael

From: guywithfrenchname@floridaaddress.com
Subject:none

My name is Marcel and I'm from Orlando, Fla. I'm not surprised by your anti-Israel bias, but to call yourself Christians that's a tall one. You seem more concerned about International law than the Kingdom of God. From your actions its clear that you don't really believe the Bible. A more accurate description would be arrogant humanistic feel good world system fixers.[Only Jesus will fix it] Your pride has deceived you. Do you believe Amos 9;14-15 ?Hahaha, Allah is a lie and thats why the Moslem world cannot tolerate Israel. Their living on land once under Dar al Islam makes Allah look dead, false or just plain weak. Your allegiance to this false god is clear, and your anti-God of Israel stand is clear. I'm going to do the best I can to let true Christians wake up to false brethren in their midst.

Marcel

---

Reply-To: militantbiblicalheroname@USAddress.net
To: cpt@igc.apc.org
Subject: I wish you would kindly drop . . . .

the word "Christian" from your name. No way could you be one, and do what you have done in Israel, especially in the Hebron area. I personally would like to see judgment done against your group for the complicity in the incitement of murder against an innocent man due to your violence and hatred against the Jews.

Jon

From: someDoctorguy@nowhere.net

To: <cpt@igc.apc.org
Subject: stop your bullshit
Date: Sun, 3 May 1998 15:46:41-0700

I recently sent you mail and yet you continue your nonsense . . .
when Christ returns you all will burn forever in the living hell you
deserve for your lies . . . its really that simple.

Subj: Re: Upcoming CPT Delegations
Date: Thu, 23 Jul, 1998 2:05 PM EDT
From: Dutchguywhoroutinelypostshatemail@netherlandsaddress.net
To: menno.org.cpt.d@MennoLink.org

I sent your recent postings to a good friend of mine in Jerusalem
and this was her reply for you to ponder.

WK


About CPT.

Yes I know of course. I know. I know about all the slander and all
the tales that were spread about the Jews ever since Abraham our
Father and Founder whom we buried in Chewron. I know the tales
and who told them. The Protocols and the blood in the Pesach-matsa,
the murder of the Christian Annointed and the stealing of Palestine
(as the enemy always calls the Jewish Homeland). I know it all.

Although to-day Israel has many very real friends in the Christian
world (and I want to mention the Christians for Israel), Christian
hatred, based on a completely false interpretation of the basics of that
religion, is still very much in evidence as is being proved again by the
e-mail I received through you. There are still Christians who want to
promote a state they call Palestine, although they must realise that
this biblical land belongs to the Jews. If they do not realise this than
they are not Christians. This is my Jewish statement.

On the political and practical level I must state that one needs a building permit in Israel for building even an extension like e.g. a porch to one's home. If one cannot put such a permit on the table one's porch, one's home (illegally built) is being demolished and it does not make any difference whether one is a Jew or anything else, e.g. a Moslim. The law is blind. Religion blind. And colour blind. Total equallity.

Emotionally speaking I want to ask how many Jewish homes are being built in the Moslim world??? But let me not get carried away by emotions. I might go on than, saying that the Moslim presence in the Land of Israel should not be pictured as an innocent presence because it is not innocent. It is directed towards annihilation of the Jewish presence. But we, the Jews do not answer in kind. We are a democracy and every citizen is a citizen. CPT does not look very knowledgeable to me. The name of the township they misspelled as Betinjan (not an Arab sound) is really Betunya and it is a very dangerous place for Jews. Even driving through it makes my bloodpressure go up. I remember all the stones thrown, all the Molotovs exploding, the killings and near killing of Jews just driving past this place: Betunya. Where CPT works so tirelessly. But not for peace. In any case not for peace with the people of Israel, the nation of the Bible, the Owners of the Land G'd promised them.

As far as disruptive effects are concerned, terrorist acts against the Jews had and have an extremely disruptive effect on the Jews. We the Jewish people will need generations in order to get over the damage that was done to our souls by the hatred, the constant war, the murder of even little children, babies in their cribs, by the Arabs of our region. What it did to us (and the whole world— almost—stood besides them as once it stood besides the Nazi's of Europe) can only be compared to the trauma's we suffer from the fourties of this century. What can I say to defend my people that do not need any defense Wim? Only this really:"ma towu ohalecha Ja'acov, mishkanotecha Yisra'el", How good are your tents oh Ya'acov, your dwellings oh Israel.

The G'd of Israel will bless the ones that bless His people, curse the ones that curse Israel.

WL

Subj: Re: HEBRON: PROVOCATION, VIOLENCE, SECURITY
Date: Thu, 18 Jun, 1998 11:23 AM EDT
From: DutchguywhoroutinelypostshatemailandcallsusAmalektoo
       @netherlandsaddress.net
To: menno.org.cpt.d@MennoLink.org

Dear misguided CPT's,
     Why don't you publish the whole truth and nothing but the truth (see enclosure about the Atrash family, who's house you helped to rebuild)? Or are you indeed completely blinded by the view points of Amelek, Martin Luther, Adolf Hitler and Ahmed Shukary? It is one thing to be engaged (and to associate) with a particular side in a conflict (even as fanatics who are looking for a remote cause, because they can harvest "respect and honor" afterwards)), but it is quite an other thing to greedily engage in lashon rah (that is the Hebrew equivalent for slander against persons) against Jews who have legal titles to their own possessions and who—as long as they are not pushed around—harm nobody while living in their own premises. Are 500 Jews a danger to 130 thousand Arabs plus Arafat's army, TIPH and you guys? You must be bloody joking! It's the Jews who need protection from you and your allies, like they would have needed protection in WWII from your spiritual ancestors in the German and German occupied areas of Europe!
     Think about it: will G'd appreciate what you are doing against His people, or will He commit you to hell for being on the side of evil incarnate? You misguided sods really have no idea what you are doing.

# CHAPTER 9

After John changed his pants, he came back to retie their blindfolds. Over the course of the next few days, other people came in to move them three times. Eugie told Tess that she recognized the Australian accent of one of the men who had first grabbed them in the Old City, but mostly, she said, the people moving them were speaking Hebrew. Because their unseen jailers had brought them eight meals, Eugie figured they had been imprisoned for two and a half days.

The food was mostly sliced white bread and chocolate spread—occasionally with a tomato or cucumber. The people who brought it spoke with Israeli accents; sometimes it was a man, sometimes a woman. They would unbind Tess and Eugie's hands and stay in the room while the two of them ate, smacking their hands or faces if they tried to remove their blindfolds. After meals, their various jailers would then take them one at a time to the bathroom and once more presumably in the evening, before it was time to go to bed.

Eugie guessed that there must be some sort of surveillance camera in the rooms where they were waiting, because she had made five attempts to wriggle her legs back through her arms so she could free her hands and each time, including the two times she attempted to do so in what they thought was the middle of the night, the jailers had intervened—rushing through the door and smacking her hard—before she could complete the maneuver.

"At least they've given us mats to sleep on," Eugie said. She also thought it was a positive thing that they had their plastic cuffs changed every night to prevent the normal tightening from cutting off their circulation.

Tess marveled again at Eugie's ability to tolerate unpleasant surroundings. She kept up a cheerful stream of chatter, and asked how Tess was doing every hour or so. When Tess found her mat too lumpy to sleep on comfortably, Eugie switched with her. When Tess decided that Eugie's mat smelled funny, Eugie switched with her again.

Eugie's idea of small talk included pulling apart creedal statements from their respective religious backgrounds and discussing what aspects of these creeds they really believed and which they didn't and why they didn't.

"I mean," she asked, "Do you really believe in the resurrection of the body? I don't think I do. I mean, it could happen, I suppose, but why was it so important to put that in? I always leave that part out when I recite the Apostle's Creed. And the part about Jesus sitting at the right hand of the Father. I mean, if we're supposed to believe that Jesus and God are the same thing, he can't really be seated at God's right hand, right? I mean, I don't even know if God HAS hands. Sometimes I wish the Reformed Anabaptists had stuck with the Mennonites and decided they didn't need official creeds."

The sheer volume of Catholic dogma that Tess had memorized fascinated Eugie, who pumped her for more, after having given up asking Tess how she related its tenets to her own life. When Tess ran out of Catholic creeds and prayers and lists of the saints and who they were patrons of, Eugie encouraged her to recite the manifesto of the Ethical Culture society, to which her second husband had belonged, and the current political platform of the American Socialist Party, of which her third husband had been a member.

"But what really speaks to you, Tess?" Eugie insisted again, on the second or third day. "I mean, what are the governing principles of your life? When you have to make decisions about something important, what of all this stuff you memorized do you think of most often?"

Tess thought back to several important packing decisions she had made before she and Yossi had flown to Israel and then she brightened.

"How about this?" she asked. She cleared her throat:

The Color Me Beautiful™ Philosophy
- Colors give expression to individual personality
- Colors create a unique sense of pride, well-being and security
- Colors influence mood, sensitivity, and attractiveness
- Colors accent an individual's best features
- Colors define a person's taste to others
- Colors are enhancements that do not depend on a person's budget
- Colors influence career, love, and life-style

We at Color Me Beautiful, Inc. have an opportunity to profoundly change the lives of others for the better.

Our work is therefore more than just a job—it is a calling.

We are in the business to be of service to others. Therefore, our mission can only be fulfilled if we are motivated by sincere and loving concern for others.

This concern must permeate all our thoughts and actions.[1]

Eugie laughed a little too hysterically and a little too long, Tess thought.

"Oh Tess, you crack me up," she said. "Okay, point taken. I'll quit badgering you. I keep forgetting sometimes that a lot of people aren't all that comfortable sharing their innermost beliefs. You know, I know you weren't being serious about this Color Me Beautiful stuff, but there were a lot of people in my hometown that treated it like dogma when I was growing up. I mean, I think it came right after the whole Slim for Him aerobics movement. My mom didn't get into either the colors or the aerobics, of course, because they were worldly, but a lot of the people that went to fundamentalist churches in town did."

---

[1]   Carole Jackson, *Color Me Beautiful MakeUp Book*. New York: Ballantine Books, 1987, p. vii.

Tess HAD been serious. She had had her colors done by a professional, who could not quite decide whether she was a Winter or Summer. Her dark hair and eyes made most experts think Winter first, but her creamy complexion sometimes made them consider summer.

"Let's face it," one of her mother's friends said as they watched Tess's colors being analyzed in the living room of her mother's house, "that girl would look good in a brown paper bag."

As Tess had contemplated the comment later while poring over the book, she had realized that only Autumns would look good in a brown paper bag.

She also realized later that blue-eyed people should not wear blue shades of eyeshadow—even though it was a basic tenet of the Color Me Beautiful make-up book. All the more recent literature on the subject recommended that people with blue eyes wear earth-toned eyeshadows and people with brown eyes think in terms of blues and greens.

But with a few exceptions, she still found *Color Me Beautiful* books helpful as a basic guideline in choosing her clothes.

After they had finished with religion, they moved on to men. Tess had noted people's reactions when she told them that she had been married three times, so she did not often do so. Instead, she drew Eugie out about her own relationships. She felt some surprise that Eugie had had so many, although, she reminded herself again, Eugie was not really unattractive. With a professional makeover, she might be considered quite pretty, even elegant.

"I sometimes wish the Reformed Anabaptists had a monastic order," Eugie told her. "I mean, I think I might be a good nun—if I didn't have to believe in infant baptism and the infallibility of the pope—not that most of the nuns I've known have cared much about what the pope thinks. The trouble is, you know, I really like men and I've liked . . . well you know, even though I think it's a sin outside of marriage. But then, I've sinned in so many ways. I mean, I wonder sometimes if God might be just as upset by the way I used to treat my little sisters as He is about extra-marital sex."

Tess considered for a moment whether she should enter into the same confessional mode. It was a mode, she recognized, that tended to sabotage Eugie's authority, and she wasn't sure why Eugie felt compelled to beat her team mates to the punch by all the self-criticism.

Her own sexual fantasies usually revolved around having an orgasm without there being any sweat or semen or sticky stuff that her own otherwise exquisite body seemed to produce. But all in all, the mess seemed worth the almost magic effect it had on the men in her life. Brash anarchists proud of not owing anyone anything—even common courtesy—became dependent slaves when sex came into the relationship.

"I would really miss sex too, if I had to give it up," Tess said.

"The thing is," Eugie said. "I know that if I have it, I'm going to be miserable afterwards and make the other person involved miserable too, and then the question is whether I'm more miserable doing without than I am doing it and regretting it afterwards. I guess it's better not to, because then at least the other person doesn't have to deal with my neuroses."

Tess did not respond, as Eugie did not seem to expect it. Her forehead was sweating behind the blindfold, and she wondered whether her skin would begin rotting soon. She would have to be sure to exfoliate as soon as she got out of this mess.

"You know," Eugie said. "Some of the best people I know, I've met since I began working with RAPT. And a lot of them are atheists and agnostics, and I sometimes envy them, because if they love someone they can sleep with him or her and feel really good about it. And then I look at the Christians I know, and a lot of them have sex outside of marriage too, but they think it's wrong, so they hide it, and you have this overlay of deceit along with the basic issue of fornication to deal with. I mean, when I found out that my fiance was sleeping with this woman in a church where he was serving as a pastoral intern, the hardest part wasn't that he was sleeping—I mean having sex. They used to do it in the four-year-old Sunday School classroom because there was a big closet there—the hardest part was that he had sworn up and down that there was no one else. He just felt like he had to break off our engagement because it didn't seem right any more. And that's when I began having sex with him, because he seemed to think our not sleeping together was the main reason why it wouldn't work out between us, and then he started waffling and saying that, well maybe we should get married after all, but he just wasn't sure. And we had set the date, and I had already ordered the invitations . . ."

Tess clucked her tongue in sympathy. She remembered the extraordinary amount of labor involved in the planning of her first wedding. People said, though, that it was the most perfect wedding they had ever seen. She had worn an off-the-shoulder tea-length lace dress, and her bridesmaids had worn a deep fuschia that it had taken her months to find.

"And the thing that hurt most was people kept telling me that he must have found someone else and I didn't believe them and finally, after I—well, I kind of had a nervous breakdown—and after that, because the psychiatrist made him tell me, he told me that there was someone else, and I asked him why he hadn't told me and he said because I wouldn't marry him if I knew. And of course I would have broken the—well, it wouldn't have been so hard for me to deal with if he had just said he was in love with someone else and didn't want to marry me. I mean, that would have been hard, too, but it was the lying that drove me crazy— and I sort of mean literally crazy—and the way he said that if I did just what he wanted and didn't put any pressure on him, that maybe he would marry me after all."

Tess raised her eyebrows. Any man who even thought about treating her that way, she would have sent packing. But there had always been men waiting in the wings for her. Eugie had probably not had that luxury. On the other hand, it was probably better, in that case, not to have a man in your life than have a man who jerked you around. It was an astonishing and troubling thought. What would it be like to live without a man whose primary interest in life was you? She shuddered.

Hearing footsteps approaching, she sat up a little straighter on her mat. Someone unlocked the door and opened it; damp air wafting into the room.

"On your feet, bitches." The man spoke with an Israeli accent. Tess braced her feet against the floor and pushed against the wall to give herself the leverage she needed to stand up. A meaty hand grabbed her arm and jerked her forward. She heard Eugie fall and yip with pain.

Once again, unknown people guided them—this time with more roughness than the previous times—through what felt like a maze of passageways. They seemed to go down more steps than they went up and at one point they were pushed down a slope. Her captor made it almost impossible for her to keep her footing, and he pinched or slapped her when she tripped.

Having never experienced physical maltreatment, she did not know how to respond. She had shown her displeasure before to men who did not treat her with sufficient consideration by walking out on them, or by entering into a relationship with another man. Neither procedure was an option at the present. She would have to think of some other way to convey that she was seriously offended.

As far as she could tell, they ended up in another room very much like the others they had been in. Tess wondered if they were just being circulated among three different rooms. Strong hands pushed her, hard, into a chair about the right size for a kindergarten classroom and untied her blindfold. In the dim light she saw a low table, also about the right size for a kindergarten classroom, in front of her, plastic laminate peeling off the edges, revealing the particle board beneath.

She rubbed at her forehead and underneath her eyes, feeling the dead skin rubbed off by the blindfold come away in clumps. She looked over at Eugie, also sitting in a small chair. The men had not taken her blindfold off, and her long hair was rucked up in clumps beneath it. Her head drooped forward. Because her hands were still bound behind her back, she had to sit on the very edge of the small chair.

Eugie's hands had turned an unhealthy purple color, with pale patches. Tess was surprised to feel a rush of concern for her, unrelated to Eugie's appearance. She really looked unwell. Her heart began to beat faster as she thought about what would happen if Eugie weren't there to deal with these snarling settlers who not only seemed to wish them harm, but seemed to be planning ways of inflicting it.

As she looked back at the two men tilting their chairs against the wall, she realized with a start that one of them was not a settler—or at least not dressed like one. His hair, standing up in sun-bleached spikes, looked both brittle and greasy, and he was wearing a short-sleeved grey shirt and pants in need of pressing. The other man, the settler, was someone whom she thought she recognized from the streets of Hebron. His torso reminded her of a garlic bulb. Rolls of flesh strained against the buttons of his white shirt and hung over his black pants.

"Your friends must not care about you very much," the settler said.

"You're from New York!" Tess said, his accent making her feel homesick.

"Brooklyn, right?" Eugie said, sitting up straight and wriggling her shoulders as though she were trying to work a kink out of her back. "You're Shlomo. And you're from Oz v'Oz."

The two men glanced at each other. The one who was not Shlomo shrugged his shoulders and lit a cigarette. Shlomo's face darkened.

"Who I am is none of your business, bitch. Slut." He shook his fist as his lips moved in search of another word. They stumbled back on to "bitch."

"Yeah, well, it's nice to know who we're dealing with."

"If you were smarter, you would be thinking of ways to persuade your friends to leave the country."

"They refused to leave." Eugie's voice was neutral, but Tess thought she saw a brief smile cross her face.

"They issued a statement on the Internet saying that you had signed a—what was it called?"

"A statement of conviction," the other man said, his eyes narrowing as he examined his cigarette.

"The Australian!" Eugie said. "See, Tess, I told you it was an Australian."

"South African, actually," the man said.

"Christian Zionist?"

"Let's just say I'm someone who knows where his best interests lie."

"What is this statement of conviction?" Shlomo asked.

"I'd be happy to tell you about it if you'd take these handcuffs off," Eugie said. "I'm afraid I'm going to get gangrene."

Shlomo looked at the South African, who indicated with his head that he should take them off. Heaving his bulk off the chair, Shlomo took a pocketknife out, walked over to Eugie, and carefully inserted the knife through the bonds around her wrists. He held his left hand high in the air as he did so, looking something like a fencer.

After a couple of his fumbling attempts to cut through, Eugie said, "I'm not menstruating."

Shlomo's face darkened. He grabbed one of her arms and jerked it upwards. She yelped in pain as he cut through the plastic with one stroke.

Tess looked back at the South African, who seemed to be regarding Eugie with both amusement and respect, now.

"Blindfold stays on," Shlomo growled as Eugie attempted to remove hers.

"Okay. Okay." Eugie began flexing her fingers, which had swollen to look like jointless sausages.

"Okay. The statement of conviction," she said, flapping her hands in front of her. "It essentially says that if we are caught in a hostage situation, or some other kind of life-threatening situation, we don't want any sort of violent intervention. Actually . . ." her brow wrinkled over the blindfold, "I'm not sure what that has to do with their not being willing to leave the country."

"Oh! Now I remember." Her brow cleared. "It says that our lives are no more important than the lives of the Israelis or Palestinians that live here and we therefore choose to stay in spite of the threats, in solidarity with both Israelis and Palestinians whose lives are threatened. We wrote it about five months ago when you guys kept telling us you were going to kill us."

Tess frowned. No one had ever told her that the team in Hebron had received death threats. She thought that Yiphat or one of the team might have at least mentioned it.

Shlomo said, "Bullshit. That's all you *goyim* ever write. Bullshit. Bullshit. Bullshit."

"Well, we never claimed to be Hemingway," Eugie said. "Or Chaim Potok," she added after a pause.

The South African reached into the puckered breast pocket of his grey shirt and pulled out a piece of paper, which he unfolded. "The message from the Internet said that the team loves you both very much, and that whatever happens you are in their hearts and thoughts and prayers every minute of the day."

Eugie smiled and Tess saw her nose turn red. "Good for them," she said, sniffling. "I just want to say that I work with some of the greatest human beings in the whole world." Wriggling her shoulders, she sat up very straight again.

"You aren't getting it," Shlomo said. "We told them very specifically what would happen if they did not leave Hebron within thirty-six hours. Do you understand the consequences? Do you understand that we will kill you?"

"Oh yeah," Eugie said. Tess thought she sounded almost cheerful.

She, on the other hand, was furious. Frank had sealed his fate. There was no question now about deciding between him and Yossi. If Frank really loved her, he wouldn't give up her life for some stupid moral principle.

Shlomo continued to stare at Eugie, mouth open. Tess thought the South African seemed to be enjoying his discomfort.

"But—but—why aren't you afraid?" Shlomo said at last. "I don't think you understand. We really are going to kill you."

"Don't worry I believe you," Eugie said, reassuringly. "So I die. No big deal."

"You really aren't afraid, are you?" The South African said, as though commenting on the weather.

Eugie twisted her mouth into a wry expression and held up her hands, flexing them backwards. Against her mottled flesh, a thick white, vertical scar ran down her left wrist, meeting a fainter diagonal scar in a sort of crooked, upside down T. On her right wrist, the scars were much thinner and crosshatched—like a tic-tac-toe board.

"It's not really a question of not being afraid," Eugie said. "It's a question of which things I am afraid of. I'm terrified of rejection," she said. After a moment's reflection she added, "And those big, black, hairy spiders. But death—no, that's not such a big deal for me."

Shlomo stumbled back to his chair against the wall and looked at the South African with concern. Tess wondered why he looked like he was afraid.

*    *    *

She had to figure out a way to get them to release Tess. Ruling out telling them that she was engaged to a Jew (they might think killing Tess was a good way to prevent another mixed marriage), she cudgelled her brain to think of ways of proving that Tess was just a tourist, had just stumbled on them through capricious circumstances. John seemed to have taken a shine to her; maybe John could intercede for her. It was a good sign that they had left Tess unbound and unblindfolded.

"Listen," she said. "I'm okay with death, really. To tell you the truth, if I was going to be kidnapped and killed by anyone, I'd just as soon be kidnapped and killed by people who think that touching me will make them unclean."

(She actually had felt some gratitude that she could be free from the fear of rape—although she didn't know where the South African fit in to this whole scenario. She wished she could get a look at him.)

"If I die, your propaganda mills can say that I brought it on myself because I was living with Arabs. You can tell them your intelligence agents told you that we were hiding guns in our apartment to give to Arabs to kill Jews—incidentally, where DID you get that information? We tried to get this *Jerusalem Post* reporter to search our apartment to prove we didn't have any, but he just laughed."

Shlomo said, "We have our sources."

"Well you have really bad sources, then. You know, it really gets to me—all the hundreds of hours I put in researching Judaism to try to understand you guys, and you can't even be bothered to open an encyclopedia to find out that Mennonites and Quakers and Church of the Brethren and Reformed Anabaptists are pacifists. Anyway, you might be able to sell to your constituency that killing me is a tragic side effect of your struggle to make Hebron safe for Jews, but I don't think you're going to be able to sell the fact that you killed an innocent tourist. Look at her—" Eugie pointed in the direction from where she had last heard Tess's voice. "Imagine her picture plastered all over the newspapers, on posters at Peace Now demonstrations, in letters to congressmen and senators . . ."

The blood running back into her fingers really hurt. She began rubbing her hands together. No one spoke for a moment. She wondered whether the men had left the room, but then decided she would have heard them if they had.

Shlomo broke the silence. "But she's seen us. She will talk to the police."

"Shlomo, don't you think the Shabak know exactly who you are and who's been involved with this? Releasing Tess would be a sign of good faith on your part. You can always say I tried to attack you or something and you killed me in self-defense."

"But you yourself have told us you're a pacifist," the South African said. Eugie thought he sounded too casual, considering the circumstances.

"Yeah, but I'm human. I slipped. 'We have all sinned and fallen short of the glory of God.' You know. Anyone who really knows me will tell you I have the capacity to really lose my temper sometimes."

More silence. "Another possibility would be to take Tess to Jerusalem in the trunk of your car or something—or you can dress her up in one of those snood thingies and drop her off at the police station with a note containing your further demands. She can say that she is not allowed to tell the police anything or you'll kill me. You could keep quiet, couldn't you, Tess?"

Tess must have nodded, because Shlomo barked, "It is not for you to be planning our strategy. I must go speak with the others."

Eugie heard the door open and close. Then the South African said, "What is a nice girl like you doing with the Arabs?"

Eugie sighed. "You might as well ask what the Arabs are doing with me."

"You really don't think there is anything wrong with them, do you?"

"Well some are greedy and some are generous and some are untrustworthy and some are honest—and I'd say they are all these things in the same proportions as other groups of people are."

"I suppose next thing you're going to tell me that you think blacks and whites are the same."

"It wasn't the next thing I was going to tell you, but I do think that most groupings of people have the same inherent capabilities and disabilities as other groupings."

"I don't understand—can't you see how much smarter you are . . ."

Eugie cut him off. "I'm smarter than most of the white people I know—and in some ways, I can be awfully dumb too, you know."

"Evidently." Eugie heard the South African push his chair back and walk to the door.

After the door closed, she inclined her head toward Tess. "I wonder what this hangup they have about intelligence is all about. I mean, I was pretty compulsive about grades when I was in school, but then, after I worked with developmentally disabled adults, I realized that intelligence isn't everything. Learning to brush your teeth or managing your finances means a whole lot more in a lot of ways than getting an 'A' on an essay."

"Why did you slash your wrists?"

Tess's voice was neutral. Eugie wished she could take her blindfold off and see her expression. She had grown used to people regarding her with fear when they found out—and it had happened long enough ago that she didn't see any need to tell most people anymore. When her first boyfriend after her fiancee told her that he had been wanting to break up with her but was afraid to because he thought she'd try to kill herself again, she realized that this reaction was something she would have to deal with for the rest of her life. The humiliation was her penance—the logical consequences, as they said in human services, of her actions. As time had passed, she felt more grateful for the penance. It reminded her not to attempt something so hare-brained again.

"I was just stupid, I guess," she told Tess. "I don't know if you've ever loved someone so much you felt you can't live without them . . ." She swallowed hard. "But that's the way it felt." She realized the lump in her throat was for Yossi and not for her fiance. Her lips twitched. This was the way she healed, she guessed. New romances cauterized the open wounds left by the old.

"You see—when I was growing up, I was afraid all the time. It had this grip on me, like I couldn't breathe. You know what I mean?"

"A fear so black and hollow it could suffocate creation," Tess said.

"Who said that?"

"Melissa Etheridge. My—an old friend really liked her."

"Well, you're right. That's what I'm talking about. I was one of those kids who always tried too hard to please adults and ended up annoying them because I was trying so hard. When you're always doing and saying the wrong thing and then you find someone who thinks that everything thing you say and everything you do is wonderful—well it's like you've entered a different universe and you'd do just about anything not to go back to the old one."

"I really thought my family and friends would understand," she said.

"I thought they would understand that I was in so much pain and I was so afraid, that I couldn't go on living. I guess that's a sign of how crazy I was. It's really impossible not to devastate people who care, I guess. What I had to learn was that God is in all the universes—the ones where you feel like you're flying and the ones where you feel you're a pile of dirt.

When people think you're wonderful it never really lasts. It's not even real. Only God is real."

"Anyway," she said. "I've been depressed since that happened, but I've never been so depressed that I would have considered trying it again. My family thinks that my RAPT work is something I do to act out on self-destructive impulses. I consider it channeling them in a positive direction."

"I'm sorry if I'm weirding you out . . ." she said, her voice trailing off.

Tess said nothing. Did she dare take off her blindfold to gauge her expression? Better not. She didn't want to upset Shlomo more than she had already.

"Tess," she said. "It's really important that you emphasize you're not with us—that you just got stuck here because Yiphat didn't know what else to do with you. I mean, that's true, right?"

She remembered that people might be listening to their conversations. "I mean, you never bought in to the RAPT philosophy, right? You would have just as soon stayed in Jerusalem. This activism thing isn't really your thing, right?"

"No," said Tess. "I wasn't planning on getting involved with you at all. Yossi was the one who got me here. I would have been happy just staying with him."

Good girl, Eugie thought. She picked up what Eugie was trying to do without the eye contact.

"I hate Hebron," Tess said at a volume that made Eugie flinch. "I hate the way it looks. I hate the way it smells. I hate not having a real bathroom and a real shower. I hate people spitting at me, and I hate people asking me personal questions when they don't even know me. I hate being tied up and blindfolded and being escorted to a bathroom. I hate pretending that I care about this whole stupid conflict. I want to go home."

Eugie heard Tess sniffling.

"There's no reason for them to hurt you," she said. "You're not one of us. You ended up with us by sheer accident."

"Yes, that's right."

"If you do get out of this—tell everyone I love them, okay?"

"All right."

After a long silence, Eugie said, "I think I'll get some sleep."

Tess told her there were no mats in the room. Eugie suggested that Tess use the small kindergarten table to sleep on and then lay on the floor against the wall. She knew she wouldn't sleep, but there didn't seem to be much else to do, under the circumstances.

Somehow she did doze off, because the sound of a key turning in a lock wakened her. Sensing a moving light of a flashlight in the room, she sat up. A hand went over her mouth.

"Not one word if you want to get out alive," a man with an American accent whispered.

# *Interim*

Actual e-mail received by the Christian Peacemaker Teams Chicago office. All misspellings are *sic.* Names and addresses have been changed.

Subject: From KACH International
Date: Sat, 17 Jan 1998 10:01:25-0600
X-MSMail-Priority: Normal
X-Priority: 3

3 of your members: Cliff Kindy, Pierre Shantz and Sara Reschly are aiding and abaiting violent moslem terrorists against heroic Jewish Community of Hebron, Israel.

Information has been forwarded to the appropriate offices of Jewish self-defense organizations.

It is advised that these 3 persons leave Land of Israel in the next 96 hours.

Subject: SWIFT PUNISHMENT
Forwarded message:
From: JewishDefenseLeagueGuy@Somewhere.USA
Date: 98-01-18 00:57:06 EST

KACH INTERNATIONAL WARNING:

It has been learned that three of your members: Cliff Kindy, Pierre Shantz and Sara Reschly help and assist arab terrorists in smuggling explosives used in recent bombings of the Hebron

Jewish Community in Israel.

Information has been forwarded to the appropriate offices of Jewish Self-Defense.

For their safety, three above-mentioned terrorists are advised to depart from the Land of Israel to their own countries in the next 96 hours.

Subj: Re: SWIFT PUNISHMENT!
Date: Sun, 18 Jan, 1998 7:23 PM EDT
From: Kathleen Kern
Subj: Re: SWIFT PUNISHMENT!
To: Jewish Defense League guy

Dear Mr. S.,

Please look up "Anabaptism," "Mennonite," "Quaker," or "Church of the Brethren" in an encyclopedia. We are the spiritual descendants of people who were burned alive, drowned, and tortured to death in other ways for refusing to participate in violence at any level—which includes participating in the military.

We believe that all human beings were created in the image of G-d, and loved by G-d, and that no one has the right to harm any human being for that reason. Participating in any action that would physically harm a human being for us is trayf.

It would be more likely that the settlers in Hebron would start serving ham sandwiches at bar mitzvahs than it would be for anyone serving with Christian Peacemaker Teams to become involved with explosives or other objects that could bring harm to others.

Thank you for bringing this to our attention.

Sincerely,

Kathleen Kern

Date: Mon, Jan 19, 1998 12:38 AM EDT
From: JewishDefenseLeagueGuy@Somewhere.USA
To: Kathleen Kern

Ms. Kern,

I am on a humanitarian mission to save the lives of those 3 members
of yourorganization in Hevron.

People are not stupid, nor can you fool anybody. Nobody will go
figure if all of your members are stupid/naiive or 1 or 2; are all of
them sympatize with Hamas or PFLP or . . . ?

Fact is: they assisted in smuggling explosives later used against
Jewish Community of Hebron.

People not connected with the Hebron Jewish Community nor
with the Israeli Government are angry and the accusing fingers are
pointed at those 3.

Federal Laws specifically prohibit assisting terrorism overseas: looks
like your church choose to violate those laws.

Time to get the 3 to Europe ASAP, before it is too late.

Date: Tue, 20 Jan, 1998 8:59 AM EDT
From: CPT Chicago office
X-From: CPT Chicago Office (Christian Peacemaker Teams)
Sender: CPT Chicago Office
To: Team in Hebron cc: Kathleen Kern

FYI—just in this morning on cptnet feedback which does not
go out automatically. Do you think we should post. I think
not. g

From: JewishDefenseLeagueGuy@Somewhere.USA
To: CPTnet
Subject: Bombing in Hevron!!!
Date: Mon, 19 Jan 1998 06:38:05-0600
X-MSMail-Priority: Normal

Grieving parents of Cliffy, Pierry and Sari sent their precious darling
ones to a very dangerous place. Brainwashed by the church fathers,
who themselves were taught that the real menno—, anabapto—
and quaker-men were persecuted, burned at stake and murdered
by their pseodo-christian bretherin, they must not fear death and
do what Jesus tells them to do. Guess what? Everyone in the Middle
East dies w/o fear. This is the end of this argument. 3 poor naiive
darlings came to a wolf's den, called "casba". Immediately, certain
people became interested and made friends. Unfortunately, on the
Middle East, even among "certain" people, there are some who tell
other people about what is going on. And other people tell things
about those people, too.

That's how it happens that some people know more then others.
To keep the long story short, there is a higher possibility on
"casba" then anywhere else, that during certain illegal activities,
carried out behind locked doors of "casba" shops by the
abovementioned "interested certain" people, things go wrong
and some pieces begin to travel at speeds around 20,000 feet
per second with temperatures reaching 5,000 degrees C. At
that time many other things around start going wrong and
people get hurt. But the most funny thing will be if in their
naiivity and stupidity, the 3 darling ones unwittingly
participated in hurting themselves by helping certain people
to get things they were not suppost to have! Of course, the
fault is not only theirs: their grieving parents are fools, along
with the stupid people who sent them there along with the
most stupid of all: their church doctrines.

Subj: Re: is this judaism?
Date: Tue, Jan 20, 1998 2:49 PM EDT
From: Tikkun-nik friend
To: Kathleen Kern

kathy,

i sent an email to the kach guy, trying to engage him, and this is
the response i got . . . definitely threatening. do with it what you
will.

>From: JewishDefenseLeagueGuy@Somewhere.USA
>To: Tikkun-nik friend
>Subject: Re: is this judaism?
>Date: Mon, 19 Jan 1998 22:33:29-0600
>X-Msmail-Priority: Normal
>
>Wednesday is fast approaching and the 3 explosive-smuggling
Hamas
>assistants got to be back home by that time.
>All shmocks with ideas better put their efforts where their big
mouthes are
>and help pay for the airfares.
>All bullshit is ignored.
>

---

Forwarded message:
From: JewishDefenseLeagueGuy@Somewhere.USA
To:Kathleen Kern
Date: 98-01-22 12:34:38 EST

Rabbi Meir Kahane, ZT"L, taught Jews never to stand silent when
other Jews are threatened. Unfinished hitlerites of the mennotite
faction, of which your are one, openly engaged in a persecution of

the heroic Jewish Community of Hevron will learn that thare are plenty of Jews willing to stand up for their People.

Mutherfucken scum like you, threatening the expulsion of Jews from their homes, engaged in bombing of a kindergarten in Hevron will end up like your spiritual father: hitler.

Subj: Re: Prayers for Peacemakers, Jan. 22
Date: Sat, 24 Jan, 1998 11:29 AM EDT
From: CPT Ontario coordinator

I was out yesterday. Did you get this? I think it should be posted to cpt.d. What do you think? G

>From: Dutchguywhoroutinelypostshatemail@netherlandsaddress.net
>Subject: Re: Prayers for Peacemakers, Jan. 22
>
>We prefer to pray for the survival of the Jewish community of Hebron, which
>is threatened by your Christian anti-semitic terrorist group and its Arab
>allies. You are inciting to violence against and the murder of Jews, just
>like your ancestors did in Germany.
>You are Amalek. You are Amalek. But you will not succeeed.
>
>>At 13:24 22-01-98 CST, you wrote:
>>PRAYERS FOR PEACEMAKERS, Thursday, Jan. 22, 1998
>>
>>Pray for the safety and steadfastness of the Christian Peacemaker Team in
>>Hebron, West Bank. They have received death threats from the Israeli
>>terrorist group Kach.
>>
>>CPT Ontario coordinator

Subj: Re: Bombing in Hevron!!!
Date: Wed, 28 Jan, 1998 10:45 AM EDT
From: CPTnet
To: Kathleen Kern

To: Unknown friend
Cc: cptnet
Subject: Re: Bombing in Hevron!!!
Date: Sat, 24 Jan 1998 05:30:55-0600

As with all people, there is a dark side to Christianity, too. We identified hypocrites of mennonite/anabaptist/quacker persuasion who talk sweet non-violence but have a leftist political agenda. They sent a Mennonite Bombmaking Team to Hevron, Israel, that smuggles explosives, acts as a lookout for bloodthirsty terrorists, helped to bomb a kindergarten, instigates mobs for attacking small Jewish community, hides criminals and provides other logistical and financial help to Hamas, Islamic Jihad and PFLP.

Already, every 4th member of Jewish Community of Hevron was attacked, stabbed or beaten in past 2 years. 17 were brutally murdered by terrorists. G-d commanded us not to stand idly by our brothers' blood. The clock is ticking.

# CHAPTER 10

When Tess had difficulty sleeping, she liked to imagine herself running barefoot along a beach in a diaphanous white gown or standing on a grassy mountain top, face tilted toward the sun, while the wind whipped her dark hair around her face. In these fantasies, she never worried about wearing sunblock.

Neither of these two images helped for a long time. She kept thinking about the ugly white scars on Eugie's wrists. She wondered whether if she hadn't been certain another man would come along to fill the void of the ones who left, the possibility of killing herself might have occurred to her, too. A strange pain clutched at her heart.

She tried to find a more comfortable position on the kindergarten table that Eugie had let her take. Just when she thought she couldn't be more uncomfortable than she already was, something worse happened.

She must have drowsed a little, because she woke up when the door unlocked. Two figures with a strong flashlight entered.

"Get up and don't talk," the larger one said.

Tess considered not complying. She had been moved one too many times and would not do it anymore. Then she heard the smaller figure say, as the light blinded her, "See, is she not beautiful like I said? Just like my beautiful Yuaad."

"Sa'eed?" She blinked.

"Sssh," the larger figure hissed. "We don't have much time." She heard the other figure saying to Eugie, "Not one word, if you want to get out alive."

Sa'eed pulled Tess to her feet, letting go of her hand with a slight caress when he reached for the flashlight the other man held out to him. Sa'eed shone the light in Eugie's face as the other man tried to untie her blindfold. The knots must have been too tight, because he eventually pulled a pocketknife out of his pants and cut the blindfold off at the back of her head. As he pulled it away, Eugie clapped her hands over her eyes.

"Take the flashlight off me," she whispered.

The large man pulled her to her feet by one arm. "There's no time. They'll realize the security camera's off and come to check any minute now. You must do exactly as I tell you. No, don't bother putting on your shoes. They'll make too much noise. Carry them."

Sa'eed grabbed Tess by the hand again. Their stockinged feet making dull thudding noises, they raced out into the tunnel. The larger man had Eugie by the hand and preceded them, but was soon puffing. Tess found it hard to keep a grip on her aerobics shoes. She didn't want to clutch the dirty soles to her clothes—though goodness knows her clothes must be filthy by now—and she didn't want to touch the soles with her hands either, so the shoes dangled from the three middle fingers of her right hand as she ran.

Eventually the large man had to stop to catch his breath, and the pace changed from a run to a walk. The passage slanted uphill and in fifteen minutes, they walked out into open air. The older man stopped beside a mound of earth and a bulldozer at the entrance to the tunnel, and pulled a kipah from his pocket.

"Sa'eed, put this on—and here, take my jacket. You two—put your shoes on."

The little man shrugged on the jacket, made of shiny fabric with Hebrew lettering on the back. Only his fingertips poked out of the sleeves. He held at arm's length the kipah made of some sort of tapestry fabric.

"I do not think . . ." he began.

"Put it on now!" the other man growled, and Sa'eed fitted it on his bald head. It hovered just above his eyebrows—like the jacket, it was too large.

Tess blinked a couple times as she straightened up from tying her shoes—surely this tunnel could not have taken them all the way to the New Jersey suburbs. Yet, all around her were neatly maintained lawns and shrubs. The large concrete apartment buildings were not aesthetically remarkable, but their uniformity had a certain charm for her after all the time she had spent in the hodgepodge of Palestinian architecture.

Overhead it was a cloudless night. Tess could see the dark, as well as the bright, half of the moon.

"We're in Kiryat Arba," Eugie said to Tess in a whisper.

"Follow me," the large man said, "and if you pass people on the street, just smile and nod. Act like we're just out for a stroll."

They saw a man and woman with a baby carriage coming toward them in the distance, but they turned onto a side street before the four of them would have had to nod and smile. Tess heard Eugie exhale a shuddering breath.

They approached a brightly lit area with a gas station. To their left was a heavy gate and a square concrete structure with an armed guard.

"I'm going to talk to you in Hebrew," the large man said. "Just nod your head and say 'ken' to whatever I say."

As they approached the light, Tess could see that his white shirt was wet under his arms. He waved cheerfully at the guard by the gate and at a couple of soldiers drinking beer in a little food court to the right, then led them into a pavilion behind the gas station. Stone benches lined the paved pathway. They stopped just short of a circular mini-plaza. Around the slab of stone in the middle were stands containing what looked like votive candles.

He gestured for them to sit, and then surveyed the area, obviously looking to see if they were in danger of being overheard.

"So, Mr. Fogel," Eugie said. "What's all this about?"

He slumped down on a bench next to Sa'eed, across from Eugie and Tess, and heaved a sigh.

"Look," he said. "I don't like what you write about us, and I wish you'd leave the country and let those of us who live here sort out our own problems. But"—he threw a sideways glance at Eugie—"I never wanted you to come to any harm. I heard about the plans to attack you on King David Street . . ."

"He means Dubboya Street," Eugie said to Tess.

"On King David Street," he reiterated, "and I thought it was just some *umshtellers* from outside talking big. And then, after you and that other girl—the Puerto Rican—were attacked—"

"Felicia is Colombian," said Eugie.

"After you were attacked, I began to pay more attention to what my sources were saying. I am"—he paused for a moment as though looking for the right word—"TIRED of all this: the rhetoric, the fighting, the hurting—the killing. When I moved to Kiryat Arba twenty years ago, I thought the Messiah was coming soon. I thought that when we redeemed the land, it would make life better for the whole world—the Arabs included, and that when they saw we meant no harm, we could be good neighbors."

"Mr. David is a very good man." Sa'eed bobbed his head up and down. "He is always very good to me. He is a much better boss than Mr. Safsarsheck was to me. Mr. Safsarsheck did not explain things to me the way I need them explained."

"YOU!" Eugie jabbed her finger at Sa'eed and poked Fogel in the throat by accident. "I don't ever want to see you again. I don't want you even to THINK about talking to us. Do you know how often I defended you? How many people I told that you WEREN'T a collaborator?"

"He saved your life," Fogel said with a sigh, looking at his shoes.

"We wouldn't have gotten into this jam if he hadn't turned us in to your Kachnik friends."

"They're not my friends," Fogel said, as though pointing out a mispronounced word. Tess wished that Eugie would shut up and let Mr. Fogel tell them how they were going to get out of Kiryat Arba.

"I don't believe what Kach or Kahane Hai or Oz v'Oz believe," Fogel said, again, as though he were stating facts rather than defending his honor. "I just want to live in peace with my neighbors."

"Okay, whatever," Eugie said. "Listen—I'm feeling a little on edge, and I could argue with you into the night about political realities, but I just realized that I should probably thank you. You saved our lives, and I know you've taken a lot of risks to do it. What do you need us to do now to keep you out of trouble?"

"I can't take you to the police station," he said. "The cops would grill me on what I know about the Oz v'Oz, and it would get back to them that I had had something to do with your escape."

"We're not going to run into them here at Goldstein's grave?" Eugie looked around her nervously.

"Not at this time of the night," he said. "But it's not safe here, either. I want you to stay put. I'll go get my car and drive you through the checkpoint. When we get to the Me'arat ha-Machpelah, you'll be safe because of the soldiers."

Eugie expelled a small puff of air and shrugged her shoulders. "Well, it's against our religion to rely on force of arms, but you're right, we should be okay. We'll wait here."

Tess anticipated the homecoming. She had never thought she would be grateful to see their very own squat-toilet—at least she looked forward to seeing the one in the women's apartment, because it had less traffic and had only laundry and bath water thrown down it. The one in the main apartment got flushed with dishwater sometimes, and the dirty dishwater in the big plastic jug sometimes began to smell really rancid.

Frank would probably want to hold her as soon as she entered the apartment, and she would have to think of some gentle way to defer the hug until she had taken a shower—or until she had poured water over herself in the bath tub with no running water. Maybe she would go to the women's apartment first and start heating water on the little single burner gas stove while Eugie made her entrance.

"You know," Eugie said, pointing to the slab of stone in the center of the circular courtyard, "I took some Norwegian journalists to the Goldstein monument once, and one of them said, 'I have traveled all over the world, including into war zones, and this is the worst thing I have ever seen.' Goldstein was the guy who killed the twenty-nine people in the Il Ibrahimi Mosque on February 25, 1994. His gravestone says that he was a martyr, because a couple guys in the mosque pulled him down and beat him to death with a fire extinguisher after he ran out of ammunition. People come here to pray—but you know, usually we don't see any when we bring groups here."

"Yes, Baruch Goldstein was a very, very bad man," Sa'eed said, nodding.

"So are you," Eugie said, looking away.

He looked at Tess anxiously. "I am very, very sorry," he said to her, "but those crazy settlers would have killed me if I had not taken you to them."

"They were going to kill us," Tess told him.

"No, no. As soon as I left you, I went to Mr. David for help."

"How much money did they pay you?" Eugie asked. "What did they give you for turning us in?"

"I do not understand this 'turning' you speak."

"Damn it!" Eugie said. "You understand exactly what I mean. How much money did they give you?"

"I did not do this for money, but because I was afraid," Sa'eed said.

"But you took the money."

"It was only a very little money," he said angrily. "They said they would give ten thousand shekels and they only gave me one thousand. They thought they could cheat because I am stupid. When I said this is not ten thousand, they laughed and said I must be happy because they did not kill me. It is like when my brother died in Haifa, and my mother said it could have been worse, and his wife said, how is this possible? And my mother said, 'It would have been worse for you to have run away with another man.'"

Tess and Eugie said nothing, so he continued. "And then my brother's wife did run off with another man, and the doctors said they could not have children and my mother said, 'And why should we not praise God?' But now I think my family has always been unlucky. If we look up in the sky for help something bad happens. If we look down on the ground for treasures, something bad happens. I am the last of a long line of pessoptimists. I have become a pessimist only."

Tess felt a little sorry for Sa'eed, but did not understand why she felt that way. She sighed. Ever since she had come to Hebron, she had been feeling things and not understanding why she felt them. She would be glad to leave and not worry about it anymore. She thought it would be easier living in Jerusalem.

She heard the sound of a car. Eugie jumped from the stone bench and walked away from the monument, not waiting to see if Tess and Sa'eed had followed. As they passed the gas station, they saw a yellow VW Beetle parked at the entrance to the park. David Fogel got out and motioned for them to move back into the shadow of the gas station. He had a bundle under his arm.

"Put this on," he said, handing a crocheted snood to Eugie. "And you, put this on," he said, thrusting a dress at Tess. "It should cover your pants." Tess took it from him gingerly. It was too dark to see what color the dress was. She hoped it wasn't purple. Purple was not her best color.

"Sa'eed—" rather than giving instructions, Fogel, stripped off the nylon windbreaker he had given him earlier, attached a clip-on tie to the frayed plaid shirt he was wearing, and helped him into a dark suit jacket.

"Good," he said. "You all look like Jews. Especially you," he said, pointing at Eugie.

"Yeah, I get that a lot. Hey, I guess it's a possibility," she said. "Maybe there's a great great great great grandmother somewhere on my mother's side . . ."

"Get in the car," Fogel interrupted her. "You in the front seat and the other two in the back. When we pass the first checkpoint, I want both of you to lie down out of sight."

Tess winced. After she been so uncomfortable for the last few days, it seemed unfair to ask her to squeeze into the back seat of a Volkswagen.

"I can sit in the back," Eugie offered.

"No. You look the most inconspicuous."

"But won't the guard who watched us go into the park, and the soldiers—"

"The soldiers are gone. And I planned to get you here just before the guards changed shifts."

The Volkswagen approached the gate. The guard waved, and the gate moved to the side as if by magic.

Fogel made a left turn toward the city. Eugie said, "Listen, if there's anything we can do to make it easier on you—"

"When you see me in Hevron"—he pronounced the "h" sound at the back of his throat—"pretend that you never met me."

Eugie said, "It's funny. Sister Madeleine has been trying for the last two years to get us to meet each other. And now we won't be able to tell her we HAVE met you."

"She is a good woman," Fogel said. After a moment's silence, he added, "But a little bit crazy." He and Eugie smiled at each other.

As they came over a rise, a young settler man in a windbreaker, white shirt, black pants and side curls stood in the middle of the road and waved his arms frantically for them to stop.

"Shit," Fogel said. "All of you. Not a word. I'm going to tell him that she's my niece and you two are friends of hers from Yerushalayim."

"*Erev tov*," Fogel greeted the young man after he rolled down his window. Tess noticed that he had a small army-style backpack. The young man leaned into the Beetle and asked some questions in Hebrew. He threw a very nice smile in Tess's direction. She responded in kind. His eyes lingered a moment, and she felt safer.

"*B'seder,*" Fogel said, and began to roll up the window. The young man's hand darted through the window and pinioned Fogel to the car seat by the throat. A gun appeared in the other hand, pointed at Fogel's forehead.

Eugie threw open the car door on her side, and was almost out when the young man shouted at her and pressed against Fogel's throat hard enough that he gurgled in protest. Eugie glanced at Tess and made a slight inclination with her head toward the hill on the opposite side of the road. Did Eugie seriously think she should make a run for it? This man had a GUN! On the other hand, she remembered a police officer she had dated telling her that it was hard for a criminal to shoot someone who was running, and that women should never get into a car with a man with a gun.

Eugie approached the young man, hands in the air. "I don't speak Hebrew," she said, "but I'm not going to run, and I won't hurt you."

The young man looked at Eugie as though she were crazy.

"I kill him," he said. "If you run, I kill him."

"I'm not going to run," she said. "Why don't you take me and let the others go?"

Tess fumbled around the back of the front seat for the lever that would move it forward. When she found it, the seat sprang away from her with a loud rasp. She jumped out of the car and ran across the road.

"Do not run!" the young man shouted. "I will not hurt you. You must stay."

His voice sounded reassuring. Tess turned and hesitated. A light came up behind them. It was an army jeep. Pulling alongside the VW, it stopped, and a soldier leaned out the window, asking a question in Hebrew.

The young man smiled and waved at the soldier. Tess couldn't see his other hand, but assumed the gun was still pointing at Fogel, because Fogel said nothing.

"It is Tessss!" the red-haired soldier she had met on her first morning in Hebron called out.

She smiled and waved.

"These are friends of yours?" the soldier asked.

Tess smiled and nodded as she looked at Eugie's paralyzed figure standing in front of the VW.

"You have many strange friends, Tess," the soldier laughed and drove on.

As soon as the jeep disappeared around the curve, Sa'eed jumped from the VW, through the door that Tess had left open, ran behind it and tumbled down the hill at the side of the road where the young man with the gun was standing. He briefly pointed it at Sa'eed as he dashed through a vineyard, but at a movement from Fogel, he whipped around and pointed the gun at his head again.

"He will die. We will kill him one day," the young man said. Tess didn't know if he was referring to Fogel or to Sa'eed.

"You," he said to Tess, "go in the car."

She began to sit in the front passenger seat.

"No," he said. "In the—other part of the car."

She got into the back seat. The young man walked around the front—keeping the gun leveled at Fogel through the windshield—and then through the open door. He motioned for Tess to slide over and then got into the back.

"You," he said to Eugie. "In the car."

Eugie got in and closed the door. The young man pulled Tess down, gently, so her head was lying on his left thigh. He pressed the gun into Fogel's side and said something in Hebrew. Fogel began to drive, and the young man drew the gun away. He then took off his backpack and jacket and put them on top of Tess. They passed the checkpoint at the top of the hill that led down to the Il Ibrahimi Mosque. The young man said something in Hebrew and both he and Fogel waved at the soldiers, who waved back in response.

They made a left turn and followed a road that wound around the perimeter of Kiryat Arba. Soon they were on a road that passed through an area of vineyards with occasional cubes of concrete houses dotting the landscape. Then they seemed to reenter Hebron, although it was a part of town that Tess had not seen before.

After directing Fogel to pull over to the side and park by a three-story concrete house, the young man whipped off his kipah, and then said something to Fogel, who did the same. He pulled a checked keffiyeh and black cord from his backpack and thrust it at Fogel, who put it on after the young man barked something at him in Hebrew.

"You," he said to Eugie, "Take away your hat."

She drew off the snood. He thrust a white scarf at her and one at Tess, and then handed each of them a white clasp so they could fasten the scarves around their throats.

With difficulty, he then managed to put a keffiyeh on his own head and slide a black cord around it with one hand.

"You. Out," he said to Eugie. "Do not run, or I kill all them."

Eugie got out and stood with her hands clasped in front of her. The young man then got out with the gun in his windbreaker pocket and pointed the pocket at Fogel through the windshield. Fogel got out of the car and started to say something in Hebrew, but the young man cut him off with a terse command. He held out his hand, said something else in Hebrew, and Fogel gave him the car keys.

The young man shoved Fogel toward the door of the house and motioned with his head for the two women to follow him. After the three of them stood clustered under a concrete balcony, the young man reached over with his free hand and rang the bell three times.

"*Min?*" a woman's voice called from the inside. The man said three words and the door opened a crack. A young woman wearing a long cotton sweater over dark leggings opened it further and moved to the side so the four of them could enter. The young man said something to her, and she nodded, frightened.

He pushed Fogel, Eugie, and Tess toward the stairs, and they began to climb. Trying a door on the second floor and finding it locked, he turned toward the young woman, who had glided up behind them. With shaking hands, she turned the key in the lock and then led them toward the back of the apartment into a large room, bare except for mats on the floor and an over-elaborate chandelier hanging from the ceiling. Three young men sat on a mat against the wall, smoking.

"*Ahlan wa sahlan,*" one of them said. He had a gaunt, pock-marked face and a moustache.

"*Ahlan bik,*" Eugie responded.

"A *moustoutinah* who speaks Arabic!" another young man wearing a red t-shirt smiled at her.

"I am not a settler," Eugie said. "I work for RAPT in the old city in Hebron."

The pockmarked man snorted. "And I suppose you will tell me that this man, too, is not a settler?"

Eugie looked at David Fogel and paused for a moment. "No, I mean, yes, he is a settler, but he helped us escape from some kachniks, who were going to kill us."

"He lives on our land. He is a settler."

The young man with the gun removed his keffiyeh, took the kipah out of his pocket and handed it to a third man who had not yet spoken. He said something to him—was it Hebrew or Arabic? Tess was no longer sure—and handed him the car keys. The third man put the kipah on his head, untucked curls from behind his ears, and left the room. Moments later, Tess heard the VW start up and drive away.

"*Tehki Arabi?*" the pock-marked man asked Eugie.

"Only enough to buy tomatoes in the marketplace," Eugie responded.

"*Adesh bandura!*" she cried, in what sounded like a quarrelsome manner to Tess. The pock-marked man laughed and said, "You speak like a Khalili."

"The best Arabic there is!" Eugie said, smiling.

"No," said their kidnapper. "Iraq Arabic is best."

The pock-marked man laughed and said something to the other two men in the room, who smiled and nodded at him.

The kidnapper said something to David Fogel and indicated with his gun that he should sit against the wall opposite from where the other men had been sitting. Fogel did as he was told, breathing heavily.

"I am very sorry," the pock-marked man said to Eugie, "but I must tie your hands and your legs."

Eugie crossed her arms over her chest and looked put out. "And why is that?" she asked.

"Because we are not sure one hundred percent that you are not a settler. Someone is coming who knows you—or who knows a Eugie Yoder, if you are not she. I am hoping you are she," he said, with a winning smile.

"Is it Hussam?" she asked.

"You mean Hussam Tawil?" The pock-marked man snorted and rolled his eyes at their kidnapper, who, in turn, rolled his eyes.

"Hussam talks like a big Marxist. He talks about Che and all the other failed revolutionaries around the world. But never acts."

"Well that's not really fair, is it?" Eugie protested. He's been in jail, like five or six times. He was in Ansar III."

"He got soft when he was in England. And from all this talking about Gandhi and Martin Luther King. He used to believe in the armed struggle, but no more."

"Well he told me that when violent attacks became a part of the Intifada, the grassroots efforts broke down, because people flocked around charismatic leaders instead of taking ownership of the struggle."

The pock-marked man looked at her blankly for a moment and then nodded at the young man in the red t-shirt, who looked vaguely like one of the Mayan Indians Tess had met when she was traveling with Barney in Central America. He came forward with what looked like clothesline.

"Please, sit," he said to Eugie and nodded encouragingly toward the wall.

Eugie sighed, turned around, and presented her hands to the man in the t-shirt. He thanked her and tied her wrists, guided her with the lightest possible touch to the wall. As the young man tied her feet, she turned to Fogel, "How are you doing?" she asked.

"It would probably be better for you if you pretended you didn't know me. I can tell them that I don't know you," he said, face expressionless.

"I have a feeling it's all going to get sorted out," she told him. After a moment she added, "I know you may not believe me, but the only agenda we've ever had here is to help promote a solution that resulted in the fewest dead or exploited people. Your life is important to us, too."

"You should be thinking more about your own life," he said to her.

"It's over for me. I am a dead man."

"No, it's not over," Eugie said. "Not if I can help it."

"You people can never leave things well enough alone, can you?" he said with the faintest of smiles.

Tess, trying to make sense of the unfamiliar undercurrents in the exchange between Eugie and Fogel, was startled to feel a light touch on her arm. "Please, come," the young woman who had opened the door said. "I am Hanan. Come with me."

Tess followed her out of the room and down a long hallway. Hanan turned on the light and motioned Tess inside the room. It was a bathroom with a floor toilet. How had Hanan known? She closed and locked the door as Hanan's footsteps retreated. As she squatted down to relieve herself, she saw a hand held shower attachment hanging against the wall. Could it be possible, or was it only her wishful thinking?

She finished and poured water down the toilet from the jug below the spigot mounted on the wall about two feet above the floor. She walked over to the shower and caressed the long, heavy silver hose. A lump rose in her throat. Did she dare take one? Would they allow her to?

Someone knocked on the door. When Tess opened it, Hanan stood there offering her a towel with both of her hands. Tess felt tears sliding down her face. She wondered why people always thought of angels as blonde, because Hanan at that moment seemed the closest thing to an angel Tess had ever seen. The idle thought sent her reeling. Hanan looked anxious.

"Are you ill?" she asked.

"No, just very, very grateful," Tess said, taking the towel.

*    *    *

"Where are you taking Tess?" Eugie demanded. "And who are you, anyway? You know our names. It's only fair that you tell us your names."

"You do not need to know our names," the pock-marked man said. "It is better that you do not know our names."

There was a shrill tweeting sound. Even after two years, Eugie had never really gotten used to Palestinian doorbells. She flinched every time she heard one.

"Hanan," the man in the red t-shirt bellowed. Eugie smiled as she heard the soft scurrying of Hanan's slippers. Revolutionaries they might be, but they still needed women to do their menial tasks.

A moment later Hanan ushered three more men into the room.

"Fucking Shit!" the first one screamed in an American accent when he saw her and Fogel tied up against the wall. He had small eyes, sandy hair, and a weedy looking goatee. "You assholes!"

It took Eugie a minute to realize that he was not yelling at her, but at the other men in the room, who looked back at him with stony expressions. She felt a little sorry for them, which surprised her, given the circumstances. "Hanan!" the pock-marked man bellowed again. She called something in Arabic from down the hall. Insistently, he called her again.

When she appeared, she had an armful of ski masks. The American grabbed one and began waving it in the face of the pock marked guy, the t-shirted guy and their kidnapper. His Arabic was very bad, Eugie thought. He might as well have spoken English.

Hanan handed the remaining ski masks to one of the other men who had entered with the American, and left again.

There were now six men in the room, and Eugie tried to sort them for future reference, before they put their ski masks on. There was their kidnapper—the young man with side curls tucked behind his ears and a scraggly beard and moustache. If he was a Palestinian, he was a Palestinian who spoke perfect Hebrew, from what she could tell. If he was Israeli, he spoke perfect Arabic. There was the gaunt-looking pock-marked man, definitely a Khalili and the baby-faced man in the red T-shirt, definitely Palestinian . . . She looked again at their kidnapper and his side curls and then leaned over toward Fogel.

"The guy with the gun," she whispered, "is his Hebrew as good as I think it is?"

"He's Israeli," Fogel whispered back. "I'm guessing his parents are from Iraq."

She must have looked doubtful, because he continued, "I don't understand it any better than you do. Some of these guys are Jewish and some are Arab."

She looked at the other two, who had entered with the American. Both were clean-shaven and olive-skinned. The taller one wore a golden cross on a chain at his throat. He must be a Palestinian. The other had a shaven head, tiny wire-rimmed glasses, and a leather jacket. Probably Israeli, although he could be a Communist from Bir Zeit University.

All of the men had gathered in a knot at the far corner of the room, yelling at each other in a mixture of Arabic and Hebrew—with the occasional "fuck" thrown in.

Eugie remembered a Sunday School teacher telling her when she was seven years old that "Hallelujah" and "Amen" were the same in all languages. She thought for years that God had instituted them as key words—after the Tower of Babel fiasco—just to remind people that once they had shared a common language. It was not until she got into seminary (even the Biblical Social Work majors had to take Hebrew) that she realized they were both Hebrew words that missionaries had brought to other cultures along with the Bible.

She wondered if she should tell that Sunday School teacher from her home church in Pennsylvania that "fuck" was now nearly as universal as "Hallelujah."

There was a light tapping at the door, and the young woman entered with a silver tray and tiny, steaming coffee cups. Eugie counted—it appeared there was one cup for each of them. The smell of cardamom made her mouth water. A cup of hot Arabic coffee was exactly what she wanted.

The young woman threw a sideways glance at the knot of arguing young men and then crouched gracefully in front of Eugie and Fogel. She laid her right palm on her chest. "I am Hanan," she said.

Putting the tray on the ground, she tilted one of the cups to Eugie's lips. It was not scalding, so Eugie was able to finish it in three swallows—half the cup was filled with coffee grounds. She smiled and wondered whether she should ask Hanan to read her grounds. She thought of George, a Palestinian Christian friend in Bethlehem with a brother who had become an evangelical/ charismatic preacher. George would read the grounds in people's coffee cups like a fortune teller just to drive his brother crazy. ("This is from Satan," George's brother would mutter.) The funny thing was that George's readings were all the same. "You have traveled a long, long distance and you will meet a dark, handsome man." Didn't have to be psychic to see that that applied to all female internationals working in Israel and Palestine.

Hanan now crouched before David Fogel, eyes averted as she tipped the cup for him to drink. Eugie tried to imprint the image on her memory. If this whole thing blew up—became the disaster she suspected it would become—she wanted to have this memory of Hanan treating a settler with kindness.

The door opened and Tess appeared with wet hair. Another young man in a leather jacket and with a red and white keffiyeh around his neck had his arm around her shoulders. She had her arm around his waist and appeared to be giving him some support. His free arm gripped a black nylon backpack. Both were smiling.

That was odd, thought Eugie. She had realized by now the tendency of men to fall in love with Tess if they came within ten feet of her, but she wasn't sure that Tess should become involved with these guys, even if it was a strategy to keep them alive.

She looked more closely at the man. "Oh my God," she whispered.

Hanan shot her a look of concern. "You are ill?" she asked and then turned to see what Eugie was staring at.

"Eug!" Yossi said, letting go of Tess and striding over to where she sat. "You don't look so hot," he said. He frowned, "Did these assholes do something to you? I told them hands off you and Tess."

"No, I'm fine," Eugie said. "You just surprised me with the moustache and everything. Did you lose weight in the hospital?"

Yossi flung back his head and let loose the belly laugh that Eugie had loved so much.

"Poor old Eug! It's just like you to be obsessed with details like that at a time like this."

He took a small knife from the pocket of his jacket and moved behind Eugie to cut her bonds.

"Yossi, what the fuck are you doing?" the American with the scraggly beard demanded. The seven men turned and stared as Yossi continued sawing back and forth on the clothesline.

"Son of a bitch," Yossi said. "What are these cords made of, kryptonite?"

The Iraqi-Israeli who had kidnapped them said something in Hebrew to him.

"Sorry, Uri," Yossi replied. "My Hebrew's not so great; you'll have to use Arabic or English."

Uri switched to Arabic and Eugie understood enough to know that he was asking whether she was a settler.

"I TOLD him," Eugie began, but Yossi shushed her and answered him in Arabic.

"These assholes have fucked up the whole operation," the weedy American guy said. "They were supposed to grab the girls and kill the collaborator. Instead they let the collaborator go and brought us this big, fat fascist—" he motioned with his hand toward Fogel as though the words were too vile even to speak, "SETTLER back here instead."

Uri looked sullen. "I do not say I will kill. Only if I must. Sa'eed say to us the girls in Kiryat Arba. It was no need—" he finished the sentence in rapid-fire Arabic.

"Shut up, Adam," Yossi addressed the other American. "No one appointed you Führer. We operate on consensus, remember?"

Adam's face by now had turned a deep plum color. "A:," he said counting on his fingers, "I was put in charge of this operation, if you remember. B: These assholes have let your girlfriend and the other two see their faces. What do you suppose I bought all these ski masks for, my health? C: We wanted to send a clear message to all Khalilis who collaborate with the fucking settlers. D: Now that we have a settler on our hands, we're going to have every goon squad in the IDF at our doorstep. We could have killed the Arab without anyone caring. Kill this guy, and our asses are fried."

"If you kill him, you're going to have to kill me too," Eugie said, wishing there were a way she could say it without sounding theatrical.

"Shut up, Eugie," Yossi said wearily. "Look, Adam, Tess and Eugie are cool. They aren't going to tell the police anything."

Was that true? Eugie thought. Could she figure out a way of not telling the police the truth, without actually lying? In the end she always broke down at airport security when they kept hammering at her with questions. She thought it possible that grilling by the Shabak might be more intense. She envisioned the headlines in the American media, "Pro-Palestinian activist refuses to identify terrorists who kidnapped her," or something like that. She might be in jail a long, long time.

"We're not at the point where we have to kill anyone, yet," Yossi said. "What's your name?" he said, turning to David Fogel.

"Fogel. Are you a Jew?" the settler asked in wonderment.

"I'm a communist in theory and an anarchist in practice," Yossi said. "But you've guessed correctly on the gene pool."

Fogel said, "Look, Yossele. I've got seven children—four of them still living at home. If something happens to me, there will be no one to support them. My wife's health is bad; she can't work."

Uri called over something about Baruch Goldstein, and Adam expounded. "Yes, what about all the orphans that Baruch Goldstein left behind? What about Sabra and Shatila? What about Qana? You settlers all think your shit is worth a million fucking dollars while Arabs are worth less than three cents."

Fogel said, "I'm asking for my children, not myself. And I was as appalled by the massacre in Me'arat ha-Macpeleh and the slaughter in Lebanon as you are. I don't believe the children of Palestinians miss their parents any less than the children of Jews."

"What a load of bullshit," Adam began, and Yossi cut him off.

"You're worried about the guys not wearing ski masks, but you don't think shouting at a thousand decibels in English is going to attract attention?"

"Yossi, who are these people and what's going on?" Eugie asked.

Yossi stared at Fogel for a minute and then addressed the group,

"I'm going into the kitchen to explain what's what to the women," he said.

"Ismael, Uri—no one touches Fogel until I get back, *f'himtu*?" The pock-marked guy and the kidnapper nodded, and Eugie thought they looked relieved.

The thought crossed her mind that the whole interchange was reminiscent of most Israeli/Jewish/Palestinian dialogue groups of which she had been a part. It seemed that the Palestinians never talked in them.

Hanan walked with them to the kitchen and ushered them inside. She disappeared, and returned moments later with three white plastic chairs, stacked together. Yossi told her in Arabic that she was welcome to stay. Pressing her hand to her heart, she smiled, and left.

"First of all," Yossi said, "it's great to see you again." He threw his arms around Eugie and swayed with her a moment. He didn't get an erection. "I'm really pissed you didn't come see me in the hospital," he said, holding her away from him and giving her a broad smile that caused all the blood in her body to rush to her genitals.

He motioned to the chairs, and the three of them sat down. He moved his closer to Tess's and took her hand, caressing it as he spoke.

"Our group is called *'Adel*," he said. "That's 'justice' in Arabic," he said, turning to Tess. She nodded with a serious expression on her face.

"I met Shukri and Khader a couple years ago when I was studying Arabic at Bir Zeit," Yossi said.

Bingo, Eugie thought.

"Shukri met Uri when Uri was doing his army duty near Ramallah. He had been detained by a group of soldiers while he was driving to classes, and he and Uri had a long talk about Zionism, the occupation, blah blah blah. Uri's parents had come from Iraq in the fifties and his father had been part of the Black Panthers in the 60's."

"Black Panthers?" Eugie asked. "Not the ones in—"

"Duh. Of course not those Black Panthers," Yossi said. "But I think that's where they got the name. It was a group of Mizrahi Jews who rose up against the fascist Labor Zionist institutions because of the way they and their parents had been treated when they immigrated to Israel. Anyway, Shukri and Uri started meeting together in *al Quds* and bringing more friends each time. They decided that they had more in common as far as how they were treated by the establishment than they did different and that by joining forces they might be able to bring an end to the occupation and establish a bi-national state with equal rights for all. I met Adam in New York, and he began organizing some of our anti-Zionist, Trotskyite friends to become part of the coalition."

"But Yossi—the guns," Eugie began.

"Don't start on me with that pacifist bullshit, Eug," he said. "Arafat has become a collaborator by giving up the armed struggle before the settlements are evacuated. Hamas and Jihad want to set up a fascist Islamic state. People need an alternative."

"An alternative terrorist group? Geez, Yossi, this isn't like—you make it sound like setting up a new radio station or food co-op. People could get killed."

"We're not going to kill anyone who isn't actively promoting the occupation. No buses. No marketplace bombs."

"Yossi, you said yourself we're all a part of the occupation. The people in Peace Now benefit from the occupation even though they're against it. Our tax dollars make settlement expansion possible."

"Eug, I'm not going to get into pointless argument number 563 with you," Yossi said. "You just need to understand where we're coming from."

"Right, and when you don't want to keep arguing it's always you who gets the right of veto." Eugie felt tears coming. Yossi's eyes widened and he looked puzzled.

"Why didn't you tell me you were a part of this group when you asked me to come here?" Tess asked.

"For your protection, Tessie. The less you knew the better. I was going to get you set up with Yiphat and then, once we had our strategies in place, I would have introduced you to the rest of the people in 'Adel."

Tess stared at him, expressionless, for a moment and then said, "If I had known you were involved in this, I wouldn't have come."

Yossi looked as though she had slapped him. "But I thought— I explained the struggle, the urgency, and you never—"

Eugie stood up. "I'll leave you two alone," she said and walked out the door.

She ran into Hanan in the hallway. "Hanan," she said. "*Mumkin . . .*" Damn it, what was the Arabic word for shower. She knew it. "*Mumkin* shower?" she said, pointing down the hallway at the bathroom.

"Of course," Hanan said. "Wait one minute." In less than thirty seconds she reappeared with a towel and a silky blue robe embroidered with flowers and birds—the standard type of house dress that women wore if they were not planning on going out. She wondered why Hanan had not given Tess a robe.

"Welcome," Hanan said, gesturing toward the bathroom.

The toilet had a large, light brown stool floating in it. Eugie turned her back on it. Sometimes she thought that her biggest handicap in her RAPT career was her fear of feces. By the end of her last assignment in Haiti, she felt that she would break down in tears if she saw another pile of animal or human waste in the middle of a path. She knew that for the rest of the shower, that stool would be beckoning, calling her to look and become ever more deeply repulsed . . .

She stripped off her clothes and hung them on a hook. A sliver of white soap sat in a nook built into the wall. On the floor was a bottle of pearly green-blue shampoo called *Gleem-o*.

The water was tepid, but it felt wonderful. She forgot about the stool for a moment and watched the accumulated grime of the past few days course down her body in gray rivulets. She sucked in her stomach and clutched the bulge of fat on her abdomen. Yossi had told her that he loved her body, and that she should stop comparing herself to the anorexic models that pass for beautiful women these days. He had told her he thought she was beautiful, every part of her. But then he had fallen in love with someone who was slender and a whole lot better looking.

She lathered up her hair furiously, disgusted by her train of thought. Why couldn't she stop whining about the way the world worked? Why couldn't she just accept the fact that even if Yossi had never met Tess, he and Eugie would no longer be together because of their religious, philosophical, and a ton of other—ical reasons?

And why, given that she was now involved with an operation that could get a whole lot of people killed or imprisoned, was she obsessing over a failed relationship and a turd floating in a squat-toilet?

She rinsed her hair. It was going to be really hard to comb out the tangles that had accumulated since she was first grabbed—how long had it been since they had been with the rest of the team?

How could she stop someone from getting killed?

She had to go to the bathroom. She squatted and held her breath, banishing sternly thoughts of the stool jumping up to get her. When she poured a jug of water down, the stool refused to sink.

After toweling herself dry she turned her panties inside out and put them on along with her bra and the blue robe. She wadded her blue skirt and stinking blouse into a bundle, opened the bathroom door and threw them outside. She then grabbed the long-handled squeegee and pushed the water from her shower into the drain in the center of the floor.

She wandered into the kitchen, where Hanan was preparing platters of cucumbers and fruit. She looked up as Eugie entered and smiled uncertainly. "Welcome."

"*Shukran,*" Eugie responded. "*Kief halik?*"

"*Al humdullilah,*" Hanan said.

"So I take it you are not an atheist," Eugie said.

"I am sorry, I do not understand," said Hanan.

"You said *al humdullilah.* That means you believe in God."

She laughed. "Maybe, maybe not. It is just something we say instead of 'Very well, thank you.'"

"You are part of 'Adel, too?"

"I am here because of my brother Ismael," she said. "He sometimes does foolish things. Working with the Jewish. This is foolish."

Eugie sighed. The hardest part about working in Hebron was forming relationships with people who made broad generalizations about what "the Jewish" were like. She knew they meant soldiers and settlers, and when she mentioned all the American and Israeli Jews who fought the occupation, the inevitable response was, "Oh yes, there are many good Israelis. I used to work for an Israeli man. He was very good to us . . . . " But they continued to refer to "the Jewish."

"Do you think some of them may be Shabak?"

"Maybe." Hanan's large, dark, and thickly lashed eyes looked worried. Eugie realized that she was asking rather personal questions.

"I am sorry. I should not be asking you all these questions. You will think *I* am Shabak."

She laughed. "No, no. We know the RAPT people are good people. Some think you are a little crazy, but we do not think you are Shabak." After a pause, she said. "I saw on the TV when the soldiers carried you from the roof."

"Oh. Yes." Eugie never knew how to respond when people placed confidence in her because of small (and in that case futile) gestures that had caused her little discomfort.

A moving blue and white light passed over Hanan's face through the window as she put the finishing touches on a platter of fruit. She and Eugie looked at each other for a moment and then turned to run toward the stairs. As they passed the room where the men were still arguing, Hanan paused and said something in Arabic while Eugie continued up the stairs. On the top step, she tripped on the hem of her robe and caught the edge of the step hard on her knee. One of her sandals went flying down the stairwell. It felt as though her knee cap had popped off, but Eugie was able to keep her exclamation of pain down to a low grunt.

Hanan came up from behind her and helped Eugie to her feet. She was able to put weight on her injured knee. Crouching and limping, they made their way to the concrete parapet and cautiously looked over.

Three army jeeps stood in the street below. Soldiers had begun pounding on all the doors in the vicinity, shouting short Arabic phrases. In the time-honored response to night raids, the neighbors were pretending to be asleep or not at home.

Below, in the stairwell, all the lights went out. That was dumb, thought Eugie. It's sure to catch their attention.

It had. She and Hanan fled down the stairs and to the sitting room, where the arguing continued fiercely, but now in whispers.

"They saw you turn off the lights," Eugie said.

"SHIT," Adam said. "You fucking assholes! Do you want to get us all killed?"

"Adam, shut your fucking mouth," Yossi said in a low, reasonable voice. "What will get us killed is your losing your cool. We don't want another Nachshon Wachsman fiasco. Now, let's look at our options. We've got three Jews here, and two of us are Americans. We need to let the goons outside know that. We've also got Fogel, which I think they must already know or they wouldn't be here."

Ismael said something to Uri in Arabic. Eugie caught the words "Yaron" and "Shabak." The young man to whom Uri had handed the car keys was named Yaron? Could he have been a plant? It was likely. She would have to ask Yossi at another time.

By the light coming in from the outside (was it the moon or soldiers' high beam siege lights?), Eugie saw Uri shrug his shoulders and bite his upper lip. He turned away from the others and looked up at the ceiling. Was it a trick of the light, or were those tears on his face?

The baby-faced man in the red t-shirt walked over to Uri and put his hand on his shoulder. Uri turned and they embraced. Eugie felt like crying. Uri had trusted Yaron too much.

A voice from a loudspeaker shattered the whispered conversations. Was it speaking Arabic or Hebrew?

"I think they're trying to say that if we come out, no one will get hurt," Yossi whispered to her. "But it's really garbled."

Everyone in the room had frozen. In a quiet voice, Ismael said, "We must discuss together our options. Shukri, translate for Uri."

"We need to let the women leave the house," Ismael said. "We will send with them our manifesto demanding an immediate end to settlement expansion. We will tell them we are Jewish and Palestinian. We will tell them we have Fogel."

Eugie turned to see Fogel slump against the wall. She crouched beside him and patted his leg to reassure him. Then she remembered he was Orthodox and touching him probably violated his religious beliefs. She turned back to the huddle.

"We have guns," Uri said. "We must fight. I want—" he waved his hand, searching for a word, and then lapsed into Arabic.

"He says he wants to avenge his father for what the Mossad did in Iraq," Shukri translated.

"Yossi and I will fight, too," Adam said. "We've practiced— back in New York. We'll stand by you."

The Palestinians looked at each other. "It will go worse for all of us if we shoot. They may kill us all, but they will certainly kill US," Ismael said. "If we fight and they capture us alive, we will be tortured." There was a moment's pause. Ismael looked straight at Yossi. "But not you," he said.

"We will insist that they treat us the same way as they treat you," Adam said.

Shukri translated and everyone looked at the floor.

"No," said Yossi, straightening up. "We won't say anything. They probably know who we are anyway." The bull horn crackled again, more demanding this time.

"Quick," Yossi said. He unwrapped the red keffiyeh from around his neck and gave it to Adam, who wrapped it around his head. Uri then drew out a pocket knife and cut off his side curls. From his pocket, Yossi drew out a kipah and handed it to Ismael, who handed it to the baby-faced man in the red T-shirt, who was handing it to Shukri when Yossi said, "Oh put the fucking thing on already." The young man in the red T-shirt did so.

"I am very sorry, Mr. Fogel," Ismael said. "But we need your clothing."

From below, they heard something like a battering ram crashing against the door. Hanan jumped up and closed shutters over the window, making the room even darker.

"Come," she said to Eugie, "we must close all of them before they use gas."

She led Eugie into the kitchen and rummaged in a low cupboard, while Eugie fastened the metal shutters in that room. There was the sound of a match striking, and then the dim light of a gas lantern lit up the room. Hanan handed the lantern to Eugie who then followed her from room to room as she closed and fastened all the metal shutters in the house.

"There is nothing to close the roof." Hanan looked up at the open staircase and bit her lip.

The demands from the bullhorn had become more frequent and more insistent. When they reentered the room, all the young men sat without speaking in the corner. Against the opposite wall, Fogel sat in his underwear. The boy in the red T-shirt now wore Fogel's over-size white shirt. In the dim light of the lantern, Eugie could not tell who was wearing his pants.

"Please," said Fogel. "It is against my religion to have women look at me like this."

Eugie and Hanan turned their backs on Fogel, and Ismael said something in Arabic to his sister. She nodded and left the room.

Yossi, Adam, and Uri now had keffiyehs wrapped around their heads. Ismael was wearing a kipah. Shukri and the young man with a cross were the only ones without some sort of identifying clothing. Shukri might be okay with the wire rimmed glasses. She looked at the other young man thoughtfully.

"What is your name?" Eugie said, pointing at him.

"Khader."

"Would it be possible for you to dress like a woman?"

"No," he said.

"But you might be the one they shoot because—"

"Then I will die with honor," he said.

"So you're telling me women do not have honor?" she said, shaking her finger in his face.

"Eug, you're not helping," Yossi said. He reached over to Khader and said something in Arabic, patting him on the arm.

At that moment, Hanan appeared with a *jilbab* and *hijab* draped over one arm. Eugie started. Could Hanan read minds? Maybe she could persuade Khader to wear it.

Hanan, however, walked over to Fogel. With her head turned away, she presented the garments to Fogel.

"Welcome," she said.

Fogel took the garments from her and arranged them over his body like a blanket. "I can't wear these," he said. "The Torah specifically forbids Jewish men from wearing women's clothing. Don't you have a *jalabiya*?"

"My uncle is very small and my aunt is very big," Hanan said using her hands and arms to denote their relative girths. She then folded her arms across her chest and glared at him.

"You may be safer, Mr. Fogel," Eugie said, "if you put them on. The soldiers will be less likely to shoot a woman."

Adam snorted, "Right."

"And isn't there something in the Talmud about it being okay to break certain commandments to save a life—" Eugie continued.

A sharp cracking noise from outside interrupted. "Tear gas," Ismael said. He asked Hanan something in Arabic. She spoke a couple sentences and pointed toward the roof.

"We've closed all the shutters," Eugie explained for Adam and Fogel's benefit, "but the stairwell is open. If a canister lands on the roof and rolls down the stairs, we may be in trouble."

Ismael said something to Uri in Hebrew, and then to Yossi in Arabic. Yossi walked over to a backpack and pulled out a legal pad. He handed it to Uri, who felt around in his pocket for a pen. Adam fished one out of a pocket in his shirt and handed it to him. Uri then walked over to the lamp, sat down, and pulled it close to him as he began writing.

"Eugie, you and Tess and Hanan are going to leave us in a few minutes and give the letter that Uri is writing to whoever's in charge," Yossi said. "It says that none of you were involved with this, that we are a group of Palestinians and Israeli and

American Jews who came together to rescue you from the Kachniks. We will put our guns outside the door after we have received some assurance that we will be turned over to the civilian police instead of the military. We're going to say that we have Fogel and he will not be harmed, provided that we have these assurances. We want the military to agree to these conditions in writing, and we want to have the written message delivered by TIPH."

"I will stay," Hanan said, looking at Ismael. He barked something at her and pointed toward the door. She responded in even more cutting Arabic and folded her arms across her chest. Eugie caught that she was saying something about their parents—perhaps Hanan had promised them she would look out for Ismael? Or was she saying that she didn't want to be the one to have to explain to her parents why their son was dead?

"It's okay," Yossi said to Ismael in English. "Eugie and Tess can go."

"I think not!" Eugie said. "You idiots are in a pickle now, and the more women who stay in here, the better. I am not going to be standing outside watching them shoot you."

"Excuse me please," Ismael said. "But you must go. Reason number one: Someone must deliver this message to the soldiers. Reason number two: It would violate our customs if you were to stay, and that would be cultural imperialism on your part."

"Nice try," Eugie said. "But no dice. I'm staying. Tess can take the note out. They will be no less likely to shoot two people than one people. I mean," she said, realizing that didn't sound right.

"Enough," Ismael said. "You will go."

There was another gunshot, and a moment later they heard the sound of a metal object rolling on the roof. Eugie could taste as well as smell the acrid, peppery gas released, but apparently the canister had not come bumping down the stairs.

"There's no time," Eugie said. "Tess should go now." She ran over to the corner of the room and grabbed one of the white *hijabs* that she and Tess had worn when they got out of the car. Racing down the hall, she almost skidded across the floor—still wet from her recent shower—into the bathroom door. Reaching inside, she grabbed the long handled squeegee.

"Here you go," she said to Tess as she tied the scarf by one corner onto the handle. "They should be able to see this pretty well." Tess did not reach her hand out to take it as Eugie thrust it forward.

"Tessie, come on. We're counting on you." Eyes pleading, Yossi looked at her. "You'll be safer this way."

Slowly she reached out and took the squeegee handle. Her eyes would not meet Yossi's. Although goodness knows Tess has a right to be angry, thought Eugie, she still felt sorry for Yossi. She recognized his look of yearning. She felt sure that was how she had looked when Yossi and she had decided that, given all their differences, it would be better if they didn't pursue the relationship any farther.

"Come on, I'll walk you down." Yossi put his arm around Tess, who stood in the same posture, wooden and unmoving.

"No, Yossi," Ismael said. "You must stay here. It will be safer if Hanan takes her to the door." He said something in Arabic to Hanan who nodded. He then looked at her sadly and said something more, and she shook her head. Evidently, Ismael had given in.

Yossi embraced Tess, hard. She struggled at first to maintain her stance, but after a moment, lay her head on his shoulder and moved her arms around him. They broke the clinch when Hanan laid her hand on the gauzy sleeve of the settler dress that Fogel had provided for Tess earlier that evening.

Ismael called out several more instructions to Hanan, who nodded and then disappeared, her arm around Tess's waist.

Yossi stared at the entrance to the room as if he could still see Tess walking away. "And she disappeared," he murmured.

"What?" Eugie asked him.

He shook his head as if to clear it.

"Oh, when you said, 'I think not,' it reminded me of that joke you told me once about Descartes on the airplane. You know, the flight attendant asks if she can sit on his lap and he says, 'Young lady, I think not,' and he disappears."

He smiled at Eugie and she smiled back. Maybe, she thought, she could learn to like this man and stop loving him, after all.

The sound of stockinged feet on stairs. Metal and leather creaking. Automatic weapon fire.

"Down!" Uri shouted. Later, Eugie was to wonder whether he had indeed spoken the word in English or whether adrenaline had performed the translation for her.

Fogel shouted something in Hebrew, and one of the invaders responded with more weapons fire. Looking behind her from her prostrate position, Eugie saw the settler, who had put on Hanan's aunt's clothes after all, reel backwards from the shots. She wiggled her way over to him on her elbows, G.I. Joe style. Blood was spurting from his chest and right arm. Pulling the white scarf from his head, she wadded it up and applied it like a compress to his wound.

"They must have thought—" he gagged, and blood began trickling from his mouth. "They must think I am an Arab."

Behind her, the sound of men shouting in Hebrew and Arabic. She heard a sickening crunching sound at the same time that the lights went on, blinding her for a moment. A soldier stood over Shukri's motionless body and brought his gun butt down for a second time on his head.

"I'm an American, you fucking assholes," Adam was shouting at the two soldiers who had him pinned against a wall. One of them punched him in the stomach. Uri, Ismael, and the other Palestinians were lying face down on the ground, hands behind their heads as soldiers kicked them.

Yossi was swearing at the soldiers in Arabic. Two of them had him by the arms and a third was punching him in the face. He spit a tooth out as strong arms began pulling Eugie away from Fogel.

"No," she shrieked. "Someone must apply direct pressure to the wound, or he will die." Fogel murmured something in Hebrew as two sets of hands lifted her from the floor. Above her, someone was speaking Hebrew. A hand grasped her still damp hair and pulled her head back. The question was repeated in Arabic. She caught "yahuud,"—Jews.

"I don't speak Arabic or Hebrew very well," she said. "Someone needs to—she pointed in Fogel's direction and tried to look at him, but the grip in her hair was too tight.

The man wrenching her head back was tall and burly, with dark skin and grey eyes. He shouted at one of his men, who came over and began translating for him.

"He wants to know whether there are other Jews here."

"Please," Eugie said. "Someone needs to keep pressure on Fogel's wound, or he will bleed to death."

"A doctor is coming," the young soldier said. At least his voice sounded young. Eugie was still not able to move her head to get a look at him. "We need to know who the Jews are."

Her head and body were turned toward the wall against which Yossi now slumped, head lolling to the side and blood streaming from his mouth and nose.

"Is he a Jew?" the young man said.

Yossi raised his head, wincing with the effort, and looked at Eugie with the eye that had not swollen shut.

"Is he a Jew?!" the tall man holding her hair shrieked, giving her shake.

Yossi's olive skin looked grey in the fluorescent light. He moved his good eye toward the ceiling and made a nearly imperceptible kissing motion with his bloody lips—Middle Eastern shorthand for "No."

That slight effort seemed to use all the energy he had left and his legs gave out. The soldiers holding him by the arms staggered with his dead weight.

"Yes, he is Jewish," Eugie said, knowing with complete certainty that Yossi would never speak to her again.

# *Interim*

Part of an article from *The Black Panther* 11/9/72, a newspaper that represented the interests of Jewish immigrants from Arab countries.


. . . In Iraq, the Jews controlled many national institutions. Most of the banks and big shops were under Jewish ownership. Even the poorest Jews lived on a higher level than the average Iraqi. Their coming to Israel involved great sufferings. The absorption transit camps (Ma'abrot) of those days represented for them a drastic lowering of their standard of living. Most of their possessions were left behind in Iraq, and only very few of them succeeded to arrive with all their belongings. To immigrant children, the transition period in the country caused a long interruption in their studies, while the emphasis was being put on learning the language and acclimatising themselves to the new life . . .

The bitterness grew up, and then rulers of the country sent to the transit camps teams of teachers in order to instill the new immigrants with some Zionism. In spite of this, the mood didn't change and one of the most popular songs of these days speaks with the nostalgia about the old country:

> What did you do, Bengurion?
> You smuggled in all of us!
> Because of the past, we waived our citizenship
> And came to Israel.
> Would that we had come riding on a donkey and we
> Hadn't arrived here yet!
> Woe, what a black hour it was!
> To hell with the plane that brought us here!

This is a word-by-word translation of the song they used to sing, even at weddings and at any other kind of festive occasions. It remained popular throughout the fifties and then it disappeared. But one can hardly say that the nostalgia disappeared, too . . .

The many suspicions which accompanied the coming of the Iraqi Jews crystallized. One of the most splendid and rich communities was destroyed, its members were turned into indigents, most of its descendants were turned into undereducated people . . . .

A community that ruled over most of the resources of Iraq—which was the most developed of the states of the area—was turned into a ruled group, discriminated against and oppressed in every aspect. A community whose own ethics together with charity were its most important values was turned into a group caught between the wheels of the Ashkenazi culture, which is totally foreign to it. From a unified and cultural community, delinquents of every kind grew in Israel from amongst its midst. A community which used to produce splendid sons, could raise only "handicapped" sons in Israel.[1]

---

[1]　"The Iraqi Jews and Their Coming to Israel," in *Documents from Israel 1967-1973: Readings for a critique of Zionism.* Uri Davis and Norton Mezvinksy, eds. (London: Ithaca Press, 1975), pp. 132-33.

# CHAPTER 11

She spent the next week in jail with two Russian prostitutes and two Israeli low level drug dealers. Mindful of the time that Felicia was incarcerated with Sister Madeleine, who had kept narcking on their cell-mates, Eugie turned to the wall whenever she saw the pot come out. She even resisted joining in on the conversation when the Israelis and the Russians began arguing about trading land for peace with the Palestinians—in broken English, since the Russians knew little Hebrew and the Israelis knew no Russian. It surprised her how right-wing the dealers were. The Russians seemed to have picked up the prevailing propaganda that Arabs were inherently violent, but they thought a case could be made for throwing them some territorial bones in exchange for promises to never bother Jews again.

Later in the week, an Israeli Arab woman named Abeer joined the group and the argument. Eugie lay on her bunk and blew soft puffs of breath to create eddies in the clouds of cigarette fumes that hung in the air. When it came out that Eugie had been arrested in connection with the raid on 'Adel's bunker, Abeer deflected the anger of their cellmates by saying that 'Adel had almost no support among either Israeli or West Bank Palestinians.

"I told them in Hebrew that half of 'Adel are faggots," she confided to Eugie later as they were eating white bread and chocolate-spread in the cafeteria. Eugie thanked her, thinking that this was one of those things you didn't share with a church congregation during a slide show. She felt grateful to Abeer for taking her mind off Yossi for even a few seconds.

Eugie had annoyed Yiphat on the first day of her incarceration by refusing to sign a statement in Hebrew saying that she would not return to Hebron for three years.

"You've been arrested before," Yiphat told her as they sat in the room where clients met with their lawyers. "They're trying to make a case that you got Tess involved with this purposely and only pretended to be kidnapped."

"Have they talked to David Fogel?"

"He says that you tried to save his life, but he also said you obviously had met at least one of the people in 'Adel before."

"Yossi."

"Yes." Yiphat sighed.

"Are you representing Yossi, too?"

"No. I thought he should have a lawyer who could resist smacking him every other minute."

"How is he?"

"His face still looks pretty bad, but it's beginning to heal. He was still weak from the head trauma when he took off for Hebron—the doctor told him to stay in bed after he left the hospital—and the beating the soldiers gave him really set him back. Since he's an American citizen, the consulate is keeping on top of his case, making sure that he gets medical treatment and everything. The army says he had a gun."

"He didn't."

"You know that. I know that. Fogel and Tess both have testified he didn't have one. The IDF says he did."

"How is Mr. Fogel?"

"Stable condition. Had no problem talking with me, which was kind of surprising. He actually seemed sort of sane. I wonder what he's doing in Kiryat Arba?"

"And the others?"

"Well, as you might expect, they're in pretty deep shit. Uri's family got him a good lawyer. He tried to insist that the same lawyer represent all of them, but right now he doesn't have a lot of *wasta*. Khader's family want me to represent him, but I haven't been able to get in to see him yet."

"Hanan?"

"I haven't been able to find out where they put her. Her parents don't want to talk to me. I don't know about any of the others," she said, before Eugie had a chance to ask.

Eugie nodded. "Can you—can you tell Yossi I'm sorry. I thought they were going to kill him."

She saw from the expression on Yiphat's face that she was thinking of a way to downplay Yossi's fury.

"Well, also as you might expect, he's pretty pissed off at you." She took out a pack of cigarettes and lit one. "However," she said. "I want to—I'm really grateful for what you did. My brother can be totally clueless, but I'd like to have him around for a few more years."

Eugie could not stop the tears from coming. She wiped at her eyes with the palm of her hand. Yiphat rummaged around in her purse and handed her a tissue.

"You know," she said, after she took a drag on her cigarette. "Sometimes I think that only people who have had their hearts broken understand what it is like to live or work over here. You fight so long and so hard, thinking that if you just care enough, people will change, that you'll be able to convince people about the right thing to do. But your heart just keeps getting broken over and over again."

"And," Yiphat said, blowing a stream of smoke toward the ceiling, "maybe we stay because we know you can survive a broken heart."

Yiphat had brought her some back copies of *Harpers* and *Tikkun*. Normally a fast reader, Eugie pored over the magazines to make them last. Her mind was so taken up by Yossi, however, that she needed to reread most of the articles anyway.

Why was it that she kept losing him? She had seen herself losing him when he had lost patience with her religion, her efforts to maintain team cohesiveness, her reminders that settlers and soldiers were children of God too.

She had lost him again when they finally signed the death certificate of their relationship, making all sorts of mature comments about how it was for the best, that neither was at fault, that it was a case of rebound, that it was a case of cultural differences, that they would always be friends.

She had lost him when he returned to the United States and never e-mailed her from home.

She had lost him when he returned, engaged to Tess, and Yiphat had asked, "Didn't you and he have some sort of thing going for a while there?" and she denied it.

She had lost him when he greeted her cheerfully on the phone, asking why the fuck hadn't she come visit—oblivious to the fact that the thought of seeing him was like a knife in her guts.

She had lost him when he walked into the room smiling, with his arm around Tess, delighted to see her.

And she had lost him for good when she told the soldiers he was Jewish so they would stop beating him.

Each time, she had thought that this was it, that she would never have to face the pain of losing him again. And each time she was wrong.

Why was it that she got over old romances only when new romances came along? Here she was at thirty-five, still hoping. It didn't seem right somehow. She knew that God ought to be enough for her, and she wondered why He wasn't.

Maybe she was like an alcoholic. She should just accept the fact that she couldn't handle romantic relationships in constructive ways, and renounce them all together. It would at least stop her from losing the men she loved, again and again. There were so many other people in the world who needed her love and would be glad to have it.

She didn't realize she was weeping until she turned her head on the little pillow and felt an unfamiliar dampness beneath her cheek. Her cellmates ignored her tears, for which she was grateful. After having had one too many classmates point at her and say, "Waterworks, waterworks," in elementary school, she had learned to cry without being noticed. If her cellmates did notice, she could always blame it on allergies.


A judge released her after one week, when no one from the military showed up for her hearing. Yiphat told her that the Shabak had rounded up some Oz v'Oz people, who had confessed to the kidnapping under light torture. (The police had found her waistpack in their possession.) The government was going to deport John, the Christian Zionist, whose real name was Earl. They had not been able to find the South African.

The day before Eugie's release, Yiphat ran over some pithy statements Eugie could quote to the media to draw attention to prisoners living under administrative detention, to the ongoing confiscation of Palestinian land for settlement expansion, to the danger posed by the Israeli religious right and their Christian allies.

But after she had retrieved her waistpack and walked out into the bright light, she saw no one waiting for her besides Yiphat, who was speaking into her cellphone.

"The schoolteachers have just announced another strike," Yiphat said, closing her cellphone and shaking her head. "So *Ha'aretz* isn't sending anyone. I just don't get it. You're an American and the embassy lodged an official complaint on your behalf. Your RAPTor friends in the States sent a gazillion faxes to your congressional rep, but no one here seems interested."

"Well, the *Intercourse News* will probably print something," Eugie said. "It's my hometown paper," she added when she saw Yiphat's blank look.

"Whatever. You guys should really try to see if you can work the national and international media more, though."

"Oh don't worry, we're shamelessly self-promoting," Eugie said. "But it's like the whole leading-the-horse-to-water thing."

"I'll be down in about a week," Yiphat said. She gave Eugie a brief hug. "Take some time off, okay? You don't look so hot."

"Must be all the chocolate spread," Eugie said. "I've had a whole week's worth of rest."

"Yeah, well, bye."

Eugie walked down Jaffa Road and turned at Notre Dame. She thought of splurging on a dessert and cappucino at *Bint il Bilaad* in the Old City, but decided she'd rather get home. People would be anxious to see her. She reminded herself to be grateful for that. Yiphat had told her in the courtroom that there had been a problem at the Qurtuba girl's school in Hebron, so the team hadn't been able to send someone up for the hearing.

She walked past the taxis at Damascus Gate and bought some *ka'k*—a two-foot-long ring of chewy sesame bread that one could not buy in Hebron. She told the vendor she didn't want the salt and thyme in a twist of newspaper that came with each purchase. She remembered Yossi's telling the story of a friend from Bir Zeit who talked about how much she loved *kike*. "You talking about me?" Yossi had asked. As he recounted the story to Eugie he said, "You should have seen how red her face turned."

Eugie made a point of over-gutturalizing the *ayin* in *ka'k* after that. She smiled as she thought of all the Arabic lessons Yossi had given her. The sessions had always ended up with them in a clinch, furiously making out. She felt bad about that afterward, because she knew that was what their conservative Muslim neighbors assumed that Americans did whenever they had privacy and she hadn't wanted them to be proven right.

After she picked up a *Jerusalem Post* at the newsstand, she walked over to the white mini-vans that went directly from Jerusalem to Hebron. A tall, bald man cried out, "*Al Khalil, al Khalil, al Khalil, al Khalil,*" as he fingered a loop of black prayer beads. She called, "*Al Khalil*" to him, and he directed her to one of the vans in the parking lot. Two young men sat in the back of the van, so she sat in the first row of seats behind the driver. It was difficult to tell sometimes, whether men were touching her to get their jollies or whether they were squeezed in so tightly next to her they couldn't help it. She smiled when an older woman climbed in, and motioned to the seat next to her.

The old woman returned her smile. She was wore a black polyester doubleknit dress, with yellow embroidery that indicated she was from the village of Samua'. Eugie had heard that village women had to wear the dresses they received on their wedding day for the rest of their lives, and that polyester doubleknit probably had a half-life of 500 years, but she shuddered when she saw women in those black dresses in the heat of summer—especially since she knew they were often wearing another complete outfit underneath. Maybe the gauzy white head scarves helped deflect some of the heat.

Eugie offered the woman some sesame bread. She smiled and bobbed her head and twisted a piece off with some difficulty. She then reached inside her black dress, through the neckline, and pulled out what looked like a piece of tile grout. Her gestures indicated that Eugie was supposed to put it in her mouth. It tasted of cloves and had the texture of silly putty. Thanking the woman, she then wondered whether people would think she was a settler if she opened her *Jerusalem Post*.

It took another ten minutes for the van to fill up, and then they were off. Rush hour traffic had begun, and the two blocks to Notre Dame, where the van turned south toward Hebron, took ten minutes more.

The old woman got off at Al 'Arub refugee camp, and a young mother with a baby on her lap left her seat beside a teenage boy and moved next to Eugie. Eugie offered her some sesame bread and she answered "*Shukran*," meaning, "No thank you."

By the time the taxi van arrived in Baab iZawiye, the commercial district of Hebron, people in the market had begun to pack up their wares for the day. Israeli soldiers called to her from the Dubboya St. checkpoint one block up, and she increased her pace into the market, knowing that they wanted to tell her that she faced imminent death by entering there.

Vendors returned her greetings and invited her into the shops they were closing. The two restaurants with identical chicken-roasting spits side by side were still open. The team could never remember which restaurant they had patronized last, and Eugie wondered whether either of the owners ever got upset when he saw the team taking visitors into the other restaurant.

She paused for a moment at a shop where the proprietor was using a long hook to take down the dresses and head scarves hanging from a green awning. Wistfully, she looked at the hair clasps in the window. She especially liked one made up of a black velvet bow and black nylon mesh tubes with little golden balls inside. Ahlam, their upstairs neighbor, had one, and Eugie enjoyed watching the balls race through the tubing when she moved her head. The price in shekels was about two dollars—approximately the daily wage of a Haitian woman in one of the Disney sweatshops, she reminded herself.

But she had lots of black clothes, too, she thought, and it would go with everything and the barrette would keep her hair looking nice with almost no effort on her part.

The shopkeeper gestured that she could come inside and take a closer look and she said, "*mar'a tani*," "another time"—one of the most useful phrases in Arabic she had learned. Their first months in Hebron it felt as though the team had drunk about a gallon of tea a day because they hadn't known how to refuse hospitality with grace.

As she approached the back of Beit Hadassah, she walked closer to the building to avoid bottles and other objects that settler kids threw down at passersby. A group of Palestinian boys glared at her, arms crossed, as she approached them. She greeted them in Arabic, and they relaxed. She had learned to be proactive with boys that age, so she wouldn't get stones thrown at her back. The *keffiyeh* that she had used to tie on her backpack had helped, but she had stopped wearing it since the attack on Dubboya St. When she knew she would be walking in Palestinian areas, she had started wearing pants, so the residents wouldn't mistake her for a settler.

"Hey you!" a soldier called from on high. She looked up at the roof-top checkpoint across from Beit Hadassah.

"Hey yourself," she said. "Where are you from?"

"Portland, Oregon, originally."

"I have a cousin in Beaverton," she said.

"Hey! I'm actually from Beaverton," the soldier said, "but I tell people Portland because more people have heard of that."

Eugie turned to go.

"Where are you going?" the soldier asked.

"We live in the market—you know where the chickens are?"

"Shit!" the soldier said. "Aren't you afraid?"

"I'm more afraid of walking by Beit Hadassah."

The soldier laughed. "That's cool," he said. "See you around."

"Yeah, see you."

As she emerged from the section of the market covered with tarps into the open area near Beit Romano, where the construction crane remained poised, dangling a huge cement block for all eternity, another soldier called from a rooftop checkpoint.

"Wait! Wait!" he called, when she ignored his shouting, ostensibly because she didn't speak Hebrew. She hurried into the next stretch of the market. Here the only place still open was the sweetshop.

She looked at the piles of baklava and fried pastry of every kind. She had had better baklava in Philadelphia than she could find in Hebron. The teenage boy in charge called out, "Good day, Eugie! How are you?"

"Very well, thank you." Another phrase the team had learned early on in the Hebron project, after the response "fine" was met with blank stares.

"Welcome," the boy said and held out a long spoon. She took the fried ball soaked in syrup and put it in her mouth.

"*Yisalaamu idek*," she said. The dough ball was unbearably sweet but at least it was small.

She had never thought she would be homesick for the smell of chickens, but now the familiar stench told her she was almost home. The chicken vendors were letting down their awnings and closing the metal doors to their shops and greeting her as she passed. Soldiers called out to her from the checkpoint as she entered the yellow metal door with the large black diamonds painted on it. She pretended not to hear them.

"Hi," she said, after she opened the door to the apartment. Bruce and Hussam jumped up from their chairs. Bruce embraced her, pulling her up off her feet. After he put her down, Hussam kissed her on both cheeks; then Frank and Felicia approached to hug her.

"So Yiphat told you why we didn't come up?" Felicia asked.

Seeing Felica reminded Eugie. "Sa'eed—you were right about him," she said.

"Yeah, well," Felicia said. She shrugged, and Eugie knew that the anticipated "I told you so" would not be coming.

"It's not bloody likely he will show his face in Hebron in the near future," Hussam said. "As a matter of fact, if he's at all intelligent, which I highly doubt, he has made his way into Israel proper by this time."

"Or Israel improper," Eugie said.

"Yes. That's very good. Israel improper," Hussam laughed.

"Tess is upstairs. We need to talk about Qurtuba school," Felicia said, heading out the door. She then took one step backwards and smiled at Eugie. "Welcome home," she said.

*    *    *

Tess had a headache. She had had it ever since the soldiers had grabbed her coming out of the house with the letter and the white scarf tied to the squeegee. They had wrested it from her grip so violently that she had gotten a splinter and twisted her wrist.

At first she thought they were going to beat her up. She had never been manhandled in that way before, but she realized after a moment that they were anxious to get her away from the house. It took her a while to get the soldiers to look at her note.

"There are Jews in there?" the man who seemed to be an officer asked her, an incredulous expression on his face. He shouted something toward the house, and for the first time, Tess saw soldiers climbing up a rope ladder onto the roof. They all had guns. One of them—just about to climb up—turned when the officer called and came running over in stocking feet. The officer handed him the note and continued talking while the soldier read and nodded.

When Tess heard the shooting begin, she said, "I only saw one little hand gun in there. You don't need—"

They ignored her and hustled her into the back of a jeep. As they drove her to the police station, she tried to tell them that Yossi and Eugie were in there and that she didn't think Ismael and all the rest of them were planning on fighting. She thought about Hanan offering her the towel. She remembered Yossi's face when he had seen how angry she was. She thought Eugie might do something stupid like running in front of someone else and taking the bullet for them. And no one would listen to her in the jeep or in the police station where she sat for the next couple hours.

The days that followed passed in a blur. The police in Jerusalem asked Tess the same questions hour after hour and her answers never seemed to satisfy them. Yiphat took her back to her miniscule apartment and then demanded that she remember the exact wording of the questions the police had asked—particularly as they related to Yossi.

While Yiphat had screaming, tearful phone conversations with her mother, who evidently held Yiphat to blame for her brother having turned out badly, Tess had tried to sleep on the couch.

She was actually glad to return to Hebron—squat toilets, cold showers and all—although she was disappointed that Eugie hadn't been able to come with her. Yiphat was angry about Eugie refusing to sign something in Hebrew.

"She could say she wasn't going to go back to Hebron and then just go," Yiphat said. "I mean she only has two weeks left in the country, so it's not like getting deported would be a huge big deal. This integrity thing she has can really get on your nerves."

Frank had come up to Jerusalem to meet her and bring her home. For the next couple days he treated her as though she were a piece of china—and for the first time in her life, she realized she needed this sort of attention at this moment, and was grateful for it, rather than assuming she was entitled to it.

Frank's treatment of Tess annoyed Felicia, who had made it clear several times that Eugie was the one who needed sympathy, and Tess should be grateful she wasn't stuck in jail. When Felicia appeared at the door, Tess adjusted the wet washcloth on her forehead, pulling it over her eyes as she lay on her mat.

"Eugie's back. We need to meet."

Tess sat up. She realized that she was every bit as glad to hear that Eugie was back as she would have been to hear that Yossi was back. As a matter of fact, she was still angry with Yossi and had pretty much decided that she would go with Frank, so she might be even more glad to see Eugie than Yossi. She had never felt this way about another woman, perhaps with the exception of her mother.

After swallowing another couple of Tylenol, she went downstairs. Eugie was telling people about her prison experience. Even at a distance of ten feet she smelled of stale cigarette smoke and unwashed clothing.

"Great! We're all here," Bruce said. "Break out the Cremisan altar wine."

"You got altar wine for me!" Eugie looked delighted.

"Yup. Fresh from Freij's grocery at Damascus Gate. I got it after we brought up that change of clothing for you on Tuesday."

"Oh my goodness, did I appreciate that!" Eugie said. "The clothes I was wearing pretty much were able to stand up by themselves. Thanks for making the special trip. Yiphat was supposed to tell you that I had decided to give you my firstborn child."

"Didn't," said Bruce. "But she was preoccupied. And I have kids anyway, so go ahead and keep your firstborn."

"Thanks, Bruce!" Eugie beamed at him.

"Maybe we could give Eugie a chance to wash up and change her clothes before we start the meeting," Tess said.

Eugie looked as though Tess had just handed her an expensive gift.

"Oh that would be so great," she said, looking at the rest of the group for affirmation. "I had a shower this morning, but I didn't have any shampoo, and I've been around five chain-smokers for the last week."

"Go ahead," Bruce said. "We'll wait."

"But make it snappy," Felicia said. "We've got a lot to talk about."

Tess wanted to follow Eugie upstairs, but decided it would look strange. Since it was her turn to cook tonight, she went into the kitchen and picked out a huge head of cauliflower. She brought it back to the kitchen table and began dissecting it into individual florets. Felicia and Hussam went into the office and seemed to be holding an urgent conversation. Bruce started mopping the kitchen floor. Frank sat at the table with her and helped her break up the cauliflower. He was really a very helpful person. She smiled at him and he blushed.

Tess had not finished with the cauliflower when Eugie reappeared, her long hair hanging lank and wet. She was wearing the brown t-shirt over the brown pants that made her look so shapeless. Tess shook her head sadly. If only Eugie would listen to her. Tess felt sure that she could do a makeover on her that would make her look stunning.

"Okay, peeps," Eugie announced as she walked in. "Meet away!"

The team reassembled. Bruce pulled the cork out of the bottle of wine with the corkscrew on Felicia's pocket knife.

Hussam took a glass along with the rest of them. "Hussam!" Eugie laughed. "*Haram!*"

Hussam raised his glass. "I never claimed to be a GOOD Muslim."

"You know," Eugie said, "I find it interesting that we drink way more on assignment, surrounded by neighbors who think drinking alcohol is a mortal sin, than we do at home."

"Well," Bruce said. "At home we're surrounded by people who think drinking alcohol is a mortal sin, too."

"Maybe you are," Felicia said. "My family has no problem with it."

"Mine neither," said Frank, "But then, we're Lutherans."

"A toast to all Lutherans and the good work they do." Eugie held her glass up and they all clinked.

"And a toast to the Muslim Peacemaker Team and all the good work they do," Hussam said.

"Muslim Peacemaker Team?" Eugie said.

"So far, I am the only member, but I am recruiting," Hussam said.

Tess wrinkled her nose. "This is very sweet," she said.

"The more it tastes like something you pour over ice cream the better, as far as I'm concerned," Eugie said.

Tess found the idea a little nauseating and decided not to drink the rest of her wine.

"So," Eugie said, draining her glass. "What's up with Qurtuba School?"

Bruce and Felicia began talking at the same time, stopped and deferred to each other, and then both began talking again.

"Felicia," Eugie said. "You first."

"Two days ago," Felicia began, "was the first day of school. And since education has been turned over to the Palestinian Authority, Qurtuba raised a Palestinian flag over the school and the girls sang, 'Biladi.' Settlers from Beit Hadassah charged the school and ripped the flag down. They burned it and began to throw rocks and bottles at the teachers and the students. It's been a little difficult to get a clear idea of what happened next. An ambulance came and some of the girls had cuts and bruises treated, but it seems like several of them fainted."

"After years of little settler boys threatening to slash their throats, maybe they thought the time had finally come," Eugie said.

"Maybe," Felicia said. "But anyway, for the last two mornings we've been walking with the girls past Beit Hadassah and sitting in the schoolyard. This morning, the school had Stars of David spray-painted all over, and there was a huge load of trash and dirty diapers in front of the school door. Someone had also tried to seal it shut with rubber cement. The police didn't appear to be very interested in investigating. I pulled a letter addressed to someone in Hebrew out of the pile of trash, but the police said that just because it was in the pile of trash doesn't mean that it belonged to the person responsible for throwing the trash in front of the door."

"So," Eugie said, "how long can we keep this up?"

"Well," Bruce said. "The police insisted we leave this morning, and we did when the head mistress asked us to, too. Settlers tried to climb the stairs up to the school, and the police kept stopping them, so we figured the girls were probably reasonably safe."

"Even with the curses," Felicia said.

"Curses?" Eugie raised her eyebrows.

"Oh, there were a couple teenage settler girls praying—what do they call it? Davening?" Bruce said.

"They were swaying back and forth, and Hussam told us they were putting curses on the girls and teachers in the school."

"They kept referring to the little girls as Amalekites," Hussam said. "If I were you people, I would jolly well consider editing your Bibles a bit more carefully."

"But that's not our problem," Bruce said. "The problem is that we're essentially defending the right of the girls and the school to raise a flag, and there are some theological problems with that."

"Or ideological," Hussam said.

Tess sighed. She knew that this conversation could very well go on for another hour.

It did. Bruce and Eugie kept bringing up something called the Kingdom of God and primary allegiance. Frank and Felicia kept pointing out that since the settlers had practically carpeted the rooftops of their buildings with Israeli flags, it was only fair that Qurtuba School be allowed to raise a Palestinian flag. Hussam said he had had friends arrested for having a Palestinian flag in their homes, so there was a matter of principle involved, even though he agreed that nationalism tended to bring out people's baser instincts.

"Sister Madeleine had a suggestion," Frank said at one point. "She talked to the settlers, who said the Palestinian flag represented terrorism to them. After they had talked some more, she brought a proposal to some of the people at the school. Get this: She said the settlers would feel okay about there being a Palestinian flag on the roof of the school if they raised an Israeli flag, too."

"Oh no, she didn't," Eugie said.

"Oh yes she did," Hussam said. "It was a good thing she doesn't understand Arabic, because some of the parents who had walked their children to school were calling her some rather nasty names."

"I don't blame them," Felicia said. "I wish there were some way of telling her that she really botches things up."

"She wouldn't believe you," Eugie said. "She has complete confidence in herself. I wish I could feel that way sometimes," she sighed.

"Well, you'd be a lot less popular if you did," Felica said. Eugie smiled. "I'm popular?"

"Don't let it go to your head," Felicia said.

The headmistress of the school asked them to stop coming every morning, because it attracted the attention of the settlers. Tess reflected that this outcome seemed to be the result of most of their long discussions—something always came along that rendered all the effort they had put into decision-making pointless. Frank told her that that didn't happen one hundred percent of the time and that it was better to be overprepared than underprepared.

What took up their time for the next three days were the clashes. To protest what had happened at Qurtuba School, Palestinian boys—mostly teenage and younger—threw stones and bottles at the soldiers at the Dubboya St. Checkpoint. The broad road leading from Baab iZawiye to the checkpoint provided a natural theatre for this activity. The boys would taunt the soldiers and throw their rocks and bottles. Waiting for the word from their commanding officer to advance, the soldiers would smack their batons against their hands. When they finally did charge, they would grab young men at random from the throng and drag them away.

Tess noticed that the young men who instigated most of the activity never got caught by the soldiers. Once she saw them grab a boy who looked to be about 10 years of age and had his arms full of groceries, so he couldn't have been throwing things. Felicia and Eugie tried to intervene, telling the soldiers that the boy had been passing through, that his home was in the market, and this was the only way he could get to it. But the soldiers pushed them aside.

Tess walked with Frank on night patrol the first night of the clashes. Bits of broken glass on the asphalt gleamed like a sky full of stars. Frank asked the soldiers, "Been busy today?" The soldiers smiled. One of them waved his hand to encompass all the glass on the ground and said, "They are all animals."

The team discussed ways to intervene—including lobbing balloons and blowing soap bubbles into the crowd. Eugie told Tess that they weren't doing the obvious—interposing themselves between the boys and the soldiers—because they had tried it before and it hadn't worked. Tess hadn't thought that option was at all obvious. In fact, it had seemed like a thing one should obviously NOT do, but she just nodded as though Eugie were making a good point.

As in the case with the Qurtuba School discussion, by the time the team had arrived at a decision, it was rendered moot. On the third day of the clashes, vendors in the area and other older men intervened when boys began throwing stones and bottles. They had lost too much business over the last three days.

Yiphat called to tell Tess that her mother was flying over again to see if she could pull some strings to get Yossi out of jail, and that she should therefore stay away from Jerusalem for a while. When the call came in, Frank was with her and he asked her to come up to the roof with him afterward for a talk. It seemed that most emotionally taxing communications between team members happened on the roof, and Tess hesitated when he asked.

"Please, Tess," Frank said in a low voice, looking over his shoulder at Bruce, who was clattering away at the computer in the office.

She decided that he was probably entitled and followed him upstairs. Their upstairs neighbor, Umm Rishad, was hanging laundry, Tess noted with relief. Frank wouldn't be able to get too personal.

"I need to know," Frank said. "I've been going crazy for the last month thinking about you and Yossi being engaged. Is your engagement for real? You don't act like it."

"What do you mean?"

"I mean, the way you've been with me, you don't act like you're engaged," Frank said.

"Are you accusing me of coming on to you?" Tess raised her eyebrows.

"No, no. I mean, well—yes. You act like you really like me, but then you get these phone calls, and you were up in Jerusalem forever with Yossi, and I mean, he did try to rescue you and everything—"

He ran his fingers through his sandy hair. "I'm sorry. I don't know what I'm saying."

Tess smiled. Apologies were always a good sign. They gave her room to maneuver.

"Frank, as you can tell, I'm torn. I'm really angry with Yossi that he brought me here without telling me he was involved with—that group of guys with guns. However, it would look kind of bad now if I dropped him while he was in jail, right? I'm trying to think of the best way I can break up with him, and I just don't know yet how. But you will be the first person I tell when I do."

Frank slouched against the roof's parapet wall. "I see your point," he said. "But I'm finding it's too much for me to be around you and keep hoping that you'll make up your mind to choose me. If it looks like I'm avoiding you, that's why, okay?"

Tess looked over at Umm Rishad, who was watching them without smiling as she hung out her laundry. A kiss and an embrace were not an option. She knew that Umm Rishad would never let either of her two older daughters come up on the roof with a man.

She looked down at two of the chicken vendors arguing. The older man with salt-and-pepper hair had blood on his hands from butchering chickens or rabbits. The younger man was waving his cigarette at him. Israeli soldiers were pointing and laughing at the two. The old man who sold sunflower seeds and candy noticed and came up to the men and motioned with his head that they should come inside his shop if they were going to continue the argument. Both of them looked toward the soldiers, hung their heads, and shuffled away in opposite directions.

Frank often brought sunflower seeds from that shop owner. Tess thought they must be covered with dust from the chickens and the chicken manure. Frank would pop a handful in his mouth, storing them in one cheek like a chipmunk, and shell them with his teeth, spitting the shells out on the ground. Tess had been meaning to bring up the inherent distastefulness of this activity, but she decided now was not the time.

"I understand," she told Frank.

Following him downstairs, she summoned up the effort not to frown, so as to avoid wrinkles. She really was going to have to think of a way to break up with Yossi, because she could no longer count on Frank as a back-up. Over all, had someone put a gun to her head and demanded that she choose, she thought she would probably choose Frank anyway, given all the unpleasantness Yossi had put her through.

But how to gracefully break up with Yossi, who might at this very moment be undergoing torture by the secret police, or so Yiphat had said? Eugie told her it was not likely that they would treat Yossi as badly as they would treat a Palestinian, but Eugie herself had described Yossi's bloody face to her, and the swollen eye. Tess shuddered. Yossi was so handsome; how could they have done something so disfiguring?

Eugie. She had broken up with Yossi before. Maybe she could tell Tess the best way to go about it. She found she missed the long talks that she and Eugie had had in the tunnel. Sometimes she found herself going into Eugie's room just to hear her start up a conversation. Eugie had made her realize that some people never stopped thinking. Now, sometimes when she walked the streets of Hebron, she looked around at the men, women, and children and wondered whether they too were thinking about issues and theology and other people the way that Eugie did.

"Hi, Tess." Eugie was pulling clothes out of her laundry bag and sniffing them. "I'm trying to decide what I need to wash and what I can last for ten days without. I like to go home with a suitcase full of dirty laundry so I can just pitch it all in the washer. I thought maybe I could get by without washing any more of my short-sleeve shirts, but it was pretty warm yesterday."

"You're leaving in ten days?"

"Yup. Pete and Wendy will be coming to take my place. I worked with them in Haiti. You'll like them. Everybody likes them—that is, if you're staying."

"For a little while longer."

"Good. I'll tell the Minneapolis office that you've been a real asset to the team here."

"I have a question," Tess said.

"Shoot," Eugie said.

"How did you break up with Yossi?"

Eugie lowered the blouse she was sniffing and let out a puff of air, extending her lips. She then inhaled deeply.

"Mind if we talk while I wash my clothes?"

Without waiting for an answer, Eugie carried an armload of clothing into the room that had once been a kitchen, but now served as a laundry room for the women.

Tess watched as Eugie filled a plastic bucket with cold water and then dunked her beige pants in it. She reached inside a plastic bag, took out a pinch of laundry detergent and began rubbing it into the crotch.

"That detergent is really bad for your hands," Tess said.

Eugie raised her hands, red from the cold water and looked at them critically. "You're probably right," she said. "I'll be sure to put some lotion on after I finish my laundry."

"I can lend you my rubber gloves."

"No, that's okay. I only have a few things to wash."

Careless, careless Eugie, Tess thought with fondness. Some things were just more important to her than taking care of her skin.

"So me and Yossi—" Eugie frowned at black marks on her pants' hem. She rubbed in more detergent, took a toothbrush out of a glass jar, and began scrubbing away at the stains.

"Well, you know that he and I met in Chicago, and he got really excited about the work that RAPT was doing in Hebron, and I persuaded our director to let him work with the team, even though he hadn't had training and even though he wasn't a Christian. And you know, he was really useful to have around. He knew enough Arabic to get by, and it was really good for a lot of the young men here to meet someone who was Jewish, but still cared about their human rights; who would even get arrested for them. He helped some teenagers that the military had detained escape once by standing in the way of the soldiers who were chasing them, and he got arrested for that—well, detained, anyway. A lot of the older people around here used to work in

Israel or used to meet Israelis when they were still allowed to travel to Jerusalem, but the young people, the ones under thirty—some of them have never met an Israeli or even a Jew who wasn't a soldier or a settler."

Good old Eugie, Tess thought. Always changing the subject. But she had learned that, given enough time, Eugie always came around full circle.

"So anyway, we had what I guess you'd call a fling, and I kind of lost perspective. You know that my primary allegiance has always been to Jesus, but I really do think that God loves all people equally, and I thought—well I thought Yossi would come to see that not all Christians are dogmatic about doctrine or intent on sending everyone to hell. And he said it didn't matter that I believed in God. And well, in the end it did—not so much because of the God part, but because the logical extension of God is that you have to treat everyone like a child of God, and Yossi thought this loving your enemies thing was stupid. You know, when he typed up our phone list, he broke things up into sections: journalists, human rights workers, and then, this one section with numbers of the Civil Administration and settler spokespeople, he headed 'Children of God.' Which was kind of funny."

She began filling up another plastic bucket and put her pants in to rinse. She then went to work on a pair of grey socks.

"So there were these ideological and theological differences. And it was my job as team coordinator to make sure things got run the way I thought our church constituency wanted them run. I mean, if something bad happens, the buck sort of stops with me. And that led to a lot of friction. And one day we took a day off in Jerusalem together—Yossi used to call it 'liberated territory' because we could hold hands and stuff. And we had a huge fight and just decided together we were better off breaking up. In retrospect, I should have seen it coming. It's not like he didn't warn me, like he pretended to be someone else. But he's so, you know, intense, and the fact that he fell for me was kind of intoxicating, and maybe I should just become a nun, because I seem to have lousy judgment when it comes to men."

Tess analyzed the information Eugie had just given her to see if any of it could be useful in breaking up with Yossi. She supposed she could plead religious differences. Being around Eugie had certainly made her think about God more. Becoming religious would alienate Yossi, but she knew he would also demand that she fill in details—what had made her decide that believing in God was a good idea. Maybe telling him that she had become a pacifist would be better. His taking up with a group of militants certainly had made things unpleasant for her, and she could certainly say that she abhorred violence. It was loud and messy and generally something that all people should be against if they thought about it.

Eugie threw her socks into the rinse water and began rubbing detergent into the armpits of a blouse. "You thinking of breaking up with Yossi?" she asked.

"It seems like it might be for the best. But breaking up is hard to do."

"Well I'm not exactly an unbiased observer, you know, so you can take what I've said with a grain of salt."

"Okay."

"One thing though—I'd wait until he was out of jail and healed up. It's probably something he could handle better when he's feeling stronger."

"Okay."

"Coming to church tomorrow?" Eugie plunged her blouse up and down with a violent motion in the sudsy water.

"No, I think I'll go with Frank when he shows that tour group around."

"Okay."

Tess could not read the expression on Eugie's face. Was she in pain? So many things seemed to hurt Eugie, and she found herself wishing she could do something about it. But right now, breaking up with Yossi was more important.


Frank looked annoyed when she said she planned to go with the group of Swedes he was showing around Hebron. Tess wondered whether it was safe for her to wait until Yossi was out of jail and in better physical condition. Frank might not wait, she realized. She deducted some points for his impatience.

Several of the Swedish women looked like they had just undergone a chemical peel, and she shook her head. Fair-skinned people should know better than to walk around in the Middle Eastern sun without some protection. Frank greeted the foreman of a road repair crew as they walked up Shuhada Street. Rajeh spoke passable English and told the Swedes about several instances in which settlers had attacked his workers—sometimes pushing them into the ditches they were digging for water pipes and on two occasions shooting out the windows of heavy construction equipment.

"You are thinking, why does this man have no teeth?" Rajeh said. The Swedes murmured politely. Tess didn't think they had been thinking that at all, but she herself wondered. And she wondered why he had not thought to buy himself some dentures.

"Yes. I will tell you," Rajeh said. He reached into his back pocket and pulled out his wallet. He shook some objects from the wallet into his palm. Tess craned her neck to look over the shoulder of a willowy girl in a sarong and saw that Rajeh held in his hand several teeth, yellow and brown with cigarette smoke and decay.

"A woman settler did this to me," he said, extending his hand so that everyone could see his teeth. "It was Yehudit Levine. She came to my house, over there." He pointed to a white concrete-and-tile house behind and to the left of Qurtuba School. "She said my house belonged to the Jewish, even though my grandfather built it. I said she could not enter my house, and she beat me in the mouth. The police came and they took her, but the next day— she is free."

Yehudit Levine really ought to be held liable, Tess thought. She should pay for dentures for Rajeh.

After the Swedes had made the full circuit of the Hebron settlements and the Il Ibrahimi Mosque, Frank and Tess walked back to the apartment in silence. Hussam, Felicia, a young maroon-haired woman in a crocheted shirt and lacy black bra, and a young man with a huge nose and ugly brown glasses were in an intense discussion. They stopped and stared at Frank and Tess when they entered, in what seemed to Tess an unfriendly way.

Hussam smiled at them and said, "Haim and Shira, I want you to meet Frank and Tess. Tess is Yossi's fiancee. Frank has been with the RAPT Hebron project since the beginning."

"You were the one that Yossi and Uri and Khader and Shukri and the others got arrested for?" Shira was American. Tess noted the heavy black hair on her legs. Why would someone decide that dying her hair maroon and piercing her eyebrow was more natural than shaving her legs?

"Well, it's not like she asked them to," Frank said. Tess looked at him, surprised. He regained a couple points.

"It was a stupid operation," Hussam said. "It was very badly planned. I told them so from the beginning. But Shira and Haim have another plan that I think may work better."

Shira and Haim said nothing, but looked uncomfortable, as though they did not want to speak in front of her. Well fine. She wasn't interested in what they had to say. She would rather work on Frank a bit.

"I'll go upstairs," Tess said, hoping Frank would follow.

"No, she should stay. I will vouch personally for each and every member of the R.A.P.T." Hussam said, spelling it out.

"What is the meaning of this word, "vouch?" Haim asked. Shira said something to him in Hebrew. Hussam then asked her a question in Hebrew, as though questioning her translation. She responded and he raised his eyebrows in a "well, you learn something new every day" way.

"All right," Shira said. "The plan is this. We think 'Adel needs to undertake another mission, to show the Shin Bet we're serious. We were thinking we should go to the Goldstein monument on some weeknight and pour acid on it. Just Israelis this time, so we'll have no problem getting into Kiryat Arba. Haim can get the acid from Hebrew University. We were wondering if one of you wants to do it with us and get deported. We figure it's right up your alley." She paused and translated the expression into Hebrew for Haim. "You'd be attacking something symbolic instead of a human being. What do you think?"

"I think we better wait until Eugie and Bruce get back from church," Frank said. "That's pretty radical."

"Bruce is spending the night with Neil from World Vision, remember," Felicia said.

"Oh yeah, that's right," Frank said. "But we should wait for Eugie. She's leaving in a few days, so she could afford to be deported."

"But she wouldn't be able to get back in the country," Felicia said. "So she might not be willing to do that. I'm not sure *I* think it's a good idea. With the project in Chiapas just getting off the ground, we don't exactly have a lot of expendable workers. I mean, Minneapolis is talking about sending me there, and that would leave just you and Margaret as the people who were here from the beginning, Frank."

"If you're going to Chiapas, anyway, maybe you could get deported," Shira said.

Felicia and Hussam exchanged glances. "I don't think it very sensible to risk Felicia," Hussam said. "We need her here in Hebron."

Frank said, "I'd rather not be deported, but if Eugie thinks this is a good idea, I suppose I'd be willing to consider it. What about you, Tess?"

It sounded like an inconvenient and dangerous idea. From Eugie's description of prison—all the cigarette smoke and chocolate spread—she thought it might be unbearable for her. On the other hand, she had survived three nights underground with her hands tied. Maybe doing this would endear her more to Frank.

She knew one thing. She would be happy never to have to see Israel, Palestine, and anything in them again.

The door to the apartment opened and Eugie entered, face white. Her hands trembled as she pushed the door closed.

"Eugie! You look ill!" Hussam said, getting up and offering her his chair.

She held her hand up and shook her head. "I need some water. I'll be right back."

When she emerged from the kitchen, glass in hand, Felicia gave a summary of their discussion. "What about it?" she asked as she concluded. "Would you be willing to be deported?"

Eugie leaned against the doorway of the kitchen. Her hands were still trembling as she drank. "What about this acid?" she asked. "Will it be a hazard to people? I mean, what if children came along and played in it?"

"When it is dry, it will not hurt any people," Haim said. "We only want to—" He said something in Hebrew to Shira who responded, "dissolve."

"Dissolve the writing on the stone which says Goldstein is a martyr."

"We're planning on staying and waiting to be arrested," Shira said. "We can tell the police they should close off the shrine to people because it's a hazard. It will kill two birds with one stone—attack the institution that makes Goldstein a hero and prevent people from coming to worship at his grave."

"Eugie!" Felicia cried out as Eugie slid to the floor. Frank walked over to the kitchen doorway, sat beside her and put his arm around her.

"There was a bombing," she said. "In the Ben Yehuda Mall. I walked there after church to get dreidels for my nieces and nephews. I was a couple blocks away when I heard the explosion. It shattered some of the glass in the shop windows near where I was."

She stood up and staggered toward the kitchen.

"You sit," Felicia ordered.

"I need more water," she said.

"I'll get it," said Frank, disappearing into the kitchen.

She leaned against the door jamb and closed her eyes. "When I got there," she said, "I saw the head and spine of one of the suicide bombers against the door of a T-shirt shop. His eyes were closed. His head was completely intact, and his spine was so white. White as—I guess the right simile isn't all that important." She began laughing and then sobbing. She put her head down on her knees and shook. Frank embraced her and swayed with her.

"We'd better go before they clamp a closure down on the territories. I don't want to have to ride the settler bus and in another couple hours it will almost impossible to get through the checkpoint in an Arab van," Shira said.

As she and Haim stood up, Eugie raised her head and began trying to talk while she hyperventilated.

"Does—Yiphat—know—what—you're—planning?"

"No, and she doesn't want to know," Shira said. "She's already under surveillance because she's representing the rest of 'Adel."

"Anyway," Shira concluded, "maybe we need to table this for a while."

Before they left the room, she looked at Eugie, who was gasping for breath.

"Take care of yourselves, okay?" she said.

"Shira!" Eugie called out, with a sob.

Shira came back inside the room, nearly bumping into Hussam, who had begun to follow her and Haim out. "Yes? What?"

"Next time you come," Eugie said. "You should wear a less revealing shirt."

\*Interim\*

## The Day of the Bus Bombings
by Kathleen Kern

I first heard about the bombings during the morning service at the Lutheran Church when the pastor asked the congregation to pray for the families of the victims. Several people told me afterward that they had heard the explosion but assumed it was a sonic boom.

I needed to run an errand to Jerusalem's International Convention Center after church, three blocks away from the site of the bombing. Listening to the Hebrew commentary playing on the radio of the Egged bus, I heard the words "Machpeleh" and "Ayyash." I guessed that the announcer was speculating that the bombings were done in reprisal for the killing of "The Engineer" fifty days ago and for the Baruch Goldstein massacre of the people praying at the Cave of Machpeleh/Il Ibrahimi Mosque two years ago today.

As the people on the bus listened to the radio, the lines on their faces seemed to deepen. A man sitting across from me said,"Zeh Shalom?" to his friend in exactly the same inflections that I have heard Palestinian men in Hebron use when they say "Hada salaam?"("This is peace?") after witnessing acts of violence committed by the Israeli military and Israeli settlers living in Hebron.

On the way back from my errand, I stopped at the site of the bombing. There was no indication that a bus had ever been there. Dozens of Orthodox Jewish men wearing rubber gloves were picking up fragments of charred flesh still lying in the road or stuck to cars. Across the street one young man was up in a tree carefully trying to reach ashy tatters draped over twigs and branches. A boy in a black velvet yarmulke said to his friend, "They found a really big piece of skin hanging up there." Over on the next street I saw more men carefully scanning the street, walls, bushes, and trees for human remains—so that they could have a decent human burial.

In the evening, the rest of the team went to visit a friend whose house frequently gets stoned by settlers from Kiryat Arba. I stayed home to write this story. At seven thirty I received a call from the team asking me to call the police because our friend's house was being stoned again. The policeman at the Civil Administration told me I had to go to the station near the mosque. As I stepped outside, a soldier from the checkpoint near where we live approached me.

"Why are you living with terrorists?" he asked. "Did you hear what they did?"

I told him about what I had seen in Jerusalem.

"They are animals. They are shit," he said. "They want to kill you, and you just don't know it."

He kept yelling as I walked away—long after I had stopped understanding what he said.

# CHAPTER 12

Felicia was treating her with far too much consideration; it gave Eugie the creeps. As she packed her last-minute purchases of pottery and glass in her suitcase full of dirty clothes, she reflected that the team's solicitousness was yet another thing that made her glad she was going home. Last night Felicia had insisted on doing dishes for her. About an hour ago, after Eugie had said that she was going to miss *kanafi*, Felicia had appeared in her bedroom with a plateful of the warm cheese dessert covered with orange shredded wheat. It was good, but it was also about a zillion calories, and Eugie was determined to go on a diet as soon as her plane touched down in Philadelphia.

But she wasn't in Philadelphia yet. Twenty more hours to go.

It was Tess who listened to her, without appearing frightened or shocked or grossed-out, when Eugie described what she had seen at Ben Yehuda Mall. The sirens and the police; the ultra-orthodox burial society collecting severed limbs, pieces of hair and skin, an ear in one case. At a certain point, one of the ultra-orthodox men brought a walnut-sized, blackened chunk over to a policeman and asked him to scrutinize it under his magnifying glass. Were they deciding whether it was human flesh or rubble? Maybe a piece of chicken from the KFC restaurant down the street? Maybe part of a bagel?

But no, she had told Tess, it was hard to find a decent bagel in Jerusalem, although a young rabbinical student, who had come down to visit once, had insisted that one could, indeed find bagels in Jerusalem. They were just a little off the beaten track.

She knew she was talking crazy, but the more she talked, the more the horror oozed out of her like pus from a wound. When she had seemed to begin—as they said in human services lingo—

*perseverating,* Tess had broken in and brightly suggested that she do a makeover on Eugie.

First they started with makeup. Tess said she didn't have the right foundation or powder for Eugie, because of her tan, but suggested that Eugie look into a bronzing powder when she got home. She further extracted a promise that Eugie would start using sunblock every day.

Eugie's eyes began watering and her nose itching as Tess plucked her brows while telling her they were very full and dark, *a la* Brooke Shields, but that just a little shaping would open her face up in ways that would surprise her.

When Tess let her look at herself in the mirror, Eugie had to admit they did look nice—and she could probably get by with it at her home church. No one would ask her if she were wearing makeup.

They had a little more difficulty with the eye-makeup. Eugie couldn't stop blinking as Tess put on "smokey taupe" liner, and Tess had to fix the damage with Q-tips. She then used "khaki" shadow on the outer third of Eugie's lids, sweeping it up to the eyebrows. Eugie could just feel that she looked like a freak even without seeing herself in the mirror. She found the mascara wand a little frightening, as Tess aimed it at her lashes.

After Tess had done Eugie's upper lashes, she stood back, wand pointed toward the ceiling and looked at Eugie for a few seconds without speaking, the tip of her tongue touching her upper lip.

"You know, I'm not going to put any mascara on your lower lashes," she said to Eugie, as though she had proposed something slightly dangerous and exciting. "It will look less made-up."

Before she allowed Eugie to look at the finished product, she brought out a forest green blouse she had brought from home. It had a scooped neckline and what could barely be called sleeves. Eugie had told her the blouse was too revealing when she first came to Hebron.

"I can't wear your size," Eugie protested. Tess insisted that on top they were probably about the same. It was in the hips where they differed. She said the neckline would show off Eugie's elegant collarbones.

To her surprise, the blouse did fit. And it hinted at a cleavage. When had she gotten a cleavage? True, the buttons gapped when she pushed her elbows backwards, but Tess told her she could wear it without doing that.

When Tess brought her over to the mirror of the non-functional sink in the living room of the women's apartment, her eyes widened. She leaned on the sink with her hands so that she could get a closer look. Only by getting about four inches from the mirror could she tell for sure she was wearing makeup. Even the eyeshadow looked like it might be natural.

"Wow." Eugie stood back and crossed her arms over chest. "This is amazing."

"I got this shadow as a free sample when I bought a bunch of other stuff at the Clinique counter," Tess said. "Your eyes have green flecks in them, so it looks better on you than it does on me. I want you to keep it. And I think you should keep the blouse, too. I brought it along because I usually try not to bring clothes I care about when I travel. There's too much chance that something will happen to them, and the blouse looks better on you than it does on me, too."

Eugie laughed. "Tess, there is nothing in this world that I could wear that would look better on me than you."

Tess appeared to consider this for a moment. "I can make almost anything I wear look good, but this makes you look good."

Eugie smiled as she wedged a bag of pine nuts in the corner of her suitcase. She really appreciated Tess's honesty. And she hadn't told her that she'd never wear the eye shadow. Although the blouse—she laid it tenderly over a plastic poncho to separate it from her dirty clothes.

She sighed when she looked at the chunks of rubble from the Abu Jaber home. She would not be able to take it all with her. Margaret had sent an e-mail saying she had had no problem getting her rubble through airport security at Ben Gurion. The young female inspector had given her the fish eye when she saw the bag of crushed cinderblock and glass. "You realize this was broken before I touched it?" she had asked Margaret. Margaret had responded, "Yes, I know," and that was the end of it.

Oh geez, Eugie thought, I am not up to airport security this evening. She would have to get in line by at least two in the morning to be sure she made her five A.M. flight.

She looked back at her rubble and at the broken coffee cup that she had picked up on the sidewalk near Ben Yehuda mall. Some poor trendy kid or a tourist had been sipping capuccino when the world had exploded around him or her.

As she ran her finger along the sharp edge and then the smooth handle of the cup, she thought of the *Martyrs' Mirror* sitting by the German Bible on her parents' coffee table. Second in importance only to the Bible for Mennonites and Reformed Anabaptists, *Martyrs' Mirror* chronicled the stories of Christians who had died for their faith from Jesus's crucifixion through the worst of the persecutions of Eugie's Anabaptist ancestors in the sixteenth century. The etchings of people being burned alive, drowned, hacked to death, and tortured in a variety of imaginative ways had fascinated her as a child. She had lain awake at night, wondering whether she could have remained loyal to Jesus and his teachings the way her ancestors had, even while facing excruciating physical pain.

A gust of mirthless laughter escaped her chest. She had wavered in her faith at the mere possibility of losing Yossi's love.

Wavered, she reminded herself, but not succumbed. Still, she was not certain that she would not have recanted under torture.

Now why had she been thinking about *Martyrs' Mirror* in the first place? Oh yes, it was the story of Maeyken Wens, burned to death in Antwerp in 1573. Wens had written letters from prison to her oldest son, fifteen-year-old Adrien, asking him to take care of his siblings and adjuring him to follow Jesus as she had, even if it meant losing his life. She said she would see him in the New Jerusalem.

Adrien had watched his mother's death at the stake with his baby brother, Hans. (Eugie frowned. He should have known better than to bring a young child to something like that.) Adrian fainted, and when he recovered, his mother was a pile of ashes. *Martyrs' Mirror* had an etching of Adrien sifting through the ashes at the stake to find the tongue screw the authorities had put in his mother's mouth to prevent her from testifying her faith before the crowd as she burned. Somehow, the Dutch Mennonites had gotten ahold of the tongue screw and handed it down from generation to generation to remind themselves of what their people had been willing to die for.

Eugie held up a chunk of marble countertop from the Abu Jaber home and the broken coffee cup, and wondered if these were the tongue screws she must show to the people back home, to make the suffering of Palestine and Israel real.

Maybe they were the opposite. The tongue screw reminded the descendants of the early Anabaptists that they were a people willing to die for what they believed. The broken cup and the chunk of rubble demonstrated only that the people in these lands were attacked, killed, and exploited for who they were. They could be right-wing or left-wing, religious or secular, good-hearted or vicious. It didn't matter. Their homes were destroyed; they were shot for looking the wrong way at a checkpoint or for trying to pass through a clash to get to their homes; they were blown to pieces because they wanted to sip an expensive cup of coffee in a hip sidewalk cafe in West Jerusalem.

New Jerusalem indeed. If Maeyken Wens could have seen Jerusalem today, she would have picked another metaphor.

Eugie wrapped the broken cup in a pair of dirty panties. She sorted through the rubble to find the pieces that would best say "demolished house" to RAPT's church constituency. She settled on two chunks of cinder block, a shard of window glass, the piece of marble countertop, an electrical outlet, and a length of PVC plumbing. The rest could be given to tour groups when they came to visit the team's apartment, with the reminder to pray for the Palestinians facing homelessness.

"Eugie. Are you in?" It was Kefaah. She had decided to accompany Eugie to Jerusalem. When Eugie had told her she might have to take bus number 160, the settler bus, because of the closure, an unholy gleam had appeared in Kefaah's eye and she had said that she would very much like to ride the settler bus with her.

Eugie sighed. In principle, she supported Kefaah's refusal to be cowed by the settlers, but there was no question that she liked to provoke incidents some time. Walking with her past Beit Hadassah was like wearing a sign, "Please spit on me."

"In here, Kefaah," she called. She reminded herself that Kefaah wasn't really provoking the settlers. She was just walking by the settlements, knowing that her presence provoked them.

Today, Kefaah wore a cream satin blouse with fringes around the yoke and shoulders, a tight denim skirt with a hemline about an inch above the knee, and red high heels.

"Kefaah, what does your mother say when she sees you in outfits like that?"

"She does not like it, but she does not like me going to visit Israeli friends either, and that is where I am going. One of my friends from Bat Shalom is getting married in Haifa."

"You're not going to have a problem getting there?"

"I have my press pass from the Israeli government. I can go wherever I want."

In reality, Eugie knew, Kefaah was in constant danger of losing that pass because she sometimes published rumor and hearsay about abuses by soldiers in her newspaper articles. When people followed up on her stories, however, they turned out to be true most of the time.

"Why do you have all this garbage in your room?" Kefaah asked.

"This is from the Abu Jaber home. We will take it back to show the people in our churches what is happening to Palestinian homes in Area C. And I will take a piece to my congresswoman's office and to the offices of my Senators and ask that they demand that Israel stop demolishing Palestinian homes."

"They will never stop, because the Jewish are in control of your government." Kefaah examined her nails. Her pale polish matched her blouse. Eugie wondered why she hadn't painted them the usual red to match her shoes.

"Well, there are a lot of American Jews that don't like Israel demolishing homes—just like your friend in Haifa."

"Oh, Yael is different. She is very nice."

Eugie sighed as she thought about all the interpreting she was going to have to do in the coming weeks. Interpreting Palestinians to American Jews. Interpreting Jews and Israelis to anti-Semitic church people. Interpreting the Israeli-Palestinian conflict to churches and civic groups without demonizing anyone. Hurting the feelings of Jewish friends in Lancaster a whole lot. In many ways, Haiti had been much easier. There, the purveyors of disinformation had been the CIA and the State Department, and most of the people in her church regarded those institutions with distrust, anyway. But with Israel and Palestine you had people of goodwill who saw no reason not to believe what the *New York Times* was publishing.

"I think we must go," Kefaah said. "The bus will pass the vegetable market soon."

"Yup," said Eugie. "Just let me say good-bye to the others."

Her suitcase weighed a ton. Kefaah carried Eugie's backpack and the wheelie thing that would be no use to her until she was on level ground. Eugie maneuvered down the stairs backwards, letting gravity work for her as her suitcase bumped from step to step. She left it on the patio, where Naseem, encumbered by the now one-week-overdue baby, was hanging laundry while her two-year-old daughter, Warud, played with the clothespins.

"I am leaving today, Naseem," she said.

Naseem kissed her on both cheeks. "You will return soon?"

"*Inshallah*. I really want to see your baby."

"*Inshallah*," Naseem responded and continued hanging up her clothes.

Hussam was translating a tape of Marcel Khalifeh songs to Felicia who sat on the couch listening intently. Bruce was at the stove frying eggplant, and Frank was working on the computer in the office.

"Hey! Ready to go?" Bruce called out and turned the gas burner off.

"Yup, 'the time has come, the walrus said.'" Eugie wriggled her shoulders. They were sore already from just getting her suitcase downstairs. How she was going to shlep it all the way to Ben Gurion she didn't know. But Christmas was coming, and people always liked Hebron glass and pottery.

"What is a walrus?" Kefaah asked.

Hussam said something in Arabic to her, then recited "The time has come, the Walrus said/to talk of many things/of shoes and ships and sealing wax/of cabbages and kings/and why the sea is boiling hot/and whether pigs have wings . . . Am I right? Not quite Shakespeare, of course."

"Close enough," Eugie said. "*Inte shater.* I never fail to be amazed by how much Shakespeare the Palestinians I know read."

"It's the poetry," Hussam said. "We are a nation of poets. Many bad poets, but poets nonetheless."

"We must go," Kefaah said.

"Right-o," replied Hussam. "I'll come with you."

"Maybe it would be better if Kefaah and I went by ourselves," Eugie said. "We don't want to attract any more attention at the settler bus stop than we have to."

"Nonsense, strength in numbers," Hussam said, pushing a button on the cassette player. "Besides, it might be a bit until I see you again."

"I'm coming too," Bruce said.

As Eugie began to protest, he said, "Save your breath, babe. You ain't stopping me."

Felicia stretched and yawned. "Yeah, I'll come too."

"Where's Tess?" Eugie asked.

"She went out to buy some yogurt and tissues." Frank came out of the office and hugged her.

"Oh." After all they had been through, Eugie would have liked to say goodbye. "Well, tell her I said good-bye, okay?"

"Will do," Frank said. "Take care of yourself."

"Will do. Make Pete and Wendy feel welcome, okay? It's their first time here."

"Will do."

"Enough already!" Bruce said. "Let's go!"

He swung the suitcase off the patio as if it were filled with feathers. Eugie took the backpack and wheelie thing from Kefaah. She tried to put the suitcase on the wheelie thing when they reached the bottom of the stairs, but Bruce said it would be easier for him to carry it to the bus stop.

The chicken vendors and the man in the nut shop waved goodbye to her as the group made their way out of the alley and on to the street. Eugie sighed when she thought of all the people to whom she hadn't said good-bye—who would reproach the team until she returned, when they would reproach her. Palestinian social mores could be so exhausting—especially for introverts. Eugie had begun to wonder in the last couple years whether introversion was a North American luxury, like private rooms and regular water and electricity. She had felt exhausted in Haiti, too.

As they passed the checkpoint, she waved at the soldiers, who nodded at her without smiling.

Hussam offered to take the suitcase from Bruce and staggered under its weight when Bruce released his grip. "I say, what have you got in here? Bricks?"

"Well, yeah, sort of," Eugie said. "I have part of the Abu Jaber house and some pottery and glass."

Hussam laughed. "Only one house? It feels as though there are at least two in here."

"This was the one we didn't save."

Hussam let Bruce take the suitcase back. "Good man. I wouldn't have guessed you to be so strong," he said.

"Comes from loading hay bales," Bruce said.

There were no settlers waiting at the bus stop and Eugie heaved a sigh of relief. She usually saw teenage settler girls at the stop on their way to or from Jerusalem, and for some reason, they scared Eugie more than the teenage boys with automatic weapons.

The bus came up from the mosque. Felicia smiled and gave Eugie a mock salute. Bruce embraced her and Hussam kissed her on both cheeks. Very culturally inappropriate, but it didn't matter, because she was going home.

The only other passenger was an elderly woman with a curly red wig that Orthodox women sometimes wore. She sat in the front seat and didn't bother looking at them when they climbed aboard. The bus driver didn't seem to care either that she and Kefaah were riding. Eugie thought Kefaah looked disappointed that she didn't have to take out her press pass.

They chose to sit about six seats back, and Eugie pulled her suitcase with difficulty into the seat with her. Kefaah sat in the seat across the aisle, took out her cellphone and began talking in English to her friend in Haifa. They passed Tess carrying a black plastic bag. Eugie pounded on the window and Tess looked up briefly, but the heavy screens that protected riders from stones and molotov cocktails must have prevented her from seeing Eugie, because she did not react.

The ride away from Hebron and Kiryat Arba was uneventful. They picked up a handful of people at the Gush Etzion bus stop. Just as the bus was pulling away, a soldier came running down the road leading to the settlements. The driver grumbled, stopped the bus, and let the soldier on, berating him in Hebrew. The soldier gave a monosyllabic reply and swung his heavy duffel bag into the seat behind the woman in the red wig, who was now sleeping. Like her, he lay his head against the window and closed his eyes after he sat down.

Suddenly Eugie felt more tired than she had ever felt in her life. As the bus turned onto the bypass road, the construction of which had decimated acres of orchards and olive groves, she put her hand against the window. Its outline stood out sharp and dark against the setting sun. She felt a vague surprise that she wasn't fading, that the last four months had not rubbed part of her away.

It was time for her to be going home—back to people who knew who she was instead of what she represented. The first thing she would do when she got there would be to take a hot bath and just let the accumulated grime and dust of the last four months soak off. Then she would distribute presents to her nieces and nephews and sleep for twenty-four hours straight. In reality, she never slept that long, but knowing that she could if she wanted to was heartening.

If she could just get through the airport departure procedure with a little grace.

Everyone who had worked on the RAPT project in Hebron had their personal horror stories about the Ben Gurion interrogation procedures to which they had been subjected when they left the country. A friend who worked with the World Council of Churches in Bethlehem had told them that bureaucrats in charge of security picked those IDF recruits who had scored high for paranoia on their psychological profiles to do the airport interrogation when people left the country.

One time when Frank had flown home via Ben Gurion, the security person had demanded to know what he did as part of his work in Hebron. When he told her that he did a lot of visiting, wrote press releases, etc., she wanted him to prove he could write a press release. He pulled out a piece of paper and a pen and said, "Well, at the top you write the date and FOR IMMEDIATE RELEASE and then you put a number 30 at the bottom, but I don't know what that's for." She had waved him aside crossly and begun checking his baggage.

Eugie had learned to say up front that she had been in Hebron for three or four months, because it always came out anyway—even if she gave the evasive, "Well I was touring the holy sites in Galilee and Jerusalem . . ." beginning. Even after they found out she had been in Hebron, they always asked, "Did you talk to any Arabs there?" Yiphat had told her that she could say she had an Israeli lawyer friend who told her that it was illegal for them to ask for the names of their landlord, etc., but they always asked anyway. And she always refused. And they always took apart her suitcase.

At least she had never had a body cavity search. The closest she had come was getting her breasts and thighs patted down by a female security person. She smiled as she remembered the time she had left the country with Margaret, and the two security people had lifted out Margaret's enema bag and demanded to know what it was. Margaret asked them if they knew what an enema was. It had taken a moment for them to translate and then they flung the object back into the suitcase. Eugie had said, "Bet you're glad you were wearing gloves, huh?"

Then there was the time she was flying home and told the security woman that she was traveling at this time because she was going to speak at a church conference about the situation in Hebron. After the security person had seen the faxed agenda Eugie had in her folder, she had become almost deferential, and Eugie had asked her, "So, how many bombs do you find in a given week? One? Two?"

The security person had just smiled and said, "We can't give out that information."

The last time that Eugie had flown home, her suitcase was full of *News from Within* and *Challenge* magazines. The other non-Arab they took to the back room (Arabs always went to the back room) was a German-Jewish physics student who had the same magazines with him.

His security person had treated him much more harshly than her security person had treated her. Freckled face impassive, his security person demanded that he explain why he was reading those magazines, and he said, "I plan to be studying physics here for the next five years and I wanted to have relationships with different peoples. I thought these magazines would help me understand different points of view."

His interrogator looked at him as if this were about the dumbest thing she had ever heard. She waved his Hebrew-English dictionary in his face. "At Hebrew University, your physics class will be taught in English, yes?"

The German-Jewish guy had nodded.

"Then why do you need a Hebrew-English dictionary?" she asked. He looked at her as if she were some alien creature. "Because I wanted to have actual conversations with people outside of class?" he said.

Eugie's interrogator just took the magazines into the mysterious inner sanctum where questionable objects went to be scanned.

Eugie usually had the most success by coming into the interrogation with a "You-have-a-ridiculous-job-and-you-ask-ridiculous-questions-but-I'm-going-to-humor-you" attitude. She considered whether to try Felicia's usual tactic this time, which involved humming through the whole procedure—always coming to the end of a stanza before she answered the security person's questions.

She leaned against the window and closed her eyes. She hated having to go through this rigmarole at two or three in the morning, barely having time to repack all her stuff before boarding. Her friend Frieda had once missed her plane because of the security procedures, and when she finally got to Frankfurt a couple days later thought to herself, "At last I'm in a free country." Frieda had then had a moment of cognitive dissonance, because her parents had fled Germany in the thirties.


The bus was coming up past Jaffa Gate and the Old City of Jerusalem. The gold Dome of the Rock caught the rays of the setting sun. It was one of the most aesthetically beautiful sights in the world, Eugie thought. She smiled as she thought of the Christian Zionists and Israeli right-wingers referring to it as "that abomination on the Temple Mount." In the eighties the Israeli authorities had stopped, in the nick of time, a right-wing Jewish underground cell from blowing it up.

She sighed. She would be glad if she never had to see another holy site in her life.

She thought of the summer when she had visited cousins in Ohio and they had gone to visit the President Rutherford B. Hayes Memorial near Fremont. Inside the gift shop at his home, there were commemorative coins, fake parchment copies of the Declaration of Independence, postcards, mugs—and little plastic cubes with real goldfish embedded inside. They were selling better than anything else in the shop, Eugie had noticed. Her aunt and uncle wouldn't have let her spend her money on something so frivolous anyway, but Eugie had wondered what a goldfish in a plastic cube had to do with Rutherford B. Hayes, or the presidency, or American history.

The holy sites and holy things in Israel and Palestine gave her the same strange feeling. What did these ancient buildings, relics and bric-a-brac have to do with God?

A Jewish friend (former friend—after she told him about her work in Hebron he had pretty much dropped the friendship) had told her he thought the whole Temple Mount should be turned into parking lot.

"There's a real shortage of parking space and a huge surplus of religious monuments in Jerusalem," he had said.

Made sense to her.

Kefaah was still talking on the phone. Eugie smiled over at her. She smiled back and continued talking. Eugie wondered if she would have enough time to go to the bathroom while Kefaah watched her luggage, or whether Kefaah would have time to do that before she made her connection to Haifa. No squat-toilets for two months, she thought, feeling more energized.

She would only have a week at home before she had to start making presentations to church and civic groups. Her sister set up her speaking schedule for her when she was out of the country. At least for the first month they were all pretty close to home. The ten-day speaking tour of Mennonite and Reformed Anabaptist congregations in Kansas had taken a lot out of her last winter.

She had given one presentation in Manhattan, Kansas and a Palestinian man from the local Islamic Center had attended and come up afterward with tears in his eyes, saying he hadn't realized there were Christians who knew what his people were going through, and he was so very, very grateful. The conversation had then switched to the dearth of news coverage of events in which U.S. policy in the Middle East was challenged.

"Like last weekend," the Palestinian man had said. "There was a huge demonstration in Washington DC against the U.S. sanctions in Iraq. And the networks chose to cover a demonstration about homosexual rights instead. You know we Muslims do not believe in homosexuality."

Eugie had nodded, feeling that she was betraying her gay cousin but not knowing what else to do. She hated having to choose between competing solidarities. Her denomination was currently being torn apart by the issue of homosexuality, and sometimes she just wanted to shake people and say, "You know what? There are children dying of malnutrition and bombs and torture in this world and you're concerned with an issue that Jesus never said word number one about."

She wondered if someday she would be excommunicated, and then caught herself, recognizing that she was indulging in one of her emotional downward spirals. She had gotten pretty good at stopping them in time since her hospitalization.

Looking for something positive, she thought about her nephews and nieces, who would be ecstatic to see her again. She thought about cuddling their warm little bodies in her lap and reading to them. She thought about the looks on their faces when they saw the presents she was bringing them—glass fish of different colors and sesame cookies and a drum and a little embroidered dress for Tabitha . . .

A weight seemed to lift from her chest. While holding children was no substitute for being held by a man who loved her, it did take the edge off her craving to be held. The love of her nieces and nephews was not a substitute for the love of children of her own she had once longed for, but it was enough.

She thought of Yossi sitting in jail and realized that the strongest emotion she felt was concern for his safety, not a yearning to return to those few months when he had told her he adored her. There was a lot of residual pain, but she realized that some day it, too, would be gone. He would never be hers and she could live with that.

The young soldier who had gotten on at Gush Etzion had a triangle of sweat on the back of his uniform. Odd, given the coolness of the early evening. He turned around, and she thought he looked familiar. Had he been stationed once in Hebron? He mirrored her uncertain smile, his face slick with perspiration, and nodded a greeting. Eugie thought he must be ill. The Orthodox woman took a mirror out of her purse and adjusted her red wig. Two teenage girls in jeans, who had gotten on at Gilo, were laughing over something that one of them had attached to a key chain.

At a bus stop past the post office on Jaffa Road, a grey-haired woman wearing a black sweater and a silver cross got on with two whining children whom she scolded in Arabic. A cluster of older Chasidic men also got on, one in a fur hat, the others in homburgs. A sulky looking, blue-haired boy with multiple piercings in his ears, eyebrows and nose followed them and sprawled across the aisle from the teenage girls. They didn't look up, and he rolled his eyes in disgust.

Eugie wondered if she had remembered to tell Frank to record that donation from the Methodist tour group in the financial log. Maybe she should call from the airport. Had she unplugged the heater in her room after she finished packing? Tess would probably notice and unplug it if she hadn't. Had she told Felicia to save the clothes for which she had not had room in her suitcase? She would need them when she came back. Had she—

*     *     *

Tess had become an expert at making tea. Bruce had shown her how after the first two waves of visitors. It gave her an excuse to get away from them. She'd rather watch the pot begin to boil than sit in the midst of all those sympathetic expressions.

While they were at Wisam's house, Rabbi Hillel Cotton had called to tell them about the bus bombing. Frank was carrying the cellphone at the time, and the air around the table had grown cold as everyone watched his face.

Rabbi Cotton said that he and Yiphat would go identify the body, or parts of the body. Eugie's waistpack had been found amidst the wreckage, and the passport and visa inside were unscathed. Eugie had put Rabbi Cotton's name and address in the "Address in Israel" box. ("Because Hebron isn't in Israel," she replayed Eugie's argument with Yossi in her head, "and I figure if they have a legitimate reason for getting hold of me, Hillel can always point them in my direction.")

Tess broke off a few sprigs of dried sage attached with a clothespin to a piece of twine strung over the trashcan and put them in the copper pot.

After Rabbi Cotton went to identify the body, he refused to give them any details, even when Bruce pressed him. It was much better for them to remember Eugie the way she had been the last time they saw her, he said.

The last time Tess had seen Eugie she had been packing her suitcase. She felt vaguely cheated that she hadn't had a chance to say good-bye. Bruce and Frank told her she had just missed her. She thought about the man in the hotel that first day in Jerusalem, with his hands and feet blown off and his skin boiled red. Hamsy Hamsy Hamsy, he had said. What did that mean, anyway? And is that what Eugie had looked like?

Rabbi Cotton told them that Eugie had been killed instantly. The suicide bomber had been sitting three or four seats ahead of her, dressed in a soldier's uniform. Kefaah, likewise, had been killed instantly. Frank said he wondered whether the police said that to all the families of people on the bus.

Ever since they heard, Felicia had been a wreck. She lay on her mat in her bedroom and refused to come down and talk to anyone—even Hussam. At night, Tess heard her speaking tormented Spanish in her sleep.

Hussam was in their main room, chain smoking, with tears in his eyes. "Those bastards," he kept saying, "Those bloody fucking bastards."

Bruce and Frank just sat on the chairs saying very little. Sitting in silence with ten or twelve people seemed to be the acceptable way of mourning here.

Yiphat had called and told Bruce that Yossi had requested that a judge let him out to sit *shiva* with them, but the judge had refused, saying that Yossi couldn't decide to get religion just when it served his interests. She had passed on no personal comment from him for Tess, and Tess found she didn't care.

She found she was not caring about a lot of things. She pinched her waist out of habit, but not from any real desire to monitor her weight. The day after they had heard the news, she had even run around the corner for toilet paper without putting on sunblock.

Kefaah's mother had stopped by and told them, with a neighbor translating, that Kefaah had not been the most dutiful of daughters—her wardrobe had indeed been rather shocking—but that she had been her father's favorite child.

Tess realized that she didn't care about Kefaah's awful clothes anymore either.

Their neighbors brought them mounds of chicken and rice and salads and cheese soup and then insisted that she and Bruce and Frank eat while they watched. Israeli friends brought cookies and cakes but did not insist that they eat them.

She put ten little glasses on the decorative aluminum tray and then filled them with syrupy tea.

"Tess," Hussam pleaded as she entered the main room. "Please let me go up and see Felicia. It's been three days, and she hasn't come down. Isn't it overdoing it a bit to be so caught up in social conventions at a time like this?"

"The rule is, no men up in the apartment," Tess said, wondering why Hussam was treating her like an authority figure.

"Told you, man," Frank said. "We can't make her come down."

Tess didn't recognize half the people in the room. There were some young men who said that Eugie had taught them English last summer, and a couple of Lutheran girls who knew Eugie from church.

"But surely she—if I could just talk to her, I think I could help."

"Hussam," Naseem broke in. Two-year-old Warud tipped the glass of sweet tea from her mother's hand into her mouth.

Throwing her an irritable look, Hussam asked, *"Eish?"*.

The normally calm Naseem launched into an Arabic tirade at Hussam, who at first slumped into his seat, looking ashamed, but then said something back in Arabic, his voice cracking.

Naseem responded with greater vigor, spilling tea into Warud's lap. Maintaining her balance against her mother's pregnant abdomen, Warud pulled her leg upward so she could suck the tea out of her pants. Tess had wondered how it was that all the gorgeous, young Palestinian women she knew turned into the solid older women haranguing their sons, soldiers, and shopkeepers on the street. Naseem's furrowed brow and jabbing finger gave her a clue.

"*Yallah*, Hussam," Naseem said, arranging Warud's leg around her stomach and preparing to exit the apartment.

"Naseem says she will chaperone me," Hussam said, rubbing his forehead with the same two fingers that were holding his cigarette. "I suppose that is all right with you folks?"

"Fine with me," Bruce said, handing Hussam the tray that still had a couple tea glasses on it. "Why don't you take up some bread and rice and chicken for her, too? I don't think she's eaten anything for three days."

Naseem whirled around and looked with astonishment at Bruce. She asked Hussam something in Arabic to which he nodded. "Why you not tell me she does not eat?" Naseem said. "That is very bad. Why you not tell her she must eat? *Ya haram*!"

Bruce opened and closed his mouth several times, failing to find the right words as Naseem glared at him. She ordered Hussam to heap a plate with rice and chicken and insisted that he bring a bowl of the cheese soup that Tess knew Felicia detested as much as she did. Raising his eyebrows at Hussam, Bruce handed him two rounds of the flat bread.

"Thank you," Hussam said. "I'll give you a status report when I come down. Perhaps it is for the best that Naseem will be there. She seems to know what she's doing."

The young men who had somehow known Eugie stood up and bobbed their heads at Bruce. "We want to go," one of them said.

Frank, Bruce, and Tess just nodded at them. The two Lutheran girls said they had better get back, themselves. The soldiers had allowed them to park their car downstairs on condition that they not stay long.

As the door closed, the cellphone rang and Frank groaned, but he pulled down the flap and said, "Hello?"

He listened for a minute, saying "uh-huh" a couple times, and then closed the phone.

"Rabbi Cotton said he has been in touch with Eugie's parents and plans to meet them at Ben Gurion when they fly in on Tuesday.

"He's a really great guy," Bruce said

"I don't think I could do it," Frank said.

They sat together in silence.

Tess's head was aching with thoughts. She felt a little bit like she had felt when her third husband left her, but worse. She was alone, now, with two men, and had no desire to charm them or wait for them to come to her like magnets to a refrigerator. And she didn't care that they hadn't made her the center of attention.

For the first time in her life, she understood those girls in junior high and high school who never seemed to have boyfriends, but didn't seem to care because they had each other. What she had had with Eugie was more than what she had with Bruce, maybe about the same as she had with Frank, more than Yossi . . . ? She found the comparisons too difficult.

She only knew that what she had had with Eugie was something she would miss. A lot. And Felicia and Yiphat—none of the other women she knew, except maybe her mother, could make her feel the way she felt with Eugie. She rubbed her head hard. But she hadn't even known she had something with Eugie. What if Eugie was the only girlfriend she would ever have?

The shrill tweet of the doorbell broke the silence. "Oh, make them go away!" Frank said under his breath. Bruce sighed, trudged to the door, and opened it.

"Oh, hi, Erland. Hi Wisam," Frank said, shoulders sagging. Tess pushed herself up off her chair and went to the kitchen to put the water on the burner.

"No, Tess, we do not have time to drink tea," Wisam said.

That was unusual. Tess sighed. Making tea was easier than making small talk.

"We wanted to come yesterday," Erland said. "But we thought you would have enough visitors."

None of the three of them said anything, and Wisam exchanged glances with Erland. "I have some very good news," Wisam said. "I thought it would help to hear good news in this sad time."

"Yeah. Good news would be great," Frank said, closing his eyes.

"Very well," Wisam said. "I wanted to tell you two nights ago when you were at my house, but then the Jewish man called you about Eugie."

She bit her lip as she looked into their faces and then looked with concern at Erland.

"Maybe we should tell you another time?" he asked.

"No, no," Bruce said, forcing a smile. "We want to hear your news."

Wisam's straight, white teeth gleamed as she put her hand in Erland's. "We are going to be married!" she said. "I was not sure whether to tell you, but then I thought, Eugie would have wanted to know as soon as possible, so telling you will be a little like telling her."

Tears came to Tess's eyes and she didn't know why. She didn't know whether she felt grief or pleasure, and not knowing scared her.

"All right!" Frank said, trying harder to sound excited. "But your parents are okay with this?"

"Erland has become a Muslim!" Wisam said. "That is even happier news to me than becoming engaged. He made the decision himself," she said. "It was not because of me."

"Really?" Bruce asked.

"I realized that becoming Muslim would bring me some peace I did not have," Erland said. His lips twitched for half a second.

"It is very good news, yes?" Wisam said. "And I have even more news like, how do you say, the icing on a cake?"

"Whoa, I don't know if we can take any more good news," Bruce said.

"Erland has many connections with important people in the Norwegian government. And I have many connections with the mayor. We are going to what is the word?" she turned to Erland.

"Propose," Erland said.

"Yes," Wisam continued. "We are going to propose that Hebron become a colony of Norway. It will be very good for us. The Norwegians are very humane."

"Some of us," Erland said. "I think that we could argue that since we started the whole Oslo process and it has been such a failure, we are willing to take the responsibility for Hebron on ourselves."

"Erland is very clever!" Wisam said. "He will suggest that the grandchildren of the Jews who lived here in 1929 move back into the houses that the settlers are living in, and he will arrange with the mayor of Hebron to give them posts."

"Posts?" Bruce said.

"You know—one will be in charge of electricity, one will be in charge of tourism. Like that. We always lived well with the Jews of Hebron before 1929."

"And the springs are so beautiful here," Erland said. "In March, Norway is still a very depressing place, and we will build hotels for Norwegians to come here and enjoy the almond and apricot trees."

"And the most important thing," Erland continued, "is that in twenty years we will feel very guilty about having a colony, and we will give Hebron its independence."

"And with the Israelis we would have to wait much longer to get our freedom," Wisam said.

"Wow," Frank said. He nodded, began to say something and then nodded some more. "Wow."

"This would have made Eugie very, very happy," Bruce said. "*Mabruk* to both of you."

"Where is Felicia?" Wisam asked.

"She's upstairs with Naseem and Hussam," Bruce said. "She's been refusing to come down since she heard. Naseem brought food up to her, because she hasn't eaten in three days, but I don't know if she'll be able to make her eat."

"She has not eaten for three days?! That is very very bad!" Wisam said. "How could you permit her not to eat for three days!"

"Come, Erland," Wisam said. "We must go and—how do you say—check to see that she eats."

She marched out the door, with Erland following after her. He turned as he left the room, shrugging his shoulders, and smiled at them.

"You know," Frank said, "let's turn out the lights and go out for a long night patrol, even if it is early. I just don't want to deal with any more visitors."

"Good idea," Bruce said.

"I'll get my hat." Tess had taken to keeping her hat in her bedroom so that no one else would use it.

When she entered the woman's apartment, she heard sobbing. In the sitting room, Warud was playing with Felicia's black velvet hairband. She shook her finger at it, lecturing in unintelligible syllables, and then made it run around the room like a toy horse.

Wisam and Erland stood in the doorway of Felicia's room. Tess poked her head inside and saw Hussam sitting on the floor, stroking Felicia's hand, while she stared past him at the wall across from her mat.

"Please, Felicia *habibti*." Tears ran down his face, and a little mucus hung on his upper lip. "Come back, talk to me. I can't bear to see you like this."

Felicia made no response. Her hand hung in Hussam's and dropped to the floor when he released it. Naseem threw Tess an anxious look. Eugie had once said they should thank God daily for neighbors who put up with some pretty unusual aggravations. She had said this after Naseem had asked, with much hesitation, whether they could try to sweep the patio they shared a little more often.

Wisam shook her head, reached into her purse for a tissue, and handed it to Hussam.

"Hussam, with your permission." She pushed Hussam out of the way before he had a chance to respond.

Taking Felicia by the shoulders, Wisam lifted her up and propped her against the wall. She then took Felicia's face in her hands and shouted, "Felicia!"

After Felicia made no response, Wisam slapped her hard.

"Huy!" Felicia said. "*Ya basta!* Stop that!" She grimaced and then seemed to try to focus on Wisam. "Wisam!" she said. "What are you doing?"

Wisam slapped her again.

"Ow!" Felicia said. "Quit it!"

"If I stop beating you, will you eat something?"

She looked at the platter of food on the chair she used as a night stand beside her mat.

"I'm not hungry," she said.

Wisam raised her hand again.

"Okay, okay! Jesus Christ! I'll eat!"

Felicia selected a piece of bread. Tess left the group, retrieved the hat from her room, and went downstairs.

As they exited their building, the crazy man who often stood in the middle of the street, preaching to bystanders or directing pretend traffic, accosted them. Waving his hands in the air, wide sleeves of his brown robe falling back to his shoulders, he began his sermon in Arabic. They stayed for a moment, watching him, and then turned to go. He grabbed Tess by the arm and swung her back, screaming into her face. Bruce and Frank tried to release his grip, but his fingers clutched Tess with more intensity, pressing on the bone.

She heard footsteps behind her coming down the stairs from the apartment. Wisam spoke a command in Arabic. The crazy man let her go and responded to Wisam. Wisam replied with something even more forceful.

"What is he trying to tell us?" Bruce asked.

"It is not important. Ignore him," Wisam said.

The crazy man became even more upset, holding his hands out, palms up, in a pleading gesture.

"He is saying that he is very sad about Eugie's death," Erland said. "Because she did not become a Muslim before she died. He wants you to know if you die tonight without becoming a Muslim, you will go to Hell."

Wisam looked down. "Ignore him," Wisam said. "He is very crazy." They turned to go back through the market and then Wisam thought of something else. "If Felicia does not come downstairs tomorrow, you must beat her until she does."

Frank said, "Uh, thanks for all your help, Wisam."

Shoulders hunched, hands held out in supplication, the crazy man followed Wisam and Erland, pleading with them in a hoarse voice.

"Wonder where our soldiers are tonight?" Bruce said, pointing to the empty checkpoint across the street. As they emerged into the area lit by spotlights, they saw a group of soldiers and settlers clustering around six young Palestinian men spread-eagled against the wall across from the army camp.

The settlers were spitting on the young men as the soldiers stood by and laughed. One of them, who seemed to be egging the settlers on, wore dark glasses, which seemed strange at that time of evening, even though the spotlights around the camp were very bright.

Frank pulled out the phone and dialed TIPH as they walked toward the gathering. Bruce went to stand beside the young men against the wall, assuming the same position.

"Nazis!" one of the settlers said, as Tess stood a little closer to Frank.

"Yeah, hi," Frank said into the phone. "There are some young men being detained across from the IDF camp on Shuhada street. There are also a bunch of settlers and it looks like things could get ugly."

Yehudit Levine spat in their direction. "Why don't you go to hell?" she asked. "I hope you all get blown to pieces like your friend did. It serves the bitch right, living with these terrorist murderers. Go away. Get out of Hebron. You are not wanted here. Do you need any more proof that Ha-Shem does not want you here? "

They said nothing. Tess wondered what all the other people who died on the bus proved.

The soldier with the dark glasses walked up to the young man on the end and kicked him hard in the kidneys. The young man cried out and fell to his knees. The soldier kicked him in the back of his head.

Something lifted inside Tess—like the casing coming off a radioactive core she hadn't known she had. She launched herself at the soldier.

"Stop it stop it stop it stop it stop it," she shrieked, pounding her fists against his chest.

She saw her crumpled face sobbing back at her in the lenses of the soldier's dark glasses. Behind him, she saw a young soldier with frizzy yellow hair and a prominent Adam's apple staring at her. It was the first time in her life that someone had looked at her with fear.

## *Interim*

Date: Thu, Jun 27, 1996 7:39 AM EDT
Subj: Four Guys Named Amin

# Four Guys Named Amin by Robert Naiman

During our last arrest, while Wendy Lehman had the misfortune to be with Israeli criminal prisoners, Randy Bond, Tom Malthaner and myself had the comparative fortune to be held with Palestinian political prisoners. Whether this was the result of happenstance or a deliberate attempt by the Israeli police to isolate and break one of our team members I don't care to speculate. Amongst those with whom the men were detained were the two Palestinians arrested with us, two Palestinian police, and four men from the village of Dura named Amin.

In an earlier release we spoke of the Palestinians arrested with us. They made the mistake of giving a ride to a bunch of Americans and hanging around after we were detained. For this crime they were arrested. In the Kiryat Arba police station we were all offered bail; the Palestinians accepted the conditions of the bail, but when the CPTers refused, the Palestinians were sent to prison along with us, even though they had agreed to the conditions of the police for their release.

Of those we met when we got to the prison, the two Palestinian policemen had been arrested for working in Hebron as policemen. Apparently they were caught in their uniforms. Since the Israeli army has not redeployed from Hebron as agreed to in the Oslo accords, the army does not allow Palestinian police to work in Hebron.

The four men from Dura named Amin had apparently been arrested because they are all from Dura and all named Amin. It seems that the authorities were looking for someone from Dura named Amin, but not knowing exactly which Amin from Dura they wanted, had arrested four of them. (Amin is a very common Arabic name.)

I had the opportunity to talk a bit with one of the Amins from Dura. Amin said he was an architect, and had been arrested from his office. We spoke about our love of books and our frustration about not having any reading material. "You know," he said, "my whole life I never wanted any trouble with the authorities. Nor did I have any. During the whole Intifada I was never arrested or detained, not one single time. And now they come to my office to arrest me. Just because my name is Amin."

The day before we left Dura prison the Palestinian police officers were released. But when we were released the four guys from Dura named Amin were still in prison.

# GLOSSARY

**Abu . . .** (Arabic) Father. In Arab culture, men and women are referred to as father of or mother of the eldest son, e.g. Abu Hussam. "Abu" is also often part of a surname. In the Hebron area the Abu Sneinehs are the largest clan. However, there are no Abu Jabers.

**Adesh bandura?** (Arabic) How much are the tomatoes?

**aliyah** (Hebrew) literally, ascent. When non-Israeli Jews immigrate to Israel and become citizens, they **make aliyah.**

**Ahlan wa sahlan** (Arabic) Welcome and double welcome. The correct response is **ahlan bik** m or **ahlan biki** f in Hebron, **ahlan fik, fiki** most everywhere else.

**Al humdullilah** (Arabic) Praise God! The polite thing to say after someone asks, "How are you?"

**'Am Yisrael** (Hebrew) **Yisroel** (Yiddish) literally, the people of Israel, which can mean actual citizens of Israel or all Jews, depending on the context.

**Amalek** Deuteronomy 25:17-19: "Remember what Amalek did to you on your journey out of Egypt, how he attacked you on the way, when you were faint and weary and struck down all who lagged behind you; he did not fear God. Therefore, when the Lord your God has given you rest from all your enemies on every hand, in the land that the Lord your God is giving you as an inheritance to possess, you shall blot out the remembrance of Amalek from under heaven; do not forget."

Extreme right wing Israelis and their partisans refer to everyone they want to get rid of as "Amalek."

**Ansar III** A notorious prison in the Negev Desert where the Israeli military sent political prisoners during the Intifada.

**Ashkenazi** Jews whose recent origins are in Central and Eastern Europe. See **Mizrahi.**

**azhnabia** (Arabic) foreigners

**Baab iZawiye** The center of Hebron where buses and taxis drop their passengers.

**"Biladi"** (Arabic) literally "my country," but also the title of the Palestinian national anthem.

**Bir Zeit** A small town near Ramallah. Bir Zeit University is the most famous university on the West Bank and was an intellectual center of the Intifada.

**bolis** (Arabic) Police. The Arabic language has no "p" sound.

**British Mandate** The period between the end of World War I and 1947, when the British controlled Palestine.

**b'seder** (Hebrew) literally, "in order." In contemporary usage: Okay. Good. Yeah.

**Christian Zionism** Although Christian Zionists are a diverse bunch, some common tenets of their beliefs include 1) That the modern nation state of Israel is a fulfillment of 6th century prophecies written during the time of Judean exile in Babylon 2) That God will bless all who support Israel and curse those who don't and 3) that in order for Jesus to return, all the Jews in the world must emigrate to Israel. Many, if not most, Christian Zionists believe that after all the Jews are ingathered, two thirds will die in Armageddon and one third will convert to Christianity. "Either way," one rabbi told the author, "You have no more Jews." The Vatican of the Christian Zionist movement is the **International Christian Embassy Jerusalem** (ICEJ.)

**CPTers** Members of Christian Peacemaker Teams (CPT), who have served on assignments in Gaza, Haiti, Hebron, Washington, DC, Richmond, VA, Bosnia, Chiapas, Colombia, and with indigenous peoples in North America.

**Druse** A religious offshoot of Islam, viewed by most Muslims as heretical. Ethnic Druse communities exist in Lebanon, northern Israel and Syria. Israeli Druse, unlike most Israeli Arabs, fight in the Israeli Defense Force, although in recent years, many young Druse have begun to identify with the Palestinian cause and become conscientious objectors.

**Dubboya Street** A relatively short road that connects the Israeli settlement of Tel Rumeida with Beit Hadassah in the city of Hebron. Called King David street by the settlers, it was the site of weekly Saturday violence by young Israeli men until the Rabin assassination in November 1995.

**Eish? Shu?** (Arabic) What? **Shu hada?** What is this?

**erev tov** (Hebrew) Good evening **boker tov** good morning **layla tov** good night.

**fait accompli/facts on the ground** The principle on which Israeli settlement policy is established. In the event of negotiations which would involved giving back some land, the Israeli government wants to be able to say, "We already have $x$ number of people living there. We can't give that back."

**Goldstein, Baruch** a settler from Kiryat Arba who, on the morning February 25, 1994, opened fire with an automatic weapon in the Il Ibrahimi mosque as more than 300 men and boys prostrated themselves in prayer. Official figures said that 29 died in the mosque, although Palestinians put the number higher. Twenty-nine more people were killed by the Israeli military as they fled the mosque and in the unrest of the next few weeks. Goldstein was dragged to the ground and beaten to death with a fire extinguisher by two worshippers in the mosque. They were subsequently shot by soldiers. Goldstein has become a martyr figure and cult hero to the radical right in Israel, who claim he had undertaken a preemptive strike based on intelligence he had purportedly received that Palestinians in Hebron were planning to attack Jews. In December 1999, the Israeli government ordered that the votive candles and prayer book cases around Goldstein's shrine in Kiryat Arba be removed, but the gravestone still remains.

**Ha 'Aretz** A newspaper sometimes referred to a *The New York Times* of Israel. It is associated with the left-wing of the Israeli intelligentsia, although some weekly and monthly Israeli journals are far more left-wing.

**Hamas** From an Arabic word meaning "zeal." Hamas is a fundamentalist Muslim religious movement in the West Bank and Gaza which provides social services to the poor. It also has an armed, militant wing. The founding of Hamas was encouraged by Israeli intelligence in order to drain Palestinian support for the PLO.

**Ha-Shem** (Hebrew) The Name—a term that very religious Jews use to refer to God, because the word "Adonai" (or "Lord") is too sacred for mortals to speak aloud.

**Haram!** (Arabic) It is forbidden! More colloquially, it can mean, "I don't believe that happened!" or "I can't believe you said that!" or even, "that's so bad!"

**hijab** A scarf worn by Muslim woman that fastens under the chin.

**IDF** Israel Defense Force, i.e., the Israeli army. Some partisans of Israel seem to believe the name proves that Israel's army is used for defense only. It never, ever, ever goes on the offense.

**Il Ibrahimi Mosque/Me'arat Machpelah** The term one uses usually indicates one's political convictions. Tradition has it that Abraham, Sara, Isaac, Rebekah, Jacob and Leah are all buried in a double cave beneath the building. It is a focal point of tensions in Hebron.

**inshallah** (Arabic) If God wills. The proper response to questions about what one might be doing in the future. Also used when you plan on not doing something and it wouldn't be polite to say, "no."

**inte shater** m, **inti shatreh** f (Arabic) You are clever (often said to young children.)

**Intifada** In Arabic the term refers to a "shaking off." The Intifada began in Gaza in 1987 after several Palestinians were killed by an Israeli driver. It quickly spread to the West Bank and lasted (roughly) until the Oslo Accords were signed in 1993. The broad grassroots movement among Palestinians living under Israeli Occupation caught the Israeli government, Yassar Arafat and other PLO members living in exile by surprise. Palestinians went to prison for holding meetings of more than ten people, reading forbidden books, boycotting goods produced in Israel and participating in strike days that paralyzed the Israeli economy, which was dependent on cheap Palestinian labor.

**jalabiya** long tunic worn by Arab men.

**Jebal Abu Ghneim/Har Homa** a hill on the outskirts of Bethlehem confiscated by the Israeli government to expand Jerusalem. Again, the terminology indicates one's politics.

**jilbab** long coat-like dress that some Muslim women wear over their clothes when they go out in public.

**Kach** A political party in Israel founded by the late Meir Kahane, whose primary platform was the transfer of all Arabs out of Israel, the West Bank and Gaza. Members of Kach are called **kachniks** and geographically, many are located in the Kiryat Arba/ Hebron area. The U.S. State Department and the Israel government have classified Kach as a terrorist organization.


**Kahane, Meir** Brooklyn-born rabbi, founder of **Kach** (see above). Famous quote: "I say what you think." For more information read Robert Friedman's *The False Prophet: From FBI informant to Knesset Member*. Brooklyn: Lawrence Hill Books, 1990.


**kanafi** In Jerusalem and the West Bank, it is a melted cheese dessert, soaked in syrup and covered with crushed pistachios and orange shredded wheat. In other places the cheese gets left out.


**ka'k** Chewy bread in long oval rings or in flat rounds, covered with sesame seeds.


**keffiyeh** Scarf that Palestinian men wear on their heads or around their necks. Black and white checks can indicate sympathies for Fatah, the political party of Yassar Arafat, and red and white checks can indicate sympathies for the Progressive Front for the Liberation of Palestine (PFLP), led by George Habash, or for the Palestinian People's Party (PPP).

The color of the checks may also have no political significance whatsoever.


**ken** (Hebrew) Yes


**Khalifeh, Marcel** Lebanese poet and song-writer, much admired for both his art and his progressive politics in the Arab world.

**Khalili** a native of Hebron. In Arabic, Hebron is referred to as Al Khalil, "the friend," meaning Abraham, who was a friend of God. The Hebrew name, Hevron, also derives from a word meaning friend for the same reason.

**Kief halik** f, **halak** m (Arabic) How are you?

**MAMNOUA ITTJOWAL** (Arabic) Curfew!! It is forbidden for you [Arabs] to move outside!!

**marra tani** (Arabic) Another time.

**mazbut** (Arabic) right, correct.

**Min?** (Arabic) Who, who is it?

**mish mushkelleh** (Arabic) No problem.

**Mizrahi** Jews whose origins are in North Africa and other Middle Eastern countries. See **Ashkenazi.**

**Muscobia,** See **Russian Compound**

**NGO** Non-Governmental Organization. Includes any religious, human rights, development, peace etc. organization that has no direct ties with a national government. NGOs proliferate like rabbits in Israel and Palestine.

**Nesher taxi** A franchise of taxis that travel between Jerusalem and Ben Gurion airport.

**The Occupation** The control that Israel has wielded over the Palestinian population in the West Bank, Gaza,and Golan Heights since it captured these territories from Jordan, Egypt and Syria during the 1967 war.

**Oz v'Oz** Strength with Strength. Not the name of a real right-wing Zionist terror cell.

**Peace Now** A mainstream peace group founded in the early 1980's to protest the Israeli invasion of Lebanon. It has also criticized the Israeli Occupation of the West Bank and Gaza, but the cautiousness of its members when it comes to taking action makes a lot of groups further to the left of it impatient.

**il Quds** The Holy. Arabic title for Jerusalem.

**Russian Compound** A collection of buildings that used to house representatives of the Russian Orthodox Church and the Russian government. Many prisoners, political and otherwise, are held there.

In addition to the jail, the compound contains a police station and the Jerusalem Magistrate's Court. The Church is still used as a church.

**satyagraha** truth force. A term that Mahatma Gandhi used to characterize nonviolent action against oppression.

**settlements** Israeli towns or cities built in the West Bank, Gaza and the Golan Heights since the 1967 war. Some residents of settlements are there for ideological reasons and some are there because of cheap government-subsidized housing. See **fait accompli/ facts on the ground.**


**Shabak** nickname for the **Shin Bet,** or General Security Service (GSS.) Israeli secret police. Roughly comparable to the FBI, just as the **Mossad** is roughly comparable to the CIA. Emphasis on "roughly," however. It is perhaps more analagous to the Iranian "Shavak" under the Shah.


**Shin Bet** See **Shabak**


**shukran** (Arabic) thank you.


**Tehki Arabi?** (Arabic) Do you speak Arabic?


**TIPH** Temporary International Presence in Hebron. A group of unarmed or lightly armed observers from the European Community. They were first sent to Hebron after the **Goldstein** massacre. Three months later, the Israeli government refused to renew their mandate. At the request of the Palestinians, they were reinstated in Spring of 1996.


**todah** (Hebrew) Thank you.


**Tzedek** (Hebrew) Righteousness. Not the name of any actual human rights center in Jerusalem.

**Umm** (Arabic) Mother. Men and women become known by the name of their oldest son. Hence, Umm Rishad and Abu Rishad.

**Wachsman, Nachshon** A soldier kidnapped in October 1994 by **Hamas** militants, who demanded that Israel release political prisoners as stipulated in the Oslo Accords. When the Israeli army stormed the place where he was being held, he and his captors were all killed.

**wasta** (Arabic) pull, leverage. If you are an ordinary person and need to cut through a bureaucracy to get a permit of some sort, or need a person to intervene on your behalf in some other way, you look for someone with wasta.

**Ya haram**! See **haram** (Arabic) **Ya** is an intensifier. It is also used to address someone, e.g., "Ya Eugie" could be roughly translated as "Hey Eugie!" or "Oh Eugie!"

**Yallah** (Arabic) Come on! Let's go! Get moving! Hurry!

**Yerushalayim** Hebrew name for Jerusalem.

**Yeshiva** a secondary or post-secondary school concentrating on Jewish and religious studies.

**Yisalaamu idek** m, **ideki** f (Arabic) Bless your hands. A way of thanking someone who has served you something or given you something.